Stevie Nicholson is an engineer fi   .. retired and
fulfilling his dream of full-time w   ҆ worked and lived all over the
world, he has a lifetime's experience of places and people on which to base
characters and situations. This is Stevie's debut novel. He is in the process of
writing a continuation novel based on the Knox Family members.

Stevie Nicholson

THE KNOX LEGACY

Austin Macauley Publishers™

LONDON · CAMBRIDGE · NEW YORK · SHARJAH

Copyright © Stevie Nicholson 2024

The right of Stevie Nicholson to be identified as author of this work has been asserted by the author in accordance with sections 77 and 78 of the Copyright, Designs and Patents Act 1988.

All rights reserved. No part of this publication may be reproduced, stored in a retrieval system, or transmitted in any form or by any means, electronic, mechanical, photocopying, recording, or otherwise, without the prior permission of the publishers.

Any person who commits any unauthorised act in relation to this publication may be liable to criminal prosecution and civil claims for damages.

This is a work of fiction. Names, characters, businesses, places, events, locales, and incidents are either the products of the author's imagination or used in a fictitious manner. Any resemblance to actual persons, living or dead, or actual events is purely coincidental.

A CIP catalogue record for this title is available from the British Library.

ISBN 9781035866274 (Paperback)
ISBN 9781035866281 (ePub e-book)

www.austinmacauley.com

First Published 2024
Austin Macauley Publishers Ltd®
1 Canada Square
Canary Wharf
London
E14 5AA

Chapter One

11 February 1921

As she sat on the step at the front of the tiny two-bedroom house in a small mining community, Mary Knox looked down at the dark grim Colliery below and considered what life held in store for her. As the eldest of two sisters, she was beginning to reach the age where her parents would need to decide what form her future would take and how she was to supplement the family income before finding a husband and raising a family.

She did not know what her parents were thinking but she did know that they were agreed that marriage to a miner was out of the question. Her father had known nothing but mining all his life and he was determined his daughters would not suffer the same poverty and grime he had endured for the thirty-eight years that God had inflicted on him. Her mother too was of mining stock and as one of eight children she had to resort to joining the men at the pithead, sorting coal at thirteen years of age to supplement the family income. Her wages had meant the difference between starvation and having enough food to fill every mouth.

It was down the pit that Davey Knox had met Annie Garvey and after a brief courtship they married. It was a marriage of mutual convenience, Davey was in his twenties and looking for a wife, Annie was desperate to escape the turmoil of the squalor that was home and the back breaking shifts she had to endure daily. When Davey proposed she agreed on the condition she did not have to work. Once married, she ensured this by producing two daughters in quick succession. This was followed by a son, unfortunately stillborn and the long-complicated labour ensured there would not be any more offspring.

The daughters, Mary and Rose were very different characters. Mary was strong willed, Organised and feisty, with an ability to talk anyone round to her way of thinking. Rose, on the other hand, suffered from ill-health, with a never-ending cough, wheezy chest and who lacked the self-confidence of her elder sister. Mary found herself protecting Rose from all the other kids, who picked on her because she was smaller and weaker than the rest of her age group.

Home was a small terraced cottage that was part of a row of twelve other cottages that were rented from the mine owners. It consisted of a front room, a kitchen with a cooking range and a built-in boiler for heating downstairs and two bedrooms upstairs. Outside was a coalhouse to store the concessionary coal and at the end of the garden was an earth privy which was shared with three other houses, which was emptied once a fortnight. Water was drawn from a standpipe at the bottom of the street, which was better than some pit villages which still had to rely on a well. All this meant that although they had enough to satisfy their basic needs, it was still a miserable existence.

Life in the village was a pretty sombre existence, there being very little in the way of amenities. There were 2 pubs, a small school and a general shop that sold basic provisions and doubled up as a bakery. Any major provisions had to be bought in Blackstone, which was the nearest town and a lot bigger than Westry.

Evenings for the girls were spent practising needlework, their grandmother had been a seamstress who had the misfortune to fall pregnant by a local lad and so ended up marrying into the coal mining community, a decision she regretted for the rest of her life.

When she died, she handed down the needlework tapestries she used to practice with to Annie and the girls. Night after night was spent re-creating these delicate pieces of coursework and when completed they would be unpicked and the whole process would begin again. Annie could not afford to keep providing new materials and would scavenge for bits of thread and lacework wherever she could. Although tedious the girls did not mind this form of recreation, especially in winter where the dark nights did not provide much in the way of entertainment. The girls were only 11 and 12, but they were proving to be very proficient with a needle. Annie knew that these skills could prove useful in later life and might lead to their escape from Westry and the poverty that was coal mining.

Getting up from the step, Mary heard the familiar rasp of her sister's cough as she came around the corner. "You sound like an old pit horse," she teased as Rosie spluttered into view.

"And you look like one," Rosie retorted. "Don't go too near the pithead or they might just hitch you up to a tub."

"Where have you been?" asked Mary, looking concerned as Rosie struggled for breath.

"Playing with the McCreadie twins down by the brook, but they ran off and left me."

The cold damp February air was not good for Rosie and she found every winter increasingly difficult, Mary knew this and became more and more protective as each year passed.

"Come on, it's getting dark, Let's go inside and help Ma with the supper," said Mary as she guided Rosie into the house.

As they entered the tiny cottage, the smell of the evening meal on the range hit their nostrils, the same smell they smelled most evenings, a stew of mixed vegetables and scraps of whatever meat was available, which sometimes was none at all. On the odd occasion, they would feast on rabbit if Dad had been out in the fields on his day off. They did not particularly like rabbit but it made for a change so it was welcome.

"Ah Mary, I'm glad you're here, you can light the fire in the front room, save me a job," said Ma. The fire was only lit at night, it gave the girls somewhere to sit while Dad was getting cleaned up in the kitchen. "Rosie can set the table, then you can both practice your needlework until your supper's ready."

Mary lit the lamps in the front room and was just about light the fire when she felt a rumbling sound beneath her feet and a loud explosion that rocked the whole house. The next thing she knew her mother let out a piercing shriek.

"NO, PLEASE GOD, NO, IT CAN'T BE," screamed Annie dropping the cooking pot spilling the contents on the floor as she rushed to the front door. Mary followed and as they entered the street, she saw plumes of yellow flames and black smoke engulfing the whole area that was the Colliery. Suddenly the whole street was out, with women wailing and men rushing to the pit, putting their coats on as they ran down the street.

"What's happening?" cried Mary.

"There's been an explosion down the mine," said one old woman wrapping her shawl around her. "It's going to take all the village to muck in and help," as she shuffled in the direction of the flames.

Mary looked at her mother, her face was ashen with an expression of terror and bewilderment filling her gaunt features.

"Get back inside and look after Rosie, I must find your father," Annie said as she hustled Mary back towards the house. Mary dutifully obeyed, not quite taking in what was going on, as her mother followed the increasing throng of people heading down the road, both men and women carrying shovels, axes, in fact any tool that might prove useful in digging out the trapped men below ground.

When she arrived at the pithead, Annie struggled to make any sense of the mass confusion there and stood around with the other women, not knowing what to do, so waiting there helpless as she observed the vain but valiant attempts to bring the fire under control.

Gradually, after a few hours the flames subsided and the slow painful process of trying to find survivors and recovering bodies began. News travelled quickly to other villages and volunteers flooded in to help. All through the night, teams would take turns hacking away at the debris and replacing props as they hauled ton after ton of rock back to the surface, mostly by hand. The dust was everywhere and Annie would never forget the faces, all with the same expression of determination and fear for what they might find, mingled with the blood, sweat and grime that was ingrained in their skin.

Mary had cleaned up the contents from the spilled pan and sorted something to eat from the remnants for herself and Rosie. They sat in the kitchen quietly eating and listening to the chaos from outside, not sure what they were supposed to do.

"Shall we go and see if we can help?" offered Rosie.

"Not much we could do, besides it would make your breathing worse, we'll just have to wait and see what happens."

"Will Dad be alright?" Rosie asked, "Is he safe?"

Mary knew that the situation was serious, she remembered when there was a similar accident at a pit a few miles away, a lot of people died, the whole village talked about it for weeks.

"I'm sure he'll be fine, we'll leave some supper out for when they get back, come on, let's go to bed," said Mary trying to sound convincing but not sure if she had succeeded.

The girls shared a bed and after undressing and changing into a rough cotton nightdress, they huddled together to share each other's body warmth, Mary listening to the wheeze of Mary's chest as she slowly dropped asleep. Once Rosie had settled Mary got up, dressed, went downstairs and wrapped some food up. She then put her coat on, picked up her mother's coat, slowly pulled the front door shut and went to look for her parents. She found Annie standing alone on a bank that gave her a good vantage point looking over the pit entrance. She slipped her mother's coat around her slender shoulders and offered her some food.

"What's happening, have they brought anyone out yet?" she asked not knowing if she wanted to know the answer.

"There were five men brought out before, but they are all badly injured, no-one has walked out yet," Annie sobbed as she tried to maintain some composure. She needed to be strong, the girls had to rely on her.

"Here, you need to eat something," Mary passed her a couple of pieces of bread with a wedge of cheese inside.

"You must go and see to Rosie, I will probably be here all night, the work is slow and your dad was working at the face, so will be one of the last out," said Annie and putting her arm around her shoulder she turned her back towards the streets above. Mary realising there would probably not be anything she could do and that her mother would not move until she knew what the outcome was, turned and returned home to care for Rosie.

Finally, as the pale watery sun was rising on cold frosty February dawn, the first bodies were recovered. As they came out there were gasps of horror as the burnt and mangled remains of the victims were stretchered to a temporary mortuary at the rear of the main office in a building used as storage. The bodies were laid in rows, covered in sacking, the entrance being guarded by a policeman. Women pushed forward craning to see if their loved ones were among the dead, but not many were recognisable, the force of the blast and the flames having ripped the skin off their faces. Now and again, someone would call out a name when they saw someone they knew and word would be passed back along the line. There were survivors though and as they emerged, they were bombarded with requests about other survivors, although in their shocked and confused state, they were not in a position to offer any information.

Annie watched as the digging continued, making slow painful progress as the rescue team went deeper into the mine. A second team was working on clearing the ventilation shaft, which was partially blocked, but was still allowing air into the mine.

Eventually, enough room was created to be able to start propping up and clearing at a faster rate and organised clearance replaced chaos.

The work continued into a second night, until at 3am a loud cheer went up and a body of thirty something survivors emerged all unscathed, accompanied by half a dozen terrified pit ponies. Slowly more men were dug out until there were only forty men unaccounted for, Davey was one of them.

News filtered back that there had been a secondary explosion, this time at the face. This was the news that Annie dreaded, her heart sank and she feared the worst. Work was then halted for six hours to allow the gas build up to be cleared, eventually the teams began to dig again.

By now Annie was exhausted, she had been awake for two days and was beginning to feel it's affects. With a promise from her next-door neighbour that they would tell her the minute there was any sign of Davey, she went home to see to the girls and try and get some sleep. As she stepped over the threshold into the cottage the girls immediately rushed to her for any news.

"I'm sorry, there's nothing I can tell you, but everyone is doing all they can and there are survivors," she tried to sound optimistic but she knew the longer time went on, the less chance there was of anyone surviving, especially when you were at the coalface. She then made herself a cup of tea and sat in front of the range and promptly fell into a fitful sleep.

At 10am Davey's body was recovered along with the rest of the lads at the face, all of whom had suffocated when a collapse had left them trapped in a 50ft chamber. Gas seeped in and within hours they were all dead. When rescuers discovered the bodies some of them were found on their knees, as if in prayer.

Mary looked out of the window and saw Margaret McGinty walking purposefully across the street towards the house, a grim expression on her face, it did not look as though it was good news. She woke her mother just as Mrs McGinty entered the room, Annie jumping up and rushing towards the door.

She then gave Annie the bad news. "They say the last of the bodies have been brought up and there are no more survivors, I'm sorry, but I didn't see Davey, you need to go to the mortuary, behind the office."

Mary and Rosie instinctively moved to support Annie who struggled to stay on her feet, moving her gently back into the chair she had just left. Mrs McGinty sensed that there was nothing she could say or do, so she made her apologies and left, leaving the three of them sitting in complete silence as the gravity of the situation began to sink in. After what seemed to be an eternity, Mary grabbed her coat and turned to Rosie, "Look after Ma, I'm going to see if there's anything I can find out."

"No, we're coming with you, we must do this together," called Annie.

Slowly, the three of them walked back down the hill and joined the queue alongside the now growing swell of families that were also looking for their loved ones. The queue moved slowly and as they edged their way inside the shed the policeman at the entrance asked them who they were looking for. The men at the face were the last bodies recovered and were near the front. The bodies were covered in Hessian sacking with just the face exposed, Mary instantly recognised most of the faces, many of which were boys not much older than her. As the slow procession crawled along, there were cries of anguish from relatives as they discovered their husband, son, or brother. As they walked down the third row, Annie suddenly stopped and held her hand to her face. Mary and Rosie looking down to see their father's face looking up at them, his face contorted and barely recognisable. After confirming the identity of the body, it was placed in a basic wooden coffin, labelled and taken away for a post mortem. This process was repeated 86 times until eventually all the bodies were claimed.

The funeral of all the men took place 3 days later, starting at mid-day and continuing through until 5 o'clock. There were various processions taking place, all greeted with the same respectful silence. As the whole village lined up along the lane that led to the churchyard, the silence was broken only by the sound of the metal rims of the wheels on stone and the cries of young, cold, bored children who were unaware of the solemnity of the occasion. Many of the families did not have the money for a private funeral and were taken to the open grave that had been prepared for them, on trailers containing up to ten coffins at a time, the priest blessing each one as it was lowered into the ground, placing relatives next to each other wherever possible.

David Thomas Knox was one of those unfortunates and as his name was read out Annie clutched the girls' hands and squeezed them gently. Mary looked around at the scene, Hundreds of men, women and children, all with the same anguished look, all sharing each other's pain and all angry at the tragic waste of human life.

The occasion was too much for Rosie and as she struggled for breath Mary led her away, sat her down on a bench and tried to console her.

"How will we manage, we have no money coming in or any savings, what will we do?" cried Rosie to Mary, who had turned away as she knew their future was looking very bleak indeed.

"Mam will have a plan, but God knows it won't be an easy time for us," she eventually replied, her head spinning as she realised they were now destitute and that in a short time they could be homeless as well.

As Davey's body was lowered into the ground, Annie turned and saw Mary comforting her sister. She knew that somehow, she had to be strong and protect them, but she was very worried about the future and at that moment in time did not have any idea how they were going to cope.

Eventually all the bodies were lowered and gradually the mourners made their way back down the hill to the village, where the woman congregated into small groups and the men headed for the local public houses to try and ease the pain of the last few days.

That night as the girls were asleep in their bed, the only sound to be heard was the crackling of the fire and the drunks fighting in the street outside. Annie sat in the darkness and the anguish of the last couple of days began to take their toll on her, the momentum building until her tears were uncontrollable and her sobs, stifled to begin with, gradually got louder and louder. Eventually the sound reached the ears of Mary, who was not able to sleep anyway and she crept downstairs to comfort her mother. As they sat huddled around the fire Mary eventually broke the silence.

"What do we do now mam, will we have to move and where will we go?"

Annie struggled to answer, she knew that for the next few weeks they were safe as the mine would not be working, but that eventually the mine owners would need the house for the new workers they would eventually be taking on. She was torn between telling her that everything was going to be alright and the reality of the situation. She knew that Mary was too bright to try and deceive, so she decided the only option was to be honest with her.

"We are in a desperate situation, I will know better when I have been to the Colliery Office tomorrow, but it does not look good. The Miners Welfare will be able to help us for a while, but I don't know how long for. Now come on, away to your bed, I need you to get some rest and be strong for your sister."

The following morning Annie joined the queue outside the Colliery Office and awaited her fate. As she shuffled along, slowly working her way to the front she looked around at the other women waiting patiently with their shawls wrapped around their stooped shoulders, heads bowed to protect them from the bitterly cold wind and Annie realised that there were others in a position at least as perilous as herself. Mrs Johnson was in front of her, a small frail looking woman who looked far older than her forty years, her hair grey and lank. She had lost a husband and two sons, now there was no-one to provide for her and her other four young children. As the queue in front grew smaller, Annie noticed that most of the women that came out were distressed, this worried her. Eventually Annie reached the front of the queue and stood outside a door with a small sign that bore the inscription 'Colliery Managers Office'.

As she was ushered in, she noted there were two men sat behind a desk, one of whom she recognised as the Secretary of the Miners Welfare Fund. It was set up for the benefit of miners and their families and was funded via a levy of one percent of the value of the coal extracted from the mine.

"How are you, Annie?" asked the secretary. "Davey was a good man and a good friend who will be badly missed." Annie was not really listening to his words, which he had probably spoken to every mourning widow he had tragically seen that morning.

"Bearing up, it's too early to tell how we will cope, but we will manage. Is it you I have to see about moving to an alms house?" she enquired. The Alms Houses were set aside for widows and children of miners and were the main source of refuge in cases such as this.

"I'm afraid there are not enough houses to go around, so it has been decided to allocate them according to greatest need and I am afraid you do not qualify," was the answer to her question.

Annie's head reeled and after a couple of minutes small talk that she did not really take in, the secretary finally told her the sum to which she would be entitled to from the fund. For herself she was granted the sum of five shillings a week and for each of the girls she was allowed an extra shilling, a grand total of seven shillings a week. She was also informed that she could stay in the tied terraced house for six weeks after which it would be required for another family.

Although the news was what she was expecting it still came as a shock when it was confirmed.

"Where will we go?" she eventually asked, looking directly at the two men in front of her. "We have no money and we cannot live on seven shillings a week."

"I'm so sorry but the houses are needed for miners, there are other families with more mouths to feed who are in the same situation," the other man said, with a genuine look of regret on his face and a tremulous tone to his voice. "The mine must stay open, no matter what, for the sake of the rest of the community."

The next few weeks were traumatic, no matter where they went, they could not find anything they could afford and so on the day they were due to leave they moved in with Margaret McGinty and her two children, on the understanding they could stay for a month in the parlour. Thomas McGinty, her husband, knew that if he had died instead of Davey then he would have expected nothing less of the Knox's, so did not considerate the situation to be a burden. It was to be expected that miners would support each other in such times.

The weeks passed into months without any sign of an improvement in their circumstances, Mrs McGinty was beginning to feel the pressure of living in such crowded conditions, but agreed to allow them to stay for yet another month, after which Annie agreed to move out. Things however, came to a head before that!

Thomas McGinty liked a drink as did most of the miners in the village, but the fact that his house was now not his own gave him the excuse to stay out in the pub most nights, an excuse he took to with relish, after all his wife was a very intimidating woman. Reeling his way home one night, he crashed the front door open and staggered into the small terrace, tripping over the threshold in the process. As he lay on his back in the front room that now doubled as a bedroom for the Knox's, he spied Annie out of the corner of his eye, lying on a mattress on the floor a couple of feet away from him, her figure silhouetted against the background of the embers of the fire behind her. Reaching over he slipped his hand inside her nightgown and roughly groped her breast, at which point Annie squealed and jumped up.

"What the hell do you think you are doing," she whispered. "Get upstairs to your wife, before the kids wake up." She then stormed off to use the outside lavvy leaving Thomas still on the floor in the front room. Thomas got up and crawled on his hands and knees into the kitchen where he waited for Annie to come back into the house. As she entered, she noticed that he was stood blocking passage to the front room, leaning first one way then the other, his face flushed and leery.

"I think it's time you gave me something for the rent," he sneered, his breath reeking of beer and tobacco as he put his face inches away from hers.

"I give Margaret five shillings a week, it's all I can afford to pay," she replied trying to edge past him.

Suddenly, he grabbed her round the waist and tried to kiss her. "There are other ways to pay and you can start now." He then thrust his hand between her legs, knocking her off balance and causing her to fall to the ground. Thomas climbed on top of her lifting her nightgown and exposing her flesh beneath. He then forced two fingers deep inside her causing her to cry out. "Please don't, my children are next door and your wife will hear you."

"TOO LATE, SHE'S ALREADY HEARD," boomed a voice form the bottom of the stairs, which caused a startled Thomas to jump up and protest his innocence. "She has been trying to get me to give her one for the last two weeks," he bleated.

Margaret then marched towards Annie her face crimson with rage and slapped her face, forcing a trickle of blood from her nose. "I think you have outstayed your welcome, I want you to leave in the morning," she snarled. Then turned and grabbing Thomas by the scruff of the neck, marched him up the stairs. Annie wanted to explain but knew that Margaret was not in the mood to listen, so took herself off to bed.

Annie could not sleep and spent most of the night worrying about what would happen when the dawn broke. She was still laid there when she heard the sound of pots rattling in the kitchen. Getting up she put on her gown and entered the kitchen to find Margaret stoking the embers of the range to get the flames going.

Margaret then turned to Annie and spoke in a very apologetic voice, "I'm sorry I hit you, I heard it all and know that you did nothing to encourage him."

Relief flooded through Annie as she heard the words, but the relief was short-lived.

"But I stand by what I said, you must leave today. Thomas may have acted like a fool, but he's my fool and me and my children need him, nothing can be allowed to come between us."

Annie tried to protest but Margaret wouldn't change her mind, though accepting that she would not be able to take all her belongings at once, allowed her to store the bulkier items and to allow the girls to stay for an extra week. When the girls had got dressed and ready for school, Annie explained that she was going to look outside the village for somewhere for them to live and would be back in a couple of days. Once the girls had set off for school, Annie packed some clothes, left the house and walked the eight miles to Blackstone, a town that might offer her the chance to find a secure roof for her and the girls.

Chapter Two

As she approached the town, she saw that though it was quite a lot bigger than Westry the people had the same drab, grey, downtrodden expression on their faces and she knew that this was just another mining town, where there were few opportunities to escape the grime and blackness of the coal dust that hung over everything. This sight made Annie's heart sink and she walked very slowly into the centre of the town, trying to see where there might be an opportunity to find a new life. In the centre was a stone cross with a fountain in the middle, Annie took a drink and then looked around to see where she would begin her search for work and a place to live. The prospects did not look too good, so she decided to accept anything that was on offer, even, God forbid, returning to the pit, if nothing else was available.

For the rest of the day she asked, begged and beseeched anyone to give her an opportunity, without any success. After the failure of the day she was now feeling very tired and knew she had to find somewhere to stay the night.

After such a long walk her feet ached, so she sat down on a bench by the town cross and took her shoes off. As she sat rubbing them, she noticed a little man with a bald head, stubbly grey beard and generally dishevelled appearance looking at her intently from across the street. Pretending she hadn't seen him, she bent down and started to put her shoes back on. As she stood up, she noticed he had disappeared, so gathering the belongings she had bundled up, she set about looking once again for somewhere to live and a job. She called in all the shops down one side of the main street, none of which were offering any hope, most of which were very dismissive and some very rude.

After 4 long hours of rejection, she was beginning to lose hope and her thoughts turned to where she was going to sleep that night. She called into a couple of public houses to ask if she could bed down somewhere in return for washing the beer glasses, but was offered nothing.

As she reached the end of the last street, she caught her reflection in the shop window and was shocked at the bedraggled, gaunt, bleary eyed, pathetic excuse of a woman staring back at her. Her hair, normally kept tight in a bun on her head, was hanging down in clumps and strands were falling onto her face.

"Oh my God, what a mess you are, no wonder you can't find anything," she muttered to herself as she used the window as a mirror to try and tidy herself up. As she did, she noticed the little man she had seen earlier in the background of the reflection in the window. As she turned round, he smiled and asked if she needed any help.

"Just somewhere to live for me and my kids and a job, not asking too much." She uttered wearily, as she realised he was the first person she had spoken to all day.

"I can't help you with a job but I can find you a bed for the night," he said, squinting at her and rubbing his beard, "Don't worry. I don't want anything in return," he exclaimed as he noticed the look of anguish and bewilderment on Annie's face. He then went on to explain that his name was Billy Thorpe, he was a verger at the local parish church and that he had noticed her futile attempts to seek lodgings and work.

Annie was not convinced and was walking away when he shouted after her with an offer to stay at the church with the housekeeper. Annie stopped after realising she didn't have any other options and listened to what he had to say. As they talked, she realised they had walked to the entrance of the Holy Trinity church.

"Wait here," Billy shouted as he nimbly sprinted up the steps and entered a door at the side of the church. After 5 minutes he re-emerged with a short, grey haired, small woman and introduced here as Miss Simpson, a spinster who looked after the needs of the clergy.

Miss Simpson said nothing, but ushered Annie up the stairs and into the church. As she entered the church Annie was struck by the peace and tranquil surroundings she found herself in, and relaxed for the first time all day. She was then taken through the church to a rear wing which served as Miss Simpson's quarters.

Not a sound had Miss Simpson made up to now, but Annie was taken aback when she finally spoke. "Your room is the next one down. I will make you some supper while you prepare yourself," The clipped, precise manner of her speech was something that Annie had never heard before, spoken without any sign of an accent.

She showed her to the bathroom and after filling a basin of fresh hot water, which fascinated her as she had never known running water, she sat on the edge of the bed and for the first time in months she let her feelings go. She broke down and cried, all the emotion that had been bottled up came out in one long outpouring. For the next 10 minutes she just sat there completely lost in her anguish. Finally, she washed and dressed and lay down on the bed to collect herself. As she lay there, her thoughts turned to Mary and Rosie, she knew they would be worried about her, she also knew that she had one more day to find lodgings and work before she had to head back to Weston. What she was going to do she didn't know and the reality came flooding back to her.

Suddenly there was a knock on the door and Miss Simpson called to tell her supper was ready, she answered and after composing herself, she followed her into the kitchen. Supper was a simple affair some bread, a little piece of ham, a small cake and a cup of tea. Annie suddenly realised how hungry she was and as she gorged on the ham, she looked at Miss Simpson who was daintily picking off small pieces of ham and gently chewing at each forkful for what seemed an eternity.

"Tell me Annie, it is Annie, is it not?" Miss Simpson asked. "How do you come to find yourself in this unfortunate predicament?" As she sat there eating Annie surprised herself by opening her heart to a complete stranger and went on to explain about the death of her husband and the loss of her home, the incident at the McGinty's and her quest to find a new life in Blackstone. As she listened, saying nothing, just nodding her head and trying to take in the enormity of her ordeal, Miss Simpson offered her sympathy and told Annie she would offer up her prayers for her. This troubled Annie as she had never been a religious person and had certainly never had anyone pray for her before.

As they sat at the table in silence Miss Simpson explained that she was once betrothed to a soldier who had died in the Crimea and had never got over his death, she had found solace in God and had decided to devote herself to him. She had considered joining a convent, but had decided that she was not pure as she had been sexually involved with her fiancé. She thought therefore that a housekeeper was a more suitable way to serve the lord. The thought of Miss Simpson being sexual was so unexpected that Annie almost choked on the last morsel of cake she was devouring. She also found it extremely funny, how could this little old lady sit there and tell her such intimate things? They talked for what seemed hours and Annie found herself warming to this very strange but endearing woman. Finally, supper was over and as she climbed into bed Annie realised just how tired she was and within minutes a deep and heavy sleep overtook her and she slept like no other night before.

When she woke it took a few seconds before she realised where she was and after washing and dressing, she went downstairs where Miss Simpson and Billy were enjoying a cup of tea. Offering her a seat, Miss Simpson then proceeded to make tea.

"Did you sleep well, you looked very weary last night?" asked Billy as Miss Simpson poured into a cup.

As Annie sipped her tea, they began to discuss religion and the wonder of the Lord. Annie, sceptical at first, began to listen and for the first time in her life she wondered about life after death and the power of worship. Gradually, she began to ask questions and was drawn into the conversation. The more she heard, the more questions there were to answer, all of which were answered and provided solutions to her woes. This went on for about 4 hours and Annie was engrossed, she wanted to know more about the church, its workings and how religion was the way forward for her. Eventually they were joined by the Reverend Evans, who expanded on the thoughts of Miss Simpson and Billy, adding depth to the conversation and quoting from the gospels. He then went on to explain about his charity works and how the church helped to provide for the poor.

This was illuminating for Annie and she felt the heavy burden she had been carrying start to lift. There was now a light at the end of the tunnel and she felt enlightened. Annie now knew the way in which her life was to turn and there was a spring in her step that had been missing for most of her life.

Eventually the Rev Evans left to carry out his business and she was left with Billy and Miss Simpson, who continued the conversation in the same vein, making tea and conversing about the Lord. A procession of people came through the house over the course of the day and Annie was struck by the serenity and calmness they all displayed.

As the afternoon wore on, it became time for prayers and as they entered the plainly decorated church there was an aura that Annie felt an uplifting that reached deep inside her. The prayers themselves, though simple, were accompanied by a number of hymns that were sung with such gusto that the sound resonated around the building as though angels were in the chorus.

It was becoming dark as Annie wondered where the time had gone, she would not be able to go and find lodgings and a job today. As she looked out of the window, Annie realised that the day had gone, she could not look for work or accommodation now and she knew it would be dangerous to travel back to Weston tonight.

Sensing her discomfort, Miss Simpson arranged with the Reverend Evans for Annie to stay over another night. While Annie was uncomfortable at not having arranged anything or seeing the girls, she knew this was a safe place, a place where she could escape the problems of the world and so she gratefully accepted the offer.

The following morning she awoke, gathered her belongings and after breakfast said goodbye to Miss Simpson, Billy and the Reverend and set out to look for work with renewed vigour. "God will provide," she kept saying to herself over and over again. She decided to spend the morning retracing her route, searching for somewhere they could call home. She decided to set off home and pick the girls up, they would all be fine, the Reverend and Miss Simpson had said so.

The walk back to Weston was cold and wet with a steady drizzle of rain that was freezing with a biting wind that cut through Annie's weak, feeble body which was offered little protection by the thin shabby wool coat she wore. But she didn't feel it as she steadily wound her way home to collect the children. She was offered a lift for the last few miles by the dray wagon loaded with barrels of beer for the pubs in the village and, after thanking the Draymen, she walked the last few yards to Margeret McGinty's house.

As she approached the house the girls rushed out to greet her and as they hugged, she told them everything was going to be alright. Margaret came out of the house, took one look at the bedraggled Annie and ushered them all inside, where she sat her down by the fire and made her a hot drink.

As Annie sipped her tea the girls asked if she had managed to secure lodgings for them. She explained what had happened and the kindness that had been shown from all at the church and how she now realised that the way forward was with the Lord.

Mary and Rosy turned and looked at each other open mouthed, was this really their mother speaking, their mother who had never been in a church in her life, who had never even had them baptised. Mary was the first to speak. "But where will we live, have you found us a home?" As she looked into Mary's eyes there was a strange vacant look that she had never seen before, this was definitely not her mother.

"The Lord will find us lodgings, Miss Simpson said that as long as we believe in the Lord, he will look after us," said Annie in a manner that suggested she believed every word she was saying.

Margeret was the first to react to this startling news, in a voice that showed she was clearly troubled by what she saw, she tried to bring some sanity to the situation. "Let me speak with your mother, go and get me some bread from the bakers," she said as she shuffled in her purse for some coppers.

After the girls had gone, Mary put a comforting arm around Annie and spoke very slowly and softly, trying to reach into Annie's head. "You can't just go and move over there without somewhere to go to," she implored. "you can stay here a while longer until you are feeling better."

"I have never felt better, I know what I must do for me and my girls. I would appreciate it though if you could find it in your heart to bear with us for one more night," her voice was completely lacking in emotion. With that Annie stood up and took her coat off revealing a sodden body underneath.

"Of course, Annie, of course," Margaret was beside herself; she had known Annie for years, this was not normal.

As Mary and Rosie walked to the shop, they discussed what they had just heard. "Mary how can we move when we don't where we are going, what are we to do when we are there."

"Mam knows what she is doing, she won't see us harmed," replied Mary, not sure if she sounded convincing. She herself was not convinced, but how could she doubt her own mother.

That evening was a very strange affair with no-one wanting to raise the subject of leaving. Margaret kept busy cooking and sorting her own children out, her husband Thomas stayed out of the way, fearful that this lunatic in their midst would seek vengeance on him. Mary and Rosie sat in the dark in the parlour, not daring to speak, each with their own fears churning around in their young confused heads. Annie helped with the evening meal then joined the girls in the dark, cuddling them, uttering words that she thought would comfort them.

"We will be fine, the Lord will provide, he will look after us, don't worry," The words did not provide much comfort, if anything they enhanced the girls' fears.

As they set off on this new adventure to a different life in a strange town where they did not know anybody, Mary reflected on the change in her mother's demeanour and a positivity that had been missing for the last couple of months and hoped that it was sign that things were going to get better. Life had always been hard but had become unbearable recently. The walking was slow and Rosie was struggling to get her breath, so they had to stop and rest regularly and this was slowing down their progress. She was also bringing up phlegm which was a concern. Rosie had always been chesty but not shown any of these symptoms before. Eventually a dray wagon was passing after having made their ale deliveries in Westry and the dray lads took pity and gave them a lift to the outskirts of Blackstone in the back of the wagon squeezed in between barrels.

The spire of the Holy Trinity church was in sight and Annie felt her spirits being uplifted and now had a spring in her stride. As they reached the steps leading up to the church entrance, Mary was now in a confused state, on the one hand she knew her mother would always try and do what is best for the girls, but this was stepping into the unknown, religion had never played any part in their life before. They walked to the side door that was the entrance to the Rev Evans' house and Annie confidently knocked on the door. After a short while, Miss Simpson opened the door and looked at Annie with a quizzical look on her face.

"Hello Annie, this is a nice surprise," but before she could finish speaking Annie pushed past her and ushered the girls into the house. "See girls, I said the Lord would look after us, we will be safe here," she then sat herself down at the dining table.

Mary could tell by the look on Miss Simpson's face that it was not alright, but she was tired, so ushered Rosie to sit down as well. Rosie, by this time, was exhausted and not capable of making any judgement and slumped wearily with her arms resting over the dining table. Miss Simpson was looking a little flustered, not knowing what Annie was doing here so decided to make some tea and try to get some sense of what was going on, the Rev Evans would be back soon anyway so it would all soon get sorted out.

As they sat there, Mary could not help but feel this was not going as Annie was expecting and had to say something.

"Ma, why are we here, what's going on?" The same thought was going through Miss Simpson's mind as well and she was a bit shocked at Annie's response.

"The Lord will protect us, we will stay here until we find somewhere suitable," was Annie's response, which nearly caused Miss Simpson to drop her cup. Mary was still confused but said nothing more, she looked at Miss Simpson and immediately knew this had not been prearranged.

After about 10 minutes of awkward silence, the Rev Evans returned and Miss Simpson immediately jumped up and ushered him into the kitchen. Having explained the situation to the Reverend he spent a couple of minutes contemplating what he was going to do about the predicament, then decided as it was getting late, he would allow Annie and the girls to stay the night and he would confront the matter in the morning.

Miss Simpson made a light supper of cheese and bread and Annie and the girls were shown to the same bed room Annie had previously slept in. They bathed and climbed wearily into bed, where Rosie promptly fell asleep. Mary still felt uncomfortable but after hearing Annie state they would be safe here she eventually drifted off as well.

In the morning, a pensive Reverend Evans began the conversation by asking Annie what her plans were.

"We will stay with you until the Lord finds us a home and some money to live on," was Annie's confident reply.

This was not what he wanted to hear but, but was what he was expecting. He took a deep breath and began to explain, "I am sorry, Annie but that is not possible, the Lord's house is a broad protection of the spirit and faith, it is not a place of refuge that anyone can just expect shelter on demand. There are many deserving cases and it is impossible to allow favour of some over others, there is no financial means of doing so."

He then went on a 5-minute sermon about people making decisions in their life based on the fact that God will eventually give them the inspiration and self-belief, which in turn will provide them with the strength to improve their lives, but God alone cannot do it, it must come from within.

During this speech, Mary kept looking across at her mother whose expression started as a look of serenity, changing eventually to disbelief until finally expressing complete rage, her face twitching and her fists becoming clenched. Finally, all the months of pent-up anger, frustration, hurt and misery emerged in one massive eruption and Annie launched herself at the Reverend taking him completely by surprise.

"You told me the Lord would provide, you told me he would protect, you told me, me and my girls would be safe," and picking up a fork proceeded to attempt to stab him. Luckily, he only received a couple of the strikes, but it drew blood from a cut to his right hand. Annie wasn't finished yet, she then proceeded to grab his hair in both hands and such was the force she inflicted, both hands had large clumps where she literally tore the hair from his head, resulting in blood streaming down his face. This was too much for Mrs Simpson who made a swift exit out the door looking for some assistance.

Annie, by now was a lost cause, "You bastard, your God has done this to me and my girls, what do we do now?" she then started to cry uncontrollably, Mary had never seen her mother like this and was I powerless to either help or take control of the situation. The Reverend managed to escape and was rushing down the church garden when Miss Simpson returned with the local constabulary. The police arrested Annie and along with Mary and Rosie was taken to the local police station. They were all in a cell for about 4 hours and eventually the girls were moved and placed in a room and made to wait for someone to tell them their fate. Little did they know this was to be the last time they saw their mother.

The news was not good, the officer sat them down and explained that their mother was being sectioned for her own protection and would be taken to the workhouse and looked after there until she was considered fit to be released. The girls would also be taken to the children's wing of the same workhouse and assessed as to their health and school requirements. Mary had never been in a workhouse but had heard tales that made her shudder, she was very scared and knew Rosie was going to suffer even more than she would.

Chapter Three

The girls did not see Annie being taken away from the station, but they heard her, the agonising shrieks and screams of a desperate woman with nowhere to turn and nobody to help her, a woman that was now losing her children and unable to control her life anymore.

Mary was very frightened now, she didn't know a lot about the workhouse, but what she did know was that it was not a good place and that life would never be the same again. A constable accompanied the girls along with Miss Simpson to be interviewed and registered at the workhouse.

On the front of the wall next to the gateway that led to the entrance was a large sign bearing the inscription "BLACKSTONE WORKHOUSE." A Large wooden gate filled the gateway and set into the gate was a door with a large knocker on it. The constable lifted the knocker and after pausing for what seemed to be an eternity the door was answered by a stocky, bald man who peered at them over a pair of spectacles that sat on a very large red nose.

"What can I do for you, constable?" He asked, looking the girls up and down as he spoke.

They were then ushered into a waiting room, where they sat and waited. Looking around Mary saw that the walls were painted a drab grey and the furniture very basic, two wooden pews that faced each other with a paving stone floor. There wasn't any sign of decoration on the wall, save for a single crucifix. It was not intended to make you feel welcome.

Eventually a tall, elderly man with a very upright stance came in and introduced himself as the Workhouse Master. After the constable explained the situation and handed over various documents, the Workhouse Master thanked the constable who then left, leaving Mary, Rosie and Miss Simpson alone with him. He told them to wait for someone to register them and left through a large imposing door, where he locked them in. After an hour or so a lady appeared who introduced herself as the Matron, informed the girls they would be admitted immediately and thanked Miss Simpson for her time and patience and showed her to the door. She barely looked at Mary and Rosie, but once Miss Simpson had gone, she ushered them through the same door she had entered from.

They found themselves in front of a long bench in a room that was as bare as the previous room except for a large book cupboard, a coat rack and a large sign in black against the lime whitewash walls that read **GOD IS YOUR SALVATION.**

Behind the bench was the Master who was joined by the Matron. Mary was feeling very confused as God just seemed to have placed them in the worse position of their lives. The Master then told them they would be detained for the next 2 days until a full meeting of the workhouse Board of Governors, at which point formal entry into the orphanage wing would be confirmed. Until then, Mary and Josie would be held in a receiving ward, Matron would explain the rules and regulations, he then stood up and left the room. Mary took an instant dislike to this arrogant man, with Rosie was barely able to concentrate on events and wheezing very badly. Mary tried to ask if they could see their mother but was immediately dismissed with a wave of the hand. The Matron then stood up and informed them they would be bathed, changed into the standard workhouse uniform and given a dormitory to sleep in. It was now the afternoon but the day had seemed like a week, Mary was exhausted after the last couple of days and not in a position to ask any more questions, so meekly complied with whatever the Matron wanted them to carry out.

They were ushered along a long straight corridor that was decorated in the same dour colours as the rest of the rooms and when they reached the end turned left to face a door indicating this was the women's dormitories. The Matron opened the door with the biggest key Mary had ever seen and looking at the size of the lock on the door it was clear to see why.

They then followed Matron to the bathing rooms where they were ordered to strip and bathe. There were 6 small tin baths in the room, Rosie was struggling to undress she was that tired and wheezy, so Mary helped her and proceeded to wash her body and hair. When Rosie was cleaned, she was given a rough linen towel to dry herself, but when she turned around to get dressed she discovered her clothes had gone, to be replaced by a calico shift, a grogram dress, worsted stockings and wooden clogs. Mary looked and saw her clothes too had been removed and replaced with identical clothing. The Matron had left the room so Rosie got dressed while Mary bathed.

The water was tepid and the soap smelled of carbolic, the whole process was very unpleasant and although Mary had a small frame, she could not straighten her legs and struggled to clean herself in the confined area. As she was struggling to get out the bath the Matron returned and told her to hurry up. As she was dressing, Mary asked where her clothes were and was informed, they would be returned, cleaned and laundered when they left the establishment, but until then they would wear the standard dress.

As this was being explained, another women came into the room wearing a similar uniform, brandishing a large pair of scissors and a bucket. As Rosie was already dressed, she was told to sit in a chair and a sheet was placed around her shoulders.

"What's happening, what are you doing?" cried Rosie.

Matron explained that all children were to have shorn heads on entry to eliminate the transmission of head lice. Mary wanted to shout and resist but knew their position was futile, they were at the mercy of these people and nothing she said or did would make any difference.

"Mary please stop them," Rosie cried, looking at Mary with floods of tears rolling down her face. Mary could do nothing to protect her little sister and the best she could offer was a feeble. "Don't worry, it will soon grow back."

Then it was Mary's turn, she was sitting facing Rosie who by now was struggling to breathe through the tears and trauma and who could only sit and stare at her hair that had half-filled the bucket. Mary feared for Rosie, who was also coughing a lot more and so she asked the Matron if they could get someone to attend to her as her breathing had got progressively worse over the day. The Matron informed them that all new inmates would be presented to the Medical Officer the following morning and that for tonight they would sleep in the receiving ward.

The receiving ward consisted of 10 iron beds with a straw filled mattress and pillow covered by 2 thin woollen blankets, the beds being separated by a small table with a small candle as a nightlight. A large wooden table was in the corner of the room on top of which was a Bible and a couple of badly worn books. A coat peg was fastened to the wall beside the beds, on which was a calico nightdress for each of the girls. As they had not been medically examined, they were to be kept in isolation in the ward and not allowed to take meals with the rest of the inmates.

At 6pm dinner was brought to the ward, which consisted of a bowl of oats, a chunk of bread and a jug of water. Mary realised they had not eaten all day and suddenly felt hungry. Rosie on the other hand just lay on the bed hardly moving, so Mary sat down and put her arms around her to try and get her to sit up and eat. She was surprised how hot and sweaty she was.

"Come on, Rosie, you need to keep your strength up," as she passed her the bowl of watery gruel.

Rosie took a small mouthful, then spat it out, "That is terrible, I can't eat that, anyway I am not hungry."

Mary decided to leave her for now and eat her own meal. She tore a lump of bread and dipped it in the bowl, and as she was about to put it in her mouth, she noticed green mould on the crust, which she removed, then proceeded to chew the remaining piece. It did not taste like any bread she had ever eaten before, it was completely tasteless and had a very dry consistency. Mary found out later that chalk was added to the flour to make the quantities go further. The gruel was also barely edible, consisting of oats, 2 small pieces of potato along with a tiny sliver of carrot and a quarter of an onion, not appetising at all. Turning back to Rosie, she knew she was very sick so forced her to drink some water and eat a mouthful of the broth, but all she wanted to do was sleep. Her coughing by now was considerably worse and Mary was very worried.

30 minutes later the door opened and the inmate who had brought the meal proceeded to gather up the plates from the table. She was accompanied this time by another woman in a black dress and white apron, with her hair scraped tightly back under a white mop hat. She introduced herself as Miss Evans and that she was the Workhouse nurse. She was there to examine the girls for infection and lice. Within seconds, she realised that Rosie was in a very bad state and said she was going to arrange for her to be moved to the infirmary. "Please don't take her away, she is very scared, we have never been apart in our lives, taking her away will make her worse. Please, let her stay with me just for tonight," Mary begged the nurse, tears welling up in her eyes.

Taking pity, Miss Evans relented and said she would bring something to relieve the wheezing and try and cool Rosie down, but Mary must make her drink. With that she left the room and returned 10 minutes later with a bowl of steaming water and a towel and forced Rosie to sit at the table with the towel over her head, breathing in the steam. Miss Evans was very concerned about Rosie's welfare, she showed all the symptoms of consumption, a big killer of the poor and infirm. She knew that Rosie should be isolated, but as it was now after 7pm, she knew there would be no further admissions that night and Mary had already been in close contact anyway so they were both better placed to remain together in the Reception Ward.

Rosie was breathing a little better but was still coughing and very hot, so the nurse reminded Mary to make Rosie keep drinking water, then left the ward, stating that the medical officer would come and see them at 8am.

That night was a very fitful sleep for Mary, she was exhausted but her 12-year-old brain was having to rationalise what was going on. She kept thinking about her mother, where she was and was she ok? She worried about Rosie and was afraid she would get worse. Although it was cold in the ward, the heat from Rosie's body was intense and she really was burning up, with the wheezing and coughing gradually increasing to the same intensity as before.

At 6am they were told to get up, make the bed and prepare for breakfast. A bowl of water along with the same carbolic soap as the bathroom was presented for them to wash themselves. Breakfast then followed which was a chunk of bread with cheese and a cup of weak tea. Mary tried in vain to get Rosie to eat, but did manage to get her to drink the tea.

The Medical Officer and Miss Evans entered the room promptly at 8am, Mary noted the strong smell of whiskey and tobacco which permeated as he set his large medical bag on the table. Having been prewarned about Rosie's condition he proceeded to sit on the bed next to Rosie, who was now lying down after the exertion of washing and forcing the tea down. He then proceeded to ask Rosie a number of questions as he felt the glands in her neck. The questions concerned Mary…

"Are you coughing up sputum?"

"Yes."

"Is there any blood in the sputum?"

"Sometimes."

"Did you have any stomach pain?"

"Yes."

"Have you lost weight recently?"

"Yes."

"Are you constantly tired?"

"Yes."

"How long have you had this condition?"

"As long as I can remember."

After a few other questions Mary realised that this was a very serious situation and she was frightened, not only for Rosie but also for herself.

Eventually, the medical officer took the nurse to one side and they had a brief discussion, then turning to Rosie, he informed her she was to be transferred to an isolation room as in all probability she was suffering from consumption and should not be in contact with any other inmates, including Mary. Miss Evans then left the room to prepare a cell for Rosie in the sick ward. Turning to Mary, the medical officer then asked the same set of questions to her and then proceeded to feel the glands in her neck. After answering negatively to all the questions, the medical officer then stated that she appeared to be clear but as a precaution Mary would also be transferred to an isolation room for a period of one week to assess whether there was any chance she too was infected.

Rosie was taken away by Miss Evans, there was no tears or protestation, she was too tired and sick to resist. Mary watched and did not say anything, but thought Rosie looked very frail, she wasn't a big girl to start with but now had lost a lot weight and as she shuffled out taking tiny steps, her body shape from behind resembled an old woman.

Miss Evans returned about 15 minutes later and escorted Mary to her own solitary bed. As they walked the short length of corridor to her room Mary asked Miss Evans a number of questions.

"What will happen to Rosie now? When can I see her?"

Miss Evans explained that consumption was very serious and very contagious, with no cure, so in all probability she would either have to stay in an isolation ward in the workhouse or in a dormitory with other sufferers. It was not possible for Mary to be able to see Rosie. if Mary proved to be free of infection and that she would be transferred to a children's dormitory after the incubation period. Mary was completely floored by this statement, they had been together all their lives. She also knew Rosie could not survive without her big sister to lean on, her head was spinning as she was shown into her tiny room.

Sitting on the bed, Mary looked around to survey her surroundings. The bed was identical to the ones in the Reception Ward with a chamber pot underneath, a small table and chair. On the table was a jug and a basin to wash in. The window was small with just enough light to allow for reading during the day. There was also a well-thumbed copy of the Bible on the table, Mary and her family never had time for God back home in Westry and so she was a little bewildered why so much attention was given to him in a sad, desperate place such as this. Suddenly she heard the familiar sound of a chesty cough and realised that Rosie was in the next room.

"Rosie, it's me. Don't worry, I am near, we are still together," There was no reply, Rosie was too weak to respond.

The rest of the day was quiet, lunch was delivered at 12 promptly which was the familiar lump of cheese and a chunk of mouldy bread to be washed down with a mug of watery tea. Mary had never been given a variety of food and her meals back home were fairly monotonous, but at least it was edible fodder, these offerings were not.

By day 3 in isolation, Mary's thoughts turned to her mother and how she had changed since their father had died. How the confidence and authority she had always shown to Mary and Rosie had evaporated and, more importantly, where was she now?

The children were due to appear in front of the Board of Governors to assess what their long-term needs were to be, but as they were both possibly infectious the board met and made their decision *in absentia*. The board consisted of elected and non-elected local dignitaries as well as the Chaplain and the Medical Officer.

The case of Annie Knox was item 4 on the agenda and discussion took place about how she had attacked a man of God and that she had no control of her senses. The police had wanted to charge Annie with assault but the Reverend insisted that she just needed time and that prison was not the place to cure her. She had been transferred to the sanatorium within the workhouse and was being kept in restricted conditions for her own safety. The chairman of the board asked how long the mother would be mentally unstable, but no end date was offered. The medical officer then declared that both girls were in isolation, one of them was confirmed with consumption, the other being isolated as a precaution and so neither could be present.

The master provided to the board the court order that was enforced after the mother of the children was sectioned, that enforced an application to stay in the workhouse.

Having taken all this into account, the decision was made that both girls would remain in blackstone Workhouse until such times as either their mother was fit to resume her parental responsibilities, or the girls were old enough to be apprenticed or placed in service. The whole process took less than five minutes.

By day 4, Mary was really starting to suffer, she called constantly to Rosie next door but never got an answer back. She knew she was still there as she could hear the coughing and wheezing and the clanking of doors opening and closing.

The only time she saw or heard anything else was when her meals were delivered, or the chamber pot was emptied and a fresh jug of water supplied. When she asked the inmate tasked with these chores about Rosie, she was told to ask the nurse.

Rosie by now was in a state of semi-consciousness all the time and had the nurse in attendance for long periods of the Day. The Medical Officer attended at least once a day and informed the nurse that he didn't think Rosie was long for this world and that Rosie's consumption had been in her body for a very long time in a latent condition, but the trauma and events of the last few months and the lack of immunity had allowed the consumption to accelerate and become active.

Finally, Mary's week in isolation was over and she as transferred to the children's dormitory, which housed 16 inmates varying in age from 6 to 13.

The day started at 6am when they were awoken by the ringing of a bell. They then washed, dressed and cleaned their shoes. An hour was then spent concentrating on the Word of the Lord and Bible Study. This left about 45 minutes during which they could socialise and relax. She noted how subdued the other children were, only speaking in quiet whispers to each other. At 8am, they were taken to the refectory, where they were seated in benches one behind the other with no facial contact with each other. Breakfast was the same gruel of oats and a chunk of stale bread, washed down with a cup of weak tea.

Before eating they had to sit and bless the offerings put before them. Mary still couldn't understand why this strange ritual occurred at every mealtime, especially as what was on offer was not exactly a feast. At 8:30am, they were marched down a corridor to a classroom where they were taught the basics of reading, writing and arithmetic. There they stayed until 12 noon, where they were marched back to the refectory for lunch with the obligatory thanking of the Lord for the offering. lunch was the most substantial meal of the day and was comprised of small cuts of mutton or beef, accompanied by a sliver of carrot a small lump of potato and a quarter of an onion… and yet another chunk of chalky bread. Mary noticed some children were only given bread, she later found out that withholding food was a punishment for misdemeanours, especially with girls as boys over 7 could be lashed but girls were spared the rod.

The afternoon was spent working on needlework skills, knitting or domestic chores such as washing laundry. Mary was luckily placed with the needlework class and found the work to be simple repairs to clothing and the like, which was very easy for her and distracted her mind from the dire situation she was in. The day passed quite quickly and they were then allowed to play in the recreation area outside for an hour. Although the air was cool, she appreciated the open space after the claustrophobic week she had just endured and the ability to walk and stretch her legs. A girl about the same age approached her, asked her name and said her name was Lizzie.

Mary realised she was in the same dormitory, so was glad she might have found a friend. As they chatted, Mary found out she had been in the workhouse about a year, her father brought her and her mother here because they had been made homeless because her father was sacked due to his liking whiskey too much. She was hoping to leave soon, her father having been sober for a while was more likely to get a job. She also said she had an appointment to see her mother this evening after supper. Mary then asked how this was possible and she was then told she was allowed 30 minutes once a month to see her alone in a private room.

At 5pm, they received supper and then were then escorted back to their dormitory, there they could relax until 6pm, before resuming the same chores as in the morning.

As they returned to the dormitory, Lizzie was summoned for her meeting with her mother by the matron. Lizzie returned after her visit and as Matron was leaving Mary asked how she could make an appointment to see her mother, Annie Knox.

"I am afraid that at the moment that is not possible," was the unwanted reply. "Your mother is in the sanatorium wing and as such is not of a fit mind to see anyone."

This was not what she either wanted or expected.

"Well, when will I be able to see her?"

Matron took hold of Mary's hand and placed it in hers, "Your mother is a very sick women, her fate is in the Lord's hands. She might have to be transferred to an asylum if the doctors decide she cannot be cured. I am afraid you might never get to see her again."

Mary was devastated, this latest blow really hit her hard and she reeled onto a bed and cried incessantly, initially she was shrieking then it subsided to a sobbing. Matron decided she was not in a fit state to carry out any work tasks so escorted the rest of the girls out and left her on the bed. Eventually Mary fell into an exhausted sleep, she had not slept properly for about a month but the sheer tiredness had built up and was now taking its toll. The rest of the dormitory returned at 8pm and everyone changed into their nightdress and knelt down for evening prayer. Throughout the prayer process, Mary was being told that God is good, God is powerful, God sees everything and God makes all the decision. Mary decided she hated God for what he had done to her family.

The days were boringly repetitive for the next 3 weeks, the same routine every day, the same food every day, the same gloomy faces every day… but things were about to change.

Chapter Four

Rosie was now in a critical condition, she had not eaten anything for 2 weeks and her emaciated body was now refusing to keep liquid down. Miss Evans asked the Matron if Mary could be allowed to see her sister for the last time. Matron at first refused on the basis that Mary could still become infectious, but eventually relented when it was pointed out that Mary had already been in isolation and that there were other cases in the workhouse anyway. At 5pm on 2 August, Matron summoned Mary to her office and informed her that she was allowed to see her sister, but Rosie was a very sick young girl. Mary's head was spinning, on one hand she realised that Rosie must be in a bad way, but it was also the first opportunity to see her for over a month.

As she entered the room, Mary was shocked at the sight that confronted her and struggled to recognise the tiny frail body that lay under the sheets. Rosie was sweating badly and her wheezing was incessant. Sitting on the bed, Mary took Rosie's tiny hand in hers and asked how she was.

"It's Mary, we are together now," she whispered, but Rosie did not respond, her eyes remained closed and not a flicker of recognition appeared on her gaunt face. Mary now realised that Rosie was dying and that was the reason she had been allowed to see her. Struggling to hold back the tears, she talked about how things will get better soon, even though the reality was clearly different. Miss Evans told Mary to say her goodbyes informing her that she would return in about half an hour, so she lay down next to Rosie and cuddled her scrawny body, talking incessantly but not really making any sense. In all this time, all Rosie could manage was a coughing fit which brought up globules of blood and the never-ending wheeze.

Eventually Miss Evans returned to escort Mary back to her dormitory, so she gave her one last kiss and a hug and whispered, "Sleep well my darling, you will soon be at peace," Then stood up and without looking back accompanied Miss Evans back to her wing. As she was walking down the corridor, the Chaplain passed her, Mary knew where he was going and wanted to tell him not bother with all the religious hypocrisy but knew she would just store up trouble for herself. She also knew that none of it would register with Rosie, so she just carried on walking.

In bed that night, Mary reflected on the day, she was beyond tears now and knew that Rosie was never going to survive and that death was a release from the pain she had suffered. Her thoughts then began to wander to her mother, how was she coping, did she know about Rosie, would she ever be released?

At 3am on 4 August, Rosie passed away, the medical officer entering in the workhouse register that Miss Rosie Knox had died from consumption, aged 10 years old, then without any ceremony her body was transferred to the workhouse cemetery for interment into a communal grave. Mary was informed as she awoke and was given the day off from any work duties so she could grieve in peace.

Annie was struggling with the realisation that her husband had died, they were homeless, she was separated from her children and that she was not in control of any aspect of her life. She was unaware of Rosie's death as those responsible for Annie's wellbeing had decided not to increase the madness within her. The people that were supposed to be treating her were just jailers and whenever she protested about her situation, she was fed doses of laudanum to suppress her anger and outrages. This had been the case since she was first admitted and with no sign of improvement the medical officer referred her case to the to the board of governors.

On 6 August 1921, the board met and the medical officer proclaimed that Annie Knox's condition had not improved and that Rosie had died, He further stated that in his opinion Annie was never going to recover and she would never be able to return to a normal sustainable life.

"What of the other child?" asked the chairman of the board.

"She is strong of body, mind and character," replied the medical officer.

After ten minutes discussion, the decision was made to transfer Annie to the Lunatic Asylum for treatment, this in effect meant she would never see the outside world again.

Mary was now classed as an orphan and as such was to be sent to the local orphanage to be schooled ready for her to enter service. Mary was nearly 13 and a year of service training and betterment of her education was the logical outcome. Neither Annie nor Mary was present when their fates were sealed and there was no discussion about whether they agreed to the outcome, the whole process taking less than 15 minutes.

Annie was subsequently transported in cuffs, for her own safety, to the Deakin Sanatorium for the medically insane. Here she would remain for the next 6 years, subject to various forms of treatment including being submerged in ice cold water for long periods, constant restraint and being fed daily doses of sedatives. Her body gave up the will to live in 1926, but in reality, she had mentally died the minute she entered the sanatorium.

Mary was informed that she was to be transferred to an orphanage, which to her made no sense as she already had a mother. Matron then explained that her mother was taken to the sanatorium and as such she was now under the care of the Board of Governors, who deemed that Mary's welfare would be better managed in an environment where she could learn and be trained in readiness to go into service. When she asked if she would ever get to see her mother, Matron stated that as her mother's mental condition was extremely unbalanced with little chance of a recovery.

She now knew she was all alone in the world, everything she had ever known in her entire life had now gone, the enormity of it left her head spinning. She had no tears left just a big empty hole where her emotions had been assaulted and she was completely numb inside. She was nearly 13 but instead of enjoying a childhood she was now looking at her life as a survival exercise. This was it, nobody would take care of her except these heartless, uncaring, God besotted officials, who had no interest in her emotional welfare and who only saw her as a commodity that provided them with the piety and religious credit they craved from their God.

Mary hated the constant prayers and religious education and only went along with the routines because she was well aware of the consequences that would result from any dissent. She hated this God that had stripped her of her family, home, happiness and replaced it with the cruel regime that she now had endure every single day.

On 12 August, Mary exchanged her workhouse clothes for her own gingham dress that she noticed was tighter than when she last wore it, she was also a little taller and her shoes pinched. It felt strange after so many months of wearing the drab, heavy workhouse uniform and Mary felt so much brighter and alive. She was escorted to the same drab room she had first entered 5 months previously and was met by a lady in a grey dress with a black cardigan, who introduced herself as Mrs Thompson.

Mary took an instant liking to her, she actually smiled which was a something Mary had never seen on Matrons stern featureless face.

"Hello Mary, I am here to take you to your new home," she explained. She then thanked Matron and guided Mary through the door and the big wooden gate to the street outside. Mary noted how warm it was, compared to the cold air when she had entered the workhouse and walked with a spring in her step to the next adventure in her short life. She estimated that whatever the future was it could not be any worse than all she had endured in that terrible institution.

The walk to the orphanage was only about 20 minutes but Mary's shoes were too small now and her feet had started to blister. Mrs Thompson noticed this and said that if it was more convenient then she should walk barefoot and she would get the nurse to tend to her feet when they arrived. Mary noted that nobody at the workhouse would either have noticed or offered any solution to her predicament and although it was uncomfortable she would carry on and walk the remaining distance with her shoes off. As they walked, Mrs Thompson asked Mary about the circumstances that led to her being in the workhouse and as she related the whole experience of her father's death, her mother's breakdown and the loss of Rosie, Mary struggled to keep herself together.

Mrs Thompson saw that Mary was really suffering and put a motherly arm round her, at which point Mary broke down completely and wrapped her arms around Mrs Thompsons waist. They stayed like this for about 5 minutes, eventually Mary regained her composure and so they resumed their journey.

The orphanage was a large imposing building with a large front garden and was accessed up a long stoney drive, Mary stepped onto the lawn and it felt good to feel the grass under her feet. As they approached the main door, Mary could hear the sound of children laughing and singing. Mary had a good feeling about this place and for the first time in months she began to relax.

On entering, Mary was introduced to the nurse who took her to the medical room and bathed her injuries. She was then issued with the standard uniform, which was similar to the workhouse but a lot more comfortable and lighter and a heavy-duty pair of shoes rather than the wooden clogs that used to irritate Mary, due to the noise they created on the stone corridor floor.

By the time Mary had been registered, it was time for lunch and Mary was pleasantly surprised that the food was of an edible quality and actually had some taste. It was a basic stew with the obligatory chunk of bread, which tasted like bread. This was followed by a jam suet pudding and custard. Mary was not used to such a feast and felt her stomach swell… but she was determined not to leave any.

As she surveyed her surroundings, Mary noticed that the children were talking to each other in whispers and not being reprimanded, this all felt very strange. The rule was supposed to be no talking but the staff appeared to turn a blind eye, as long as the noise was kept to a minimum. After lunch, they were given half an hour to play outside in the garden, some were sat down chatting while others were playing hop scotch, spinning tops or jacks.

As a new entry, Mary attracted quite a bit of attention from 4 or 5 girls who seemed quite chatty and in good spirits. The oldest was just a little older than Mary, the youngest being about eight years old. Mary was asking lots of questions about where they were, how strict was it, did they work, what did they do?

The orphanage was named Willard Hall and been established in 1910, thanks to the patronage of Mr Charles Butterworth a local industrialist who made his fortune providing weaving machines to northern mill owners. He died in 1908 after having lived in the house for over 30 years. He had no heirs so insisted the hall be turned into an institution for the betterment of the education of the working classes and laid down strict covenants about how it was to be run. He had seen firsthand how young girls put their lives in danger cleaning under machines as they were producing linen and was shocked at how little regard was made as to their welfare.

The Covenant stated that the girls should receive 2 hours recreation time a day, 3 meals of which at least one must contain meat and vegetables and a sound education in the skills of the 3 R's. There was also a stipulation that vocational training in the form of tailoring, cooking and housekeeping be applied for 4 hours a day. The orphanage was run by trustees, comprising of local dignitaries, magistrate, local bank manager and the obligatory reverend from the local parish and there was a healthy allocation of financial investment which allowed Willard Hall to be run efficiently and with ample staff to supervise the children's wellbeing.

Apart from the Matron there was a housekeeper, a seamstress, nurse, cook, and general handyman to manage 50 girls.

The girls were from varied background some were orphaned sent there because their father had died in the Great War and the mothers could not cope, some were orphans from birth as their mother had died giving birth. Talking to them they all seemed to say the same thing, life was regimented but in general they were treated well.

After lunch they assembled to go to their afternoon classes, which were the basics of reading, writing and arithmetic. Mary's school in Westry was small and all the children hardly benefited from the personal attention of the teacher who took no notice of the different levels of the various ages and just used to rattle away with her teaching, oblivious of who could and could not keep up with the pace of the lesson.

Because of this Mary struggled with her reading and writing, but she had a natural flair for mathematics that was far ahead of the others in the class.

As she settled down in class, the teacher who was called Miss Brierley, sat Mary in the front row so she could assess what her standard was. The first hour was reading, Mary hated having to take a turn reading out aloud for the rest of the class to hear and as she struggled, she became very aware of the rest of the class focusing on her and started to get flustered. Miss Brierley helped her through her half page and congratulated her at the end, even though Mary knew her reading had been poor. There were some girls at the back of the class that didn't have to read aloud and she discovered later this was because they were already proficient and so they were allowed to read other books alone. Mary was determined to get to this standard at all costs.

The next lesson was writing, again Mary struggled. At Westry, they were given chalk and slate boards on which to practice the letters of the alphabet, here they were given a pen that was dipped in an inkwell and transferred onto a sheet of paper. Mary could not handle this whole new process very well and proceeded to fill the sheet with blobs of ink, the pen was much thinner than she had been used to and she struggled to manoeuvrer it to the correct position. Miss Brierley noticed this and managed to locate a pen with a thicker girth which was marginally better, but she still struggled.

By the time it came to mathematics Mary had lost all confidence and was feeling very low, but to her surprise she excelled and was one of the better girls in the class, her long division being highly praised by Miss Brierley.

After three long hours, it was over and Mary's head was spinning and she was surprised how tired she felt. It had begun to rain outside so playtime was restricted to 30 minutes in the day room, which housed some chairs, a small library and some board games.

She sat down on a long sofa and a girl that she recognised from earlier sat down and introduced herself as Molly. "How was your first school lesson?" asked Molly with a slight smirk on her face, as she had seen Mary struggling.

"It's so different," Mary sighed. "It's nothing like I had back in the village."

"I was exactly the same but at least your sums are good, I was useless at everything," Molly then related how her father had died in 1915 in the war and that her mother remarried just after the war ended, but her stepfather didn't want her so she was sent away. She had grown up in a village school just like Mary and the teacher was just as unsympathetic as Mary's teacher.

"I can't help you with your writing, but we can read these together, they helped me get better," With that she produced a well-thumbed copy of a book called 'The Story of Doctor Dolittle'. "We can read this together if you like."

Mary was grateful for anything that would help her progress, so they sat down for the next half hour and read a few pages.

By now Mary was mentally exhausted, it had been a very long tiring first day. But it was not over yet. They then had the Evening Service which consisted of half an hour of prayers during which Mary took no part and just mimed so it looked as though she was participating, before being wheeled out for tea. Mary by now was hungry again and welcomed the bread and cheese that was on offer.

Finally, at 6:30 there was what was termed 'useful work', which consisted of the older girls being split into various groups where they were tasked with carrying out tasks that might provide them with a future career. Some learnt cooking skills, some tailoring, others had laundry and general housekeeping. For today, Mary was shown how to make pastry, which she quite enjoyed.

At 8pm the younger girls were put to bed and the older ones allowed to read or play games until 9pm. Mary decided to ask Molly to help her with her reading, which she obliged and although she was finding it difficult, Mary was determined to make progress.

This routine was repeated every day except Sunday which was a day of religious contemplation in the morning and the afternoon was considered free time, this was when the girls could go out as a group for a walk by the river or in the woods. They were instantly recognisable when out as the green uniform was distinct, the local kids used to tease them for not having parents and shout names, but they all became immune to the catcalling after a while.

Mary was at her happiest when it came to the tailoring, she was after all very good working with cloth and sewing. The standard of Mary's work was also noticed by the seamstress who after discussion with Mrs Thompson agreed this was to be Mary's career path, so she remained learning various aspects of tailoring for the duration of her stay.

One day, an opportunity arose that was to be the highlight of her stay. The seamstress and Mrs Thompson had designed an outline draft of a new school uniform, then Mary was asked to assist the seamstress in creating a sample to present to the board for approval. After a number of alterations, the final design was agreed and Mary was tasked with producing the finished article. This was warmly accepted by the board, who noted the quality of the workmanship.

Mary was also beginning to get confidence with her reading, the time spent with Molly was producing excellent results. Over the next few months Mary not only matched her peer's ability but was ahead of the majority of the class. She still struggled with her writing though and no matter how hard she tried she could not get the pen to paper in a presentable form. It was legible and the structure was good, but with all the blobs of ink on the paper, the physical appearance of the note resembled that of a Frisian Cow.

All this good work was being noted by Mrs Thompson who knew that in a year's time Mary would be fourteen and of an age to commence work, she had an idea that would be of great benefit to Mary. On 2 October, Mary's thirteenth birthday passed off without any recognition, after all with 50 girls in Willard Hall, it was someone's birthday nearly every week. Mary herself didn't realise until evening time and then spent over an hour alone contemplating where the last year had taken her, how her life had changed and the loss of her family. She knew nothing could change the past so put all her efforts into making sure she would carve out a life for herself, she was determined not to be at the bottom of the pile, she would be self-sufficient in every way.

The next year saw her begin the journey from a child into a woman and she noticed her breasts develop and her body shape change, by the following summer the caterpillar became a butterfly, her confidence was soaring because of her tailoring skills and Mrs Thompson knew she was ready for her next steps.

Chapter Five

It was a cold autumn evening as Mrs Thompson alighted from the train at Manchester station. The journey, though short and uneventful, had had given her the opportunity to consider how she was going to present her suggestion in regard to Mary Knox. There to meet her was her sister who was a few years older than her, in her fifties but with similar features, though a little slimmer.

"This is a pleasant surprise Sarah; it must be at least two years since we last saw each other."

"Yes, at least, we have a lot to catch up on Martha," she replied handing her bag for a porter to carry as they walked off the platform and hailed a cab.

As they travelled the couple of miles through Manchester centre, Sarah was struck by how busy and hectic it was, compared to the relative peace and quiet of Blackstone. The constant movement of people, the sound of cars and lorries, this was a city that was alive and vibrant.

The cab pulled up outside a dress shop in a busy street in a suburb of Manchester. Entering the shop, Sarah was struck by the delicate nature of the embroidery and the quality of the linen used on the dresses in the shop window. They were met by a young shop assistant who took the bags through to the back of the shop. Putting the bags in a bedroom, she then left the sisters to discuss the reason for Sarah's visit.

Martha, poured a cup of tea and passing it to her younger sibling asked, "So why are you really here, your letter merely said that we needed to meet as you have something I might be interested in."

"How are your hands, still having trouble with them?" Sarah knew that Martha's rheumatism was getting worse. Although they hadn't seen each other for a while, they did write on a regular basis and Martha's handwriting had become more spidery and harder to decipher.

"And your eyes, how are they?"

"Fine, fine, fine… now what is on your mind!"

Sarah took a deep breath and told her all about Mary and her tragic tale, of her potential and the fact that Martha did not have a child of her own to pass her skills on to.

"Why would I need the trouble of taking in a child? I am of an age where I do not need the trouble that such a child would bring."

"Mary is a good girl, who should be given a chance in life. Yes, she has some rough edges, she is from a mining background, what do you expect? But she deserves better than the life that she has." Sarah then proceeded to tell her about Mary's needlework skills and painted a picture of how she could be developed to become a skilled dressmaker, someone for Martha to pass her knowledge on to, someone who in turn would look after her as she aged. Finally, she produced a sample of Mary's work and placed it in Martha's hands. Martha studied the cloth and felt the stitchwork, this was indeed work of a high standard.

Sarah went on. "You have no family except for me, you need someone to bring some joy into your life. Someone you can help and nurture, to become a daughter to you."

Martha knew Sarah was telling the truth. "I will reflect on it and let you know tomorrow."

The rest of the evening was spent catching up on how Sarah's boys were, and the sad loss of her eldest. The other two were now working on the railways with their father, who was still grieving for his son.

Eventually they retired to bed and as Martha lay in the darkness she thought about her own mortality, her business, her future. Sarah was right, she did need someone. After the Great War, it had become more difficult to find young women that would enter the dressmaking profession, they simply wanted the freedom, money and respect they had gained by working in the factories during the Great War, they wanted to explore the new horizons that were opening up, not working in a shop that still traditionally was poorly paid. The girls she had were capable but no more than that. And certainly did not have the skills of the calibre she expected.

After breakfast, they went for a walk in the park, the cold autumnal wind piercing the air. As they walked and as young women passed them, Martha realised that fashion had also changed and she was making dresses that no-one except her own age group were wearing, the type of dresses she made looked dated.

Finally, Martha spoke, "Your proposal has certain merits I must admit, but before I can consider taking this young child into my home, then I must meet her, I make no promises."

"Of course, Martha, you will not be disappointed, I'm sure."

It was agreed that they would tell Mary she was going to stay with Martha for the week to gain some experience that would assist her to get a permanent placement somewhere. After agreement from the trustees, Mary was informed she was to stay at 'The Castlefield Fashion House' to gain an insight into what to expect for her future life.

Three days after her 14th birthday, Mary was informed that she would travel with Mrs Thompson to see her new employer. Her old clothes that she had outgrown were replaced with new and a small case with extra clothing provided. She was also given a coat that actually fitted, Mary had been used to second-hand hand me downs that were either too small or too large and something she would eventually grow into, so she felt rather special as she accompanied Mrs Thompson to the station. This was something of an adventure, Mary had never been on a train before and found the whole experience exhilarating. As they travelled Mrs Thompson explained about Martha being her sister, that she was a spinster and that while she appeared to have a very abrupt nature, she was really a caring person. She went on to further expand and said that Martha was at an age where her dexterity was suffering and she needed a trainee to develop as her own skills waned. Mary sat quietly taking it all in and although she had developed a lot of confidence over the last year or so, she knew this could be a daunting experience.

The Castlefield Fashion House was on the corner of a very busy street that had shops selling various products along its length. Next door was a ladies' shoe shop and next that was a haberdasher's selling all kinds of cloth. Mary also saw a cinema and was intrigued to see inside it. Upon entering the shop, they were met by a shop assistant who promptly showed them through to see Martha. Mrs Thompson introduced them to each other.

"This is Mary Knox," and gently ushered her forward to Martha who was in the middle of sewing a hem on a very lavish dress. Turning to Mary Mrs Thompson added, "And this is Miss Shorrock, who will be your new employer," Mary was not allowed to address Martha by her first name, she was first and foremost her employer, so such personal terms were totally unacceptable.

Beckoning them both to sit down Miss Shorrock ordered some tea and they began to talk about Mary, Miss Shorrock asking all the questions with Mary responding quite confidently, after all she had nothing to hide and the questions were straightforward.

All the while she was talking, Miss Thompson was busy attending to the dress, until finally she looked up and asked Mary to look at the stitching and work she had done. Mary noticed that there was about four inches of unfinished stitch left to do. "Do you think you could finish this off?"

Mary looked at the work—the stitching was with a fine silk thread and the material very light; she could quite easily get this wrong. She was used to heavier materials, but the principles were the same. "I reckon so, Miss Shorrock," and so she moved in position and picked up the needle and thread. She could normally work at twice the speed but knew this was all about getting it right, so steadied her hand and took her time. When she finished, Miss Shorrock scrutinised the work, it was difficult to tell the difference but she had to be critical. "You were a little slow, it would take you a long time to complete a whole section, but the standard is passable," Mary explained that she was not used to working with such fine materials and that she was bound to speed up as she became familiar with working with finer quality. Mrs Thompson could tell by the look on her sisters face she was happy with both the work and Mary's response, this was going to be a good match.

Finally, the initial meeting was over and they had tea and cakes, Mary had never tasted such splendour. Mary was then shown to her room by Mrs Thompson and as they entered the small bedroom she sat on the chair in the corner and informed Mary that she now had a good chance to live a good life and that Mary must not waste the opportunity, Mary was well aware that she had to get this right. Mary was then left to sort her small amount of clothing into the wardrobe and chest of drawers and as she did so her mind wandered to her mother and how she would be happy that Mary had this chance.

Mrs Thompson and Miss Shorrock were in the parlour talking about Mary and Mrs Thompson was curious as to the first impression Mary had made. "She seems a likeable young lady and the standard of work was fairly good, but her speed needs to improve. This time next week, I will know if she will make the grade," Mrs Thompson knew her sister very rarely gave praise so this was a good start.

As they sat down to supper it was explained that she would stay above the shop for a month, there would be no wages but she would have everything she needed. The hours would be from 8am until 6:30pm and she will be expected to work on any task as requested. Miss Shorrock employed two other girls in the workshop and a shop assistant who doubled up as a general dogsbody. They didn't live in and their skills were varied, Mary would be introduced to them tomorrow.

After breakfast Mary said goodbye to Mrs Thompson who was returning to Willard Hall and was given a cream pinafore to wear before being shown into the workshop at the rear and introduced to the other girls.

The first impression of the room was how large and organised it was. Row upon row of cloth in different colours, shades and textures adorned the rear wall. There were 3 mannequins with dresses in different styles and state of readiness, a large cutting table and 3 tables with sewing machines surrounded by baskets and bundles of linen. A young lady named Daisy who was not much older than Mary was sat working away at one of the machines and Mary sat down at the machine next to her. Miss Shorrock informed Mary she was to work every morning for the next week making blouses exactly the same as Daisy.

The blouses were very plain but were also the staple income and although they were not expensive, they paid all the bills and were very popular, Miss Shorrock sold them to other shops and markets in smaller communities. They were all the same basic shape but were useful in that they could be adapted by introducing beads, braids and overlaid in silk so were very versatile.

As Mary settled down to this mundane task, she struck up a conversation with Daisy, who was also from a mining community near Ashton in Makerfield. Daisy's father had succumbed to Black Lung in 1916 and she was the main earner in the family. There was only her and her mother, who had shown her how to sew from childhood, a very similar background as Mary and they immediately bonded. That morning, she managed to make six blouses, Daisy had managed seven, so Mary was quite pleased with her output.

Miss Shorrock spent most of her time either in the shop at the front or in the workshop supervising the work of the other girl, who was making the dress that was draped over one of the mannequins. The dress looked lavish, but Mary thought it a little over elaborate and old fashioned.

Lunch was a 30-minute break, the other girls brought their own food and Mary lunched with Miss Shorrock, a bowl of vegetable soup and a couple of slices of bread and butter. Mary smiled to herself… still soup for dinner, but at least the bread has butter, she thought to herself.

In the afternoon, Mary worked with the other girl on the mannequin dress and also some fine stitching to a silk blouse that was designed to be worn under the dress. Mary immediately noticed the difference in quality from the plain linen blouses she had been making in the morning. The other girls name was Millicent but who preferred to be called Milly. Mary noted she seemed to be a rather serious young lady. She told Mary she was 19 and had been with Miss Shorrock for 4 years, Mary got the impression thought Mary was a rival, so was reluctant to engage in any sort of friendly chat. Mary also noted that the quality of Milly's work was variable and most of what she was tasked with appeared to be areas out of sight in a finished garment. Mary was to be proved right as Miss Shorrock seemed to be the one who completed all the final touches to the dresses.

The subject at supper consisted mainly of Miss Shorrock asking Mary about the other girls but Mary did not want to be seen as unfriendly, so gave both girls a favourable opinion. Miss Shorrock then sat down and completed paperwork and said she would be there for another 2 hours. Mary thought this was a long day for an old woman but said nothing.

This routine was repeated every day but on Sunday Mary was allowed the day off and keen to see what the neighbourhood was like. Daisy lived in lodgings a 10-minute walk away and Miss Shorrock agreed Mary could meet up with her and go for a walk in the local park. Mary was so excited to be allowed out on her own, without being in a group and wearing clothes that made her stand out as a member of an institution.

As they walked, Mary was keen to know what Daisy thought about her work and Miss Shorrock.

"Miss Shorrock is ok, she pays slightly more than other dressmakers, but dressmaking is not a very profitable business so I will never get rich," Milly further went on to say she thought that too much time was spent on expensive dresses and that as they were so time consuming, it was impossible to make money.

"We are still making dresses from the last century, only old spinsters dress like that nowadays."

The exact same thought had crossed Mary's mind, but it wasn't her place to tell Miss Shorrock how to run her business.

The month passed quickly and soon Mary was back in Wardle Hall and being asked a million questions about her experience. On the second day back, she was summoned to Mrs Thompson's office.

"How did you find the month, was it how you imagined it?"

Mary informed her she had learnt much and that Miss Shorrock had been very kind to her.

"Miss Shorrock spoke highly of the way you adapted and the attitude and aptitude you presented. In fact, so much so, she wants you to be an apprenticed dressmaker at her establishment. How do you feel about that?"

Mary could hardly contain herself. "Yes, yes, yes," she exclaimed.

Mrs Thompson smiled. "It has to go to the board for approval, but you are 14 now so we will work towards you leaving around the end of the month."

The following week Mrs Thompson presented all the facts to the Board of Trustees and it was agreed that Miss Mary Knox was to become an indentured Apprentice Dressmaker at the Castlefield Fashion House. Mary's return to the shop was greeted with whoops of glee by Daisy but a more reticent Milly merely nodded an acknowledgement, which Mary noticed immediately.

Miss Shorrock sat her down at the table in the parlour. She had warmed to Mary over the month she had been there and she felt she was capable of more responsibility.

"I am an old lady now and I feel I need to step back and take things easier, therefore I want you to take more of a lead in making the more expensive dresses," Mary knew that Milly would not be pleased with that and suggested that maybe it would be better for the responsibility to be shared between her and Milly. "I have thought about that and it won't work because Milly is not as capable as you and she thinks she is better than she actually is," Miss Shorrock clarified.

Mary was not prepared for this and was momentarily stunned; this was going to cause a problem. She donned her pinafore and entered the workshop to work for a couple of hours until the end of the day, but her mind was not on work.

Supper was a very quiet affair with Mary hardly speaking, which Miss Shorrock noted and decided to leave her with her thoughts.

After a sleepless night in which all manner of thoughts went through her head, Mary decided to try and get Miss Shorrock to sit on the idea for now. During breakfast Mary suggested that a less formal transfer of responsibility might be appropriate. "Why not look at making a less formal and less complicated design, in keeping with the change in fashion?" she suggested. "The modern styles are easy to produce and cost less." She went on to say that they could probably produce more dresses for less cost if they ditched the old 'belle epoque' style that Miss Shorrock had been producing for the last 20 years.

Miss Shorrock listened intently, nobody had ever questioned her before about the style and quality of dress that she was producing, but she admitted to herself that the costs had increased and demand was low, it was only the blouses that kept her solvent at the moment. Mary was not sure what reaction she was going to get, she was worried she had overstepped the mark and was heading for a disastrously short career as a dressmaker.

Finally, Miss Shorrock spoke, "Please can you give me an example of the style of dress you would implement by supper and we can discuss your proposal in more depth."

"Of course," said Mary, as she finished her cup of tea. She then grabbed her pinafore and headed off for her morning stint with Daisy on the blouses.

Mary's head was spinning, but she said nothing for about an hour and kept her head down all the while thinking about how she was going to convince Miss Shorrock to back her plan. Daisy noticed how preoccupied Mary was and eventually asked her what was wrong. As Mary explained, Daisy started gushing about what a great idea it was and how much better things would be. Mary was not sure how to present to Miss Shorrock but Daisy had the solution. "Ask her to give you 2 days and I will get some magazines tonight, there are always examples in them."

Miss Shorrock agreed to the request and 2 days later Daisy arrived at work with a few crumpled magazines and also a sample dress she had borrowed from a neighbour. As she skimmed the magazines, it was obvious that the dresses were lighter, shorter and revealing more flesh. She laid the dress out and immediately could see there was a lot less stitching and the material considerably less rigid. It almost flowed as she handled it.

Milly had been watching what was going on and wandered over to have a look. "What you planning?" Mary had been preoccupied with scanning the dress and didn't see her peering over her shoulder.

"Mary is going to ask if we can start making a new style," Daisy offered, which Mary didn't appreciate as she didn't want Milly to work out what the reasons were.

Milly scoffed, "She will never buy it, been doing the same for years, but wish she would. Something needs to change, nobody is buying this stuff now."

This was just what Mary wanted and she couldn't wait for supper time to arrive. That night Mary waited until they had eaten and the table cleared.

"I have something to show you," then Mary produced the dress and the magazines and spread them out on the table.

"These are the latest fashion and they can be produced quickly and cheaply, we can make at least six of these for the same cost as one of the more formal dresses. The basic style can be adapted by placing sequins and creating pleats. Gone are the days of a double layer of clothing, these could be manufactured quickly and do not require the same degree of skill to produce."

Miss Shorrock was impressed, this young lady was talking sense. After looking at the materials, she knew half of her current stock was not really suitable for the new fashion styles and she made a mental note to speak with her suppliers. The colour of the dress was more pastel which she knew was the fashion and she realised there would need to be more investment in materials.

"What you say has some merit Mary and I will give your ideas some thought."

Over the next few days, Miss Shorrock made a few enquiries and had a couple of trips to various Haberdashery and clothing warehouse suppliers in the area, then made appointments for their salesman to call at the shop the following week. She was amazed at the range of materials available and soon realised Mary was right, she needed to modernise. A week after their little chat, Miss Shorrock made a proposal that shocked Mary.

"I would like you to make a dress that is contemporary and that you think might be able to be produced quickly and cheaply, you have a completely free hand, everything about the manufacturing process is your decision." She went on to say they would be seeing a few suppliers over the next week or so and that she needed to create a design over the next few days.

Mary scoured the magazines and whenever she had time, she looked at what people in the street were wearing. She had to design something that was fit for everyday wear, the exotic evening dresses could wait, functionality was the key. She made sketches and thought about how the dress would be composed, the colour, the waistlines, everything would be totally different to Miss Sharrock's current method of manufacture. Finally, she was ready to meet the cloth suppliers.

The following day, Miss Shorrock told the girls that Mary was busy and would not be with them today and she was ushered into the shop and was told to wait for the salesman to come, but in the meantime to help in the shop.

At 10am the first salesman arrived, he was a large sweaty man, who swaggered into the shop and demanded to meet the shop owner. Miss Shorrock was duly summoned and as the salesman was removing his samples from a very large bag Miss Shorrock introduced Mary. The salesman who introduced himself to Miss Shorrock as Mr Thomas Evans, barely glanced at this little shop girl and Mary did not warm to him at all.

"We have a lot of new materials in all kinds of styles and colours," he pronounced in a very distinct Welsh voice and looking around the shop stated, "these might not be suitable for the clientele you are used to."

This statement made Miss Shorrock bristle, who was this this man to tell her what she can and can't buy?

With the samples laid out on the table, Mary's eye was drawn to a fabric she had never seen before and she felt its smoothness, almost silk like, with her fingers.

"It's Rayon, a mixture of wood and some chemicals, it's been about a while but is now very fashionable," Mr Evans explained. He then produced a colour chart which was extensive, Mary was impressed. "The beauty of this product is it feels like silk but is about a third of the price."

Miss Sharrock's ears pricked up; this was definitely worth exploring. After about an hour of discussing the various cottons silks, colours and prices, Mr Evans left. When he had gone, they discussed the virtues of Rayon and they were both impressed with the versatility of the material and the applications it could be used for.

Mary then outlined the style of dress she had in mind, which was tubular with a 'V' neckline a lower waist and a hem at mid-calf. She produced a rough sketch so Miss Shorrock could visualise the finished product.

"Well, there won't be very much in material costs, for sure," said Miss Shorrock with raised eyebrows, not totally convinced.

"Please come with me for a walk to the park and take a look at what people are wearing now," said Mary and guided Miss Shorrock to put her coat on. Miss Shorrock agreed and as they walked, she began to notice the raised hems, the sometimes open neck and general smoothness of shape that was indeed the fashion now.

"Alright I agree, estimate how much material you need, how long it will take and I will cost it up."

As Miss Shorrock estimated the costs, she was very surprised at how much cheaper it was to produce Mary's dress compared to the standard attire she had produced, she would be very interested to see the finished product.

Over the next few days, the material was ordered and delivered and Mary refined the style. Miss Shorrock kept bobbing in and out of the workshop and Daisy and Milly were both distracted from their day-to-day work as they were fascinated to see what Mary was up to, which Miss Shorrock duly noted and reprimanded both girls, to Mary's amusement.

Once Mary had decided what the style of the dress was, she set about cutting the cloth and arranging it neatly on the table. The material was predominantly a fine pastel blue with a lace trim to the hem neckline and shoulders. The waist was trimmer and lower and as she set about stitching the assembled materials, she felt a wave of apprehension, if she got this wrong then Miss Shorrock would surely never trust her again. Eventually, the dress was finished and as Daisy was about the right size she asked her to try it on which Daisy was delighted to do. Looking at it on her, Mary could not help but be more than a little bewildered, the dress just did not sit right, then it dawned on her.

"Daisy, take off your underwear, its bulking the dress out." She demanded.

"I will not, you will see all my bits," Daisy responded. With that Mary took some of the linen that was used to make blouses and created a rough Camisole for Daisy to wear. "Here put this on," then she threw the makeshift garment at Daisy, who slipped around the back of the mannequins and got changed. The material did fit a lot better and Mary took note of the need to ensure that different undergarments were required for this new style of clothing. It still didn't look right so she added some sequins around the neckline and finally it was finished. Daisy took the dress off and it was placed on a mannequin.

"What do you think?" asked Mary to the girls as they scrutinised the garment. They both agreed it was the kind of thing they would both wear and that it was an improvement on what they were making.

"How many do you think we could make in a day?" asked Mary trying to anticipate Miss Shorrock's line of questioning.

Daisy was first to speak, "a lot of the work is similar to the blouses just a little more that's all, I could probably manage 6 in a day."

Milly was a little more apprehensive, she knew where this was leading and didn't consider herself to be a machinist. "Not sure, but we will not be able to manage both these and the other styles we currently do," she finally answered, hoping she wasn't talking herself out of a job.

Mary decided to leave it at that, she did not want to get into a war of words with Milly over anything, especially as this could save Milly's job. She then covered the dress with a sheet and waited until the end of the day and after the girls had gone home, before asking Miss Shorrock to cast her eye over the finished product.

As Miss Shorrock examined the dress, she noted how much less material was used and that the vast majority of it could be made on a machine. Her experienced eye also picked up that by utilising various finishes such as sequins, chiffon, etc a standard dress could be made to look so different with many options of choice available.

"Well, you are a hidden talent," she finally said. "I am quite impressed with your first effort... but will it sell, is what I ask myself."

Mary was delighted with this response, she knew Miss Shorrock was a difficult woman to please.

"I am sure it will and it didn't take long to make," Mary replied.

She then went on to say that Daisy could probably make 6 a day, if Milly spent a morning making another 3 or 4 then she could assist Mary to sew the variation in adornments to the basic dress, then 9 completed dresses could be managed easily in a day.

Miss Shorrock started to work the costs out mentally, the girls' wages a week, the material costs and the running of the shop meant a dress would cost about six shilling to make, looking at the dress before her, there was a substantial profit to be made. It was agreed that the dress would be placed in the shop window and if it sold reasonably quickly then more would be produced.

Mary was feeling very pleased with herself as the item was placed in the shop window, the rest of the day flew by as she carried on with the daily routine in the workshop.

Supper that night was a quiet affair and after clearing the plates away Mary was about to leave the room and go read a book when Miss Shorrock who had been busy looking at her accounts and diligently writing notes and doing calculations, looked up and said, "Mary we need to have a serious chat," in a very sombre voice.

This startled Mary a little as she not expecting such a stern look. Sitting back down at the table, Miss Shorrock asked her to go and take another look at the dress in the window to make sure she was happy with it.

As she turned the shop light on, she could see the dress was still in the window, and her head was spinning now, what was going on? As she got closer to the dress to get a better look, she saw there was a label around the neck... SOLD.

Mary shrieked with delight then ran back into the parlour where Miss Shorrock was smiling.

"It sold in less than 2 hours, the buyer will be back to collect it tomorrow. I want you to make a dozen of the same or similar in the next couple of days, we will go to the warehouse tomorrow and get all the material we need, so you better get your thinking head on, we are going to be very busy."

The next few days were very hectic as Mary and the girls set about producing the garments. Once they set up a production line, they soon got into the swing of it with Mary cutting the fabric, Daisy producing the basic stitched garment and Milly providing the final touches, along with Mary once the cutting was finished.

Soon all the dresses were made and Miss Shorrock then examined and accepted the standard of work. Once she was happy the dresses were placed on a rack ready for sale.

As a reward, Miss Shorrock paid for the girls to have a night out at the Gaumont Cinema down the road and some supper to eat later. She herself was not going as she was not fond of sitting in a darkened room full of cigarette smoke and flickering lights, so gave Mary enough money for the seats and fish and chips after. Mary and Daisy had never been to the cinema and were very excited, Milly said she had been once before and tried to act a bit blasé but didn't convince Mary.

The film was Blood and Sand with Rudolph Valentino and Gloria Swanson, Mary was fascinated from start to finish and immediately became a big movie fan.

It was back to normal the following day and normal service was resumed with Daisy on the Blouses and Mary flitting between her and Milly. The dresses they had made although similar had different finishes once Milly and Mary had embellished them. The two that Mary thought most saleable were put in the window, where they stayed for a couple of days before being sold. They were quickly replaced and to Miss Shorrock's amazement these also went quickly.

Mary was also busy scouring magazines for ideas on the latest fashions and when it was decided to start making the dresses again, variations were incorporated to match current styles and these too were proving to be popular. It was decided that there was a need to take on another 2 girls and so the workshop was rearranged and the area set aside for the older clumsier styles was taken over to accommodate the new fashions.

Over the next few months, word got about and the shop was busy every day, Miss Shorrock couldn't believe the effect this young girl had on the business, her enthusiasm and energy was boundless and infectious.

Chapter Six

Over the next 2 years the shop went from strength to strength, 3 more girls were recruited and business was booming. The dresses were selling well and Mary had a good eye for fashion. Miss Shorrock now decided that the turnover was such she would employ an accountant to look after the books and also appoint Mary as the manager, which was praise indeed for a young lady who was not even 18 yet.

Mary had a weekly treat she indulged herself, a trip to the cinema every Saturday night. She loved the glamour that shone down from the screen and was fully immersed in every character. One of these visits resulted in an unforgettable moment for her… The Great Gatsby came to town. The style, the panache, the whole array of emotions washed over her. She was fascinated with the dresses that the main character Daisy Buchanan wore and she was determined to produce something similar and mentally took note of the style and shimmer of the fabric.

By now, Mary was trusted to order all the materials herself and so the following morning she decided to take a trip to the wholesalers and see what was available. There really was a vast array of choice, so many options, but Mary's mind wandered back to the Rayon the first salesman had shown. She also picked some mercerised cotton, which looked very versatile, yet reasonably priced.

Once back in the shop she took the materials up to her room until she was certain of what she was going to produce, then went back to the daily routine.

Miss Shorrock was very pleased with the way the new designs and recently recruited girls were settling in and was curious as to what further plans her prodigy had lined up.

When supper was nearly over Mary decided to let Miss Shorrock in on her plans. "I would like to produce some evening wear such as is the fashion on the silver screen," she announced. "I have decided on rayon and also mercerised cotton as the main fabrics and would like to work on the designs in the evening in my own time so that the general day-to-day output is not affected," Miss

Shorrock started to have a little giggle, which threw Mary because she was not expecting it and also because Miss Shorrock very rarely smiled let alone giggled.

"I swear you can read my mind young lady, whatever you have got planned has my full blessing so let's hear what's in your plans."

Mary went on to expand on her thoughts. "A lot of young ladies nowadays are working in factories, offices and banks, etc. and earning a lot more than they used to, therefore they are more interested in going out to theatres, cinemas and have more money to spend on fashion. This fashion is being driven by the film market from America and the clothes are really desirable, but far too expensive. By using cheaper materials that act in the same way as the silks and chiffons we could get a market share that would be very profitable." She then went on to say that the shop was not big enough to accommodate all this extra work and wanted to see if it was possible to move to bigger premises.

Miss Shorrock was not expecting this last remark and was beginning to get worried, she was not comfortable with all this talk of expansion and told Mary so.

"There will be no moving anywhere until you can clearly demonstrate the workload justifies it," she retorted, suddenly getting angry at the thought of her whole business life being pulled from beneath her feet.

It was finally agreed that the new line of clothing would be introduced and the whole thought of expansion be set aside until the financial results as a result of the introduction were calculated.

Mary worked alone on the designs for 2 weeks, then spent every night in the workshop over the following 2 weeks until she was happy with the final result. In the end she produced 3 dresses that could be worn as evening attire, she was very happy with the finished product. Finally, she was ready, she decided which one of the dresses she liked the most and tried it on in the store room and asked Daisy in to see what reaction she would get and whether she liked it. Daisy liked it a lot and wanted to know where she bought it as she had no idea what Mary was doing in the evening.

"Wow, wow, wow," she gushed, "that is really nice, it must have been expensive," Mary then explained what she had been doing and when Daisy said that similar dresses had been on display in the shop window of Robinsons Retail emporium for between 4 pounds and 6 pounds, she suddenly had a thought that she needed to follow through. She then tried the other dresses on, which also got the seal of approval from Daisy. She then swore her to secrecy and said she would have to speak with Miss Shorrock.

Daisys comments about Robinsons intrigued, her so the following morning she took the short distance on the tram and entered the store, which was the biggest in the area and was busy every day. Making her way to the ladies' dress section, she spent a good hour taking a close look at the materials, the stitching, the flow of the dresses. She came to the conclusion that she could produce the same styles in artificial fabrics as the silk on sale here, at a much lower price.

A sales girl who had been watching Mary's scrutiny of the dresses on offer, eventually came over and enquired if Mary needed any help. Mary replied no but wanted to know where they were being made. "Not sure, could be anywhere, only person that would know would be the shop buyer."

Mary asked where he was and was informed that he only came into the shop on Wednesdays as there were 8 branches to service. After asking his name and being informed it was a Mr James Masheter and he was always in about 9am, she made a mental note and returned to the shop. Today was Thursday and it was another 6 days before she would be able to see what impression she could make on the shop buyer. But she decided that Miss Shorrock could wait another week before she discussed the new range.

Mary was still going to the cinema and reading magazines on the latest fashions and had taken to carrying a pencil and paper whenever she was out and about, making sketches whenever she could. Films were proving to be a big inspiration, such a film was Flaming Youth with Collen Moore, Mary loved her bobbed hairstyle and off the shoulder dresses, so much so she decided she had to have the same hairstyle.

Saturday arrived, but instead of planning a cinema trip, she left about 2pm and visited the Hairdressers. She was a little surprised at the cost but after being told you have to pay for fashion and that the world was constantly changing, she afforded a little smile and paid up.

When she got home, Miss Shorrock was in the shop and raised an eyebrow when she saw the new Mary, which left Mary not sure if it was a sign of approval or not. At supper that night, Miss Shorrock made no mention of the cropped style but did ask Mary about her new dresses.

"What stage are you at Mary, it's been a month now?"

"I have completed the dresses but I wanted to wait until next week to show you," she replied.

"Why?"

"Because I have a plan and if it works then it will make a big difference?" Miss Shorrock was beginning to get irritated.

"If they are complete, I would like to see them… Now."

Mary knew her well enough to know when and when not to play games with Miss Shorrock, this was clearly not one of those times. She went into the workshop and returned with the garments over her arm. Placing one of them on top of the sofa, she then went upstairs to her room and changed into one of them, then returning to the parlour she did a little twirl so Miss Shorrock could see the flow and movement of the dress.

Miss Shorrock's face was not one of approval. "Who would wear such a flimsy thing and where would they wear it?"

This was not going well. Mary then showed her the magazine cuttings and sketches she had done, but was getting nowhere until she mentioned that Robinsons were already selling them at inflated prices and that she was going to see the buyer next week. Still not impressed, Miss Shorrock said she would reserve judgement until next Wednesday and insisted on accompanying Mary to see the buyer, until then the matter was closed. Mary knew not to argue and meekly agreed.

The next few days dragged with Miss Shorrock giving no indication of her mood, Mary was a little unsettled by this, was she happy with Mary's course of action, was she going to cancel her plans?

On Monday morning after breakfast, Miss Shorrock announced she was going out for the morning and would be back in time for lunch, but gave no indication of where she was going. Mary didn't ask and settled into her normal routine with the girls.

It was a nice morning so Miss Shorrock took a 15-minute stroll through the park and cut through the indoor market and back on to the main street in Blakewater until she eventually found herself outside a store with Large windows and a huge double door entrance, above which was a sign in large black bold letters 'Robinsons'. Upon entering the store, she immediately headed for the ladies clothing section and sought out a couple of rows of dresses that were similar in appearance to those Mary had made. As she felt the materials and examined the styles, she noticed a distinct similarity, but these were expensive silks and natural materials, whereas Mary had concentrated on softer manmade fabrics that looked and moved in the same way as these dearer comparisons.

After about 15 minutes, of intense scrutiny Miss Shorrock left the store and made her way back, this time stopping off at a couple of stalls in the indoor market and having conversations with a couple of the stall holders.

Mary was sat having lunch when Miss Shorrock came back and as she sat down beside her, a conversation began about costs, quality, price of materials and timescales, which took Mary slightly by surprise, this was definitely not a normal lunchtime situation. Eventually, Mary went back to work in the workshop and Miss Shorrock mentioned she was going out again that afternoon, she was gone for about 3 hours.

Eventually Wednesday came round and Mary and Miss Shorrock set off in good time to arrive at Robinsons just as the store was opening, with Mary carrying a large bag that contained the sample dresses. As they approached the main counter Miss Shorrock asked to see Mr James Masheter, the lady on the counter was about to speak when a small round figure with a bowler hat, stopped as he was passing, turned, raised his hat and informed her that he was indeed that person and enquired why she wanted to speak with him.

In a very firm controlled voice Miss Shorrock then said, "I have something that might be financially beneficial to both Robinsons and myself and would therefore like twenty minutes of your time to allow me to state my case."

"I am always open to financially beneficial opportunities, please step this way," ushering both of them into a small office at the side of the counter.

Sitting himself behind the desk Mr Masheter then asked Miss Shorrock to present her case, at the same time Mary laid the dresses over the desk for his perusal.

"Your stores sell dresses that are very similar to these on offer here," Miss Shorrock stated, in a very confident straightforward manner, gesticulating towards the garments as she did so. "But unfortunately, because of the very expensive materials that are used in the manufacturing process, then the price range is out of reach for the ordinary working girl, wife and mother. What I have to offer is a dress that is comparable in style, form and feel as these dresses, but because we use latest manmade materials, we are able to produce the same result a lot cheaper and within reach of the average lady."

She then went on to talk about the fact that young ladies now have more spending power than ever before and spending money on latest fashions are a popular pastime.

Mary was very surprised, Miss Shorrock had shown very little interest in the sketches that Mary had produced and had not shown any interest in the new fashions and styles before. This was not a side of Miss Shorrock that had emerged before and she was clearly in full control of the situation.

Mr Masheter spent a good fifteen minutes closely analysing each garment, taking out a magnifying glass at one stage to scrutinise the stitching. He then excused himself and went onto the sales floor and did the same to a couple of dresses that were on sale. When he returned, he sat back down in his chair and after a thoughtful few seconds he informed Miss Shorrock that there was some merit in what she was saying, but he needed to discuss costs, quantities, delivery times, profit margins and a whole lot of topics. Mary did not have a clue what was being said, but she was mightily impressed with Miss Shorrock today. The meeting concluded after about thirty minutes, with a handshake and an appointment to view the manufacturing process with a site visit to the workshop.

Mary's head was spinning as they walked home, was this a success, what happens next, have they got a contract?

Later that night at supper, Miss Shorrock explained that Mr Masheter was very impressed with the product and agreed that an intermediary range that was more affordable would sell more products and because the trade price was lower then the retail price would also drop, thus creating a market for the young and single to get fashionable clothes without affecting profit margins. But the costs depended on how many units were bought and what discounts would apply for larger quantities.

Mary was still a little confused but grasped the basic premise that the more you sold the cheaper you can sell. She then went on to let Miss Shorrock know how impressive she had been that day, but was a little disappointed with her reply.

"I had to go, a young lady like you would have been eaten alive. He is a hard-nosed business man and you would have come away with a very bad deal."

But she perked up a little when Miss Shorrock praised her for the initiative of going to see the store and the opportunities that have now arisen.

The site visit was arranged for the following Wednesday at 2pm after Mr Masheter had finished his business in the store and he arrived promptly, stating he was in a hurry and needed to commence the visit immediately. Miss Shorrock informed Mr Masheter that Mary would provide all the information needed as she was the manager of the workshop. She would be available to discuss matters further in the parlour after the tour. The whole tour lasted about fifteen minutes with only brief comments and questions about staff numbers, storage, where materials were purchased and delivery, which Mary was able to answer without any difficulty.

After the tour they entered the lounge, Mary saw that George Davies the Accountant was present, he usually visited once a month and had only been the previous week.

All 4 of them sat around the dining table. Miss Shorrock was the first to speak.

"I hope you were satisfied with your visit and that Mary provided you with all the information you need."

"The young lady was very punctual with her answers and provided me with everything I need to know," replied Mr Masheter turning to Mary and smiling as he spoke.

He then went on to say he was happy with the way the business was managed and that he felt there was definitely an opportunity… but that he had some misgivings about the ability to provide sufficient quantities.

"I am looking at the possibility of ordering 200 units a week, your staff numbers are not able to provide me with confidence that you can supply that number, especially as this is not your only line of merchandise and you are producing other garments that are to be sold elsewhere."

Mary glanced across at Miss Shorrock who was trying to conceal a grin, "So, what do you propose then, Mr Masheter?" was Miss Shorrock's response.

"I propose we have a trial run of a variety of 50 dresses to see if they sell, then we can talk again about any production issues. If you can manage to sell the dresses, we can look at our internal structure and adapt accordingly, would that suffice in the short term?"

"That is just what I was about to suggest, Madam, when could you provide the first run of 50, assuming we can agree a unit price?" Mr Masheter meant business.

Looking across to Mary, Miss Shorrock asked her when she thought delivery could be confirmed. Mary replied that it would take a week for the materials to be delivered, then allow 2 weeks for production and delivery to the Blakewater Store, 3 or 4 weeks maximum for the complete process.

Miss Shorrock, Mr Masheter and the accountant finalised the agreed costs for the initial 50 units and also prices for any follow up orders with unit quantities attached. Miss Shorrock was very insistent on the follow up prices being confirmed and there was plenty of discussion in relation to this, but it was finally agreed and all three of them seemed to be happy with the outcome.

As Mr Masheter finally left, they shook hands, Miss Shorrock's parting words were to confirm that production would commence as soon as the order for the 50 dresses was received.

The order was duly hand delivered 2 days later and there was an immediate response. Materials were ordered and delivered, the girls workload begin reassigned to allow for this increase in production, with Mary at the hub of it and directing the flow.

At the end of the first week, they were ahead of schedule and Mary was feeling quite pleased with herself. At supper on the Thursday night, Miss Shorrock asked how things were progressing and after receiving the good news made an announcement.

"Mary, you have been a breath of fresh air to me and have made me realise that I have stagnated in the past few years before you arrived, thank you so much."

Mary was not expecting this and felt herself welling up inside. Struggling to contain herself she replied that if it wasn't for Miss Shorrock her life could have been so different and that she was very happy to be where she was now. Looking up she could see that Miss Shorrock was also struggling to control her emotions, so looking back down at her supper she quietly carried on eating. Not much was said that night and Mary retreated to her room, the last few days had been draining and she soon fell into a deep sleep.

The following morning at breakfast, Miss Shorrock appeared to be much chirpier and announced that as a reward she was going to take Mary to the theatre on Saturday where a play was being performed. Mary had never been to the theatre and asked if she could wear one of the evening dresses as it was a special occasion, which Miss Shorrock allowed.

Saturday arrived and they set off, Mary assumed they were going to the local Gaumont theatre, but when Miss Shorrock informed her, they were going to the Royal Exchange Theatre in Manchester, she could hardly contain herself.

The tram took 15 minutes and stopped just down the road from the theatre. Mary was open eyed as they approached this massive building that was so impressively lit up, with a large sign that read 'The Return of Sherlock Holmes.'

Miss Shorrock had paid for Mid-range price tickets and they were on the second level. As Mary took her seat, she realised how hot it was inside and took her coat off and folded it on her lap. As she did so Miss Shorrock noticed some admiring glances, mainly from young men, but also from a number of women who were casting an eye on her dress. This young lady has grown up she thought, no longer a girl, she is a very attractive confident, young lady.

Mary was engrossed in the play as she had read some of Sherlock Holmes when she was in the orphanage, she found the whole event fascinating.

When the intermission came, they went down to buy a drink, Mary settling for a Lemonade, but surprisingly Miss Shorrock opted for a glass of sherry. This was the first time Mary had ever seen her drink alcohol. Mary found her eyes drawn to a well-dressed young man who looked a couple of years older than her, he also spotted her and they spent several seconds eyeing each other up. Eventually he walked over and introduced himself as Tom and asked her if she was enjoying the show. She replied that it was the first time she had ever been, but yes, it was very nice. She felt herself blush, she was not used to talking to young men and felt uneasy, but at the same time a little excited.

Miss Shorrock stepped in and asked Tom who he was with, he replied that it was his sister's birthday and so the whole family was attending. With that he withdrew and the intermission over bell was ringing so they returned to their seats. During the second half of the performance, Mary found herself looking around to see where Tom might be, but failed to spot him.

As they walked to the tram stop after the show, Miss Shorrock could not help but notice that Mary seemed a little preoccupied. "He was a nice young man," she eventually commented. Mary tried to play it down but the truth was she felt something she had never felt before, a tingling sensation that excited her.

"Yes, he seemed quite nice," was the only response should could muster.

When they got home, they had a little supper of cheese and biscuits before going to bed.

As she lay there in the dark, her mind kept wandering back to this young man and the strange effect he had on her. She found her hand wandering to between her legs and she wanted to touch herself. As she did so she found she was getting wetter and wetter and a strange tingling motion was stirring. She eventually found that she was enjoying it and stroked some more, eventually finding a spot that was more inflamed, so she rubbed it some more and started to put her fingers inside. At the same time, her nipples became hard, so she caressed these as well which made the tingling stronger, until eventually she was writhing in the pleasure of her fingers inside her and squeezing her nipples, the strength of which eventually overcame her and a gush of emotion caused her to squeal, then she just lay there completely overwhelmed for over a minute, then fell into the deepest sleep she could ever remember.

Miss Shorrock was in the next room and could hear the last throes of her orgasm… yes, she thought, the child is no more.

The following week the deadline was reached with 2 days to spare and all the dress were packed into cardboard boxes and despatched to Robinsons Warehouse in Salford where they were distributed to the various stores. Mary's curiosity eventually got the better of her and she had to take a look to see where they were in the Blakewater Store. Miss Shorrock was also curious, so they both made their way to the store and found them displayed in quite a prominent position.

As they admired the way the dresses were displayed the same young assistant that had spoken to came up and said that these had proved to be quite popular and these were the last 6 in the store, which pleased Miss Shorrock immensely. They then went off to compare their product with the more expensive ones and looking at them there was quite a price difference but to the ordinary customer the quality and feel of the product was such that the price difference would make an impact on which product you would select, Mary was feeling quite smug by now, her hunch had been right.

As they made their way back to the shop, they stopped off at the indoor market to see what was on offer there. There were only about 4 stalls selling women's dresses and the style and quality was nowhere near what they could produce and Miss Shorrock noted the prices were such that they could produce dresses to a better standard and they would still make a profit, with money enough for the retailer to sell and also make money.

That afternoon Miss Shorrock spent all her time in the parlour. Making notes and writing things down in a book, stopping only to ask Mary how many dresses they had left, to which Mary replied, "Only four as we spent all our time on the Robinson contract so had to get back up to date with the day-to-day orders that were kept to one side."

"I would like you to look at some every day wear that we can display in the window here, there may be a market where we can sell directly to customers as well as to stallholders," Miss Shorrock announced, before adding, "Mr Masheter will be back for more orders, of that I have no doubt, so we need to be prepared to offer more variety."

Over the next week, Mary set to work looking at what materials worked with what styles and a long list of ideas she would love to develop, eventually settling on 6 dresses that she felt would be successful. She then presented them to Miss Shorrock in the form of a sketch and some approximation of cost.

"Some of these dresses can have a similar style but with different materials, we already have some material in stock to produce some samples," Miss Shorrock could see the potential and ordered Mary to set to work and produce one of each and to get the material wholesaler to send his salesman in so they could look at all options.

Sure enough, the following Wednesday Mr Masheter arrived unannounced, apologised and asked for an hour of Miss Shorrock's time. As he was ushered into the parlour, Mary was summoned and they all sat around the table. Mr Masheter then declared that most of the 50 units had sold very quickly and they were interested to see not only if they could produce another 400 of the same but also to see if there were any other options of units available. Miss Shorrock paused for a little before asking if the same terms and conditions were applicable.

"I think as we are asking for a large sale then we would have exclusivity of supply and that you only supply Robinsons. Everything else would be on the same terms," Mr Masheter appeared a little smug, but Miss Shorrock was having none of it.

"We are in the process of looking at several other outlets for our product and if successful then Robinsons would be a welcome customer, but not one that we fully rely on. So, exclusivity is not an option we are willing to consider, unless of course you are willing to accept that exclusivity comes with an exclusive price."

This took the wind out of Masheter's sail, he was expecting Castlefield Fashion House to be fully compliant and accept all the conditions. It surprised Mary as well and she could not believe what she was hearing, Miss Shorrock was playing a game of bluff with their biggest customer.

As she sat there perplexed, Masheter countered, "Ok, we can possibly discuss exclusivity at a further date, can we agree on the 400 and can I see what other styles you might have as well?"

Mary showed him the sketches and informed him she was in mid-production of some, but he was welcome to look at them in the workshop, which Masheter agreed to.

After examining the three models on the mannequins he returned to Miss Shorrock and confirmed there would be an order placed for the original 400 and once he had seen the new fashions when complete he could possibly want another 150. Mary was to take the completed new samples to Robinsons the following Wednesday. Miss Shorrock agreed and Mr Masheter went on his way a happy man.

Mary had to say something, she didn't understand what exclusivity meant and asked Shorrock to explain. Once she understood the concept, she then wanted to know why this would be an issue if Robinsons were prepared to provide orders for quantities that kept them fully busy.

"Because, we are going to expand and sell more dresses to different outlets," was the response, "starting with filling our own shop window and creating space for customers in the shop itself. Then we are going to investigate the possibility of a bigger workshop and recruiting more seamstresses. We cannot do this if we have Robinsons as the only customer."

Mary's head was spinning, was this the same cautious middle-aged woman that was critical of the styles such a short time ago? They then sat down to work out what was required, the cost and timescale and produced a plan.

First on Mary's list was to order the material for the new order and then to complete the prototype new styles, which were finished in time for Mary to deliver for Masheter's scrutiny the following Wednesday. Miss Shorrock decided to allow Mary to attend alone, feeling it was important Mary developed some business savvy, besides she had already agreed the rates, so it was more for Mary's morale and self-worth. Mary returned with an order for 150 of the new units, feeling very proud of herself. When she arrived back, Miss Shorrock was not there and was informed, she had gone to the bank with the accountant and would be back in a few hours.

That night Mary sat down to supper and they discussed how the day had gone, Mary gleefully confirmed the extra orders.

Miss Shorrock also had some news. "We will begin to look for a new workshop immediately I have been to the bank with George Davies and we had our business plan accepted, they have agreed to loan me the money for expansion. George is going to look at various sites, once we have agreed what our requirements are."

As they looked at what potential orders might be developed and what resources they needed to sustain that potential, Mary was suddenly struck by the enormity of the situation and how much responsibility sat on her shoulders, she began to become very afraid, which Miss Shorrock picked up on.

"I have lived in this shop for 35 boring years, in all that time I have spent my time on a daily routine that has not made me rich, but has provided a me with a modicum of an income to allow me to retain that same drudgery year in and year out. You have entered my life and awakened my ambition. Do not worry about this venture we are about to embark on, I will always have this place if anything goes wrong. I have been lucky to have a small private family income, which means I have savings that will cover a large percentage of the cost and the bank have agreed to loan me the rest, so don't worry," Mary had to admit there was a spark in Martha Shorrock's eyes that was not there when she had first arrived and she definitely seemed more sprightly. There was certainly nothing wrong with her brain, as she had observed when she ran rings around James Masheter in negotiations.

Over the next few months, the workshop was running at full speed, with Mary at the helm organising everything, eventually settling down as dresses were made and despatched, Mary was exhausted and was asleep every night by 8pm. During this period a couple of sample dresses were placed in the shop window, they sold quickly and were immediately replaced. As these were retail units, they displayed prices just below Robinsons, so creating a little more profit. Mary also noticed that accessories were as important as the dresses themselves so some investment was made to sell these in the shop and placing them strategically near the dresses in the window. Mary was becoming quite an entrepreneur.

As the dresses were selling so well, it was decided that the original cotton blouses were becoming a distraction and so the decision was made to only concentrate on the latest fashions and they were discontinued.

In the spring of 1927, a new workshop was leased and 10 more machinists employed, the workshop was in a converted Warehouse in Salford, it was fitted out, with more machines, extra cutting tables, storage space and good access for suppliers and also deliveries. There was also a nice surprise for Mary when they turned up on the first day… Her own office with the sign 'manager' on the door. She felt herself welling up when she saw it and for the first time in a long time she thought about her family and how proud they would have been of her. Later that day, she sat down at her very own desk and had a few tears, her life had changed so much and she felt almost guilty that she had forgotten where she came from.

Business went from strength to strength, new orders were coming in and old customers returning for repeat orders, Mary was still keeping up with latest fashions, ensuring that as soon as a fashion was fading it was dropped from production. Miss Shorrock was taking a back seat and Mary was flourishing. Suppliers were queueing up to provide goods and the salesmen were constantly calling, offering deals and discounts. The accessories in the shop were proving to be a very good idea and attracted a lot of interest in their own right, things were going along very nicely. Miss Shorrock now insisted that Mary call her Martha, which she found a little uncomfortable, she had been Miss Shorrock for the last 5 years and Martha didn't roll off the tongue comfortably.

Martha was spending a considerable time outside the shop and by now very rarely attended the workshop, her only input was to keep an eye on the finances and sit down with the accountants on a regular basis with Mary. The accounts were good and making a very healthy profit and because of the workload and turnover an accounts clerk was hired full time to keep things ticking over on a day-to-day basis.

One Saturday afternoon in November 1928, Mary was just coming back into the shop where they still lived and could hear voices in the parlour. As all business was conducted in the new factory and never on a Saturday anyway, she was intrigued as to who it was. As she entered the room a familiar voice exclaimed, "Ah, the fashion queen has arrived." With that Mrs Thompson stood up and embraced Mary. "My sister has kept me informed of your progress over the years and I must say I am mightily impressed."

Mary just stood there open mouthed for nearly a minute before replying, "Mrs Thompson, oh my word, oh my word… How are you?"

"I am well, I think you are old enough now to call me Sarah," Another name that didn't sit comfortable with Mary.

They sat down drinking tea and Sarah asked Mary about how she was, how proud the orphanage was of what she had become and the turnaround in her life. She also commented on the effect she had had on her sister, with Martha nodding her head in agreement and smiling.

Mary then spent the next hour or so recapping her life over the last few years, thanking them both for the opportunity and spelling out where she hoped the future direction of the business might go.

"The direction is completely up to you," Martha interjected. "There is a purpose to Sarah's visit besides a social one."

"We have a proposition you may find attractive," Sarah went on to explain that the business was owned not just by Martha but also by Sarah on a 50% equal equity status. The shop had previously been their father's tailors' shop and when he died, it passed on to both of them, but Martha was the only one with seamstress experience. Sarah had concentrated on her own family and it was agreed that Martha would run the business as she saw fit and had concentrated on ladieswear rather than gents tailoring.

Martha then went into detail about the reason she had not been getting involved as much as she would have liked and why she was spending a lot of time out of the shop.

She had developed cancer and as such was told she will probably die in the next couple of years and so she needed to step back further from the running of the business and would only be involved in an advisory capacity from now on. She then stunned Mary by announcing that as she had no children, she was going to leave her half of the business to Mary in her will. Sarah had agreed that she would retain her 50% as a sleeping partner, taking limited profits on an annual basis. The whole of the company was to be restructured to reflect this and Mary was to become a director, should she accept the proposal.

Mary sat there and said nothing for a full minute, how was all this possible? Her mind was spinning about the offer, Martha's health, Sarah's involvement, this was all too much to take in. Eventually she managed to compose herself, "Why have you not told me how ill you are, you have pushed yourself to the limit."

"You have provided me with a welcome distraction, but I am afraid I am weakening to the point I will need to rest more. I thank you for everything you are doing, I am very proud of you."

Martha had a tremble in her voice, this was not the stern, dour lady Mary was introduced to 5 years previously. "you are like a daughter to me and I want to repay you for the life you have given me and energy you have brought to this home."

Sarah then went on to say the proposed structure was for Sarah to retain her 50% and Martha was to give Mary 24%, while she retained 26% which would be given to Mary upon Martha's demise. They then discussed a salary which would be paid to her as a working director, which would give her a very healthy income. Martha would remain mainly in an advisory capacity, especially in relation to financial matters and Mary was expected to meet with her and George Davies on a monthly basis to review expenditure against income.

Mary thanked them both and then turned to the subject of Martha's health, which Martha clarified in the matter-of-fact manner Mary had come to know and expect.

"I have cancer of the liver, they have told me to expect to live for another one to three years, I do not fear death, but it is an unwelcome visitor," she said with a wry smile.

Mary had no idea this was coming, but decided to take stock of the situation before asking anything further, so merely thanked them again for their generosity and asked to be allowed to take some time before accepting their generous offer. She then hugged them both before going up to her room to absorb what had been said.

The following week, Mary accepted the offer and the legal paperwork was drawn up and signed, Mary was now a director! She now had sole responsibility for the day-to-day running of the business, she already had it, but now she was officially in charge.

Nothing changed as a result of the management restructure, except for the extra hiring of staff to keep up with demand. Daisy was promoted to head seamstress and was responsible for co-ordinating the works, for which she was extremely grateful after years of having her head down over a machine day in and day out. Milly too was rewarded, she had shown a flair for reproducing the styles that Mary was creating and was rewarded with the title of Head Cutter, which prompted some amusement from the shopfloor, who subsequently dubbed her the executioner. After a plea to Mary, the title was renamed chief stylist.

Business was good and Mary had a lot of appointments with a lot of people, very rarely did anything negative come from these meetings and she was learning all the time and becoming a very astute business woman. The monthly progress meetings with Martha and George Davies were also productive with both educating her and explaining the finer workings of finance.

So, it continued for the next few months, Mary still absorbing what was on the silver screen and scouring fashion magazines for ideas, and orders flying out the doors and onto shelves. This was to change in the summer of 1929.

Chapter Seven

Mary had been so busy working, she failed to realise the deterioration in Martha's health. They always breakfasted together and although Martha had developed a yellowish tinge to her skin, her appetite was diminished and her breathing was laboured. This particular morning Martha did not appear and remained in her room, well past her usual routine of having breakfast at 7:30, so Mary went up to her room. As she knocked on the door, Martha responded and Mary entered to see her sat up in bed hair bedraggled, propped up on pillows, not looking at all well. Martha was always immaculately groomed and made up, this was a surprise and Mary for the first time saw how frail she was.

"How are you, shall I call the doctor?" Mary was really concerned now; Martha was in a bad way.

"You can call the doctor, but I am afraid there is nothing he can do, we are at the end stage now," Martha's voice was very frail but her pragmatism was not appreciated by Mary.

"Do not be so negative, we can get you some treatment," Mary scolded Martha, which shocked her as Mary had never raised her voice to her before.

"Let's hear what the doctor says before you rattle on about dying."

The doctor was summoned and he spent some time alone with Martha, eventually appearing in the parlour to update Mary.

"Are you her daughter?" he asked, to which Mary explained she was not but that the relationship was all but that.

"Does she have any relatives at all?" The doctor's tone was very solemn and Mary knew this was not good news. After explaining to the doctor that she had a sister he then advised she be contacted and informed of the severity of the situation.

"How serious is it?" Mary asked.

"Gravely serious, I will come back to see Miss Shorrock tomorrow, if the sister can get here, I will answer any questions to her then," was the response that Mary was expecting, but dreading.

Mary went back to see Martha then once she was sure she was comfortable she went to the workshop, but could not concentrate so left early explaining briefly to Daisy and Milly what the situation was and to let her know that if there were any problems at work to come and get her.

Sarah was immediately given the bad news and arrived at the shop that evening. One look at Martha was all she needed to know, she sat on the chair and held her hand. Martha's breathing was rattly and erratic, with a high temperature. Mary sat on the other side and between them they tried to keep her cool and comfortable. They stayed all night, with Martha drifting in and out of consciousness, sometimes lucid, sometimes making no sense at all.

The doctor arrived and after examining Martha, he gave her an injection, then they all sat down in the parlour where he explained to Mary and Sarah that Martha was now in the final stages and to expect her passing in the next few days. He left, saying he would call back later that evening and they both sat there in silence for at least five minutes. Finally, Sarah spoke in a very fragile voice, "I can't believe this is the end, she has always been so strong."

Mary continued with her silence, she had been there before with Rosie and the memories came flooding back. Struggling to fight the tears, she couldn't find any words so just sat there quietly. She had been expecting this for over a year now but the impact still shook her to her roots.

Eventually Sarah faced the reality. "I will stay with her, you must go and keep the shop running, if there are any developments, I will call you."

Mary nodded and went to clean herself up, she decided that she would not make any announcement until the inevitable had happened so as not to disrupt work proceedings. The rest of the day was a blur and luckily there were no interruptions to the normal working production so she was able to finish on time and arrive home at 5:30pm.

As she entered the shop, there was a delicious smell coming from the kitchen and Mary suddenly realised she hadn't eaten for 36 hours, no wonder she was feeling faint. Sarah was in the kitchen and as she turned to face her Mary asked about Martha.

"No change, not sure whether that is good or bad but her breathing seems very rattly, she is asleep now so thought I would take the chance to sort dinner out."

Mary went up to the bedroom and sat holding her hand, not speaking, but so many thoughts in her head. Martha was oblivious, Mary was not sure if she was asleep or unconscious, so left her and went down to see Sarah who was just setting the table.

"She has been like that all day, save for the odd spluttering and struggling to breathe. I tried feeding her but she would only have a few sips of broth." Supper was eaten in silence and just as they finished the doctor called.

He examined Martha and then turned to Sarah and said there was nothing more to be done, they should just try and make her last few days a comfortable as possible. He then gave her a bottle of laudanum to issue if Martha became in too much pain.

The next 5 days continued in exactly the same manner, Martha drifting in and out, Sarah and Mary by her side every night, until eventually the inevitable arrived. When it did happen, it was over quickly, Mary was in the kitchen making a pot of tea—when suddenly she could hear a movement directly above her head and Sarah calling her name. Rushing up the stairs, she entered the room to see Martha being cradled in Sarah's arms.

Sarah had tears in her eyes as she uttered, "It's over, she is at peace now," as she lowered Martha s lifeless body back to the bed. Mary walked over and kissed Martha's forehead. A new chapter was about to begin.

The funeral was five days later and she was interred into a family plot in Didsbury, which the family had bought 5 generations before. Two days after this Sarah and Mary were summoned to the family solicitors office for the reading of the will. They were to be the only two beneficiaries and Mary was having mixed emotions. Martha was now gone and this was to be the final string to be severed, she knew a lot of things were about to change and she was not sure how to handle it, Martha was her guiding light, her strength and now she was alone.

The whole process of reading the will took about ten minutes and she sat nervously throughout the reading. The outcome was that Mary received the other 26% of the business as promised as well as two thousand pounds, Sarah received the 50% share of the house, the house contents and also some shares and bonds that had been acquired over her lifetime. These bonds were in the form of investments and the solicitor informed Sarah they were quite substantial; Martha had been very shrewd and picked her stock well.

There was another surprise that Mary was not expecting, as the solicitor was about to reveal.

"Mrs Thompson has asked me to draw up a document for you to sign, I think it best if she explains its contents." He then placed an envelope on the table which Sarah then picked up.

"I have had my investment in the company for a number of years now and although the dividends are welcome, I do not feel I have been justified in accepting them, so now I want to put that right," Sarah then handed the letter to Mary.

"This is a contract that transfers my share of the business to you outright, you now own 100% of Castlefield Fashion House."

Mary was stunned, totally unable to speak she sat down open mouthed for a full minute. Sarah broke the silence, "I have everything I need and with the house and shop, I do not need this extra income and feel you could manage the situation better if you have total ownership... Besides you have done the hard work and put the company in the good place it is now, you deserve it."

After getting over the initial shock, Mary was now ready to respond. "I owe everything in my life to you and Martha, without you... well, you I don't know where I would be, thank you so much for everything."

There was a proviso though, Sarah explained that she wanted to move into the house as her current home was proving to be too small now her sons had grown up. One of them was now married and so the obvious choice was to move into the shop and let her married son have the small terrace she currently occupied. Mary could hardly refuse and it was agreed she would be given 2 months to find somewhere suitable.

After a month of searching, Mary eventually settled on renting a terraced house in Eccles that was close to the workshop but in a nice tree lined avenue with a large garden at the rear. She was a woman of substance now and her lifestyle was beginning to reflect that. She had developed a liking for art deco furniture and furnishings and so spent a lot of her spare time selecting pieces that suited her character. At the same time, she was having to run the business alone and Mary accepted that this was too much for one person and she needed to employ a manager. The office was starting to fall behind, all the areas that Martha used to manage had been put to one side and the events of the last couple of months meant that although the business was ticking over there needed to be some hands-on management. The wages clerk was constantly chasing Mary to get bills paid and she was being overrun.

After thinking long and hard, Mary discounted anyone currently employed, there was not enough business acumen to be able to step up, so she decided to advertise.

After speaking with her accountant to see what she was able to offer in terms of salary, Mary placed an ad in the local newspaper. The response was an expected mix of suitable and clearly unsuitable candidates. She narrowed it down to three that had possibilities and arranged to meet them all the same day.

The first was a lady who was obviously well educated and who exuded self-confidence, she had recently been employed as a manager for a medium sized retail outlet. She spoke well but although she was used to managing people she had no practical experience of the garment sector and so was discounted on that basis.

The second applicant was a man with a very high opinion of himself and Mary knew they would not get on and that he would try and control everything, which Mary was not prepared to accept, so he was also discounted.

The last person she saw was a small handsome Italian who walked and talked quite effeminately, Mary was quite taken with him. He informed her he was from a tailoring family in Milan. They had a number of shops and their own workshops with over 45 staff. He introduced himself as Antonio Guido and when he spoke it was with enthusiasm, he clearly had an insightful knowledge of the trade and its workings. But when questioned about why he had left Italy to come to England, he was very hesitant to provide any information and this raised suspicion in Mary, so she thanked him for coming to see her and he then took his leave. Unable to make a decision, she decided to take a look again at some of the other applicants.

As the workshop was finishing for the day and Mary was tidying up the paperwork, there was a knock on the office door and as she looked up the little Italian man was standing in the doorway.

"I would like to explain something to you, but I ask that you treat it in the utmost confidence," he looked very nervous and Mary sensed this was an important statement he was about to make.

"I have been a little evasive when answering your questions about my life, but there is a reason for that and you seem a very open and honest lady so I will trust you with my background." He looked very nervous and uneasy, so Mary asked him to close the door and gestured for him to take a chair. As he sat with his hands clenched and sweat forming on his brow, he then proceeded to fill in the details of his life in Italy.

He was the middle one of 3 brothers who all worked in the family business, which was comfortably off and part of a very active social scene. His parents had wanted him to marry a young lady whose family were landowners with a very healthy wool trade. Arranged marriages were very common and this had been planned from when he was about 18, with a view to marrying in his early 20s once his position within the family business was established. His elder brother was killed during the Great War, in 1917 at the battle for Isonzo. This placed a greater responsibility on him to carry on the family name and eventually head the business. After the war, the families wanted to formalise the engagement but Antonio said he thought they were both too young, he by then was 21, she 19, so it was agreed to wait for another year.

This year came and went and he still did not want to commit, the young lady and her family were getting very frustrated and agitated by now so Antonio decided he had to admit to his family that he couldn't marry her because he preferred the company of men. In a land of super Macho men this was not acceptable to his father, who had been relying on Antonio to carry on the family name. The rise of Mussolini and the Blackshirt movement were also very anti-homosexual, so his position both professionally and personally was thrown into chaos.

His younger brother was 8 years younger and not of an age to be considered. Homosexuality was not socially accepted in the middle-class circles of Milan, so the excuse that Antonio was considering entering the priesthood was fabricated to the intended family and he was hurriedly despatched out of Italy with sufficient funds to last him a few years until he came to his 'senses'.

Antonio then travelled to Paris and worked in some fashion houses before eventually arriving in England, where he found that as a foreigner he was not really accepted by any class. Now, at the age of 32 he was in need a of a secure job and a stable life, and he was begging Mary to consider him for the job.

This was totally new territory for Mary, she had never met a homosexual before and didn't understand why he did not want a family. But she was intrigued, she also felt very sorry for him and wanted to find out more.

Looking at the clock she could see it was now 7:30 and she was very hungry. "Would you care to have dinner with me, I know a restaurant not far from here that is very good... my treat?"

Antonio gladly accepted and they then spent a pleasant few hours discussing life, fashion and movies, which they both admitted inspired their fashion strategy.

By the end of the evening, Mary knew Toni (as he preferred to be called) would fit in well and she decided to offer him the position, so she asked him to come and see her in the office the following morning.

Terms were formally agreed and the areas of supervision and control established, Toni was then introduced to the rest of the staff as the new production manager. Mary then explained Toni's work history omitting the personal details, production then resumed as normal. As they walked back to the office the accountant's clerk was entering the building, Mary introduced him and they then went and sat down and looked at the monthly turnover. She then explained that Toni was eventually to be the main point of contact for day-to-day affairs but that for now he would work closely with Mary to ensure continuation. They then discussed how the office was run, ordering materials, wages, etc. Toni seemed to know automatically what was required and Mary was convinced this was a good appointment.

Over the next few weeks, Toni settled in and Mary could start to take a strategic overview of the direction of the company. Toni's managing of the supervision was excellent he was a very good people person and quickly got the workforce onside with his quick wit and personality. But he was also a stickler for quality and the girls knew that standards were not allowed to drop and if anything, productivity managed to increase.

Mary had taken to inviting Toni to accompany her to the cinema, he was good company and they shared thoughts on fashion and styles in the restaurant after the movie. She found herself becoming very attracted to him, but knew it was pointless as his sexuality pointed in a very different direction. Nonetheless, they became good friends as well as work colleagues and bounced ideas off each bother and became a very creative team. Many of the creations came to fruition as a result of a drawing on a napkin. The company was becoming well known and attracting a lot of interest from various streams, including a number of interviews for fashion magazines.

Mary was now 30 and time was passing her by, she was totally engrossed in the company to the extent that she had no other life, she was also a virgin which was another source of concern. Over the months, Toni had pictured a very rosy picture of Italy, the people, the food, the wine, the history and she was totally fascinated as to what it was like. One evening as they were on their way to see a movie, Mary casually asked Toni if he ever thought about going back home.

"Yes, I often think about it, but at the moment it is not be acceptable, Mussolini has got a grip of the country and even if my family accepted my sexuality, the Blackshirts would not."

He then went on to explain that his girlfriend had given up on him and got married a year ago, so she was not a problem now.

"What if you went back with a girlfriend?" Mary offered. "Surely there could be no objection then?"

Toni looked quizzical, what was this woman babbling on about. Mary then made her proposal. "What if we pretended we were girlfriend-boyfriend to the public. Nobody would know except those that need to, you get to see your family and I get to see your wonderful country, we both win."

Toni was stunned, it was a good idea, but the biggest hurdle was his father, who would see right through this audacious plan.

Toni thought he would test the water so wrote a letter to his mother explaining the proposal and asking her advice. The response was as expected, his mother welcomed the idea but his father would never be able to accept such a deception. She also said that she was aware of Castlefield Fashion House as some interviews had been published in Italian fashion magazines. She then came up with a foolproof idea. She proposed a trade visit by Mary with Toni as interpreter, with a view to doing some collaborative work that would benefit both companies, but the approach to the company would have to come from Mary herself via the proper intercompany communication channels.

Mary drafted a letter outlining the history of Castlefield Fashion House and the current turnover, which surprised herself when she saw it written down. She outlined the mutual benefits of companies collaborating and sharing information and that she was keen to see how the European fashion houses produced such wonderful garments. She also proposed a date of the second and third weeks in July as this was Wakes Weeks when the whole of Salford closed for the annual holiday. She read it to Toni who thought she had had gone a little over the top about Italian fashion, but Mary insisted the flattery was essential in order to bolster his father's ego.

A month later they got a response to say that this was acceptable, it might be beneficial and that the date worked well for them and they looked forward to meeting her, more crucially it was signed by Toni's father.

A boat train to Paris was booked and it took three days, the journey took them vis overnight trains to Milan via Paris and Zurich. Mary was totally engrossed in the whole adventure, she had never been outside the Lancashire area, never mind travelling across Europe. The languages, food, culture, were totally fascinating and she was loving every minute. Toni was completely at ease; he could speak a little French and was busy organising everything and scurrying about making sure all was well. The sleeper trains were not to Mary's taste. The daytime was fine, she spent her time looking at the beautiful landscape as it passed before her eyes, but sleeping was impossible. The constant rolling and unfamiliar sounds meant that when they finally arrived in Milano Central Station at 11am she was exhausted.

They booked 2 rooms in the Hotel Manin, Mary quickly unpacked her case and then, after a long slow bath she lay down on the bed and promptly fell asleep for the next 4 hours. She was awoken by a knocking on the door at 5pm, it was Toni.

"I have been trying to call you for over an hour," he looked exasperated and was very flushed.

"Sorry but I am very tired, what is the hurry anyway, we are not due to meet your father until tomorrow," Mary was not in a very hospitable mood after being rudely awoken.

"I know but my mother wants to meet us tonight for dinner, she is very keen as she has not seen me for a few years. She wants to see us at 7pm," Mary was not in the mood for socialising today, but realised that some ground needed to be prepared for their meeting tomorrow.

"Ok, where are we meeting and what time shall I meet you in the lobby."

"it's not far so 6:45 will be sufficient."

Mary took a shower and laid out her dress while she dried and combed her hair, all the while thinking about whether this was a good idea or not. Finally accepting that there was nothing she could do about it now, she sorted herself out and was in the lobby at 6:40 prompt. Toni appeared at virtually the same time and informed her they were eating in the hotel restaurant, which suited Mary as she was not keen on spending time walking about.

His mother appeared within a few minutes, gave Toni a long strong hug, then turning to Mary, she introduced herself in English as Sophia. She was a tall, slim woman, which surprised Mary as she was expecting a smaller person as Toni was only 5ft 7in tall. They made their way into the restaurant and ordered a drink.

Toni began to rattle away in Italian for a minute or so until Sophia raised a hand and pointed out that as Mary didn't speak the language and they both spoke English it would be rude to speak in their mother tongue. Toni immediately apologised to them both and they all began a long evening of conversation, which Mary found fascinating. Eventually after Toni had brought his mother up to speed on where his life had been spent and how happy he was working for Mary, the topic of Toni's fathers' attitude was introduced, Toni's sexual preference was carefully skirted around as Sophia began to explain that she had only informed his father after he had responded to Mary's letter that Toni was going to come with her. At first, he was angry, more about Sophia going behind his back than the fact that his errant son was returning, but after accepting that it had been a few years, he accepted that time had given him the opportunity to reflect on the situation. The youngest son was now engaged to be married and had settled well into the family business, so it was no longer the catastrophic situation it had previously been.

On the subject of business matters, Sophia obviously was heavily involved in all areas and Mary was impressed with her knowledge and understanding. Sophia then asked Mary what she was hoping to achieve from this meeting in terms of material benefit.

"To be honest, Toni has painted such a beautiful picture of Milan in my mind that I knew I had to see it for myself and also, he was desperately missing his family, so I took the opportunity to come and see for myself."

Toni smiled at his mother. "This lady is the best, Mama," beamed Toni.

Sophie then asked how long they were planning to stay, Mary explained about wakes fortnight and that she needed to be back in time to reopen the factory so it was only practical to stay for 4 days before travelling back.

Mary then explained that while here she wanted to see if there were any fashion trends that could be adapted for the English market and to look at what was in vogue in Milan.

Sophia was very curious about this delightful, considerate English lady and when Mary filled in all about her background, her early life in a pit village, the orphanage and all the hardship, she was doubly impressed with Mary's drive and resourcefulness. Eventually the evening came to an end and Mary was surprised to see how late it was, they agreed to meet at the business office at 10am the next day and she left. At breakfast the following morning, Toni informed Mary that his mother was very impressed with her and that if she had a daughter, she would be proud if she was like her, which made her blush slightly. After a light breakfast of coffee and eggs with ham, they caught a cab for the 5 min ride to the office just off Piazza Mercanti. As they passed the Piazza de Duomo Mary gasped audibly as the magnificent Cathedral came into view. This truly was a magical city and Toni had not exaggerated its beauty.

The business was in a picturesque old building with an open stone stairway, Toni's father's office was on the first floor. Overlooking the main street. Mary could see Toni was sweating and very nervous, she put a comforting arm on his shoulder.

"Come on, he won't bite," she uttered.

"No, but he might shoot me," which made Mary smile.

They knocked on the door and Sophia opened it and welcomed them both with a kiss on the cheek.

Toni's father was a very broad imposing man and was sat behind his desk as they walked into the room. As they entered, he stood up and walked around to shake Mary's hand. Mary was a little concerned that Toni was going to be overlooked, but after introducing himself as Franco Guidi, he turned to Toni and held out his arms and embraced him for what seemed a long time, but was about ten seconds. Mary then noticed that he was quite short, even smaller than Toni, which accounted for Toni's height, she mentally noted.

Without saying a word to Toni, he eventually turned back to face Mary and in very broken English said, "My wife informs me that you are an exceptional woman, so I am intrigued as to why you have come to Milan… Have come to take over my business?"

The look on his face was very strait laced and Mary was taken aback. Eventually the poker face gave way to a big broad smile and he chuckled at Mary's temporary discomfort. Mary chuckled back, mainly at herself for taking things so seriously.

Sophia then went to organise some coffee and they all sat around a large circular table to discuss formal matters.

As Mary had used business as a pretext to visit, she didn't really have an agenda and so the chat was informal and not too heavy. She was interested however in the materials and style of clothes rather than costs and production methods, but was happy to agree to a factory visit later that day. Franco had set aside all day for the visit so it wasn't any inconvenience to him, What Mary was surprised to find was that there were more workers in the office than she employed and more dedication placed on procurement, which she noted to look into when she got back to England.

Toni spent a lot of time hugging and kissing everyone, the factory was where he was at his best, the staff had hardly changed while he was away, many of whom he had grown up with.

When they arrived at the factory which was 3 miles away, they were met by Toni's young brother, Marco, who was very similar in appearance. As soon as the Siblings saw each other the tears were flowing and they were hugging and chatting and hugging again, all this brought a tear to Mary's eye and she noticed Sophia was also filling up.

During the visit Mary could see there was a distinct difference between the English and Italian styles which were much more militaristic with broad shoulders and suits of slim skirts with pockets were more common than dresses. Sophia explained that the State Police the OVRA laid down strict recommendations and they were encouraged to adopt the Mussolini military style strategy. Mary could see this influence and saw that Sophia was wearing a black skirt and blazer that closed with one button that resembled a medal from a distance. The blazer dropping to below her waist, it was a very eye-catching outfit.

On returning to the office, a secretary took Franco to one side and had a brief conversation with him. It transpired that Mary had already attracted the interest of the OVRA and they had been asking questions about her visit. Franco then relayed the message and explained this was not unusual and that the black shirts liked to know exactly what was going on, he would visit their office and explain the situation.

Just as he was finishing there was a knock on the office door and upon opening it two senior OVRA officers entered and introduced themselves. They talked briefly in Italian to Franco then turned to Mary and in very good English asked, "Good morning, Miss, I am Captain Josef Baritelli, whom might you be? What is your business here in Milan?"

Mary introduced herself as the girlfriend of Toni, that she owned a fashion house in England and that they had come to visit his family.

The Captain eyed Toni up and down and then asked, "Why would you want to visit a clothing factory, if you are here to visit family?"

"Because I have heard and seen the fabulous Mussolini style garments that are in vogue here in Italy and have been very impressed, so impressed I may wish to take the style back to England."

Mary was thinking on her feet, and was quite pleased at her response. The Captain congratulated her on her keen eye for good taste and wished her a pleasant stay in Milan. They then left and Mary gasped, she had never experienced dealing with fascists and it had scared her. Toni, Sophia and Franco were in total admiration that this young lady could hold her own against such aggression.

"Sophia, you said this was a very impressive young lady, there is no doubt you were right," Franco was chuckling away again. "Perhaps you could convince my son to marry you."

Even Toni was taken back that his father could laugh at his sexuality and although embarrassed enjoyed the moment. That evening the whole family enjoyed a very nice meal at a Trattoria in the Piazza de Duomo, Mary was loving Milan.

Toni and Mary decided to walk the 10 minutes to the hotel and on the way discussed what Franco had said about Mary marrying Toni, they joked about the absurdity of it. Toni's room was 4 doors down on the same floor and as they came out of the elevator, he mentioned that he thought Mary would make a wonderful wife and mother, he was about to kiss her on the cheek as normal when she suddenly clasped his face in her hands and gave him a long passionate kiss. Toni jumped back and tried to make a joke of the situation, "I meant for some handsome man that can give you what you want, not a little Nancy Boy like me." With that, he scuttled off, leaving a red-faced Mary outside her door.

Mary changed into her night dress then climbed into bed, she could not explain why she had acted that way and spent an hour pondering over her action. Eventually after finishing her session of pleasure with her fingers, she decided she definitely needed to find a life partner.

Nothing was said the following morning, but they were both conscious of the situation and skirted around and ignored what had happened. After breakfast, they visited one of the family shops and Mary noted again how much emphasis was placed on controlling the costs. By selling their own attire they could achieve greater profit, something definitely to look into.

The next 2 days were spent touring the city, its shops, its architecture and its culture. She learnt a lot about Italian life and vowed to come back soon. Finally, the two weeks were over and it was time to get back to work.

Once they returned, Mary realised just how much she had needed to get away and look at her life from a completely new perspective, she had her house but it was lonely there spending every night on her own and she wanted someone special in her life. She decided to widen her social life and get out and meet people. Before then however there was another crisis to deal with.

Chapter Eight

The stock market crash in October 1929 in America caused businesses to crash with a knock-on effect over the next year in England. Many of the materials sourced came from the USA and the downturn in trade meant that parts for sewing machines became unavailable, or at least were on a long delivery time. Cotton also increased in price which in turn was reflected in the increase of the cost of linen. All these setbacks impacted on the business and they were forced to cut back production and release 4 machinists until times improved. This also meant that the cost of obtaining supplies needer a tighter control, so after seeing the way the Milan factory was run, Mary decided now was the time to recruit a procurement manager.

The new manager was tall thin gangly man with a thick Glaswegian accent by the name of William McCallister, but who liked to be called Mac. Mary found him very hard to understand, Toni did not take to him and said so very vocally to Mary, "There's something about him that is *non bene*," which Mary later found out meant not good. Mac did however manage to cut costs very effectively. One of the main suppliers was 'Bromsgrove Linen Supplies' who Mary had dealt with for a few years, Mac managed to find an importer who sold virtually the same materials and was able to undercut Bromsgrove by 25%. This was a significant saving and Mary was delighted and Toni grudgingly acknowledged it was a good deal.

Over the next few months, the marketplace remained a bit rocky, but they were holding their own. There was a downturn in turnover but it was manageable and they didn't have to lose any more machinists.

One day out of the blue, Mary received a phone call, it was from a director at Bromsgrove who was concerned at the drop off in orders, she explained that it was purely down to cost, there was nothing wrong with their products, just a financial decision. The director asked if he could come and meet Mary to discuss new terms and to see what they might be able to do to retrieve the situation. Mary agreed and a meeting was set up for the following Monday. The meeting was attended by Mary, Mac and the Director of Bromsgrove, Mr James Morris. Toni was not invited, his role was managing the shopfloor and therefore Mary decided he was not required. From the look on Toni's face when the meeting was taking place it was apparent he thought differently.

Mary studied Mr Morris as he sat down, he was good looking, confident and spoke well, she was quite taken with him. He explained that there had been various increases in basic costs over the last year and Bromsgrove had failed to absorb or try and mitigate these increases, merely passing them on to the customer. It was accepted that this was wrong and they had restructured, taking on new manufacturers and suppliers and that he was now in a position to offer much more acceptable terms.

He asked what they were currently paying for materials and Mac merely battered it back with a dismissive, "Very good terms, you will have to do better than our current deals if you want us as a satisfied customer."

Morris then countered with a 20% reduction on current costs.

"Not even close to our current supplier," was Mac's response.

This banter continued for another 10 minutes before Mary interjected, "Give us 28% and you have a deal."

Morris then insisted he could not match that and said the best he could do was 25%. Mac informed him that was not enough and the meeting ended. He wished them good luck and smiling at Mary said in a hushed tone, "Thank you for the opportunity to speak with you I hope we can meet again," and left the building.

The following day Mary was in her office when Mr Morris returned, he informed her he was prepared to go to 28% after all. He had studied the previous orders placed over the years and Bromsgrove wanted to reinstate the previous goodwill. Mary accepted, then Morris asked her if she would like to go to lunch to celebrate, which Mary willingly accepted.

Over a light lunch in the White Bull Hotel, James Morris proved to be extremely good company and Mary was fully at ease with this charming man. He informed her that the main company was based in the Midlands and he was a director that covered the north from Wolverhampton up to Carlisle and across as far as Newcastle. Because of all this travel he stayed in hotels during the week and went home at the weekend. Mary wanted to know more about his personal life, "Are you married, any children?" She was very curious.

"My wife died 3 years ago and no children, that is why I travel so much." This response gave a mixed emotion to Mary, on the one hand she was very sympathetic that his wife had died, but on the other was also very interested in the fact he was available.

The hour turned into two hours and they chatted away about everything, it was obvious there was a strong chemistry between them. James then said he was back in the area on Thursday if she would like to go to dinner in the evening, which Mary gladly accepted.

Thursday was another delightful night and this was repeated twice a week over the next three weeks, Mary was smitten. Every night James dropped Mary off outside her door, on the sixth occasion she decided now was the time to ask him in for coffee, but she had more on her mind than a drink.

As they pulled up outside her house, she turned and kissed hm for the first time. "Want a nightcap?" she was very nervous and it was noticeable. They entered the house and James sat on the sofa as Mary asked if he wanted coffee or a whiskey to which he replied coffee was fine. As he went into the kitchen Mary found herself shaking as she poured the water from the kettle, she also felt very wet… Tonight had to be the night.

She handed him the cup and as she sat down next to him, they discussed the art deco collection Mary had acquired. She found herself talking absolute rubbish and James sensed her uncomfortableness. He put a reassuring hand on her knee, which caused her to jump nervously.

"I am not used to being alone with a man in my house, I don't want you to think this happens all the time." She really was waffling now and she could feel herself sweating. She stood up and walked towards the dining table, she really was sure what she was doing, what she was going to do or even how this was going to end.

James stood up and moved towards her, placing his arms around her waist and kissed her neck. "I think you are the most incredible woman; I hope this is the start of something special," with that he turned her around and kissed her. She was helpless by now, she kissed him back and they spent the next couple of minutes entwined with each other. He reached up and cupped her breast over her dress her nipples hard and sensitive. She could feel his hard cock rubbing against her, he put her hand down there and she rubbed it, they were both ready. Suddenly he spun her round so she was bent over, leaning on the table, he raised her dress and pulled her pants down.

This is it, she thought, it's happening… then she felt him deep inside her. She found herself pushing against him, she had waited a long time for this and was ready. After what appeared to be a matter of seconds, she heard a grunt and felt a final push, then it was all over. Mary was not sure how she was supposed to feel, but she knew she wanted more than she had just experienced. She was excited, her body was on fire, so many emotions were going through her mind and body.

They stayed in the same position for a full minute before James pulled up his trousers and Mary redressed herself.

"I was a virgin," she eventually said, not sure what the protocol for post sex conversation was supposed to be. "I guessed that, it was why it was exciting and over very quickly, I can promise you that if we repeat this evening, then the next time will be a much more fulfilling time."

Over the next few months James became a regular visitor to Mary's home usually on a Tuesday and Thursday. He always left early in the morning and never stayed the night as he said he did not want to draw attention to the fact that if his car was there all night it might embarrass Mary, which she thought was sweet. Mary found she was spending less time at the office and more getting out and about shopping, dining, long walks, she was finally enjoying life.

The performances did indeed improve and she found out everything about not only her own body but also James. He proved to be a skilled lover and he was able to completely satisfy her, especially when his tongue found its way between her legs, she discovered this was the quickest way to orgasm… And she loved it. She also discovered how to please the male body; he taught her well. She was in love!

One morning after a passionate night, Mary was lying in bed relaxing, when it suddenly struck her that she had not had her period, in fact she was about 3 weeks late. This was unusual as she knew that she was regular. She had been so distracted by events she hadn't noticed. She decided to leave it a week then go and see a doctor if her bleeding didn't appear.

Mary's absence from the office was beginning to irritate Toni as he felt he was carrying all the responsibility and that Mary was not concentrating on any of the day-to-day activities. He also did not like having to interact with Mac who he grown to detest with a passion. Eventually it all came to a head and Toni asked to see Mary alone, so she invited him around to the house.

Toni came straight to the point, "I cannot continue to work like this, Mac is very uncooperative and I need you to be there to take some of the workload from me. I feel that I am having to manage the workshop as well as the office and it's becoming too much, you are never around anymore."

He went on to explain that Mac's moods were extremely erratic, he never knew what to expect, sometimes he was ok and others he would blow up at the slightest remark. Toni then said that when he is ordering materials, Mac has taken it upon himself to decide exactly what that should be.

"We are getting what he wants, not what I specify." This was worrying for Mary, she knew Toni was not a moaner and if Mac was not ordering as specified then there was a big problem to sort out. She also realised that she had let things slip and needed to be at work more often, so she told Toni she wanted examples of where Mac was not doing as specified and promised to be at work more often, starting tomorrow.

The following morning Mary was up nice and early and in the office before either Mac or Toni appeared. She wanted to see for herself what was being ordered so went through all the orders for the previous two months, but everything appeared to be as normal. There were a couple of new suppliers for various buttons, trims, etc but this was fairly routine and it was Mac's job to get the best prices so it didn't concern her.

Toni arrived promptly at 8am as he always did and went straight into Mary's office.

She ushered him to sit down and looked him directly in the eye, "You have made a very serious accusation Toni, so I came in early and looked at the orders, apart from the trims and accessories we are still using Bromford for most of the purchases and it doesn't look to me that there is much to investigate, so would you please explain what you mean when you say the wrong materials were being ordered?" She knew Toni detested Mac, but she had to be seen to be objective even though she also knew Toni was not given to outbursts.

"Come, come, I will show you," with that he opened the office door and guided her to the workshop.

Mary did not want a scene in front of the staff so she warned Toni, "Please keep your voice down, Toni, I do not want this becoming factory gossip," Toni nodded and they entered the shopfloor just as everyone was starting their daily shift.

Toni picked up some thread and offering it to Mary, he pointed out that there was a big difference in quality, it broke easily and was much thinner. "The machines are constantly stopping because the thread is poor, it has no strength." He went on to point out that this meant production was down and seams were at risk of splitting. He then showed her a piece of lace. "Look at the quality of this lace, it's very inferior to what we used to use," which indeed it was.

Mary could now see Toni's point and was getting a little worried. Toni then showed her a roll of plain white cotton, which was used extensively. He didn't say anything, just showed it to her and stared into her eyes.

"But we get our cotton from Bromsgrove and they know what our standards are, this is a vastly inferior product." By now, Mary was fuming, she told Toni not to say anything to anyone but to leave it with her for now.

She returned to the office and Mac was at his desk as usual going through some papers.

"I would like to see what we are ordering from Bromsgrove and how much it costs," Mac rose and took down the file containing orders that Mary had looked at earlier.

"It's virtually the same as it's always been, what's the problem?" Mac looked a little uneasy, but Mary didn't notice because she was scanning the orders. The specification was the same as before on the order, but the delivered material clearly was not of the same standard.

"Why does the cloth I specified not meet the standard?" she was now extremely angry and in the mood for a fight.

"Not my problem, I just order it, I never see anything that comes through the doors."

This was not the response she was expecting. Mac informed her his role was to ensure the orders were correctly sourced, as far as he was concerned this was a problem for Toni as he managed the delivery process. She summoned Toni and there was then a heated discussion with both Mac and Toni blaming each other and neither taking responsibility. It was clear this had all resulted because they did not communicate with each other and she had not been there. This needed to be sorted immediately. She was also not happy with Bromsgrove and she was going to speak to James about it as soon as she saw him which was now next Tuesday. She ordered Mac to go back to the original suppliers for the threads and lace and to place an order immediately and ensure new stock was delivered without delay, no matter what the cost was. She then tore into both of them and told them this was a result of them not talking to each other and to sort their relationship out so it does not happen again.

Mary could see that Toni was angry that a portion of blame had been allocated to him and when she returned to her office next door, he followed her and closed the door behind them.

"We have worked together a long time, we never used to have these sort of problems, but you have to shoulder some responsibility for this, you are never here now, I am left to deal with everything." He ranted on further, "I don't trust him, I have never trusted him, something is not right."

Mary knew Toni was right about her not being in the office, there had been a stagnation in the design of new garments and Toni was under a lot of pressure.

"I promise I will be here. I am sorry for what's happened but you need to have to work with Mac. You are the senior manager and you need to take control over what comes through the door and what goes out of the door. I will tell Mac that you can overrule his decisions if you don't feel they are right."

This seemed to calm Toni down and he then left to go back to the workshop, so Mary went to see Mac to explain the new hierarchy, which wasn't well received. She had wanted to go and see the doctor, but with the tension in the office being so intense, she decided it could wait until the following week. Unbeknown to Mary, the accountant, George Davies also had concerns about materials, there appeared to be a large discrepancy between materials ordered and the finished product. He had been managing the accounts for a number of years and had developed a good idea between the raw materials and cost of the finished article and this didn't seem to match up. The only way in which it would make sense was if there was a large amount of unused material being stored, which he knew both Mary and Toni would never authorise and there was no sign of any surplus anywhere. There was a monthly meeting due next week and he would bring the subject up then.

Over the weekend, Mary noticed that her breasts were getting tender and fuller, she was now coming round to thinking she might be pregnant, so she knew she could not put off a doctor's appointment any longer. The thought of being a mother preoccupied all of her thoughts and she was wondering how to tell James, more importantly how he would react. She didn't care about the social stigma, her body clock was running down and she was looking forward to being a mother.

On Monday, Mary made a doctor's appointment for Wednesday and spent the morning looking at some new designs Toni had run by her, office life appeared to be getting back to normality.

Just as she was getting ready to leave at the end of the day, she received a visitor, it was the new buyer from Robinsons who had replaced Mr Masheter who was now retired. Robinsons were still one of the biggest customers and it was a nice surprise that the new man had taken the trouble to come and see them. She beckoned him to sit down but immediately noticed he was very pensive. They exchanged pleasantries, His name was Terry Coleman, but this was not a social visit. Then he came out with a very dramatic statement.

"I won't beat around the bush, this is not a very pleasant visit for me but I have no choice, I have to inform you that after the current orders are completed, we will not be placing any new work."

Mary was staggered, the relationship between Castlefield and Robinsons had been solid for nearly a decade, they accounted for nearly 40% of the turnover.

"But why, we have always treated you as our flagship customer, if there is a problem I feel sure it can be resolved," Mary was flustered.

"The garment that Castlefield supplied is not of the same quality as it used to be. There have been complaints about stitching coming loose and the material does not reflect the standard we require, so we have sourced an alternative supplier."

This was what Toni had warned about, she needed to resolve this now before Mr Coleman left the office.

"I confess we have had issues that have only recently come to light, I can give you an assurance that all of these problems can be and will be resolved immediately if you can allow us a little time."

She then went on to explain about the buying procedure and that they had now reverted to their original supplier. She showed him the new orders placed for the replacement and assured him that no more dresses would leave the factory until the original materials were being used. She asked him to wait in the office and went to see if Toni was about, which luckily, he was. After explaining what the buyer said, she told Toni no more goods were to go out until they had been rectified.

"There are 300 dresses waiting to be delivered, what do we do with them?" Toni was flustered, he knew they were in big trouble. "I warned you this would happen, we also have another 50 in various stages of production."

Mary told him nothing was to go out of the floor until they were perfect, they needed to unpick what was salvageable and they would sell the substandard dresses in the local market. She then asked how long it would take to replace the order.

"It depends on when we can get the replacement materials, if we can get tomorrow, then by the time we have sorted out what can be saved then the best will be 3 weeks, but I think more like 4 to 6 weeks."

She returned to the office and begged for a delay in the delivery of the next order for 6 weeks. Mr Coleman stated 4 weeks was the best he could do and there was still no guarantee of follow-on work.

The following morning was chaotic, it started with her addressing the workforce and informing them there was a serious situation that needed to be sorted out that meant the next few weeks would be like no other, but not to worry there would be no layoffs and they would still get paid. She then handed over to Toni who told them to get out all the Robinson's order and to unpick the dresses as carefully as possible, if it was going to damage the material then they were to repair the damage as best they could and put it to one side and try another one. Within 20 minutes, it became clear that this was not going to work, so all the girls were told to stop and ignore the previous order as there would be nothing to salvage.

This meant all the machines were stopped and all the girls were sat around talking, Mary and Toni went back into her office to discuss what the other options were.

She rang Oldfields, the previous supplier to ask if they could deliver the thread, buttons, trim that they had ordered and were told they had not yet received the order, but if someone were to arrange transport and bring an order with them then they could sort something out immediately. Mary informed them that Toni would be on his way immediately. Toni was then despatched with a driver to travel the 14 miles to pick them up. Meanwhile, the only production was being carried out by the cutters who still had some material to work with, everybody else was sat about chattering away and asking each other questions. Toni was away for about 3 hours so it was early afternoon by the time he got back. Mary was relieved but it was not all good news, the thread was fine, but the lacework and trims were not ready for another 2 days.

"At least we can get most of the girls working," said Toni, "But we have a lot of substandard stock to get rid of, we can't possibly sell it now."

Mary then had an idea, "We could try and sell them in the local market, there's a lot of clothes stalls there, the markets open Thursday, Friday and Saturday. We will have to sell cheaper obviously but at least we will salvage something."

So, a few of the machinists were then tasked with salvaging as much as possible, by the end of the day nearly everyone was producing something.

Mary was exhausted, this had been the worse day she had ever experienced in her working life, so she was not in the best of moods when she finally got home at 6pm.

James arrived promptly at 7pm as he always did, they had arranged to go out to meet but Mary was not in the mood and looked very tired, so he went out and brought back fish and chips. She still had to see James about the cloth he had provided, but decided to wait until they had finished eating.

As she was clearing the plates, she asked James why they were now sending substandard materials to Castlefield. James looked perplexed. "We are providing you with exactly the same material as we always have, I don't understand."

Mary then went on to explain that the cotton provided was clearly inferior, then handed him a sample she had brought home with her, "As you can see, this is nowhere near the same quality."

"I can see that, but I can assure you, my dear, this has not been supplied by Bromsgrove, we do not keep or sell cotton as cheap as this… To anyone, let alone a valued customer like Castlefield," James then promised to look into it the following day.

She decided to change the subject, she hadn't planned to tell him she might be having a baby until after the doctor confirmed she was pregnant, but after the day she had, she decided that now was as good a time as any. She snuggled up to him on the sofa and spoke very softly, "There is some other news that I have to tell you… I think I am going to have a baby."

There was no response but she felt his body go rigid. She then looked up at him. "It's not certain yet, I go to see the doctor tomorrow."

There was no response from James, who just sat there motionless looking into space with a shocked look on his face. She went on, "We can hardly be surprised, we have been at it for months and neither of us thought about the consequences."

After a good minute's silence, James's response was, "Let's not get carried away just yet darling, wait until after you have seen the doctor."

She agreed this made sense, so didn't mention it again. They went to bed at the usual time of 9pm but for the first time in weeks there was no lovemaking.

Mary's appointment was for 9:30 so she went into the office first for an update and plan of action, these were serious times and she needed to be there as much as possible.

Toni was in early and reminded her they had a monthly finance meeting in the afternoon, Mary mentally noted today was going to be another busy day. She informed him she had a doctor's appointment, Toni asked if she was ok, to which she replied, "I am fine, just need to something to be confirmed," which Toni thought was a strange response, but he wished her luck then went off onto the shop floor.

Before she left the sales manager at Bromsgrove rang her, he was as confused as James had been. He assured her that there had been no change in the specification of the cotton since the day they sold Castlefield their first roll. She didn't have time to discuss the matter now with Mac or Toni and she decided it could wait until the afternoon meeting.

She was in and out of the doctors in twenty minutes, the meeting with the doctor and his nurse confirmed what Mary already knew, she was expecting a baby and she was 12 weeks into her pregnancy. Mary was full of mixed emotions, at first, she wasn't sure but as the morning went on, she decided she was happy with the situation and couldn't wait to tell James. He was due to come and see her on Thursday so it would have to wait until tomorrow.

Mary and Toni sat down to prepare some notes for the meeting, she wasn't in the mood to listen to him and Mac bickering so there was just the two of them. First on the agenda was the Robinsons contract and how much it was going to cost to put right, it was worse than Mary had anticipated.

All the downtime, the cost of replacement materials. The wasted dresses that had already been made all added up to a substantial sum. To sell the dresses in the local market alone would incur a loss, Mary knew that the costs there were significantly lower than the retail price in Robinsons, they were looking at a damage limitation exercise. The matter of the inferior cotton was a mystery, she had no reason to believe that Bromsgrove would risk losing such a regular customer and she trusted James' word on the matter. By the time they finished costing everything it was apparent that there would be no profit for at least another 3 months.

The accountant arrived and as they sat down waiting for Mac, she brought him up to date on the latest developments. The expression on his face suggested that the situation was dire, but she was not prepared for what he had to report back to her. It was another ten minutes before Toni returned, he was alone.

"He's gone, I have looked everywhere but he has disappeared, his desk has been cleared," They all stared at each other in disbelief, it was now becoming clearer as to where all the problems originated.

Mary rose and went into Mac's office, she searched all the drawers in his desk, there were a few bits of stationary but all his personal effects were gone. More importantly the ordering file was also missing, all the records of what had been ordered were filed there. Mary feared the worse.

Returning to the meeting, Mary sat down, George Davies opened the books and informed her that there was a problem with cashflow that they had never had before. Mary had been well taught by George and Martha about profit and loss accounts and the general finances of the company so she understood what was occurring here.

George began his report, "As you are both aware for the last few months, we have had a situation where we have had fluctuations that have meant we have had to rely on our bank overdraft and have just about held our head above water," he looked up briefly before continuing, "These were normal, they have happened before and are as a result of season flow and customers settling accounts on time. However, there are a couple of abnormalities that are of major concern, these cannot be explained by seasonal adjustments."

"What abnormalities, I haven't noticed anything?" Mary's voice was shaky, she looked at Toni who was sat there with a totally baffled look on his face.

George then dropped the bombshell, "Over the last four months there has been a dramatic increase in the amount of dress material purchased, it wasn't noticeable at first as there are always delays between purchase and selling the finished article, so on a month by month basis you just assume that it's a normal cashflow situation, but when you take it over a quarter it is apparent that the amount of material ordered far exceeds what the output and stock account for."

Toni was leaning forward as he spoke, "I don't understand, we are producing the same amount of dresses as we always have, we should be making a profit, not a loss."

Mary knew exactly what George was saying. "So, there has been a massive spend on materials, that doesn't match the production orders, we have over ordered dress materials."

"Impossible, I know exactly how much to order, I always keep my stock under control, anyway we don't have the room to keep large amounts," Toni was taking this personally.

Mary knew who was responsible now, "Its Mac, that's why he has disappeared and took all the works orders with him. Just how bad is it, George?"

George sat back in his chair, took his glasses off and sighed. "The stock situation is very bad, but with the added problems with Robinsons, it will take a long time to recover."

Toni then asked the question they were all wondering, "Well where is all this stock then, because it's certainly not here."

George then explained, "The materials have never been delivered, you would have noticed the increase, there is a conspiracy between Mac and another to create false invoices and payments, with the money being syphoned off to another bank account. It must involve someone in the accounts office at Bromsgrove, but I advise that you call the police."

Mary decided she had to speak with James before calling the police, so she asked what the cost of all this deception was up to present. "It's the equivalent of six months normal material costs, there has been an overorder of 50% of your annual stock, its big money, Mary."

"Can we get a bridging loan to cover it?"

"You will be borrowing against future turnover and profit; this will mean that you are relying on the continuing custom of Robinsons and other customers as a guarantee." He then explained that this becomes a compounded risk as they are going to struggle over the next couple of months anyway, so it was not certain the banks would take the risk.

George wanted to investigate further to see if he could pin down exactly how this deception worked and so moved himself into Mac's office. Mary decided the first thing she needed to do was speak to James, there were a lot of questions to answer. She rang him but he was out of the office. She left a message and then sat down with Toni to work out a strategy. There wasn't much more Toni could do, so he took himself back to the workshop and try and concentrate on making sure normal service was resumed, but his head was spinning. He also knew the next few months would be manic and he wasn't looking forward to it. His workload was going to increase due to the extra problems the material crisis had produced, but now they were a man down on the office side, so even more work was going to be piled on him.

James rang back later that day and Mary gave a brief description of events, concentrating on the overordering of 6 months of materials. James said he knew more orders were being placed but assumed that business was good. When they were together, they didn't really talk about work matters, so he was unaware of anything out of the ordinary. He said he would look into it, but as far as he could see work orders were sent and received, materials despatched and delivered as normal. He asked her to give him time to investigate and they could talk the following night as usual. Mary did not want to mention about the baby, she was totally wrapped up in the catastrophe that was unfolding.

George could not see how this stock situation had unfolded, he needed the order books to correlate all the information, this was now missing along with Mac. He informed Mary there was nothing more he could do today and left.

All of this had left Mary shattered, it was now nearly five so she decided she couldn't face any more crisis, so she went home.

Toni on the other hand, was trembling with rage, he always knew Mac was bad, but he had been made to bite his tongue. He wished he had put up more of an argument, but he also knew that if he had then he would have been called disruptive. He was particularly mad with Mary, he had always put the business interests first and she had ignored his advice. He knew how much the business meant to her and the pain she would be feeling now. He went back to his apartment, but couldn't settle so decided he would go look for Mac and have it out with him. He went to the address that Mac had given when he began employment, but the landlord said he had not been there for months He had heard him talk about the Kings Arms public house, so went there more in hope than expectation.

Upon entering, he saw it was a typical back street pub with two rooms, a public lounge bar and a back bar that was men only. The main lounge was empty, so he made his way to the back bar where two men were sat together talking and another was sat reading a newspaper in the corner.

He ordered a half of Bitter, sat at the bar and tried to make conversation with the barman, who wasn't really interested in talking to a foppy foreigner with a peculiar accent. Toni offered to buy the barman a drink, which he gladly accepted. He then felt obliged to enter into a chat, so Toni asked about the area and how busy it got in here, etc., just general chat. He wasn't getting anywhere with line of questioning so decided to be more direct.

"I am looking for a tall Scotsman called Mac, I believe he lives around here and this is his local bar."

The barman then replied, "I was wondering what a guy like you would be doing around here, but for your information we don't talk to strangers about our business... Who are you anyway?"

Toni just said he needed to talk with him and that he would be quite generous towards anyone that could help him track him down.

"I take it, he owes you money," a voice behind him called out. Turning around, he saw the man on his own had dropped his paper to shoulder level and was staring straight at him.

"You could say that, but I don't want to go into details."

"You owed a gambling debt? If you are then you need to be warned there's a big queue in front of you." The man then joined Toni at the bar and asked for a double whiskey then he turned to the barman, "This gentleman is paying," and nodded at Toni.

"You're looking in the wrong place, but for a fiver I can show you where you're likely to find him," Toni agreed, they drank up and left the pub.

Two streets down there was a quite large hotel by the name of the Imperial, that at some point in time had probably been quite nice but was now badly run down. He pointed upstairs and informed Toni there was a card school there most nights and that he knew Mac frequented it often.

"He must have been on a winning streak because he has been loaded the last few months."

Now everything made complete sense, Mac was skimming money out of the company, they just needed to know how. They also needed to find Mac, but he was now in need of food and sleep, so gave the man his five pounds and went home.

The following morning Toni updated Mary on last night's news, "There is definitely a swindle going on, but I don't know how he is doing it, we need to talk to Bromsgrove to track everything through from beginning to end."

Toni knew about Mary and James but had never said anything, if she wanted him to know she would have been more open, so it was never mentioned. Mary then said she had already spoken with James and he was looking into it, but it would be a good idea if Toni spoke with the Bromsgrove accounts people and see if they could get copies of the orders placed over the past 4 months, as they were unable to, due to Mac running off with the order book. Mary then called James and asked him to meet with her at lunchtime, which was unusual, they always met in the evening at her house, but this couldn't wait.

They agreed on lunch at the White Bull, the restaurant was not busy and they managed to get a nice table in the corner so they could talk without being overheard.

James started the conversation by letting her know what information he had about the cotton and the number of orders.

"You have been quite busy with us just lately, I knew the orders were up, but thought the quantities are generous by your previous standards. All the materials were delivered in good time and received by Castlefield as per normal."

Mary then Told James about Mac, that he had disappeared and that Toni had found out about his gambling problem. They discussed how and where it was possible for the money to find its way into Mac's pocket.

"I think I know how he is doing it," James thought he had the solution. "You are placing the order, nothing wrong there. Then the material is despatched, again nothing wrong. The problem is that you are not seeing that material in your workshop, therefore the materials are being diverted before they get to you."

It was obvious, Mac had a customer for the goods which were delivered to a different address, he was then being paid directly for the materials and Castlefield were picking up the cost and paying as per contract.

James went on, "But in order to do that he must have been in collusion with the driver from my place to divert the lorry elsewhere."

Now it all made sense, James promised to leave no stone unturned in order to find the driver responsible and Mary would now be able to go to the police with the information about Mac. She felt a lot better now she knew the detail of the fraud, she wasn't happy about it, but at least they could focus on trying to find the materials and possibly get some of the money back once they tracked Mac down.

Now was the time to break the good news to James, "That's the bad news out of the way, now for the good."

James suddenly looked uncomfortable, he had put the thought of a baby to one side, but now he recalled the conversation from last week and he realised this was really happening.

"I went to see the doctor yesterday, I am having a baby and I am 12 weeks into my pregnancy… isn't that wonderful?"

James was now sweating; he raised his hands to his head and laid his elbows on the table. "No, no, no, you can't make me a father, this was not supposed to happen. This will ruin my life."

Mary had been wondering how James would respond, but this response had never figured in her thoughts.

"What's wrong darling, I hoped you would be pleased. Yes, it's a bit of a shock but we can get married and live in my house and everything will be good. Don't worry it will all be ok." She was truly shocked but what came next completely floored her.

James lifted his head; she could see tears in his eyes.

"I cannot marry you and you cannot have my baby." He was cold and calculated in his response. "It's impossible, you cannot name me as the father."

Mary was speechless, "Why, what is it?"

James took her hand and spoke slowly and softly, looking around to see if anyone was listening. "I cannot marry you because I am already married with a son. Bromsgrove is my wife's fathers' company and I will be thrown out of my house and my job and will lose everything. I thought that what we had was an agreement to enjoy ourselves, I wasn't expecting anything to develop like this."

He went on to explain that as sales director, he was expected to travel and visit companies in the northwest and as such he stayed in a hotel three nights a week and went home at the week, which was why they only met up Tuesday and Thursday. He ushered the waitress over and asked for the bill which he settled up. Then he pushed his chair back stood up and in a hushed voice said, "If you keep the baby I will provide financially, but under no circumstances must anyone know about our relationship."

Then he leaned on the table and firmly grasped her hand and in a menacing tone said, "If anything does come out, then I will act and do whatever it takes to protect me and my family. I will never be a part of the child's life, get used to it, or pay the consequences." He then released her hand, turned around and walked swiftly to the exit.

Mary could not move, she was shaking, her head was spinning. Did he really just speak and act like that, was it really James, the same James she had come to love and adore. It was a full five minutes before she could bring herself around to realise what had just happened. She then spent the next ten minutes contemplating how and what she was to do next and not being able to come to any conclusion, went home. She couldn't face work now, she couldn't face anything.

Toni closed the factory at the end of the day and went to a local hostelry for something to eat. He was determined to chase Mac down, this was now a personal vendetta, how dare that Scottish bastard ruin so many people's lives. After eating, he made his way to the hotel, ordered a drink in the lounge and settled down and wait. He wasn't sure what was going to happen or how things might develop, he just knew that this was his best chance of finding him. It was only 7pm and he had to wait until 9pm for things to liven up. A couple of girls arrived with gentlemen and were immediately ushered upstairs. The place obviously doubled up as a brothel, which made Toni wonder if that's where some of the money had disappeared to. A number of men were gathered at the far end of the lounge, Toni counted six. They looked like business men and they were all sat around as if waiting for something.

At 10pm a man came down the stairs and summoned them, at which point they all went upstairs. Toni ordered another drink but at 10:30 last orders were sounded. He asked the barman if there was any way he could get another drink, but was told that it was not possible. Toni then pointed out that there were men upstairs and could he join them, to which the barman laughed and said they were registered guests and were entitled. He had just given up when one of the men came back down, nodded to the barman and made his way outside. Toni thanked the barman and followed the man catching up with him at the end of the street.

"Excuse me Sir, may I have a minute?" The man looked annoyed so Toni reckoned that he had just lost some money.

"I am looking for a friend of mine called William McCallister, you might know him as Mac."

The man looked Toni up and down, "What makes you think I might know such a person? I don't have time to stand here in idle gossip."

"He frequents the Imperial and I just saw you leave there. He also likes a game of cards that I understand is played there, again I just saw you come down the stairs," Toni could see the man was nervous, so he pressed further. "He has played there before so I assume you will have come across him, a tall thin man with a strong accent."

He then produced a five-pound note and waving it under the man's nose told him, "Nobody will know, I just want to find him."

The man snatched the note and quickly stuffed it in his pocket. "Yes, I know him, he upset a lot of people over the past year and owed money to some very dangerous people. But he came into some money, quite big money. In fact, he was in there last night, settled his debt and told everyone he was going back to Scotland."

The man seemed genuine, so Toni thanked him and the man walked off. As he was walking home it suddenly struck him that Mac may well have been in the hotel at the same time as he was stood outside, if he had gone into the hotel, he may well have caught him. He also realised that it was obvious there would be no money to be recovered, it had all gone to pay gambling debts.

After a sleepless night Mary rose and forced herself to eat some toast, washed down with a cup of strong black coffee. She wasn't hungry but knew she had to eat for the sake of the baby. After dressing into her increasingly tight clothes she realised that hiding the pregnancy was mow becoming impossible so she would have to confide in someone. Toni was the nearest thing to family she had so she decided to speak with him first thing. She was also struck by the fact she realised for the first time that she didn't have any friends at all. She was a loner. She never noticed it before because work was all consuming and everything, but she was truly alone in this world.

Yesterday's events kept playing over and over in her head, her thoughts now were to blame herself for being so stupid. It all added up, why he never saw her at weekend, why always the same 2 nights, why he insisted on secrecy... She was torturing herself and the worry of bringing up a child alone scared her even more.

Once in work, Toni sorted out the girls on the floor and went into the office to give Mary the news. He poured them both a coffee and explained about how Mac owed money, that it appeared he had run back to Scotland and that it was unlikely there would be any money to recover.

Mary could feel herself boiling up, the events of the last few days were beginning to take their toll, finally she was unable to control herself anymore and broke down in floods of tears.

Toni was taken aback, he had always seen Mary in complete control of her emotions, this was a very vulnerable Mary and he was unsure how he should react. He put his arm around her shoulder and let her cry. He said nothing, what could he say, he knew all of her life was tied in the business and everything was crumbling around her and he felt her pain, she was more than a friend, she was a sister he never had, he loved her like family.

After five minutes the tears subsided, Toni finally spoke, "Look, we have reached the bottom, things cannot get worse, we will both bring this company back to what it was, we will be bigger and stronger."

Mary suddenly started laughing hysterically, which really threw Toni, "You think so, you really think so?"

Mary gripped Toni's wrist and looking him in the eye, she screeched, "I am having a baby, Toni, the father is married to someone else, I am alone and my life is fucked."

Toni had never heard Mary swear before which threw him momentarily. He was not expecting this news and it took a moment to sink in. He guessed that James was the father, but didn't want to let Mary know that he was aware of their relationship, so said nothing.

She told him all about James and he sat there in total silence as she unfolded the whole scenario of the past 5 months. At the end of it he asked her if her health was ok and that she needed to take a step back and not allow herself to get too excited, then he realised the absurdity of what he had said and they both laughed hard and long.

Having finally unburdened herself, Mary felt a lot better and composed herself. They agreed the biggest priority at the moment was to try and get some money in to ease the cashflow situation.

Tony called a few of the buyers of other customers to see if they were interested in some cut-price garments, but got the same response from all of them. They all had enough stock to see the summer out and didn't want to get stuck with stock they wouldn't be able to get rid of.

Mary grabbed a couple of samples and went down to see some of the stallholders in the indoor market, she came back with a few small orders but they would still be left with the majority of unsaleable dresses. This was obviously not going to work, so the dresses were bagged up and put in the store cupboard until she knew what to do with them. The priority now was getting things back to normal as quickly as possible.

Toni asked the girls on the shopfloor if anyone wanted extra hours and weekend work, a few agreed to work until 8pm every day to meet the Robinsons' order.

George Davies called with an update on the financial situation, it was not a good conversation. He informed Mary that that there was enough money in the bank to cover the next two weeks but they needed to complete the Robinsons' order as soon as possible in order to keep afloat. There were a few other customers' orders that were outstanding, but they would not be completed until the major Robinsons order was out of the way.

Mary estimated that if they completed the work next week and submitted an invoice immediately there would be at least another 2 weeks before the payment came through. She had no choice, she had to ask the banks for a bridging loan.

She sat down with Toni and drew up a business plan for the short term, she needed money to cover a month, this was to cover wages and materials, Toni insisted they needed to ask for more than they thought they needed to cover and unforeseen problems, they agreed to ask for 15000 pounds. She then called George Davies and asked his opinion, she gave him the figures, he warned her it would only be enough for the immediate future but that figure would certainly ease the strain.

She needed to speak with Bromsgrove about extending credit, but James refused her call. This happened 4 times and she finally left a message to say that she was going to call to Bromsgrove office the following day, James responded within twenty minutes. The discussion was very brief and curt. He informed her that she was not welcome, but he was willing to discuss new terms with Toni but not to expect the same discounts, it was clear that Mary was not in a position to negotiate, so it was agreed that Toni would call in to discuss new terms and also pick up copies of delivery notes for the previous orders to demonstrate there was nothing untoward from Bromsgrove Linen Supplies. George managed to get a bank appointment the following Monday and Toni took the train to Birmingham to meet Bromsgrove.

On Monday morning, as Mary sat very nervously in a small office at the bank, she noticed that her clothes were now far too tight and people would soon be able to see her increased waistline and bigger breasts, she knew she had to buy some new outfits but felt guilty about the cost, even though it was from her own money.

George could see she was uneasy and tried to calm the atmosphere down. "You know what you need to borrow, you just need to convince them that it's a cashflow situation that is temporary."

He had been in this situation with other customers before and knew this was not going to be easy. One thing in their favour was that the business had been banking here for over forty years, ever since Martha Shorrock had first started up and they had never had to ask for a loan before.

The manager entered the room with a number of files and sat himself behind a large leather chesterfield chair.

He placed the file on the desk, looked up at Mary and smiled. "Well, this is the first time I have had the pleasure of a visit from Castlefield Fashion House. I have worked here for over twenty years and not had to have any dealings with such a respected company, it's a pleasure to see you, now how may I help?"

This was a good start so Mary decided to lay her cards on the table and went through the whole scenario of what had occurred over the past 6 months, about Mac and the missing materials, his procurement decisions and the fact that he had now left the business. She further explained that they had nearly completed the Robinsons order and were expecting that there would repeat orders. She also explained that Toni was at the moment agreeing extended credit with Bromsgrove, she thought she had given a good account of herself and was feeling quite confidant. George was concerned that Mary had given out too much detrimental information, she didn't need to go into that amount of detail.

The manager then started to go through the file on his desk, making notes every now and again. Mary could also see he was making calculations, which she took to be a good sign. Finally, after a long silent ten minutes, he put his pen down, closed the file and looked up and started to ask the type of questions that Mary was not expecting. He questioned the structure of the company, the procurement and accounting processes, how would they manage this process to ensure accountability? He wanted to know about future orders, not once did he mention money.

This is what George feared, he knew this manager was thorough and very much had a business mind, it wasn't about money it was about the ability to run a business in a responsible manner.

Mary was thinking on her feet now, she was rattled and it showed. "After what happened with Mr McCallister, the strategy is to restrict authority to Myself and Mr Guido, we will install extra office staff for administration purposes only, all the main decisions will be made by us alone."

The manager reopened the file and looked at the bank statements, "I can see that you had a very healthy account up until the beginning of this year and that I can see over the past few years there was steady growth and, on that basis alone I am prepared to lend you 10,000 pounds. Your estimate of 15,000 is, in my opinion, a little bit heavy, but then again if I was in your position, I would also want to cover myself."

He smiled as he said it. Mary could see this man knew his business; she smiled meekly back. He wasn't finished however and asked Mary a final couple of questions. "What is the possibility that your reputation is damaged to the extent that you cannot recover your position?"

Mary replied that she had a good reputation and that she had every confidence there was no long-lasting damage, which prompted a raising of eyebrows. George knew what he meant, reputations can be destroyed easily, regaining the trust will be difficult, especially as the previous buyer from Robinsons with whom they had built the trust and confidence was no longer there.

The final question was completely out of the blue. "You say that all the major decisions in relation to the business will be made by yourself and Mr Guido, is that too large a responsibility for one person to make when you have to take time off to have your baby… I take it you are expecting."

Mary just sat there open mouthed, totally unable to speak, her mind operating in overdrive. It was now so obvious?

The only response she could muster was a meek, "We have taken all scenarios into account, it is not a major concern. I will only be off for a short period of time."

George was stunned, he had noticed She had put a little weight on, but he didn't even know she was married and said so to Mary on the way back to the office.

Toni meanwhile was in the Midlands to discuss extended credit with James. It was obvious that James did not really want to trade with Castlefield and the terms on offer were very unfavourable, he was hoping Toni would walk away. But Toni was not in a position to refuse, he needed to complete the outstanding orders and sourcing other suppliers was too time consuming… for now. Toni was seething with James, not only about the new deal but mainly about how he had treated Mary. In the end he was forced to agree that the previous 28% discounts would no longer apply, which would eat substantially into their profit Margin.

After completing the deal, James showed Toni the orders they received over the past 6 months, Toni scribbled notes furiously. Then he was shown the delivery notes which proved to be very informative. Toni knew what was normally ordered over this period and 5 extra deliveries to a different site had been ordered. Matching these deliveries to the orders it amounted to double what would normally be ordered over a year let alone 6 months. The delivery address was also noteworthy for these extra orders, they were dropped off at a warehouse in Bolton instead of at the factory.

Toni didn't bother to shake James' hand when he left, which left James wondering what Toni knew about his relationship with Mary. He caught the 2:30 to Manchester Victoria and finally got home too late to go to into the office.

On the way back to the office, Mary asked George to drop her off in central Manchester, it was now obvious she needed to update her wardrobe. She got out and decided to get some lunch before trailing her way around the shops. As she sat there the enormity of the impact a baby will make suddenly dawned on her. The bank manager was right, Toni was running around in circles at the minute and stressed to the maximum, how would he cope with all the extra responsibility? This was a crisis and she needed to sit down with Toni to work out how they would cope and the impact on the business. She hated shopping, so quickly choice some bigger outfits and went back to the office.

Toni also knew that Mary being pregnant was a big issue, he tried to put it to the back of his mind, there were too many other things that needed immediate attention, that could wait for now.

Mary wandered onto the shop floor to get an update on progress and was informed that they were ahead of schedule and that the Robinsons order would be ready by Wednesday. As she walked back to her office, she was aware of a few sniggers behind her back, they too had noticed. She knew she was going to be the subject of shop floor gossip for the next few months.

The Robinsons' order was ready on Tuesday night, which was lucky as the buyer was always in the local store on Wednesdays, so Mary rang him and agreed to come to his office with some finished garments. She quickly examined the quality and satisfied with the finished article she made her way to Robinsons store.

Mr Coleman was already in his office and was on the telephone as she entered, it was apparent the call was not a friendly one and he was giving someone a roasting, so she sat there quietly trying not make eye contact. After putting the phone down, he stood up and moved around his desk, "Ok then, let's see what is on offer this time," Mary did not like his tone, he was obviously in a bad mood.

She unwrapped the three samples she had provided and laid them on the desk. He then cast a very critical eye over all of them. "Yes, that's more like it, I can sell these."

Mary was relieved and promised the remaining garments would be delivered by the end of the day. "Can I be assured then that you will be continuing our previous arrangement and placing further orders with Castlefield."

"That all depends on what you have got, I need to see your winter collection before I can guarantee you any further work."

"Of course," Mary countered. "I will let you see some of the concepts and sketches we are proposing to introduce this afternoon."

"I am not interested in concepts or drawings on a paper, I need to see the finished product. I am going to see a factory this afternoon that has garments ready for me to inspect." He leaned right into Mary's face, "I am currently placing orders for the winter and you want me to give you work based on an idea? What sort of business are you running, I only deal with professionals and your company is anything but, as far as I can see."

Mary pleaded with him to reconsider, this could break the back of her business, but he was not going to change his mind. She then got angry, "How dare you question my professionalism? I have over 30 staff, we produce good quality garments and we have dealt with Robinsons successfully for over a decade. How dare you?"

He then told her there was nothing more to discuss and opened the door for her to leave. As she stood up, she suddenly felt her head spinning, she was feeling sick, then everything went black and she collapsed unconscious on the floor.

Chapter Nine

It was a full four days of intermittent sweats, unconsciousness, crazy nightmares and fever before Mary finally emerged back into the real world.

As she woke up a familiar face was looking intently at her, Toni was there looking totally drained and exhausted. He had stayed for most of the duration. Having had the phone call from Robinsons that Mary was being taken to hospital. The only time off he had was to return to the factory and try and keep things steady. Mary immediately realised that she had lost the baby, her body felt different. She wasn't sure how she was supposed to feel, her maternal instincts were making her feel guilty, but her gut instincts were saying that it was probably for the best and that now was the time to get her life back.

Toni explained what had happened, Mary had no recollection of the meeting with Coleman and wasn't immediately aware of the situation the company was now in. As soon as he realised she could not remember, he decided that now was not the time to discuss such matters, she needed to rest and recover before facing the reality of it all. He just brushed over the fact that the dresses were now sold and that she should relax and recover. Mary was still not fully conscious and drifted back to sleep, so Toni left her and then, feeling relieved that she was back in the real world went back to the factory to try and make plans for the next stages of recovery.

As he sat down to survey the situation Toni could not help feeling that they were in deep trouble and so made a list of things he needed to sort out and prioritise them.

By far the biggest problem was getting production back to the previous level and getting orders out, everything else was secondary. They were operating at less than 40% of the previous capacity and this barely covered costs, so he had no choice he had to let at least half the workforce go. The trouble was he couldn't do that without Mary's authority. He knew he would have to talk business with her very soon, but the timing of the discussion needed to be when she was strong enough, so then he moved onto the second problem.

Bromsgrove had left them in a very difficult position, they needed to get materials and although they had the credit available it was at an enhanced cost therefore either prices had to go up or they found a new supplier. The materials from Bromsgrove were good quality and they delivered on time, so he decided to try and put emotional pressure on James to see if they could get some movement in the rates, he would tell him the baby has gone and hope there was an element of guilt that would pressure him into renegotiating.

Then there was the bank loan, this was due the following week and there was no chance of getting any of it paid off. Another appointment was required and some sort of strategy required to convince them the money could be paid at some stage. But this was dependant on everything else falling into line and there was no certainty that was going to happen. Lastly, they needed to design and produce a new winter collection.

They had both been firefighting and there was nothing in the pipeline, so no new protype of garment to develop. This was one thing he could do on his own, but he still badly needed to get Mary fit and able to make decisions.

He needed to speak with someone and as it was all financially related, he made an appointment with George Davies and met him in his office the following day.

George Davies had known Mary since she first stayed at Martha Shorrock's home and knew she was a very capable woman. He had watched her mature into an astute business woman with a flair for knowing what was in and out of vogue. The business had grown steadily and to see it in the position it was now in was very disheartening for him.

As Toni outlined the business position from where they are now to where they needed to be, it was obvious to Toni from the look on Georges face that they really were in trouble. After listening to Toni for a good ten minutes, George finally spoke.

"It gives me no pleasure at all to say this but the position looks to be unsalvageable, there is only enough money to pay next week's wages and the bank is due to foreclose on the bridging loan next week. Your customer base has diminished by 40% and your other customers are waiting to see what new merchandise you can offer them, which at the moment is nothing. The owner is sadly in poor health at the moment so no decisions can be made… so basically the position, in my opinion, is irretrievable."

The reality hit Toni hard, he knew they were in big trouble but to hear it spelled out in such a matter-of-fact way suddenly hit him hard. He knew he had to speak with Mary, but how much will she be able to take? She had just lost a baby and was very weak, but she had to make decisions. He also knew that if nothing was done, she would never forgive him, so he decided the only thing he could do was to try and salvage as much as possible from the wreckage.

He went back to the office and called a meeting with the workforce, he explained that after next week there was no money to pay wages. He was hoping to pick up work but there was no guarantee and if anyone wanted to leave now, then it was understandable. He did not elaborate, just left it short and to the point. He didn't even wait for questions, just turned and went back to the office.

Then he phoned Bromsgrove and, after being fobbed off a few times, finally got through to James and laid his cards on the table. If they were not prepared to increase the discounts then there was every chance there would be no customer to deal with at all. James was fairly dismissive and promised to review the rates and get back to him, which was all Toni could hope for at this stage.

Finally, he started work on some new designs that had previously been outlined in draft form, he needed to urgently get these in production if they were going to save the company.

The following day he went back to see Mary who was looking stronger and more lucid. She informed him she was going home the following day, Toni decided to discuss matters once she was in more familiar surroundings.

Mary wanted to know what the current situation was and asked about her meeting with Coleman at Robinsons. He told her all the dresses they produced were accepted and that the payment was due in 2 weeks, he didn't mention that that was the only money due in or that there would not be any repeat orders. Mary thankfully didn't ask any more questions so he told her he would return the following morning and make sure she got home safely.

Once Mary was home and settled, Toni knew he could not delay any longer and had to make sure Mary was fully informed of the position they were in. Mary sat back and absorbed it all, her face showing little emotion. When lying in her hospital bed yesterday, she had analysed everything that had gone on and was aware of everything, except that any repeat orders from Robinsons were not going to materialise.

"I need to get back to work and I need to do it now," Mary started to rise from the sofa but Toni held her back.

"There is nothing you can do there that you can't do here. The shop floor is winding up, the bank loan is foreclosure imminent and Bromsgrove are considering their position."

"Bromsgrove considering, considering what? If it wasn't for them and that bastard James Morris, we wouldn't be in this position." Mary was furious and reached for the phone.

She called Bromsgrove and was put straight through to James Morris. He started by saying he was sorry she had lost the baby, which they both knew was a lie.

"Toni has explained the situation, what is your decision, I need this sorting immediately," Mary was straight to the point.

I can offer you extended credit but the rates will have to be as I renegotiated with Toni in my office last week. "How would it look if I now changed them again, people would ask questions." This answer nearly caused Mary to explode.

"How would it look if I come down there and explain all about my pregnancy and our affair? If your father-in-law sacks you then I might even be able to negotiate an even better rate with your successor."

Toni looked at Mary and saw a face that he had never seen before, she was raging and was not a woman to argue with. He could hear Morris imploring Mary to be reasonable, which just seemed to make her even angrier. In the end he agreed to go back to the original arrangement of 28% discount and Mary hung up.

She then called a number of customers and assured them a new collection would be out in the next few weeks. This was met with mixed reaction; a lot had already sourced new suppliers and others thought they had left it too late for a winter collection and that it would get to the shops after peak retail season. It wasn't looking good. Now that the supply problem had been temporarily resolved they turned their attention to design, Toni had brought some drafts and they looked at those and they were forced to acknowledge that they were indeed a couple of months behind where they needed to be to get a winter collection designed, manufactured and in the shops in good time.

Mary made a snap decision, "We are going to look at the following spring collection and get ahead of the game."

This made no sense to Toni, nobody could foresee what would be in demand in eight months' time. Castlefield followed fashion acting on trends, mainly from America, but there was recession there now, not much was coming through and the future requirements were uncertain. Castlefield was not in a position to predict future demand and certainly not big enough to create one. Also, what was going to happen to the workforce in the meantime, there would be no money coming in and the cashflow would cripple them. He was convinced she wasn't thinking clearly yet, so he decided not to raise his concerns and merely commented that this needed further consideration.

There was another matter that needed Mary's attention, she had to speak to the bank manager and try and extend the bridging loan, so she called and made an appointment. Then she called George Davies, she needed to discuss how they were going to convince the bank to extend.

On Monday morning at 10 am, Mary, George and Toni found themselves in the same office where they had originally borrowed the money, the bridging loan terms had expired the Friday before, so the mood of the manager was not as jovial as had previously been, As Mary sat down, she noticed him looking at her stomach, with a look of curiosity on his face. George had advised that the only approach to make was one of total honesty, so Mary came straight to the point and explained about the meeting with Robinsons, that they had sold the dresses as per the order, but they now needed to retrieve their reputation before Robinsons would consider new orders. She explained they had a lot of ideas in the various stages of design and that they were confident that once the new lines were rolled out then there would be no more cashflow problems. She was asking for a further two thousand pounds to allow Castlefield to develop the new lines. She also explained that the whole experience and stress had caused her to miscarriage, which now meant she would be able to fully concentrate on the business.

The bank manager said nothing all the time Mary was talking, he didn't even look at the file in front of him, when she had finished speaking, he finally looked at Mary and in a slow, clear voice told her how he saw the situation.

"First off, may I give my condolences on your loss, it has obviously been a very difficult time for you and your family. We are now in a very precarious situation, so allow me to spell out the bank's position in all this." He then summarised the position as he saw it.

"Your bridging loan was granted on the assumption that your existing customer, Robinsons, with whom 40% of your business operates, would be happy to resume trading on the same basis as before. This repeat business formed the collateral on which the loan was established." He was in a very sombre mood.

"This repeat business has not materialised and so you are not in a position to repay the loan and are now asking for the loan to be increased, but without being in a position to giving any categoric financial assurances of how the loan would be paid."

Mary just sat there totally demoralised, this was not looking good. She glanced at Toni who was sitting with his head down, just staring at the floor. He knew they were now finished.

The bank manager continued, "So basically you want more money, with less collateral, with an even bigger risk to the bank. That would be financial madness. I cannot even consider an increase on the original loan… but I have a duty to the bank's shareholders to try and recover the money lent so far. Therefore, I am giving you one extra month credit to see if you can clear your existing loan. This will, of course, be subject to interest at the current rate."

Mary tried in vain to reason with him, but there was nothing to negotiate with, they had nothing to offer. The manager then concluded the meeting by saying that if the loan was not fully repaid within the month, then legal proceedings would be undertaken to recover the costs. They returned to the office and sat there in total silence, trying to absorb the predicament they now found themselves in. Mary could only think that her life was now destroyed, she had no future and over and over in her mind was the thought about how she felt she had let Martha down.

George was concerned for Mary, she looked frail and vulnerable. He felt sorry that the company was going to fold but this was business and he had other clients as customers so financially it didn't really affect him. Toni could only think about one thing, that bastard McCallister. How could one person cause such misery to so many people?

They tried to think optimistically, but were getting nowhere, it all seemed futile. Finally, Mary broke the silence, "We need to tell the workforce they are to be finished, but it has to come from me. Toni please can you let them know I wish to speak with them this afternoon." Toni nodded in agreement then left to organise it.

George left at 1pm and Mary was left alone in the office, very despondent, a defeated woman. As she sat there accepting her fate, her mind wandered to the person that caused all this, Mac. She then realised that they had not tried to recover the diverted materials, where were they? There was a lot of money tied up in those transactions and if they could recover half the money stolen, it would go some way to paying off the debt to the bank.

The afternoon meeting with the shopfloor was difficult for Mary, they had all grown together as the company grew and were close knit, almost family, but there was no avoiding it, they needed a miracle. As she spoke the whole place was silent and she could see faces of disappointment everywhere.

Toni was quick to point out the core of the problem related to Mac's behaviour and was very scathing in his assessment. Mary said that now was not the time for finger pointing, it was just as much her fault for not giving the business her full commitment and that if she had devoted more time, she would have foreseen the problems as they arose.

The meeting was over in 20 minutes with Mary promising they would be paid until Friday and that after that the factory was to close for good. She refused to answer any questions, after all what more could be said? She wasn't going to promise things would improve. Why lie and build false hope. Mary wasn't a big drinker, but that night she went home and demolished a bottle of wine then fell into a very deep sleep.

Toni had also been wondering about where the materials had been diverted to and what had happened to them. The factory was quiet and so he decided to try and track them down, and travelled the 12 miles to Bolton to the warehouse they had been delivered to. The warehouse was right on the canal and flanked either side by other small warehouses, but they were occupied and this was empty and looked like it had not been used for a while. After asking around, he found a couple of workers that remembered some deliveries of cloth being unloaded at the front on at least 4 occasions, they also informed him they had been taken straight to the back and being loaded onto a barge that was moored on the canal at the back.

Here he got another piece of valuable information, the name of the barge was the "Griffen Park," and it was registered to a company from Bolton called Hall and Sons Ltd.

Toni tracked the barge down and spoke with the Skipper, who was less than forthcoming. Eventually he offered him five pounds if he could tell him where it was all delivered and then found him to be little more talkative. It transpired that the materials were offloaded at Appleyard Bridge where the goods were transferred to a small lorry. He then gave Toni the location of the Bridge and also informed him that the lorry when loaded headed in the direction of Farnworth.

The following morning, armed with this information, Toni went to see Mary to let her know of this latest news, but she was not in a listening mood as her head was pounding.

"You go take a look and let me know if it's worth following up, but if it's been loaded onto a lorry then it could be anywhere," was all she could bring herself to express.

The majority of girls had been laid off and the few remaining were set to work using up available materials to make blouses and every day wear, that would probably finish up being sold on the market. This meant that Toni was free to try and investigate where the missing materials were.

He drove to where the Bridge was, it was a fairly remote spot and transferring materials would not have attracted any interest. From there he headed in the direction of Farnworth, he was hoping that the final drop would be local. He wasn't sure how or where to start looking but decided to seek out dressmaker shops or linen suppliers, he drove around all morning but was getting nowhere. The only likely places he found were either too small or clearly had no use for finer quality materials. By 2pm, he realised he was hungry so he called in to a little tea shop and ordered a coffee and cake. He was just sitting there pondering his next move when his train of thought was interrupted, "I haven't seen you here before, you lost or travelling through?"

Looking up he could see the shop was empty except for himself and a plump lady who he estimated to be in her late forties. He didn't want to go into details, so told her he was a salesman of fine garments and was looking for potential customers. There was no further conversation and he ate his cake in silence and considered giving up and going home. He paid the bill and as he was heading towards the door the lady spoke again.

"You're wasting your time in Farnworth, nobody around here shops for the type of clothing your selling."

Toni nodded and acknowledgement and as he reached the door she continued, "But there is a shop in Kearsley that's not been open too long and is selling some lovely stuff, you can't miss it, its on Bolton Road."

Toni thanked her and hurried to his car. Sure enough, in the middle of the main street there was a quite large dress shop and there in the window was some materials he immediately recognised. Staring through the window into the shop, he saw a thin woman of above average height. Her face looked vaguely familiar but he couldn't quite place her. He was convinced this business was the one they were looking for and so he went back and sat in the car, his head spinning, what was he going to do now?

He could go straight to the police, but he immediately ruled that out. He would go to the police when he had established all the facts, he didn't want them potentially messing things up. When they reported the initial materials as stolen, they didn't seem very interested.

He could directly confront the shop owner and ask where she got her materials from. This was also risky as he didn't know exactly who he was dealing with. He finally decided that for now he would do nothing. The shop would still be there tomorrow, he needed to discuss everything with Mary and form a plan of action, so he drove straight round to her house.

Mary, by now, had recovered and she apologised to Toni for her disinterest earlier in the day. Toni with a dramatic dismissal with his hand was in a very excited state.

"Never mind that, I think I have found where the materials are."

He then gave Mary full details of his day and finished by telling her he didn't want to go to the police yet. Mary agreed, the police had shown little interest up to now, which irked her.

She was by now totally intrigued and curious to see this establishment for herself, so the plan was to go and visit, with Mary posing as a customer, to try and establish some more facts and to confirm if this was the end destination for the materials.

On Wednesday morning, they opened up the workshop and set the girls to work, but there was very little to do, so Mary asked Milly to send them all home at lunchtime, it was pointless sitting about worrying about their futures, they may as well be at home.

It was a 45-minute drive to the shop and they pulled up outside the side street where the back alley to the shop was, Mary was to go in the front and engage in conversation and Toni would take a look around the back. As Mary entered the shop, she was very apprehensive, she didn't know what she was going to say, she would just have to wing it. The shop assistant was not a tall older lady as described by Toni, but a young lady in her twenties. Mary started to look around and noticed certain similarities in style but nowhere near as good as she had sold and the quality was definitely inferior, but the materials were very familiar. She started the conversation by saying she passed this area quite often but hadn't noticed this shop before.

"No, we are quite new I have only been here a few weeks, but we are quite busy," Mary then picked a dress from the rack and looked at the price, it was very cheap. No doubt, the local mill girls would be quite happy to pay this as it was just a cheap copy made from decent materials. If that had been produced at her factory using the same materials, but a much better finished product, then she would have expected to pay double. No wonder they were doing well!

"Wow," Mary exclaimed. "This looks very good value; how can you possibly sell it at that price."

The girl smiled, "Yes it's very good value, I am not sure how or where they are made. You would have to ask the lady who owns the shop."

"I would love to; I might be interested in making a bulk purchase is she here now?"

"Yes, she is in the back, I will just go and find her."

She then disappeared and came back with the tall middle-aged woman that Toni described. She did look familiar and as soon as she started to speak everything became clear.

"Good afternoon, my name is Gina McCallister and I believe you are interested in my garments." The accent was clearly strong Glaswegian and her face was now as recognisable as her brothers. This was obviously Mac's sister.

Mary didn't know what to say and just rattled away saying she liked her product and that she had a couple of market stalls, she was waffling and Mac's sister was looking suspiciously at her.

"What's your name and what market do you sell on?"

"Blackburn and Preston," was all she could summon up. Mary knew she need to get out of there and so looked at her watch and made an excuse about being late for an appointment. Gina McCallister was not convinced, she knew there was something wrong. "And your name?"

Mary didn't answer, bolted for the door and ran up the street to the car, slid down in the car seat so as not to be seen and waited for Toni.

As Toni peered over the back wall, he could see packaging and cardboard and all indications were that the premises had only recently been occupied. He tried the yard door latch and it opened, so he tentatively crept in to carry out further investigation. He could see into the kitchen and it was obvious nobody was living here; it was just being used for making beverages and the odd sandwich. He peered into the back room which contained more dresses and again the materials were instantly recognisable. With nothing more to be gained he went back to the car and saw Mary cowering in her seat, looking scared.

"It's Mac's sister," was Mary's first words. "She even sounds like him."

Toni nodded, "Yes, that's why I recognised the face, it makes sense now." He then went on to explain that the shop was only a shop and nobody lived there. All the dresses were obviously being made elsewhere and then brought here to sell, they needed to follow her and find out where she goes at night.

Mary wasn't keen on this, she wanted to go straight to the police, but Toni argued that unless they could track the materials then they had no case. It was agreed they would think about what they had seen today and try and find a solution. Toni dropped Mary off at home but wasn't happy to let the matter drop and decided he would go and find out the alternative address, but it was now late afternoon and too late to go back today.

In the shop, Gina McCallister, was doing a lot of thinking. Who was this strange woman, why act so suspiciously? Something was nagging in her head but she couldn't pin it down, so she dismissed it and at the end of the day locked up and went home, which was a fifteen-minute walk from the shop. She entered the parlour to see her brother sat by the fire reading the local paper.

"How was your day, made plenty of money for your business partner?" he dropped the paper and smiled at Gina.

"Had a very odd visit today," she replied and went on to explain the conversation she had with Mary. As she did so she could see Mac's face drop, turn white and his fists clenching the paper hard.

"What did she look like?" Mac's voice was raised, he looked very nervous and as she described Mary, he began to look very worried.

"You ok?" Gina could see beads of sweat begin to form on Mac's forehead.

Mac put the paper down and reached out to Gina and asked her to sit down next to him on the sofa, "There's something you need to know, I haven't been totally honest with you."

Gina was dreading what was coming next. She knew her brother had done some dodgy deals in the past and the reason they were living a very low-key life in the middle of a small town was because some of Glasgow's most notorious Criminals wanted to have more than a little chat with him.

"When I told you that I had the chance to buy some bankrupt stock at a reasonable price, that wasn't strictly true." He then went on to explain the circumstances of how he obtained the materials and that he had over purchased and then diverted the delivery point. The money she gave him for the purchase went on covering his gambling debts, which, if they remained unpaid would have put him in serious danger.

Gina put her head in her hands, "NO, NO, NO, NOT AGAIN," she screamed at him. She had heard it all before, she loved her brother but he was destroying both their lives yet again.

They both sat in silence staring at the fire, it was a full ten minutes before Gina spoke, "I am not moving again, this is my last chance to make something work, you are not going to ruin it." Tears were rolling down her face and Mac knew this was a pivotal moment in their relationship. He also knew that if Mary was onto him, he would spend a time in prison if he was caught. He had served time on a few occasions for various crimes, including assault, theft, burglary and fraud. If he went down this time it would be for a very long time and he was not going to allow that to happen. He tried to talk Gina round to moving on but she wasn't having any of it.

"You have had me running all my life, when Mother died, we had to sell the house and we have not had a proper home since. It's only because I have been careful with my inheritance that we have a roof over our head," she ranted at him. All the years of frustration came out in the open and Mac was shocked at how much pent-up anger was being released.

"You are lazy, you don't give a shit about anyone and you have fucked my life up… But no more. I want you out of here by the end of the week," The working-class Glaswegian was really kicking in now. Mac tried to pull her towards him but she pushed him away. "I mean it, I want you gone, you have 3 days to find somewhere, I don't care where, just go."

She then went into the kitchen, made herself a snack and cup of tea and remained in her room the rest of the night.

Mac's mind was working overtime, where could he go. He had very little money and no job. The remainder of the materials were stored in the dining room, so he tried to calculate how much he could get if he could sell the remainder. He might get enough to get him a month's rent on a small room, but there wasn't that much left, most had been converted into dresses. There were a few stored in one of the bedrooms, so he would start with those. He then decided he needed to take some from the shop and sell them all on the market stalls, he would get more for a finished article anyway. Eventually he worked out what he needed to do, but it was a desperate solution with a high cost if it failed, but it would take a couple of days. As far as he was concerned, Gina had now cut herself off from him, so there was no brotherly loyalty and she would have to fend for herself.

The workshop was closed now and Mary was accepting the inevitable, there were no more orders and all the girls sent home, but she went into the office anyway. Toni was there and they discussed Mac's sister and what route they needed to go down. Toni's plan was to try and trace the materials, yes, a lot of it was gone but maybe there was enough to try and start again, albeit on a much smaller scale, maybe even with just the two of them. At least they would be doing something. Mary still was not convinced, If the police were involved then they might be able to put more pressure on to find the materials and even find Mac, to get him on trial would give her great satisfaction.

Eventually she agreed to give Toni 48 hours to try and track down the materials and see what was salvageable, after that the police would be called in. Toni then told her he was going to follow Gina McCallister after work to see where she lived.

That afternoon about 4:30 Toni parked up in a side street facing the shop and waited. The shop assistant was the first to leave at 5:30pm, followed by Gina McCallister about 15 minutes later. Toni decided the best option was to follow on foot, if she went down a small lane or track then the car would be of no use. Staying a discreet distance, behind he managed to remain unseen until Gina turned into Union St and then entered a large end terraced property.

As Gina entered the house, Mac was there as usual, sat in front of the fire doing nothing, she could smell that he had made a stew, which was welcome as she wasn't in the mood for cooking and she had to go out to her weekly choir practice at the local church.

Mac was fully aware that his sister was not going to be in the house long and would be going out soon, so the stew was intended to make sure she didn't hang about. He brought the stew from the kitchen into the dining room and ladled it into 2 bowls and they sat down at the table to eat.

"Don't think that you can try and get around me by making a meal, you haven't done a thing around here since you moved in, I am not changing my mind."

Mac knew she was not for turning, his sister was stubborn and he knew the signs and that when she wanted to be she could really become hard. This was definitely one of those occasions.

"I know, I am sorry for the trouble I have caused and don't worry, I will definitely be gone by the end of the week."

Gina didn't bother to ask where he would go, she just knew he would survive and that would mean problems for someone else. She was sick of having to run because of William and liked living where she was. She knew she wasn't the best seamstress in the world, but she was good enough to make a decent living and the business was doing ok. The designs William had given her that he had obviously stolen from his employer had given her a lift up as had the materials. But she decided she had enough of a start and that she could now push on. If the police came then William would be blamed, she had bought everything in good faith and they would be looking for him, another reason to make sure he was nowhere near her, another reason for her not to know where he was going.

Gina finished her meal and went up to change, while Mac washed the dishes. Ten minutes later she came back down and informed him she would be back about 9:30, which he already knew as this was her weekly routine.

Toni was curious about the house, it was quite big and certainly large enough to contain all the materials comfortably so he decided to take a walk around the back of the house. He climbed onto a dustbin to see over the wall and had a good view directly into the dining room. He could see from the shadows being cast that there was someone in the kitchen and nearly fell off the dustbin when the shadow emerged into the dining room with 2 bowls in his hand.

So that's where you have been hiding, he thought, gotcha now you bastard! He watched for a while then saw Gina go upstairs, turn the light on and close the curtains. He decided there was nothing more to see so walked back to pick his car up, then drove up the street so he could still see the front door and waited to see if Mac was going out anywhere.

Gina was the first to go out and Toni decided there was no point following her, the main prize was still in the house.

As soon as Gina left the house, Mac made his move. He had already packed his bags and leaving through the back door, loaded them into a van at the rear of property. He then went into the spare bedroom where the additional stock was stored and loaded them into the same van. He knew Gina would see that the dresses were missing but he also knew she wouldn't report them as they were already stolen goods in the first place and she wouldn't want to attract attention.

He returned to the house and picked up 2 sets of keys, one was for Gina's shop and the other was for a lock up he had rented for a month that very day. His plan was to drive to Gina's shop and steal the stock in the shop. He would then set fire to the shop and take all the stock to the lock up, which he would then sell to stallholders in various markets and small shops. He reasoned that Gina could claim on the insurance for the stock, so she would not suffer any financial loss. He had provided her with fake invoices when she bought the goods, so she would be covered for any loss.

Toni watched a light go on in another bedroom, so knew Mac was still there, he would give it until 9pm then if there was no more movement he would go home.

Mac turned into the street and headed towards the shop, as he did so Toni was side on and could see the definite features of Mac as he drove past. Toni jumped up and started the engine, keeping just far enough behind so not to attract any attention. It was soon obvious where he was going so Toni relaxed and parked up just down the street from the shop in the same spot he had parked before. Mac however had drove around the back of the shop and parked outside the back yard door.

After 10 minutes, Toni's curiosity was getting the better of him so he eased his way around the corner of the alley and could see the back doors to the van was open. He could just make out that the contents of the van contained clothing, so decided to try and get a closer look, as he did so Mac came out of the yard with a bundle of dresses draped over his arm.

Mac had started to load the van and was on his third load when something caught his eye at the end of the alley. He couldn't quite see who it was, but threw the garments in and closed the doors. He then went back for the last load and as he entered the back door of the shop, he turned the light off and waited to see who was there. As he peered through the back window, the figure creeped into the back yard. As it got closer there was no doubt who it was, Toni had tracked him down.

Mac was panicking now; he knew if he was caught that he was finished and his life was over. His plan to steal the dresses was now in jeopardy, He had nowhere to go apart from prison and he was not prepared to let this little Wop destroy him.

Toni opened the door to the shop and entered via the kitchen, the place was in darkness but he knew Mac was there. He crept forward into the back room and as he did so he briefly heard a metallic sound.

Mac had picked up a heavy flat iron that was resting on an ironing board and swung it as Toni's head popped around the door. It was to be the last movement Toni would ever make. The blow landed on the temple and the impact of edge of the Iron immediately rendered him unconscious.

Mac was frantic now, his immediate reaction was to get rid of Toni's lifeless body and opening the door under the stairs, pushed him in and closed the door behind him wedging it so no escape was possible.

He finished loading the van and then returned to the house and placed a candle halfway up the stairs and lit it. He then left all the house internal doors open and turned on the gas to the cooker in the kitchen, then closed the back door on the way out, dashed to the van and raced to get as far away as possible.

It took ten minutes for the gas to travel along the floor of both the rooms and rise to reach the height of the flame. When it exploded it completely destroyed the house and both of the adjacent properties that were tied into it. The fire that followed also took out another 2 properties either side and it took a full day to control the situation. By the time it all died down, there was no evidence of what had caused the explosion. The fire Brigade and police were convinced it was a gas leak and reported it as such.

Gina McCallister knew different, she not only knew who had done it, she also knew why, but could not say anything.

Mary had waited all morning for Toni to make contact, but when she hadn't heard anything by lunchtime, she went around to his room, only to be told that nobody had seen him since yesterday. She decided to go home and tried to work on some designs, but her mind was not focusing, so quickly gave that idea up. Toni was a very organised punctual person, who very rarely did anything unpredictable, this was definitely out of character for him.

By the end of the day, she knew something was not right and went to the police in Salford, who immediately dismissed that anything might be wrong and told her to wait a couple of days before reporting him missing. Two days later she returned and filed a missing person's report. She tried to explain about the shop in Kearsley and the missing materials, but as it was not in Salford's jurisdiction they were obviously not interested.

Not content with this she boarded a bus and after 2 route changes found herself on Bolton Road outside what remained of the shop. She could not believe the devastation in front of her and stood there by the side of the road trying to take it all in. After five minutes, she decided she needed to report this to the police, so she turned to walk up the road and as she did so she saw Toni's car, parked fifty yards up the street in exactly the same place as it had been parked when she went there with him.

The police station was only a ten-minute walk away and as she made her way there, she was thinking all the while about how she was going to describe the incidents from the last few months. She decided to start from the beginning and tell them everything.

She approached the main desk and informed the Duty Constable that she had some information about the Kearsley explosion and that she wanted to speak to someone in authority. She was taken to an interview room where there was a detective who announced that he was the investigating officer in relation to the explosion. There was also a constable present who was taking notes.

She told them everything, how Mac had swindled Castlefield Fashion House, how they were being forced into bankruptcy, how they tracked down his sister and that the materials in the shop clearly were the stolen items. The detective listened intently, asking a couple of questions as she spoke. When she had finally finished, he then began to give her his impressions of what had happened.

As far as he was concerned Gina McCallister had absolutely nothing to do with the explosion, she had been the village hall with at least a dozen other choristers when the incident occurred. She had provided him with a list of the destroyed goods, including invoices for materials purchased. His next statement chilled Mary to the bone.

"We would like to speak with your friend and colleague Mr Toni Guido, we believe he may be able to shed some light on what happened." Then staring intently at Mary, he offered an opinion that Mary could scarcely believe.

"He obviously is carrying a very heavy grudge against Miss McCallister and it is possible that his anger may have resulted in him committing an arson attack on the property."

Despite Mary's protestations, the detective informed her that Toni was a suspect and that when she next saw him the best advice, she could give would be for Toni to report to Kearsley Police Station for interview as soon as possible. He also warned her not to trouble Miss McCallister. When she asked why would he leave his car there, there was no explanation, except to say that it was possible that with all that was going on he may have panicked and lost his keys.

The next few weeks were a nightmare for Mary, the factory was now closed and then she received a letter from the bank informing her that they were taking legal proceedings to reclaim the bridging loan, which in effect meant that Castlefield Fashion House was now bankrupt.

But the disappearance of Toni was the biggest blow, she didn't have any idea of where he was. This was so out of character for him and she genuinely worried for his safety. After two weeks she sent a telegram to his mother to inform her that Toni was missing, Sophia replied by saying she was coming to England immediately and would let her know of the travel arrangements when confirmed.

Chapter Ten

The week beginning Monday, 23 October 1934 would live forever in the mind of Mary Knox, her whole world collapsed around her.

On Monday she had a final meeting with George Davies about winding up the business. He advised that she should declare the company insolvent, which would be a better option than bankruptcy, as it gave them the opportunity to recover if there were better times ahead.

They agreed the main creditor was the bank and if they sold Toni's car which was registered as belonging to the company, as well as the contents of the workshop then that debt would be cleared. They still owed money for rent on the factory, but Mary informed him they should give notice immediately and she would stand the rental costs out of her own pocket. When this was done, the company would be mothballed until such time as it was possible to start again.

George then explained the situation to the bank manager who agreed to postpone any action on confirmation the debt would be discharged once the various sales had gone through.

Mary knew she wouldn't be able to stay in her nice house, so she also gave notice on that and rented a small room in Eccles. The art deco furniture she had acquired was far too big and there was too much of it for her to take with her, so she placed it all in the auction rooms for sale. Luckily the style was still extremely popular and Mary managed to get back most of the original cost. She was sad to see it go, this had been her stamp, her show of independence and now it was gone.

There had been a delay in clearing the site in Kearsley due to insurance assessors, police, fire, gas and everyone else wanting to make sure that all investigation was complete, but on Wednesday they finally got around to removing all the debris.

It didn't take long to discover Toni's body and work was immediately stopped to remove his remains. There wasn't much left to identify, he had been in the cupboard below the stairs less than 3 feet from where the gas was ignited. The stairs had shattered into shards and his body was completely covered in wooden splinters His badly burnt body was completely disfigured and been ripped apart by the blast. Mary had to go and identify the body as his mother would not be there for another week. His wallet, car keys and a ring that was given to him by his father was all that was recognisable that confirmed who it was. The sight of her best friend's body in such a state was too much for Mary and she broke down. Her whole life was being destroyed, she had lost a loved one yet again, she wasn't sure how much more she could take.

When Sophia arrived, she was shocked to see how gaunt and thin Mary looked, she looked a completely beaten woman. She had grown very fond of Mary and knew how close her friendship with Toni was, the working relationship they had and that she was as devastated as the family with the news of his death.

The family had already decided that Toni's body should be taken back to Italy and buried in the Guido mausoleum to lie next to his brother, so she arranged all the travel and necessary paperwork and once the dates had been confirmed She told Mary she thought she needed to rest and recover and would she come back with her to Milan.

Mary was not in the mood to argue, she couldn't think straight and agreed that she needed to get away and sort her life out. She still had some private savings, the money from the sales had cleared the company debt, so she wouldn't starve for a couple of years.

"Thank you, your very kind. I think getting away is probably the best option." Even her voice sounded weary, Mary was not at all well.

On 4 November, they set off to board the train to Southampton, the Undertaker sorted the travel arrangements for Toni's coffin, then drove down and made sure it was loaded onto the boat that was going to Genoa. From there they would be met by Toni's brother and escorted directly to Milan. Sophie had booked second class berths on the SS Conte Biancamano.

The trip was not good for Mary she was constantly sick and while the food was perfectly acceptable, she could not keep anything down. The weeks' journey was painful for Sophia as well, watching Mary get weaker by the day and not being able to help was agonising.

Eventually her ordeal was over and as they arrived in Genoa, Sophia could see her son Marco on the quayside. She handed him the documentation required to release Toni's body, then she booked into a hotel and informed Mary they would stay the night before moving on tomorrow, for which Mary was extremely grateful.

The following morning, Mary felt much better having been on dry land for a night and managing to eat without incident. Marco was now in charge of everything, so Sophia could relax, she could see that Mary was looking a little better.

As the train trundled along the Genoa to Milan route, Sophia sat watching Mary who was sleeping most of the four-hour journey, she couldn't help thinking how much pain this young lady had been through and how much she deserved a better life. She badly wanted to take care of her and nurse her back to health. The boat trip had made Mary's already frail body even weaker and she needed building up.

The rest of the journey was uneventful and when they arrived in Milan they were met by Franco and the local priest. There were also a number of curious Blackshirts looking on and Mary winced when she saw them, recalling how her last meeting felt very threatening. There were definitely more of them about now. Toni's coffin was transported to the local church, with the funeral being arranged for the following day. Sophia went inside and said a few prayers, Mary waited outside not understanding why a few words spoken while kneeling down would make any difference.

When they arrived at the family villa it was starting to get dark, Sophia informed Mary she was to treat the place as her home, she just wanted her to relax and get her strength back. Mary thanked her and said for now she just wanted to sleep, so Sophia showed her to her room, helped her unpack and left her alone. Mary immediately dropped asleep and didn't wake up for another ten hours.

When she awoke, the sun was starting to break through the curtains, Mary felt a lot better, then realised it was Toni's funeral today which dampened her mood until she realised that he was already dead, this was just a ceremony to finalise his life. She would still have her memories of the sweet, kind man she knew.

Sophia was already up when Mary got to the patio, they exchanged small talk and she explained the order of the day, which would culminate in a family dinner to celebrate Toni's life.

"Toni did not have many friends here, he left when he was young and you were the closest thing to family that he had in England." Her eyes welled up with tears. "I was not there for him, but you were and for that I am extremely grateful."

Mary, too was now close to tears. "He loved you all and missed you all the time. It's a pity that people only looked at his sexuality and could not see the beautiful person that was inside him."

They embraced each other and cried, for Mary this was the release she needed. There had been so much going on around the time of his death, she had not had time to grieve for him, she really let herself go and clung to Sophia as if her life depended on it.

Sophia was the first to pull away. "You need to rest and recover; you will be strong again. I have seen the strong woman and she will return, I promise you." Then she said the words that Mary would remember for the rest of her days. "All of your future is because of your past. You will learn lessons from what has happened and it will make you a better, wiser person, you will succeed."

After a light breakfast, Mary went back to her room and prepared herself for the funeral. She was feeling a lot brighter now having shed her tears and was actually looking forward to seeing Toni off.

The funeral cortege set off at 10am prompt and they gathered in the small Parish Church for the service. Looking around, Mary could see there was about 20 people in attendance, some of which had facial similarities to the Guido family, so Mary assumed they were cousins.

Mary didn't understand the Latin service or the hymns sung, so she just followed the rest and bowed and knelt when appropriate, thinking all the time what relevance has this got to Toni's life? After the service, the coffin was carried outside and they went to the rear of the church grounds and into the graveyard where there were a couple of monuments and mausoleums. One of the larger ones had its doors open and they walked in that direction. Mary noted it was an imposing building, larger than the rest. The coffin was led through the doors and down into the crypt. That was the last time she would see Toni; her only feeling was one of relief that now he was back with his family. She wasn't religious but she knew what it meant to the Guidos and she was happy for them.

When they got back to the villa, the mood immediately lifted and everyone started to drink wine and cheer up. She spotted Franco at the far end of the room; he saw her at the same time and beckoned her to him.

"Thank you for being his friend, you were the one person outside of the family he could rely on. You will always be welcome here." He went on to say she needed fattening up, she was too skinny, they would make sure she stayed as long as it took to get her fit and well again.

"Thank you, Franco, your family are very kind, I really am grateful to you all."

The rest of the day was spent in limited conversation as most of the guests could not speak English, but Mary enjoyed it anyway and she began to enjoy herself for the first time in months. The dinner was a sumptuous feast comprising several courses and Mary, surprisingly, managed to eat everything put in front of her.

The next few weeks were spent relaxing and going for long walks, sometimes with Sophia, but mostly alone. Winter was now upon them and she was not sure what her future plans were. There was nothing to go back to but she didn't want to overstay her welcome. Sophia solved her dilemma by asking Mary to stay on for Christmas, Mary gratefully accepted, it settled her mind and she was looking forward to it.

Christmas was a lavish affair, the Guidos certainly knew how to celebrate.

It all started on Xmas Eve, the crib was brought into the large hallway to the villa and the various figurines placed. This was followed by a lavish meal that was seafood based. At midnight they all went to mass and Mary finally got to bed at 2am, exhausted.

Xmas day was just as hectic, with presents being exchanged. Mary had taken a trip into Milan the week before with Sophia and after asking her what she should buy she was told only to buy for immediate family and items of clothing were always welcome, especially in winter when Milan could get really cold. The Guido tradition was to open presents in the evening after dinner, which was again a waist enlarging feast, accompanied with copious amounts of excellent wine. Mary was developing quite a taste for fine wine, which was always plentiful in the Guido household.

As they passed the presents around after dinner, Mary was surprised to see that for a clearly affluent family they did not buy each other expensive presents, Sophia explained that the sentiment and emotion behind it was all that mattered. They could buy anything they wanted, but it's better to buy with feeling rather than with Lira, which Mary found to be a comforting statement.

Mary gave out her presents, which appeared to be well received and in return she was given a cardigan, a scarf, some chocolates and a nice winter coat that was almost certainly from Sophia and was definitely the most expensive item presented that night. They all sat around the lounge drinking and talking, Mary was beginning to be able to understand some Italian, but was not confident enough to verbally use what she had learnt. She was really feeling at home now and the Guido's family closeness was totally engaging.

By the middle of January, Mary felt strong and she was beginning to think about what direction her life should take and one day while out walking with Sophia she confided that perhaps was the time for her to move on. Sophia stopped in her tracks and turning to Mary gave her an option.

"You can stay here, you understand the clothing business and there will always be a place for you," she implored.

Mary wasn't expecting this, she had always assumed she would go back to England at some point. She knew the offer was genuine and she had grown to love the Guidos, this was a tremendous opportunity and she needed to get back to work.

Sophia went on to explain that they had now been given quite a large contract to supply black shirt uniforms for Mussolini. The family hated fascism but had to live with it and it was better if they were not seen to be hostile. She went on to say that Marco was not able to manage all this extra work alone and they needed to find someone to help him out. This was worth serious consideration and she told Sophia she would think long and hard about it. Mary pointed out that the biggest problem was the language, how would she be able to communicate? Sophia said they could arrange Italian lessons for her, there was no rush for her to go straight to work and as long as she could make herself understood there would not be that much of a problem. Mary could see this was definitely something that was achievable.

After weighing up all pros and cons, Mary came to the conclusion she had nothing to lose and after various conversations with the family accepted a position as a manager in the Milan branch. Sophia arranged Italian language lessons twice a week and Mary was surprised at how easy it was for her to get a grasp of the basics. Within a few weeks she was able to hold a low-level conversation, she was feeling really pleased with herself.

Sophia was also surprised to see how much progress Mary had made and was delighted to see her smile again and lose the haunted gaunt features she had displayed when she saw her in England.

Mary was starting to get interested in fashion design again and spent a lot of time observing the various styles that were the vogue in Milan. At weekends she would go and sit in a small café in the Piazza Duomo and sketch ladies' dresses and get ideas. Sometimes with Sophia, but often alone.

It was during one of these people watching sessions she noticed a man sat across from her who was watching her intently, he nodded in her direction, she nodded back and carried on. This happened on 2 more occasions and eventually he wandered over and asked if he could sit with her. He seemed a nice man so she beckoned him to sit next to her.

He introduced himself as Alfonso Vialla and after she gave him her name he ordered two coffees. He asked why she drew sketches all the time and that he had seen her most weekends for the last few weeks and that his curiosity had get the better of him. He was surprised that her language skills were obviously from a foreigner and asked where she was from. After finding out she was English he then proceeded to question why she was in Milan, but Mary struggled to get her explanation across in Italian so they dropped the subject and conversed on a more basic level.

He was quite tall, with a nice smile and almost perfect teeth, Mary found him an intriguing personality. He informed her he was a pharmacist and that he had three pharmacies in the Milan area. Mary tried to guess how old he was, he looked quite young but had an air about him of an older man. His clothing was pristine and he obviously took very good care of his health. They stumbled along, making small talk and eventually, after about an hour, he got up, paid the bill and bade her a good day.

That evening Sophia asked her about her day and when she described Mr Vialla, Sophia replied she had never heard of him and that she knew the owners of the biggest pharmacies and the description did not match anyone she knew.

Sophia asked about the sketches and wanted to see what Mary had done, so Mary went to her room and came back and spread them on the dining table. Sophia scanned the contents of the sketches, then sat back in her chair.

"Unfortunately, my dear, I doubt that the ENM would approve of most of these designs." She went on to explain that they were the National Fashion Body and that they influenced the style of women's fashion as instructed by Mussolini.

She said that as an alien in Italy it would be better not to attract their attention, they could be very vindictive if she were to upset the local militia. Mary duly obliged and took the drawing back to her room. She despised the Blackshirts, everything about them was so depressing and regimented, which is exactly how they wanted the population to be.

She continued to go to the Piazza Duamo as she found it a nice place to just relax, drink coffee and watch the world go by. She noticed that the Blackshirts were very arrogant, strutting around and their very presence was upsetting to most of the local population. She could see both fear and anger in their faces, but also an acceptance of their situation.

One Saturday, she had just sat down at the table of one of her favourite cafes, when she heard a commotion at the side of her. Turning to look she saw an older lady being thrown out of her chair to the floor and three Blackshirts leaning over and telling her they were having her table and to move on. This infuriated Mary and she had to say something, so she shouted in broken Italian that they were cowards for picking on an old lady. They looked stunned and surprised that someone should dare to question them and one of them grabbed Mary by the arm and ranted something so quickly she was not able to understand what he was saying but it was obviously threatening. Mary sat back down, she wasn't going to be intimidated. She drank her coffee and left fifteen minutes later, all the time fully aware that these young thugs were staring at her.

She left and walked quickly, she just wanted to get home now. As she passed down a side street, she was just passing an alley when she was grabbed and a hand placed over her mouth. She was dragged about 20 yards into the alley and into a doorway. She could see now that it was the Blackshirt thugs. One of them uttered something threatening and tried to lift her skirt, but one of the others said something that sounded to her like 'no, that's going to far' and so he stopped, then thought for a minute. He then unfastened his trousers and got his cock out. He then said, "She can't have too much to say if her mouth is full."

The others laughed and forced Mary to her knees. He was trying to fill her mouth, but she kept turning away, he pulled her hair and tried to twist her head, but she resisted. This went on for ten minutes, all the time the others were groping her. Mary was terrified but refused to give in. Eventually the main attacker just ejaculated in her face then rubbed it in with his cock. They threw her to the ground and warned her against speaking to anyone about what had happened, if she did there would be consequences.

Mary cleaned herself up as best she could, then went home and into the bathroom. She felt the humiliation in every strand of her body and after cleaning herself, laid down on the bed. After a short nap, she woke up and began to think about her life and that every time she felt she was getting somewhere, something came along to kick her back down again. Her confidence once again had taken a hit and as she lay there reflecting about how much trauma there had been in her life, she began to get angry, very angry and she made her mind up there was going to be changes. The nice mild Mary was going and she was replacing her with a totally different person, someone who didn't shit from anyone. Sophia was right, all of her future was because of what happened to her in her past. She had learnt lessons and was now ready to impose herself and not be imposed on. She decided not to mention it to Sophia, there was nothing she could do and even if they reported it, the Blackshirts would deny it.

At dinner that night, Sophia noticed that Mary was a little subdued, so asked her about her day. Mary just said she had been walking and wouldn't be drawn into a conversation, so she didn't pursue it further.

Mary was still deep in thought and today's events had forced into a decision, she decided she was going back to England. Everywhere she would go there would be Blackshirts, a constant reminder of not only today's event, but also of the oppression that the fashion trade was enduring. She would give it a couple of days to think about what her plans would be before telling the family. She wasn't sure what she was going to do but her future was not in Milan. She made an excuse about having a headache and retreated to her room to contemplate some more.

Over the next few days, Sophia could see there was definitely something wrong and just had to say something. "What is the matter, I can see you are very troubled about something?" Mary tried to dismiss it, but Sophia was persistent.

"I have decided to go back to England next month," she finally answered. "I am looking at the politics here and the oppression that's shown towards not just fashion, but all aspects of life here. I think it will get worse as there is no resistance and I need to get away from it all."

Sophia nodded in acceptance and knew that Mary was telling the truth, things were very difficult now, but she badly needed Mary to stay. She was battling her own demons about Toni's death and now relied on her to get through her daily life.

"I understand," she sighed. "But what is there in England, you have nothing there, here you will have a family. We love you, Mary... and I need you."

Mary had never given a thought about how Toni's death had affected Sophia, but it was clear now that she had been fighting an internal battle to keep herself together over the last few months. She also knew that Sophia was right, there was nothing for her back home, she would be alone and have to start again from nothing. She now had to reconsider, she owed a lot to the Guido family and they were also her family now, the only family she had. Mary told her she would think it over, Sophia's reply was to tell her to take her time.

The next month passed quickly, then another month, Mary was beginning to think life in Milan might be alright after all. She tended to stay away from public places, especially where there might be Blackshirts. Her language skills were getting stronger, she could converse about most subjects comfortably. She now felt that it was about time she contributed, so she spoke with Sophia and Franco about working for the company. Franco was now getting old and welcomed the news, he knew that if he left Marco would never manage on his own. Sophia was dealing with the customers and making sure sales were maintained, so the options for Mary were within the factory and manufacturing. Working as an assistant to Marco would allow him the time to take on the mantle of Managing Director which would give Franco more time to ease his way into retirement.

They agreed to look at how Mary would fit into the structure and then a plan of action would be formulated. Mary now accepted that she would not be going anywhere for the foreseeable future.

Mary suggested that she go into the factory and work in the different departments to see how things were made, even working on some of the machines. Once the workforce could see that she knew what she was doing then she would gain more respect and an acceptance when she made decisions. Franco was not keen, Marco however thought it was an excellent idea as did Sophia, so it was agreed she would just float around and get a good grounding on how the manufacturing process worked.

On 2 August 1936, Mary began a new life as part of the *Guido emporio della Moda* (Guido Fashion Emporium) group. She woke early and then after a light breakfast made her way to the Milan factory, where Marco was already in the office sorting out paperwork. After a brief conversation over a cup of coffee, she was introduced to Helena, who was the factory supervisor. Marco outlined Mary's role and said that she was to show her anything she wanted to see and to co-operate fully with any requests. He did not go into any further details about Mary's future role within the organisation. Mary looked at Helena and smiled to herself, this was the same look that Milly had given her all those years ago. Helena on the other hand was feeling threatened, was this person going to replace her? Why would she need to be given access to everywhere, unless it was to be as her successor?

The first few days was a learning curve, the work was not dissimilar to the way they had worked in England and the girls, at first suspicious, relaxed once Mary managed to chat with them in Italian. They were curious, when Mary had been introduced, they were told she was part of the family, so assumed she was Italian. They were all wondering about the connection. When Mary explained that she had been friends with Toni, she did not say she was his boss, they were then inquisitive and started to ask questions. Most had known Toni as a child or as their manager, or both. She found she could talk fondly about him, everybody was too polite to ask about the circumstances and Mary enjoyed the conversations. Helena too was warming to Mary; she had grown up with Toni and knew about his homosexuality and that her relationship with him was purely friendship.

She was settling in well and even impressed some of the girls with her seamstress work. At dinner one night, the conversation turned to the factory and Franco made an announcement:

"We have received a very large order from the OVRA, they want 20,000 uniforms over the next year, all of this work will be given to the Milan factory. All existing and future other work is to go to the Brescia factory." He went on to explain that there was capacity to expand the Milan factory by 20% and that they were to begin recruitment immediately. Mary wasn't impressed with this announcement, she hated the sight of the Blackshirts and now was going to be surrounded by them all day. Franco concluded by saying that to celebrate they were going to La Scala next Friday to see Puccini's La Rondine.

This depressed Mary even more, she had only been to the opera once before and found it boring, but she put on a brave face and thanked him. Sophia asked how they would manage the increased workload for the Brescia factory which was only small, Franco countered that the output from that factory would remain the same, the OVRA contract covered all costs, it could be allowed to work at it its own pace. Sophia then pointed out that the stock for the 8 shops they had would run down, but Franco did not seem interested. He could see the political future and keeping the government happy was his main priority for now.

The night at the opera arrived and all the family were sat in a box on the 2nd floor, just to the right of stage, Franco had got prime tickets. As they climbed the stairs to their seats, Mary noticed a familiar figure, Mr Alfonso Vialla.

She saw that he was accompanied by an elderly lady, possibly his mother. He nodded in her direction and she acknowledged him. Sophia had noticed this and as they sat in their seats asked how she knew him.

"That's the man I told you about, the man with three pharmacies," Mary explained.

Sophia turned and looking Mary straight in the eye said, "That man with three pharmacies is in fact the head of all the OVRA in Northern Italy. He is one of Mussolini's most trusted officials. He is very devious, treat him with the utmost suspicion."

Mary sat back in her seat totally shocked, she couldn't believe what she was hearing. She didn't really concentrate on the opera, she didn't like it anyway, she couldn't help wondering why this important man had sought her out in the café.

At the interval, she noticed a lot of people making a lot of fuss about Vialla, with a lot of whispered messages. Eventually he spotted her and beckoned her over. Mary thought she had no choice but to go and see him, she did not know to what extent his interest in her was.

"How are you enjoying the performance?" was his opening statement.

"It's something new to me and I am trying to understand it, but I love the passion of the performers." She thought she shouldn't be so critical. He then introduced his mother, a very elderly lady, who he said could hardly hear the show, but loved the occasion.

She thought back to when they first met and the way he introduced himself to her was getting too much, so she asked him outright, "Why did you tell me you were a pharmacist, when in fact you are a senior politician in the government?"

She couldn't believe what she was saying, but the new Mary was not going to be messed with.

Vialla looked surprised, but was impressed that someone should speak so openly to him. "Because if I had said I was OVRA, you would have felt intimidated and I didn't want to worry you."

Before they could converse anymore, the bell rang to call them back to their seats and she made her way back to her box.

Sophia had noticed their conversation and asked her what she said to him. "I asked him why he lied about being a pharmacist."

Sophia didn't know whether to applaud or cringe, the OVRA were feared and didn't like to be questioned. She had briefly met Vialla on a couple of social occasions with mutual friends. He had a reputation for being ruthless and she didn't like to think about Mary upsetting him.

As they were leaving the theatre, Vialla spotted Mary getting into the car with the Guidos, Franco had also spotted Vialla and raised his hat to him. "Bastardo," he uttered under his breath as he climbed into the car. The recruitment of the additional staff was left with Marco and Mary started to become more involved in the day-to-day running of the factory as he went through the process. The materials arrived for the uniforms and it became a production line of shirts and trousers being churned out. After a week or so, it was apparent that little hands-on management was required, it was just a question of keeping the machines fed and the rest sorted itself out.

Mary wanted to know about the Brescia factory and asked Marco if she could go and see what was happening there. They had one of Francos Nephews running it, but he was more of a figurehead than a manager and Marco wasn't all that impressed anyway, so agreed it was a good idea if she spent a little time over there. Sophia agreed to take Mary for the first day, after that she could get the train which ran every 30 minutes.

The Brescia factory was about the same size as Mary's in Salford and there were many similarities in how the workload was managed and the output. The fashion consisted basically of two styles, day dresses and attire that accentuated the military look. The daytime look was as approved by ENM, it was a village Peasant look that was very basic and not at all popular. Overall sales were down because nobody wanted to spend money on clothes they really didn't want to wear, that's why the business needed to concentrate on the Blackshirt uniform.

Mary commented that the sales would never pick up until there was more variety and the fashion houses allowed to make their own decisions.

"Yes, I know, but if we don't work to their guidelines, they would make life hard for us, we would not get contracts like we have just been given," Sophia was just as frustrated as Mary, but they had to play the game. The visit over they drove back to Brescia, stopping off for lunch on the way back.

As they relaxed over lunch, Mary had an idea. "I would like to look at developing some new lines for the more upmarket styles, if that's ok."

"Yes, that's fine, I will show you the guidelines from the ENM, but I would have to have final approval, I don't want you upsetting the OVRA," Sophia smiled as she recalled Mary's abruptness in front of the Blackshirts.

"Diplomacy is king when dealing with our militia," Mary agreed and over the next few days got together her sketches and reworked them to try and produce something that would be acceptable.

It took Mary a week to put together two outfits on paper and she asked Sophia for permission to make them at Bruscia. Sophia looked over the drawings and while they were original, didn't see anything that might draw attention so gave permission for Mary to start work on the prototypes.

Mary looked around the factory and found some nice fabrics that would do nicely. It took her the best part of the week to get the look she was aiming for and after a lot of revision eventually got to where she needed to be for the finished article. Having made the dresses she then had more work to do but could not find what she wanted in the factory, so took the dresses home and went into Milan to seek out her remaining articles. It took her a full morning, but eventually she found what she was looking for and arrived home in the afternoon and put the final product together.

That evening after dinner she asked them all to wait and she went upstairs and changed into the new dress. Having put everything together she slowly walked into the dining room as if on a catwalk. Sophia could see that she had complied with the ENM code, but couldn't see what was so different about the style that Mary had improved on. She didn't like to criticise so congratulated Mary on her skills.

"You haven't seen the difference yet, wait," With that Mary took off the broad shoulders that had been disguised as a shawl, to reveal an off the shoulder evening dress that flowed elegantly. She also removed the broad belt that had accentuated the military look and had made the overall shape more hourglass. The end product was a long slim flowing evening dress in the French fashion style, which was stunning.

Sophia gasped, "What a glorious illusion, the result is sensational."

Franco was less impressed. "The ENM will never approve of this, they would give us all kinds of problems."

Mary was not giving up. "We sell the whole of the outfit as one dress. The shawl is connected by small buttons sewn discretely in the neck strap, how people want to adapt it is not our concern. We will have complied entirely with their ridiculous guidelines."

Mary smiled at Franco, who smiled back. "Let me think about this, it may have a big impact on our business."

Mary then went further and produced a full cost of producing the dress, which was within acceptable parameters, the Guido's were very impressed with this latest member of the family.

Before Franco could decide on whether to proceed with Mary's idea, international matters intervened in a way which made her plan unworkable. The League of Nations was a peace council created to ensure there was no repeat of the Great War. Mussolini was causing problems in Africa and had invaded Ethiopia, which were now being supported by Germany. This was causing tension across Europe so the League introduced sanctions of non-essential goods to Italy, unfortunately for Mary this included textiles and clothing. Franco was concerned that the situation might escalate, he was a member of a number of trade bodies and the news was not good, Italy was becoming isolated. He therefore decided to scale back at Bruscia until things settled down and concentrate on the uniforms.

Mary found herself with more time on her hands now, Mussolini's political stance was that women should be at home producing children and the Blackshirts were very much more obvious on the streets. Life was becoming very restricted and therefore social opportunities became fewer and fewer and the Catholic Church was becoming more conservative and inhibitive in their attitude towards women. Sophia was attending various church functions designed for women, more to ensure the Guidos did not upset the establishment, Mary sometimes accompanied her, purely for something to do, she despised religion but needed to get out of the house.

She noted that Alfonso Vialla's mother would quite often be at the same events and he would always drop her off and pick her up personally. On one of these occasions, she was curious about his personal life, so asked Sophia if he was married.

"No," Sophia laughed. "nobody can match up to his expectations, he will probably die alone. He has had relationships but they never last," Mary was curious as to why such a powerful man would bother about what a women needed to be, after all the government line was that women were only fit to raise children.

Over the next few weeks, she watched him at a number of separate events. He was always in conversation with men and very superior in his attitude, was aggressive at times and ultra-masculine in his manner. He avoided contact with women and when he did converse with a woman, his body language was introvert. When his mother spoke, he was very attentive and almost submissive.

Suddenly the reality struck her, he was scared of women! His mother was the driving force behind his persona, her influence over him reigned supreme. He was used to being controlled by a woman, all his previous lovers had no doubt been very submissive, but that did not impress him, he needed to be controlled. Mary was feeling very pleased with herself, she had found the Achilles heel of one of the most powerful men in Italy and the new Mary was going to test him to the limit.

Mary was still pushing to carry on with her designs, which was beginning to irritate Franco. He was not well, having recently been diagnosed with a heart condition. He was considering handing over the reins to Marco as soon as there was some political stability and therefore not really in a receptive mood. Sophia had to eventually have a word with Mary.

"You must wait, now is not the time for change, Franco is right, we must wait for the whole political situation to calm down, please do not mention it again." There was a severity in Sophia's voice that Mary hadn't heard directed at her before, so she knew she was pushing too far and agreed not to mention it again.

She hated the Italian government, especially the Blackshirts and that weasel Vialla.

He obviously did not agree with the government line about the role of women, but sat at the top table and did nothing. Mary decided to teach him a lesson and also try and strike a blow to elevate women's status in the community.

The opportunity came a few weeks later when she was at a charity fundraising event, all the Guidos were there as was Alfonso Vialla and his mother. The event commenced with drinks in the lounge of a large hotel, to be followed by a dinner. As everyone was milling around and socialising, Mary took the opportunity to speak with him. She gripped him firmly by the arm and said that she wanted to speak with him, then guided him to the corner of the room.

"I have some fashion designs I am working on and I am not sure if they would comply with ENM guidelines." She tried to look confident and in control, but inside her stomach was churning. "I don't want to get off on the wrong foot with them so would like your opinion before going ahead."

He looked at her quizzically. "Why would I be an expert on fashion, this is nothing to do with me. I am sorry I cannot help you." He then turned to go back into the room but Mary knew she had to be insistent.

"I don't want to be made a fool of in front of the fashion police, therefore I think someone of your standing would have an idea of what is and what is not acceptable. You are obviously not as well informed as you ought to be," Mary wondered if she had gone too far, he could make her disappear in an instant if she annoyed him enough.

He turned to face her and smiled, "Of course I can give you my opinion, call me tomorrow and we can make arrangements to meet," he then produced a business card and handed it to her.

She decided to push him further, "It will have to be next week, my diary is busy for the rest of this week," Alfonoso nodded in acceptance and re-entered the room, leaving Mary shaking and not sure what her next action was going to be.

Mary was jubilant, her observations of Vialla had proved correct, he was not the all-powerful leader, he was a fallible male that needed a woman's influence. She was in control and she was going to make sure he was aware of that fact. A week later Mary rang his office, they had been expecting her call and immediately put her through to Alfonso. He was polite and suggested they meet at the same hotel on Saturday, but Mary still wanted to be in control.

"Sorry, Saturday is no good for me. Monday would be better."

"That would be fine," he replied. "We can have dinner at the same time."

Mary decided to push him a little further. "Can you book a room there so you can see the dresses, I don't want to be walking around with them draped over my arm all night?"

"Yes of course, leave it with me."

Mary ended the conversation by telling him the dinner reservation needed to be for 8pm and to let her know when the room arrangements were confirmed.

Alfonso decided he liked this insistent English woman; she was not afraid of him like the other women in his life had been.

Mary woke up on Monday and was very, very nervous. If this plan backfired then she would be in big trouble. She prepared the 2 dresses she had made, wrapped them in a cover and placed them on the bed. She spent all day going over and over in her head what she was going to do. What she planned was nothing like what the Mary of old would do, but this was a new, ruthless Mary, a Mary that didn't take shit from anyone. The more she thought about it the more she realised how much it excited her the thought of controlling such an influential person.

On Monday Mary woke early and went into the Brescia factory as normal, but found it hard to concentrate and the day just drifted by. By 3pm she had had enough so decided to go home and get ready for her big night. When she arrived at the villa, she was relieved to see none of the family were in so she quickly gathered everything she needed and booked into the hotel, where there was indeed a reservation in her name, which had already been paid for.

She had a couple of hours to spare so relaxed on the bed and went through her strategy. At 7:15pm she showered and got ready. At 7:45 she received a call to say Mr Vialla was downstairs in the lobby waiting for her. She waited 10 minutes then went down to meet him. They had a drink and chatted briefly about how their day had been and then went to the restaurant.

She decided to be the person that drove the conversation, asking him about his life in general and making sure she got her opinions across clearly and confidently. Eventually the conversation about relationships came up and he was the first to ask. "Why have you never married? Your beautiful, clever, confident and good company." He didn't look her in the eye as he said it and Mary had been hoping he would say something along those lines.

"Because too many men think that a woman is only fit for breeding. I am a woman that makes decisions, not one that will sit back and be controlled."

As soon as Mary had finished speaking, "he lifted his head and looked her in the eye."

"As the head of OVRA in Milan, I have to say that what your saying does not agree with the philosophy that Il Duce wishes for the woman folk of Italy."

"Mussolini is not dining with me tonight, I answered a question from Alfonso Vialla, what does he think of what I believe."

Vialla dropped his head again and started to play with his food, Mary could see he was uncomfortable. He was silent for a moment, placed some food in his mouth and took a sip of wine, then he stared into her eyes and almost apologetically he replied, "my thoughts are irrelevant, as the head of OVRA in the North of Italy, it is my duty to ensure that all Political Policies, statements and legislation is carried out in full. I do not write the law; I just ensure it is complied with."

Mary knew now she was right in her assessment of Vialla, so decided to drop the subject. They talked about life in general and she gave him a detailed account of her life and the way she had overcome all the hurdles she had faced, making sure he knew she was a strong woman. Finally, they got around to the subject of her dresses and how she thought the ENM were being harsh by dictating what people should wear. Vialla just shrugged and said he could only give her an opinion, he couldn't dictate policy. At 10pm they left the restaurant and made their way to her room and ordered a bottle of wine from room service.

She went to the bathroom and changed into the off the shoulder dress with the detachable shawl and reappeared. He was sat sipping his drink as she walked in, as she entered, he had a look of bewilderment on his face.

"That will certainly not upset the ENM," he said, as he looked over the attire with the artificially elevated shoulder pads and big buckled belt. "There is no need to worry about that, why do you think they would be upset?"

Walking over to him, she took the glass from his hand and asked him to stand up. As he did so she placed his hand on the shawl and gently pulled so it fell to the ground. Once the gown had been revealed in all its glory, Vialla could see that her shoulders were fully revealed, but also that Mary did not have a bra on and her nipples could now be clearly seen underneath.

"What do you think now," Mary whispered as she moved closer to his face. "Is this passable?"

Vialla was breathing heavily now and Mary could see he had little beads of sweat forming on his forehead, so she knew she had him just where she wanted him.

Taking his hand, she placed it on her breast, her nipple was hard and she found herself getting excited, she loved being in control. He slipped the gown down to reveal her breast and she pushed his head down to put her nipple in his mouth. He sucked hard on it like a new born baby, Mary could feel herself getting wet.

Reaching down she stroked him over his trousers, he was hard and he groaned as she undid the buttons on his trousers. When she had him in her hand, she could feel the end all sticky and realised he wasn't going to last much longer.

She thought about taking him in her mouth but thought better of it, if she was on her knees, it would send out a submissive tone, she was in control and that's the way it was going to stay.

He tried to place his hand between her legs, but she was so wet she knew that she would not be able to resist if he started to play with her. She pushed his hand away and continued to pull on his cock and after a few more strokes he gave a shudder and came all over her hand.

He stood there breathless for a minute, Mary went into the bathroom and cleaned her hands before putting on her dressing gown and re-entering the room. He then excused himself and went into the bathroom to sort himself out. When he was in there, he looked at his reflection in the mirror and smiled. He had always been a failure with women and his sex life had been disastrous, but here was a lady that knew exactly what he needed, this woman was special.

When he returned, Mary was sat on the sofa having poured herself a glass of wine. He picked his glass up and refilled it, then turned to her and almost apologetically said, "not quite sure that was supposed to happen, but thank you anyway."

Mary was still in control mode, "Things sometimes happen because of circumstances, there is no right, there is no wrong. Please do not think that this is the start of something new, it's merely an unexplainable spontaneous act, which I am sure gave you pleasure."

Mary herself wasn't even sure what she meant by that statement, but she just wanted to make sure he knew that she wasn't just going to roll over for him when he wanted. Vialla didn't know what that meant either, but did know he had quite clearly been told that she was no walkover.

They agreed now was probably not the time to look at the other dresses, so Vialla finished his wine and as he was leaving, told Mary, "We should do this again sometime, dinner that is, not, well, you know." Mary nodded and ushered him through the door.

Once he had gone, she lay on the bed to think about how the night had gone, concluding that it had gone as well as she hoped. She was loving the new Mary, this sense of control was very empowering and now she knew just how much power her sexuality had given her, she wanted more.

She did not stay the night in the hotel as she knew Sophia and Franco would be worried about where she was all night, so packed everything and got back to the villa just after 11:30pm. All the lights were out and so she sneaked in and crept up to her room unnoticed.

At breakfast the following morning, Sophia wanted to ask Mary about the previous night as she heard her come in late, but decided against it. Mary was a grown woman and had probably met someone and it wasn't for her to pry. She was curious, but couldn't think of anyone in Mary's social circle that it could possibly be.

Mary's day was uneventful, but in the back of her mind she was wondering where she was going to go with this new found power. She was also worrying about Vialla, what after effects would be going through his mind, how was he going to react to her in future?

She arrived home at the usual time to find Sophia in the dining room with a big smile on her face. Mary looked at her quizzically. "What's with the big grin?" she enquired.

Sophia chuckled. "I don't know where you were last night and I won't ask, but you have left a very big impression on whoever it was." Mary was not happy that Sophia knew she had met someone last night, especially as she knew Sophia would equally not be happy if she knew the full circumstances. Mary still did not know what was going on so left Sophia and went upstairs to her room. There on the bed was the reason for Sophia's amusement, the biggest flower Bouquet Mary had ever seen. She wasn't an expert on floral displays but knew this was very expensive and the flowers very rare. In the middle of this presentation was a card with her name on and a simple message 'My thanks to an incredible lady'. Mary knew immediately who it was from but wasn't impressed. At least he hadn't signed it, she thought, that would really have got people talking.

As Mary sat down to dinner, Sophia was still smirking and couldn't contain herself any longer. "Please forgive my curiosity, but who would send such a lavish bouquet. That's the gift from someone who is infatuated, please tell me who it is."

Mary knew she could not reveal the true source so said she had met someone during her trips into Milan, she had met him again yesterday and he treated her to dinner. This was true, she hadn't lied, so she didn't feel the need to explain herself further.

Mary decided the best strategy was to ignore the flowers and not respond, let him do the chasing. She didn't see him as husband material so why bother? Alfonso, though thought differently.

Mary was beginning to get bored at work, the production line was trickling along in Brescia and Franco had insisted they now pick up the slack by producing uniforms, which was a repetitive and monotonous process. She was not being allowed to produce her own designs, the Blackshirt influence was everywhere and all the talk of Mussolini forming an alliance with Hitler in Germany was having a negative effect on everyone. Franco had good connections within the community and he was hearing of bad things coming from Europe, Mussolini was upsetting a lot of people. All of this was discussed around the table during their evening supper, Mary was concerned that as a foreigner she might be treated with suspicion or even arrested. The only solution was to find out for herself and the logical person to turn to was Vialla.

It had been nearly a month since she last saw him, so when she called him in his office she had to apologies for the delay, saying she had been busy producing uniforms for Il Duce. As expected, he asked her if she was free for dinner, she replied she could make the following night, so Vialla booked a table in the same restaurant. Mary wasn't sure if she wanted sex with him but the feeling of control was powerful and excited her, so she wasn't going to rule it out.

She arrived promptly and he was already waiting in the lounge. They ordered a pre-meal drink and sat chatting in the lounge. As they did so a Blackshirt arrived with a note, which he promptly handed to Vialla. Mary kept her head down, but then he spoke to Vialla. Mary froze, she knew that voice, it was the same person that had dragged her into the alley. She looked up, as she did so he turned to face her and in that moment, he winced, he was truly petrified. Vialla quickly gave him an answer to the note and he scuttled off as fast as he could. Mary said nothing, dealing with him could wait for now, but she was determined to make sure he paid for his assault on her.

The conversation over dinner mainly revolved about Mary asking questions about his work, probing but not so much that it would make Vialla wonder about her intent. She could sense though that there was definitely something happening on the international stage. She needed to dig further but was aware she needed to be subtle. As the meal was ending, Alfonso announced that he had booked a room for himself at the hotel and would she like to share a bottle of wine. Mary had been wondering how this was going to progress, she knew she needed more time to work on him if she wanted results, so accepted.

Once in the room, Vialla poured them both a drink and they sat down together on the sofa. Mary continued to ask about his work, but noticed he was beginning to seem irritated.

"I don't really feel like talking about politics, I much prefer to relax." He said as he moved closer to her, his face close up to hers. Mary replied by telling him the reason she was asking was because she was concerned about all the rumours that Italy was preparing for war and that as a foreign national, she might be arrested. He assured her that as long as he was in charge, she would be safe, especially if they were seen together socially. Mary thought now was the time to mention about the assault. "I am not safe now, so what makes you think I would be safe if the political climate changed?"

"Sorry, I don't understand, why would you not be safe now," Vialla looked puzzled.

Mary then went into great detail about the way she was humiliated and she could see Vialla's hands clenching, his face was purple and he looked as though he would explode.

"Are you sure it was him?"

"Yes, I am sure, I am not likely to forget something like that, am I?" Mary then described his accomplices and Vialla knew from their description that she was telling the truth. Mary finished her drink and poured herself another.

"All this drama has made me anxious and when I am anxious, I like to drink. Can we have another bottle?" She needed to get him to loosen up and a few glasses more would do the trick.

Vialla was still thinking about her experience and told her that he was going to make sure they were punished.

"I would expect nothing less than the severest punishment." Mary was back in a controlling mood, all her senses were heightened, she could feel herself getting excited and she had decided that tonight she was going to fuck all the information she could out of this Blackshirt wimp.

Once room service had delivered the extra bottle, Mary filled Vialla's drink, he was drinking more quickly now, he was still agitated.

"Now you know why I am asking questions, your thugs have no morals now, so what will they be like when their power is absolute," Mary moved her face forward so her mouth was almost touching his. "I would hope that you appreciate my predicament and will ensure that my wellbeing is assured, if someone like you cannot guarantee my safety, then I may as well go back to England now."

She then refilled their glasses and sat back. This news stunned Vialla, he was now in a predicament. The officer who Mary referred to was a trusted Lieutenant, he was also well connected.

Mary could see that Vialla was reluctant to discuss the matter, so decided to push on and find out as much as she could, this was her future and she needed to know what lay ahead. She leaned forward and squeezed his thigh. "Enough of my predicament, I have lived with it for a few months so I can wait a little longer for you to deliver justice… For now."

Vialla was glad to avoid the subject and turned to Mary and kissed her.

"You are a very strong woman, please be assured that it will be resolved," Mary nodded and kissed him back, at the same time she moved her hand up his leg and onto his groin. He was hard already. Determined to maintain control, she stroked him.

"In that case, I will allow you a reward," she muttered as she undid the buttons on his trousers. Vialla was not used to a woman being so upfront, but it felt a lot better than him having to take the lead. He reached forward and slipped his hand up her skirt. As he slid up her stockinged leg, Mary was unsure if letting him touch her would be classed as a weakness, but soon decided she needed him inside her, she was wet and wanted to feel something hard inside her.

Mary stood up and slipped out of all her clothes completely, she stood in front of him totally naked and told him to stand up. As he did so his trousers fell down around his ankles. She reached forward and squeezed his balls.

"I feel the need for you to satisfy me, so get undressed and onto the bed."

Vialla was now her plaything and Mary was loving it, she wanted some cock, any cock would do, even Vialla's.

Mary got on the other side of the bed and spread her legs. "Before you get satisfaction, you must ensure mine." He reached down to put a finger inside, but Mary gripped his hair and pulling him down to her very wet pussy ordered him to eat her. "Once you have completed this task, then you shall have your reward."

Vialla could not believe what was happening, women in Italy did not act like this. He found that he was enjoying the situation more than anything he had ever experienced before, he didn't care what she did, he was happy to comply with every request.

He licked and sucked, but was obviously not an expert on women's anatomy, so Mary pulled his hair and ears until he was in the right spot, then once she had him where she wanted, she lay back and enjoyed the moment. After about five minutes, she could feel herself getting ready to come, she wanted to stop, she didn't want him to control the situation, but she couldn't stop herself. She felt the emotion rising until there was no going back and she gushed a flood of juice as he lapped away.

She told him to stop, she would now reward him. She stroked him until he was hard again then straddled him and gently rocked back and forth, looking down at him all the time, exerting her authority. When she felt he was ready to come, she climbed off and stroked him.

"No, no, leave it inside," he begged. Mary just lay with her head on his and carried on stroking.

"Only a future husband gets that privilege," she replied as she reached lower and with her other hand squeezed his balls. "Are you ready to come now. I want to see you spurt?"

He gasped that he was, so she jerked a little faster and squeezed a little harder, then with a twitch he exploded all over his stomach.

They lay there for a while and Mary tried to get more information out of him, but was met by a resistance that told her she was wasting her time, so she went and cleaned up, then got dressed. She felt that Vialla was not going to divulge any information, so decided to go home. Vialla tried to get her to stay, but Mary knew there was nothing to gain by doing so.

The following day, Vialla asked his secretary for all the information in the file of Mary's three assailants, which she did, but because of time constraints didn't have time to read them, so put them in his desk.

Chapter Eleven

Mary stayed away from Vialla for the next 6 months, despite his several desperate attempts to contact her. Life carried on, but the Mussolini influence and fascist ideology was still growing. Italy was becoming more involved in international matters. The Spanish civil war was in progress and Italy sent 60000 troops, planes and artillery. Mussolini's Fascism and Hitler's National Socialist Party were closely aligned in ideology. Even Marco Guido was falling under its spell, attending various rallies and forming friendships with some unsavoury characters, much to the disgust of his mother and father.

He was also utilising the Brescia factory to alter uniforms for officers when the standard uniform did not fit. This appeasement to vanity was proving to be quite popular and one particular customer reminded her of an unfinished matter. One of the assailants against her in the alley turned up with a uniform and asked for a fitting, which was carried out in a storeroom. Mary was walking past and recognised him straight away. He did not recognise her and smiled as she passed.

Mary was very concerned about the situation in Europe, she did not want to be stranded in Europe, or even worse detained. She decided to try one last time with Vialla, but this time it was going to be more official, she would go to his office, she didn't want to sleep with him. She tried a number of times before finally getting an interview, he was obviously not happy with her.

Vialla had already given up on Mary and didn't want anything that would resurrect his feelings so was quite happy to meet in his office. He was just thinking about what she might want when it occurred to him he had not done anything about investigating the assault, so he dived into his desk drawer and retrieved the files. As he looked at them it was clear that the main protagonist Gianni Bertoli was trouble. His father was a wealthy industrialist in Rome and Gianni had a reputation for being spoilt and used to getting his own way. Reading through the file there was a reference to a rape four years previously. No charges were brought but Bertoli was transferred to Milan, no doubt someone had brought some influence into play with the local authorities. Vialla was not pleased that nobody had sought to warn him about this officers previous behaviour.

Mary arrived on time, she only had 2 matters to discuss, the first was how safe she would be in the current climate and secondly what had been done about the assault on her.

As she sat down, Vialla could feel his feelings for her coming back, but tried to play them down. Mary asked about what was happening, she was concerned. The outlook had got bleaker since the last time she spoke to him about it. Vialla knew she was right, he didn't want to try and give her a false prediction of the future, so he told her that he agreed things had got more serious and while he could not guarantee her safety, he would do whatever he could to assist her if the situation worsened. Mary then asked about her attackers and Vialla was forced to admit he had done nothing.

"But I have the files here," he replied waving them in his hand. "I will certainly complete my observations today."

Mary was not impressed and snatched them out of his hand. "Let me help you, then maybe we can be sure it will be completed." She then opened the file of Bertoli and started to scan the page before Vialla could get around his desk to take them back. He winced when he noticed that she was obviously reading the section about the alleged rape in Rome and his transfer to Milan.

He grabbed the file back, "These are confidential, you do not have the authority to read them."

Mary spoke very slowly but deliberately. "So, you have a man in your employment that was transferred to you in order to escape a rape charge and who then was given the opportunity to strike again, and you did nothing."

"I did not know about his history until I started to read his file, if I had known I would have blocked his transfer."

Mary looked at him wide-eyed. "So, you have a man in your employment that was transferred to you in order to escape a rape charge and who then was given the opportunity to strike again, and you didn't even know about it?"

Mary approached the desk, her voice trembling with rage and getting louder, "Are YOU telling me that YOU, who is supposed to be the boss around here, doesn't have a clue about who works as a senior official for you?" She went on, "Also that YOU are going to whatever it takes to make sure I am kept as safe as possible."

Mary was fuming now, Vialla tried to speak but Mary was having none of it and waved her hand as he was about to speak, "You promised me that they would receive the severest punishment, but months later they are still free to swagger about and do as they please. Are you sure you are in charge here, it seems to me that the monkeys are running the zoo," Mary was going too far now and knew she had to back off or she would be in serious trouble.

Vialla was also fuming, but for different reasons. He was not made aware of the history or reason for the transfer, He knew he should have looked into and didn't, he knew Mary was right. He also knew he looked like a fool in her eyes for saying he would guarantee her safety… but he wasn't going to listen to her ranting anymore.

He stood up, face purple and spitting as he shouted back to her, "SHUT UP NOW, WHO DO YOU THINK YOU ARE TALKING TO."

This was a different Vialla than Mary was used to dealing with, the mild-mannered submissive man was now transformed into a formidable animal, she was scared. Had she gone too far? She sat back down in the chair.

"THIS MATTER WILL BE DEALT WITH QUICKLY, I CAN ASSURE YOU, NOW GET OUT OF MY OFFICE." His face looked ready to explode, the look was that of someone she did not recognise, the look of a dangerous man. Mary didn't need telling twice, she grabbed her bag and coat and scuttled away as fast as she could, almost running down the stairs. She walked around the corner and needed to sit down and recover, so entered a little café and ordered a cappuccino. As she was reflecting on what had just happened, she realised her time in Italy was now up and she needed to get back to England as soon as possible.

That night at dinner she told the family of her plans. Sophia looked resigned, she had seen it coming and although sad, accepted it was probably the right decision. Franco said nothing but she could see he was almost relieved. He had good connections and what the connections were saying was not good news, she was better off back in England.

Mary sat down to establish her financial status, she knew she had enough money in her English account to last a few years and that since working in Italy Mary had received a generous salary that she hardly ever touched, as she lived at the villa and never really had any outgoing expenses. She decided to clear out her Italian bank account, she wasn't sure how much was in it but thought there would be plenty to cover her train fare home at least, what was left she would convert into pound notes to take with her.

On Wednesday, she enquired at the railway station about times and prices, then decided she would leave on the following Monday and booked her ticket. She then went shopping to buy some farewell presents for the family, stopping off first at the Galleria Vittorio Emmanuel. She was a little more relaxed now she had finally made her mind up, she still didn't know what she was going to do, but that felt sure that little problem would resolve itself. After about an hour, she decided to take a coffee and found herself by a cafe the edge of the Duomo, so sat down to enjoy watching all the people as they passed by. She then saw approaching the tall imposing figure of Vialla. She kept her head down but he had already seen her.

As he reached the table, he raised his hat and stood directly over her. He bent down slightly and in a hushed tone said, "Your little problem with the Lieutenant has been resolved, he will not cause you any further distress." With that, he turned away, but then stopped and turned back. "I hope your journey back to England is incident free," then turned on his heels and walked off.

On Saturday night Sophia made an exceptional dinner in Mary's honour, all the family was there along with Helena who Mary had grown quite close to when she first started work. As they had just finished, Franco informed them all of the latest news from the various forums and trade meetings he had attended, which was pretty standard as all the meetings fell under the Blackshirt control. He finished by informing them of the death of a senior figure of the militia.

Marco was the first to comment. "Yes, I knew him, not very well, but enough to know that his suicide was most unexpected." Marco then went on, "Gianni Bertoli did not appear to have any problems that would force him to take a bullet to the brain, but I suppose nobody knows what goes on inside a person's mind."

At the sound of his name Mary froze. She knew he hadn't committed suicide, this was Vialla making good on his promise to sort things out. Unable to think straight she made her excuses and went for a walk in the garden. She now knew she had to get away from Milan as soon as possible. What did Vialla mean when he said he hoped her journey was without incident, had he got plans for her as well? Her head was spinning. Sophia could see that Mary was distressed, but allowed her 10 minutes alone before going to see if she was alright.

"What's the matter are you ok, you look worried?"

Mary knew she could not tell Sophia, if she did, she would have to tell her about the assault and sleeping with Vialla, she wasn't going to do that.

"I am fine, I think it's just the fact that it's all becoming clear that I probably won't see you all again for a long time, if at all," was the best she could think of.

Sophia accepted that excuse and put a comforting arm around her. "We will be together again, I promise you."

On Monday, she arrived at the station ready for the 11am departure, Sophia and Franco came to see her off and there were a few tears and hugs on the platform. Eventually Mary settled into her seat on the sleeper train. She had booked a two-seat cabin all for herself, it obviously was twice as expensive, but she wanted the privacy and security it allowed. As the train pulled out. She saw a figure that made her skin crawl. There at the end of the platform was Vialla, he raised his hat as she passed him, a cold sweat formed on her brow. Had he got plans to kill her as well? She was truly terrified now and locked the cabin door to be safe.

The journey took 8 hours and they pulled into Zurich at 7pm, Mary was so relieved to get out of Italy. The passport check took a couple of minutes and after refuelling set off again for Paris at 8pm. She realised she was very hungry, but she had not dare leave her cabin before. Venturing to the buffet car, she sat down at her table and after ordering a cheese fondue with roast potato, she relaxed sipping a soothing glass of wine. Looking around and listening to the various conversations Mary concluded that the majority of the other passengers were German, with not a Blackshirt in sight. The meal was very filling and all the tension of the day had made her tired so she made her way back to the cabin, where she saw her bed had already been made up. She undressed and without getting her nightdress on lay on the bed and immediately fell asleep.

When she woke, she quickly washed and dressed, then opening the blinds, could see that it was early morning and they were just arriving in Dijon. She then went to breakfast and returned to her cabin an hour later and was pleased to see the bed had been converted back to a seat and she then enjoyed the last couple of hours without any problems. From there, it was all change at Paris onto the boat train to London, then the final route up to the northwest of England.

Mary managed to get back to Salford at 4pm on the Wednesday. It was too late to be running around trying to sort all her things in storage, so she booked into a local hotel for the night and planned for the following day. She knew she needed a room or apartment that was big enough for her to carry out dressmaking and tailoring and was fairly local. This proved a difficult challenge and after the first day it didn't look good, there was nothing that seemed suitable. She then booked in a second night in the hotel and spread her net a bit wider, until she finally found herself a terraced house that was attached to a builder's yard in the Trafford area.

The next few weeks were a settling in period, she ran up curtains, bought new furniture and spent time just adjusting to life back in England. She had forgotten how cold and damp the north of England was, so needed to buy some new coats and wear more layers of clothing. Milan was cold in the winter but this seemed a different type of cold, a wet cold.

Finally, she was ready to face the world. She put out advertisements in Shops for Tailoring alterations and bespoke dressmaking, but didn't get much joy. Then one day on the bus she was reminded of something Marco had picked up on. The Conductors uniform was a really bad fit, all the uniforms were standard sizes, but people are not standard, they come in all shapes and sizes. She went home and thought about all the various professions that wore a uniform and decided to concentrate on those. Policemen, nurses, bus crews, ambulance men, soldiers, the list was endless. She then bombarded local hospitals, police stations and army barracks with leaflets and at all the local buildings she offered to collect and deliver as well.

Then response was encouraging and she found herself working 14 hours a day to keep up with the demand, but she needed extra help as the constant picking up and delivering was too time consuming and it was all a struggle. She sought out Daisy who lived fairly central and asked her if she was interested in carrying out alterations, which she gladly accepted. Mary bought her a machine and Daisy then set out collecting uniforms and carrying out alterations at home.

This continued for the next three months with a steady flow of work producing a steady income, but not making her a fortune. Mary was getting frustrated, the work was just a constant churn of alterations, she wanted to stretch herself and this was not getting her anywhere.

A regular source of income was from the Salford Royal Hospital, it was the biggest in the area and doubled up as a teaching hospital, Mary was going there a couple of times a week. During one of these trips, she noticed the entrance to the laundry, which she hoped would give her a short cut into the wards where she dropped off the alterations. As she wandered through the lower levels, she saw there were a number of side rooms that were used for storage of various materials and goods. There was plenty of space for her to set up a small alterations room, which would save a lot of trips. She made enquiries to see if it was possible and after being sent from department to department, she finally found herself outside a door with the sign **Head of Nursing** and politely knocked on the door. A female voice beckoned her in and she found herself in the secretary's office and sat behind a desk was a fairly formidable looking woman with her hair tied back in a bun.

Peering over her glasses, she asked what Mary wanted and when she replied she was looking for somewhere to carry out alterations and repairs to uniforms, she was shown a seat and told to sit down. The secretary then left and entered a second room that was adjacent to the desk. After a couple of minutes, she was ushered into the second room, which was surprisingly spacious and had a large Bay window that looked out over the main entrance. A tall slim woman was there with her back to Mary looking out of the window and without turning around she asked in a very prim and proper voice.

"So, what is it you would like from the hospital and what can you offer us?"

Mary thought her a little rude for not facing her, but replied to the back of her head anyway. "I am an experienced dressmaker and we currently carry out alterations to your nurses' uniforms so they don't look as ill-fitting as they do when issued, these alterations are popular and they make the nurses feel more comfortable. Currently I am having to take them away and work from home, I would like to be able to carry out this work here at the hospital, which in turn means I can offer a better service."

The faceless body turned around and Mary could see she was a quite attractive woman in her mid-forties. She also noticed a scar that ran for three inches down the left-hand side from her ear to her cheek, which spoilt an otherwise attractive face.

Mary tried to ignore this and continued, "You have a lot of unused space in the basement areas and I would like to rent some from you, not much, just enough to operate a couple of machines. I could also carry out any other alterations or repairs to curtains, etc."

"Ok, please can you take me to where you think might be suitable?" With that, the Face walked out of the room.

"Come, I am a busy woman and do not have time to dawdle."

They walked down into the basement, but Mary was a little disoriented as she had not been down these corridors before. Eventually she found some signs that gave her general directions, they were near where she had expected to be.

"Any rooms in this area would be sufficient, I can work wherever is suitable for yourselves." Mary was struggling to keep up with this whirlwind, she was certainly a determined woman.

Eventually they came to a corridor that had three rooms side by side with only a handful of packing cases and boxes.

"Would these be suitable for what you need, there is electricity available and we could improve the lighting for you?"

Mary could see this was a great opportunity, she wasn't going to turn it down and the only stumbling point would be the rental costs.

"This is just what we need, who do I need to speak to for authorisation and how much would you want as rent every week?" The response was not what she was expecting. "I am the Matron of this hospital and I have just given my authorisation. There is no rental cost except for a token figure for the electricity."

She went on to explain that she had served as a field nurse in the Great War and was well aware of how uncomfortable and ill-fitting the uniforms were. She was determined to raise the status of nurses and morale was important, if the nurses felt better dressed than they would feel better about themselves. What a stroke of luck, thought Mary, she was now warming to this enigmatic character who was obviously committed to her nurses.

Over the next few weeks, Mary dug into her savings and set up a mini factory in two of the rooms, bringing in three machines and sorting out shelving as well as a small office set up in the third. Daisy had continued to work from home, but there was a small backlog developing. The nurses were told where they could go to for alterations when they were being fitted, so life the work became a lot more efficient. There was also a nurses' teaching hospital on site which meant every year there were new recruits to furnish.

Life was ticking along, Mary spent most of her time working, her social life was non-existent. There were the odd nights to the cinema or a show, sometimes with Daisy, sometimes alone. On one of the nights to the cinema, she happened to spot the Matron in the queue and wondered who she was with. She could only see the back of their heads; her partner was obviously slim with short black hair and wearing a fedora hat.

As they received their tickets they turned and the Matron saw Mary and approached her as they passed.

"How is business in the basement?" She smiled.

Mary noticed she had covered her scar quite successfully with makeup. "Everything is good below ground, thank you."

Then Mary turned to the Matrons partner and was surprised to see it was a woman, probably about five years younger than Mary. The Matron smiled at Mary and wished her a good evening, then they went to take their seats in the circle. The film was Angels with Dirty Faces starring James Cagney, which she enjoyed but Mary was concerned Pathe News clip showing what was happening around Europe, especially where it showed Hitler going into Vienna. Mary could sense this was the beginning of something that would cause problems throughout Europe.

The following day Mary was at her desk when there was a tap on the door, when she looked up it was the Matron.

"I have been meaning to take a look at how things were and seeing you last night reminded me to come and see you. Did you enjoy the movie last night?"

"The movie was very good, I enjoyed it, but the news clips were a little disturbing."

The matron then asked, "Oh, not many people care about matters outside of England, why does it interest you?"

Mary then explained about her experiences in Italy and how she came to be there, the matron appeared totally fascinated in hearing her story. They sat talking for quite a while and Mary found herself becoming fascinated with this woman. She then opened up about her experience in the orphanage and how she came to be a successful business woman and how Mac had ruined her.

The Matron surprised her by informing her that she too had spent three years in an orphanage, her father was killed in the Boer War and her mother contracted cancer and died when she was eleven. She lived in Derbyshire and was raised by nuns. When she was of suitable age she was indentured into nursing, then at 18 she was sent to the warfront and served in the hospitals at Ypres. That was where she got the scar when a stray shell bombed the hospital, she was working in.

Mary told her she must get very tired and lonely, having such a responsible position, to which Matron replied, "My life is what it is, I chose it. I have my yoga which my friend, Chloe is teaching me, this is a very calming influence and helps to clear the mind, I find it very therapeutic. You met her last night. I noticed you were on your own, no boyfriend or husband?"

Mary shook her head, "Don't have the time, or particularly the inclination at present," was the best Mary could respond.

The Matron then told her she had spent far too much time talking and had to get back to work, then as she was about to leave, she turned and with a thoughtful expression asked Mary, "You say you used to make dresses and uniforms, is that correct?" Mary confirmed and the Matron then went on her way.

The following week, Matron sent a message to ask Mary to come to her office on Wednesday, when she turned up the previously pompous secretary was very welcoming and showed her straight into the office. This time Matron was sat behind the desk reading through some notes. As Mary entered the room, she stood up and walked around to a small sofa in front of which was a small coffee table and two more small chairs. On the table was some sample size pieces of various types of cloth. Matron beckoned her to sit down and asked if Mary was wondering why she had been asked to come to the office, Mary nodded.

"I have been giving some thought about the current arrangement in so far as uniforms. I have also visited the stores to see what is available and have to admit it's not the best selection. The chief buyer says we are getting the best value possible, but I am not so sure, what do you think?" She handed Mary a sheet with prices for the various uniforms and also a sample of linen. Mary scanned the list and could see it was as much as she had been paying for linen of a far more superior quality.

"Is this the price for a full uniform, or just the material?"

"Full uniform in batches of one hundred. Is that value for money?"

Mary was sure that she could have produced a better finished uniform and used better quality linen for a cheaper price. "I don't think it's particularly good value and the quality of the finished product is not very good, who monitors quality?"

Matron looked at Mary, "Good question, not sure anyone does. Can you go away and make a uniform then tell me how much it would be."

This was a great opportunity, Mary assured her she could produce a better result for less money and said it would take 2 weeks to source the materials and another 2 to produce the finished article.

Mary stood up and shook her hand, "Thank you for this opportunity, Matron, I will not let you down."

"When we are alone, you may call me Claire, but obviously when there is company, I expect to be called Matron." She smiled at Mary, then went on, "I am having a small yoga get-together at my house next Saturday afternoon, if you are free then you are most welcome. Nothing special, just wear loose clothes and expect to stretch a lot."

Mary accepted and after getting the address, went back down to her small office. That was an interesting meeting, she thought. She spent the next few days looking at how the uniforms could be improved and spoke to some of the nurses as they collected garments, who gave a her a couple of ideas.

On Saturday, Mary woke early and felt strangely apprehensive, she wasn't sure if it was due to the fact she knew nothing about yoga or whether she felt intimidated by Claire. She wasn't sure what she should wear but settled for a flowing skirt and loose-fitting blouse.

At 2pm she arrived at Claire's house, which was a large semi-detached house in Worsley. She rang the bell and the door was answered by Chloe, who was wearing a bright coloured sari, which Mary thought was beautiful. She was shown into the parlour where the furniture had been cleared to the side of the room, in the middle, Claire was laying out a large rug. Mary was surprised to see Claire in a large pair of shorts with a white singlet vest, a completely different look to the starched Matron's uniform.

The session itself was led by Chloe, who explained every step as it happened. It was unlike anything Mary had ever experienced before, a combination of breathing exercises, stretching, concentration and meditation. It was very relaxing and Mary found herself becoming totally immersed in herself and when it eventually ended, she realised that 2 hours had flown by. It also made her very tired and as she just lay on the mat looking at the ceiling. Chloe went to make some tea and Claire explained that Chloe had been brought up on a plantation in Ceylon and had learnt the art of Hindu yoga over many years. Chloe returned with a large teapot of tea and they sat in quiet meditation as they sipped it. Mary had never known such tranquillity and was feeling extremely relaxed. Chloe then told Claire it was time for her massage and summoned both of them to follow her to the bedroom. Mary was not quite sure what was going on but Claire grabbed her hand and showed her the way.

They entered the bedroom, where a large double bed had been covered in towels. Chloe slipped off her sari to reveal she was only wearing a pair of panties, then immediately pulled Clair's vest over her head. Mary was shocked to see that

Claire's body was full of ugly shrapnel scars, there must have been at least a dozen, including a 12" scar that ran across her stomach. Claire turned to Mary.

"Not only soldiers bear the scars of war, I have learnt to live with it, but I won't ever be allowed to forget it."

Then she lay on the bed and Chloe rubbed essential oils that smelled divine, all over Claire's legs and back, massaging into every crease and orifice with a slow, deliberate action that Mary found quite erotic. As Chloe worked away on her body, there were little sighs and moans coming from Claire that suggested she was quite happy with the position she was in. After about 20 minutes, she was turned over and the process repeated on the front. Mary could not help but notice how hard Claire's nipples were and that she seemed to shudder every time Chloe massaged between her thighs. Sometimes a hand would wander to the top of the leg and this resulted in a deep sigh. Eventually Claire's massage was over and she sat up and said she was going for a shower and that it was now Mary's turn.

Mary sat up startled, she hadn't been expecting that and tried to wave Chloe away, "Maybe next time, this has been enough for the first time."

But Chloe was insistent and started to unbutton Mary's blouse, who by now was in a very confused state. She was fascinated to watch Chloe massage Claire, but was not sure about another woman rubbing oil into her body. By the time she had gathered her thoughts together she realised that she had been undressed to her panties and was being led to the bed, so she submitted and lay down on her front.

Chloe's hands were very soft, but at the same time strong and she worked oil onto her back and was caressing it deep into Mary's muscles, which was very, very satisfying. The combination of the yoga and massage was making her drowsy and she was in a complete state of relaxation. She was lying there and enjoying every moment, but then realised that Chloe's fingers were rubbing the inside of her thighs. The sensation was incredible, she wanted her to stop but also to carry on. When one of her fingers slipped inside her panties and then into her, she gasped, but not a gasp of surprise, more of anticipation of something more. Suddenly she came to her senses and wriggled and Chloe immediately stopped.

"Time for the front, please turn over." This sounded more like a command than a request, Mary's head was spinning. She decided to turn over anyway and as she lay on her back, she was aware that Claire was back in the room and sat on a chair watching them, dressed only in her dressing gown.

Mary felt very self-conscious, being semi-naked in front of 2 women she barely knew, she also felt aroused. Chloe set up rubbing oil onto her chest and Mary felt her nipples stiffen. She had always had sensitive nipples and this was sending them into overdrive. She felt completely helpless as Chloe set about her upper body. She looked across and Claire was sat upright in the chair looking on intently.

"Are you enjoying it dear, Chloe is very good, isn't she?" She asked, Mary could only utter a faint confirmation and nodded.

"Perhaps I could help? I need some practice," Claire asked as she stood up and without asking for permission moved towards the bed. Claire then picked up a bottle, rubbed some oil onto her hands and then began massaging it into Mary's feet.

Chloe was working her way down to Mary's stomach and Claire was working her way up Mary's leg, the effect of both of these actions was getting Mary very wet, she had never experienced anything like this in her life.

Suddenly everything became very blurred for Mary, she felt Chloe's hand reach down inside her panties, then she gently started to rub her clitoris, slowly, very slowly. At the same time Claire's hand was massaging her inner thigh very erotically. Mary began to tremble, her body wanted more. Chloe sensed this and gentled tugged Mary's panties down, Mary was in no position to resist and raised her body so they could come off.

Claire pulled them down and spread Mary's legs, then pulled her down to the edge of the bed where Claire then got on her knees and began to lick her dripping pussy. At the same time as this Chloe moved up to Mary's breasts and started to kiss and suck her nipples. Mary was gone, she grabbed Claire's hair and pulled, begging her to eat her forcing her to rub her mouth against her. Chloe placed a nipple in Mary's mouth and she gladly suckled it, then Chloe slipped off her panties and placed Mary's hand between her legs, Mary was enjoying the whole experience and found another woman's wetness stimulating and placed 2 more fingers inside her.

Suddenly, it was all too much and Mary exploded with an orgasm like she had never known before, her head was spinning, her body was tingling, and she almost passed out with the overwhelming emotion of it all. She looked down and Claire was smiling at her, gently licking, which was still making her body shudder.

Chloe moved to lie down next to Mary and spread her legs. Claire now began to give Chloe the same experience as she had given Mary, so Mary turned on her side to watch, she was totally fascinated. She found herself kissing Chloe, a long slow smouldering kiss, the sort reserved for lovers. Chloe then responded by reaching down between Mary's legs and gently stroking her. Mary could feel that she wanted to come again and encouraged Chloe to put more fingers inside, which she did. Claire's licking of Chloe was having the desired effect and she then began moaning and crying out, until it reached a stage of no return and she shuddered then collapsed in a breathless state. After getting her breath back she then looked down at Claire, smiled and informed her, "Now it's your turn."

"I am not sure Mary is ready for my preferences," Claire replied, looking up at Mary and smiling. The statement was a strange one and the look that accompanied it was even more intriguing. "We had better leave that for another time, but we could at least make sure our guest is fully satisfied."

All the time she had been talking, Chloe had been working her fingers inside Mary and she was ready for some more action. Mary gave a little squeal as Claire moved her head back between her legs and as she did Chloe removed her fingers and began to stroke Mary's nipples. It didn't take long for another explosion to take place and at the end of its Mary's body lay limp on the bed. They all talked for a little while and then Mary fell into an exhausted sleep for the next three hours.

When Mary awoke, it was just beginning to go dark outside, there was a small table lamp that illuminated the room and as she slowly became aware of her surroundings, she slowly evaluated what had occurred that day. Her mixed emotions were troubling her; it was without doubt the biggest sexual high of her life and she had found it extremely satisfying. But at the same time, she had never before considered having sex with another woman and also where would this leave her professional relationship with Claire?

After lying there for half an hour, she heard footsteps coming up the stairs, she felt very apprehensive. The door opened and in stepped Claire, with a cup of tea.

"How are you feeling, you soon fell asleep, yoga can have that effect."

Mary took the cup and sat up in bed. At first, she tried to cover her naked body, but then realised that was a pointless gesture in light of what had happened a couple of hours before.

"Erm, yes I slept well," Mary was unable to think straight, she didn't know how to react. Claire was acting as if it was a normal day and nothing was untoward. She then asked about the yoga and if she had enjoyed it, which Mary admitted was very therapeutic, they chatted about its benefits and how it can be good for mental wellbeing.

Mary said she had to go, so Claire showed her where the towels were and ran the shower for her. "I will be downstairs when you're finished."

As she dried herself, Mary noted that overall, the experience had been good, the yoga was interesting, the massage pleasant and the sex sensational, but did she want to repeat it… she wasn't sure.

Claire was waiting in the parlour, but there was no sign of Chloe. When she asked where she was Claire replied that she had gone home to her husband, which surprised Mary.

"We hold yoga sessions every Saturday, your most welcome to join us if you like, I find it very stress relieving," Claire looked straight into Mary's eyes as she spoke. "You would be very welcome." Mary said she would consider it, then asked how many other ladies had been invited to partake in yoga lessons.

"None, but you are a most interesting person and I feel that we think along similar lines. I do hope you will consider it." She rose to show Mary the door and as she was leaving gave her a close affectionate hug and whispered, "I know I can rely on your utmost discretion." Then pulling away, added, "not everybody understands yoga," and smiled, which also made Mary smile.

The next couple of weeks were busy for Mary, she received the materials and proceeded to run up a couple of options for a new uniform, taking on board the opinions of the nurses and the practicalities involved in wearing something that needed to be both practical and comfortable. It also had to comply with the expectations of the board and Claire and be compatible with the current uniforms. The pricing was not a problem as whoever had agreed the current prices obviously didn't have any idea of the cost of producing a uniform. Eventually she was satisfied with the result and informed Matron via the secretary that she was ready to present her finished product.

She was then asked to meet with Matron beforehand to discuss and finalise any small areas that might require fine tuning, so on Friday morning they met for the first time since the yoga session.

Mary was nervous as she walked through the door and into the room. Claire was alone and already seated by the coffee table. She waited until the secretary closed the door then Claire stood up and embraced Mary.

"How are you, I was hoping to see you again," The way it was said seemed to Mary to be a sign of a very lonely person who was desperate for friendship.

"I have been very busy, but finally I think I have got what you are looking for," Mary then proceeded to lay out three alternative types of dress, one for a standard nurse, one for an auxiliary nurse and one for a nursing sister.

She then produced a list of costs and sizes. "I can produce these for 75% of your current costs, as you can see the material is superior and the uniforms are crisper and attention to detail greater."

Claire looked them over, this was really good work and without doubt a massive improvement on the current issue. Mary went on, "In addition, I am prepared to offer a bigger size range, which would mean less alterations are required. But in order to offer this service I need a guarantee of work and minimum orders per month over a fixed period."

"I feel sure that can be agreed, let me arrange a meeting with the board, they will no doubt agree if it means we are saving money. Leave these samples with me and I will get back to you soon," Claire seemed confident that this would happen, so Mary agreed.

As Mary was leaving Claire asked her to come for yoga tomorrow.

"Just yoga?" Mary asked as she raised her eyebrows.

"That is entirely your choice, if only yoga, then only yoga it is." She smiled at Mary, hoping she would take up her offer.

Mary spent the rest of the day thinking about whether she should go to Claire's, she had thought constantly about what had happened and she had to admit to herself that she had enjoyed the whole experience. Another thing that ate away at her was Claire's statement about whether 'Mary was ready for her preferences', which she thought was a strange thing to say.

In the end, curiosity got the better of her and she decided she had to go at least one more time, so she turned up at exactly 2pm, this time the door was answered by Claire, who led her into the parlour.

Chloe was already there and had cleared the room, she smiled at Mary, a smile that said she was very pleased to see her. The yoga routine was the same as the previous session, but Mary was finding it hard to concentrate. At the end of it, Claire asked Mary if she was ready for a massage, the wetness between her legs told Mary she was more than ready, so she nodded. Mary was told to lie on the bed face down, which she did. The first thing that happened was she felt her panties being pulled down and her legs spread then the warm sensual oil was poured over the full length of her body and rubbed in by two pair of hands.

The hands proceeded up and down her body, one person on either side of her. She could feel that little by little more attention was being paid to her inner thighs and an odd finger finding its way between the cheeks and just tickling the ring of her bottom. She raised herself slightly to meet it and the tip of the finger slipped just inside and worked its way in and out. She moaned and then felt the other person slide 2 fingers in her pussy and gently rub, at the same time applying light pressure on her clitoris. There was no going back now, and Mary could feel herself rocking up and down on the digits inside her and asking for more, she wanted to be licked and so tried to turned herself over, but she was forced back down.

"Please finish me, I need to come now," Mary whimpered… but then it all stopped, the fingers were taken out and hands removed from her body, this was not what she wanted or needed. She lay there writhing and begged, "Don't stop, please don't stop."

Then WHACK, she felt a belt across her backside and winced as it slapped down hard onto her skin, then again and again. The mixture of the expectation of an orgasm and the reality of the pain left Mary in a state of utter confusion, but it was an emotion that really had her wanting more, but also less, she didn't know where she was, her body was screaming for attention.

"You don't get to decide, we will tell you when you are finished," Chloe's voice was very dominant and Mary could only sob gently. Then Mary found her backside being propped up by 2 pillows so that her rear was in the air, then could feel a tongue working its way inside her thighs and also licking her anus. She was on the edge now, she was nearly there, the tongue was everywhere and she nearly screamed when it reached her clitoris…

"I am coming," she shrieked and was about to come when it stopped again. The slap on the backside brought her back down… Except it didn't she found herself liking the heady mixture of pleasure and pain.

This went on twice more and Mary felt that her body was not her own, she didn't know how she felt, it was unlike anything she had ever known before.

"Would you like me to let you finish?" This time, the voice was Claire's. Mary could only nod. She was turned over on her back and her legs spread wide, then she felt the tongue on her clitoris and at the same time 2 hands were pulling hard on her nipples. This time there was no stopping and Mary felt a gushing erupt from her body, A literal gush. She exploded and juices went everywhere, mainly over Claire whose face was right into Mary's pussy.

It took at least 15 seconds for Mary to stop coming, never had she felt such an overwhelming emotion. When she finished, she could only lie down, not daring to move. She felt that her body was in shock, her head was spinning and her insides felt like they were coming out. Then she fell asleep.

When she woke there was nobody there and so she had a shower and got dressed, went downstairs and found a note on the dining table which said that, 'You looked so peaceful I didn't want to wake you; I have gone to the shops and will be back around 7pm. You are welcome to stay and eat with me later if you want.'

Mary wasn't in any hurry, she was still tired, she had been through an exhausting experience. She went upstairs and made the bed, but then curiosity got the better of her and she decided to take a look around the room. In the wardrobe there was a variety of clothes that were not exactly day-to-day apparel and in the corner were some straps and whips. Quickly shutting the cupboard doors, she opened some of the drawers and found more items of intrigue. There were large dildos and straps and other items of restraint. Mary closed the drawer and as she turned around Claire was in the doorway, which startled her.

"I am sorry, I don't know what came over me," was all Mary could manage to blurt out.

"You mean you were curious, it's understandable after today," Claire smiled.

"I did wonder if you were ready for my preferences, Let's have some tea and I will explain."

As they sat on the sofa sipping their tea Claire explained that the war had been traumatic for her, she had seen dozens of men die from horrific pain and she herself had suffered greatly. The wounds inflicted on her had been life threatening, she was not able to have children and pain was all around her for more than 2 years. She had become immune to everything relating to suffering and the mental strain left her with a fixation for giving and receiving pain, she found them both very stimulating in equal measures.

Mary was forced to admit it was the most intense emotional experience she had ever been through and the satisfaction at the end of it was off the scale. Claire then went on to say she liked to receive pain; it was the main outlet in order to make herself come. No man would ever want her due to her scars and she could not bear children. She also said that she had been sexually mistreated by quite a few soldiers and this had put her off men, women were much nicer.

Claire asked Mary to stay the night but Mary thought she needed to get away and back to some sort of normality, so declined the offer.

Mary wasn't in contact with Claire until the following Thursday, when she got a message to say the board were very interested in the uniforms and would like to see her at the next Board meeting which was 2 weeks today. She also said that Mary was welcome to discuss the matter at her home on the Saturday afternoon. Mary replied that she was available for the meeting but not able to see her on Saturday. This whole lesbian thing had shaken Mary and she wanted to step back, even though she had enjoyed it.

The board met with Mary and they agreed a 2-year contract on terms that were better than they already had, but not everyone was in agreement. The dissenting voice belonged to Mr Richard Grice, who had appointed the previous uniform provider, who also just happened to be his brother. He argued that Mary was a failed businesswoman who now had no collateral or factory and they were taking a huge gamble betting on such a loser. Mary explained the circumstances regarding the previous failure and gave assurances she could revive her business once confirmation of orders was placed.

The board then questioned Mr Grice about why he recommended they remain with an uncompetitive supplier with a clearly inferior product. This did not sit well with Richard Grice who struggled to support his argument. It was agreed that Mary would be given an initial six-month contract, with a following 2-year contract if the initial terms were fulfilled satisfactorily. Mary thanked and left the meeting. As she was leaving Claire asked if she could see Mary later that afternoon.

"Sorry Matron, but I am going to be very busy over the next few months," Mary's reply was a confident, firm statement to Claire that she should leave her alone.

Mary knew she needed some capital investment and need it quickly, so she arranged to go back to the bank and arrange a meeting. It was with the same manager in the same room as before. He was once again sat behind his large desk and stood up to meet Mary as she entered the room.

"Every time we have met it has been under differing circumstances, what do you have for me today, young lady."

Mary was very nervous, she knew that her previous experience was not great, but all she could do was to present the facts and see what the outcome, but she wasn't confident. She explained about the nursing contract, about the alterations, about her experiences in Italy, but then emphasised that although she had been in debt, it was a debt as a result of being defrauded and that she had learnt from that experience. She also pointed out that she had paid off all her debt before she had gone to Italy.

The manager said nothing as Mary opened up, Mary presented all the facts, what her outgoings would be, she had already agreed prices for materials, all she had to do was find a new factory. He listened intently, then when he had finished, he leaned back in his big leather chair and ran his hands through his beard.

"I have to admit, you are a very persuasive lady and you are in a better state of mind than when I last saw you. Your numbers appear to add up and your whole presentation has merit."

This sounded promising, thought Mary to herself.

He continued, "However, the fact remains that you proved to be an unsafe investment the last time around and the bank was forced to chase you for repayment. I personally think you have a chance, but professionally it is a risk too far. If the bank lent you the money and you defaulted again, then serious questions would be raised as to my credibility and competence... Therefore, unfortunately I have to decline your request, but wish you well."

This was the knock back Mary dreaded, but she wasn't surprised, she had hardly covered herself in glory the last time she was here. She thanked the manager and decided to go home and think out her options.

"As she was turning the key to her front door an unfamiliar voice called to her. She turned around to see a lorry turn into the yard next to her house."

"I wondered who my new neighbour was, how do you do, my name is Billy, Billy Reddy, and who might you be?"

Mary was confronted by a large man with curly black hair, with a large friendly grin on his face.

"Hello Billy, Billy Reddy, my name is Mary Knox, pleased to meet you. He jumped out of the cab and walked towards her, extending his hand, then wiping it when he realised how dirty it was. From his accent, she guessed him to be an Irishman, he seemed a very friendly man. They talked for a short while and it turned out that he was actually the owner of the house, but didn't like legal formalities so relied on representation to sort out the paperwork. He lived in a flat within the yard itself. He was a general builder who could turn his hand to most things, but as he had been brought up in a remote village in Cork, he was barely literate. Mary told him about her alterations business but didn't say any more than that, so Billy, ended the conversation by asking Mary if she would like to go for a drink sometime."

"That would be nice," she replied. "But I am very busy at the moment," and left it at that, he did not appear to be the sort of man she wanted to spend a lot of time with.

Mary set about getting her new venture up and running but capital was still a problem, there was no way she could fund it herself, she only made enough of a living to pay her and Daisy a wage. She needed to buy new machines, rent a factory and buy sufficient stock to keep production moving, but she was running out of ideas.

Claire came down to her office after a couple of weeks to ask when production was going to begin, Mary had to be honest with her and let her know there was every possibility that she would be unable to fulfil the order and that she wasn't going to start producing uniforms until everything was in place.

Claire was sympathetic, but was unable to provide a solution and could only tell Mary that she had to begin soon or there would be no chance of completing the initial contract within timescales. Mary nodded; she already knew that but she could not see any way out of her predicament.

Claire then asked if Mary wanted to come and see her at the house, she said she missed her, as did Chloe. Mary was having problems coming to terms with the yoga days, much as she enjoyed them. She did not like the lack of self-control she had, she was like a jelly once Chloe and Claire got their hands on her. Mary refused but was curious about Chloe, so asked what Claire's relationship was and also whether her husband knew about the yoga parties.

"It's quite simple my dear, Chloe prefers women but her husband is extremely rich so she hasn't got around to telling him that she doesn't want him, but she is prepared to tolerate his lifestyle. It's a marriage of convenience, he doesn't know and doesn't really care as long as he has his freedom to fuck anything, which Chloe obviously turns a blind eye to." Claire then went on, "We have been friends for a few years now and I suspect something will give soon, he wants an heir and Chloe has no intention of providing one, children have no place in her world."

Mary tried not to want to go to the yoga party, but she was really down because it looked as though her business opportunity would not be fulfilled, she needed a distraction. It was also so extremely arousing and fulfilling that she found herself at the house once again on Saturday, but this time she was determined to be the one in control. Mary was willing for the yoga to finish and when it did, she led the way upstairs.

"Chloe first this time, I want to give something back," Mary wanted to be in control, she was still getting very wet at the thought of making the other two squirm. Chloe undressed and lay on the bed face down. She had an athletic body, toned with very defined muscle and hardly any fat. Claire was on other side of the room watching and Mary noticed her gown was partly open and she was rubbing her nipples underneath as Mary worked away on Chloe's body. As she massaged, they talked and Chloe mentioned that Claire had informed her of her failure to raise finances. Mary wasn't happy that Claire had told her and looked across at Claire and frowned.

"My husband might be able to help you," Chloe uttered as Mary worked her way down her back. Mary's ears pricked up at this statement.

"Really, it would just be a temporary loan until I am established, I could pay it off within a year."

"You wouldn't have to pay it back at all if you are in agreement with what I propose."

Mary was confused, what sort of offer was this?

Chloe then went on, "I do not want children under any circumstances and my husband needs an heir."

"What's that got to do with me?" Mary was confused now.

"It's really quite simple, you give him an heir and he will support your business and also provide you with an allowance."

Mary was getting angry now, she was being treated like a brood mare. Chloe went on, "I have already spoken with my husband and he has agreed to whatever arrangement we can come to, money is not an object." Mary was now fuming, this bitch was treating her like an animal and was even making arrangements behind her back. Chloe was still not finished.

"You will go to him twice a month until conception, then you will remain confined to an agreed place and will hand over the child after birth, after which you will have no further contact."

"What makes you think that I want to participate in such an arrangement and why did you not feel it necessary to discuss it with me first?" Mary was finding it difficult to control herself, her week had been bad and she was in no mood to be treated like an animal.

"Surely a working-class girl from an orphanage would appreciate the security my husband can offer," Chloe's condescending tone was the last straw.

Mary slowly reached down to the side of the bed and picked up a belt and hit Chloe in the middle of the back causing her to scream. These were not blows for sexual pleasure; these were designed to hurt, to cut and to inflict maximum pain.

Claire was slow to react, Mary had Chloe hunched up in a foetal position and got 4 blows in before she reached her. She tried to grab Mary. "Chloe does not like to receive pain; she only likes to please others."

Mary shook her off and laid even more strokes on Chloe's body, the buckle of the belt causing welts all over her back and thighs.

"Well, she is pleasing me now, this is just what I need," Mary then turned and slapped Claire across the face with the belt, she was out of control now. Returning to Chloe, she inflicted another dozen blows, before breaking down into tears.

"How dare you think you can treat me like something you can own, nobody owns me. Nobody, understand?"

She turned to Claire who was sat on the floor holding her face.

"I take it I won't be working at the hospital anymore, no worry, I will survive, I always do."

She took one last look at Chloe, whose body was covered in welts and blood and was trembling on the bed, "I would think twice about reporting this, just think of the scandal that would arise." Then calmly got dressed and made her way back home.

Chapter Twelve

The following week Mary had the machines transferred to her home, she wasn't going to try and maintain the uniform alterations business. The hardest part was telling Daisy, once again, that there was no more work. Daisy started to ask why but it was obvious that Mary was saying nothing, so she collected her personal items then went home. The machines were being delivered when Billy Reddy was in the yard, he noticed the activity and shouted over asking Mary what she was doing.

"Looking for a job," was Mary's short response, she wasn't in the mood for chit chat. Patrick walked over to her.

"If you're any good with accounts then I might be able to help you out. I am hopeless with paperwork and it just clutters my office up."

Mary was interested, she was good with figures and so asked Billy about the hours and pay.

"I will have to think about it, because it's only just come into my head. We can discuss it tonight over a pint, ok?"

Mary agreed and Billy carried on loading his van, "see you at 7pm, prompt."

Billy called on time and they walked to the Aquaduct Inn which was near the canal. It was quite a large pub that was quite busy, but they managed to find a quiet spot and sat down to talk. Billy was a very amiable man, quick witted and self-deprecating, with no pretence of any ego, Mary quickly warmed to him. They chatted for a few hours and Mary discovered he had a son who lived with him part of the time. She mentioned she had never seen him and Billy explained that his mother had left him for another man a year ago and taken the son with her, he only saw him on rare occasions. He also said he came over from Ireland 5 years ago and set up building maintenance business, which was doing well, but the office side of things was a complete mystery to him. At the end of the night, it was agreed that Mary would work fulltime until all the backlog was cleared, then the hours would be reviewed once everything was running to order.

She started the following day, the office was nothing more than a desk and chair with a few files scattered about. There were piles and piles of paperwork and Mary wondered how he had survived and told him so.

"It's simple," said Billy. "I wait until someone starts shouting for payment then I dig out their bill and pay it… but I always make sure that I get my bill in on time, then I do the shouting."

Mary could see this work procedure had flaws and so set about sorting all the bills and creating some order. After a week or so, it was looking a little more organised and some sort of order was in place. Billy seemed to appreciate that he wasn't running about chasing paperwork and was especially pleased when he realised Mary had a head for figures, so Mary was offered a fulltime position.

The world was becoming a very dangerous place. Austria had just been annexed by Germany and the Munich agreement allowed Germany access to a large area of Czechoslovakia. But the Germans were not happy with this and in March 1939 invaded Czechoslovakia, causing panic across Europe. Britain tried to negotiate a settlement but was unsuccessful and in September 1939 war was declared, life would never be the same again.

At first there appeared to be little change, life was fairly normal with no real impact on daily life. There was however conscription, but Billy as an Irishman was exempt. He was also a builder so his skills were required in Britain, not on the frontline. Once Germany invaded Poland then the war cranked up and more munitions factories and production lines for the war effort put in place. The Manchester area, in particular Trafford docks, was a very busy area with a lot of war related activity. Gradually the intensity built until troops were landing in France, the war was very much under way now.

In December 1940, the war landed on Mary Knox's doorstep. The Germans had been bombing London Liverpool and Coventry heavily and now it was Manchester's turn. For 2 nights, on the 22 and 23, December incessant bombing took place and the Manchester area was hit badly. Luckily for Mary, she found shelter in Billy Reddy's Anderson shelter at the back of his yard, there they stayed all night. When morning came the smell of burning from the incendiary bombs was over␣whelming, there were fires everywhere.

Billy was out first thing and the priority was to make safe as many buildings as possible, which was an impossible task as there were fires everywhere. Over the next few weeks, it was all work, from first thing in the morning until late into the evening, always hampered by the wintery lack of daylight. When as many buildings were made secure as possible, the task of removing debris and demolition of unsafe properties began, Billy was still working long hours and was exhausted, but there was a serious lack of manpower due to the conscription into the forces for the war effort and Mary was spending more time working alongside Billy on site, loading truck after truck with rubble. She learnt that good solid timber, roof slates, lead and anything that was salvageable was to be taken to the yard and the rest was to be taken to a quarry and dumped. Billy was making good money and he made sure he looked after Mary. He recruited men from Ireland who were experienced builders and work was flooding in.

The work then began to expand from salvage work to rebuilding and again Patrick was very much in demand, there were not many decent building companies about, they were all fighting a war on the frontline. The priorities were the public utilities and government buildings, a lot of which had suffered damage and needed to be repaired. Some were just boarded up and made secure, Billy was winning on both counts.

Mary gained a lot of experience about various buildings, what needed to be repaired and the methods of construction. Because of Billy's illiteracy, she became more involved in the finer points of costs, she was a quick learner and Billy knew he needed her to run the finances. There were various meetings with government officials about different contracts and Billy sent Mary along to represent him. At first, she made mistakes in terms of estimating costs and how much labour was involved, but she was a quick learner and soon adapted to the game that needed to be played in order to make money. This is when she realised that all form of business is a game and once you know the rules and how to bend the rules in your favour, then you can be successful playing the game. It was also apparent that there was a severe lack of auditing control, invoices were paid without question. Billy would tell her what work had been done and what the labour hours were, Mary worked out the materials used and priced up accordingly. She noticed that Billy often overstated the hours worked, but never queried anything and it was always paid.

She also noted there was a store cupboard in one of the rooms in the yard that was always locked and only Billy had the key. When she asked about it, she was told that it contained specialist equipment that was quite valuable and he didn't want it stolen, which seemed a plausible answer.

Following on from the bomb related work there were other contracts from the various authorities, such as the railways, water companies, etc., life was very busy.

In 1941, the War Damage Commission was set up to co-ordinate rebuilding works and Mary was in constant conversations with them about work. This meant that private property owners could claim for works arising from the bombings and so even more work was needed, Billy brought in more workers from Ireland to meet the demand. Business was booming and Mary soon had to get some help in the office, when she approached Billy about it, he just shrugged, as far as he was concerned, she could do as she pleased, he had never been wealthier.

Mary was feeling a little jaded by now, it had been all work, long hours and no time to relax, she need to get a break. She noted that there was a new film starring Humphrey Bogart at the Appollo and she mentioned to a secretary at the end of one of the many meetings she attended that she might go and see it.

"If you want some company, then I would like to see it as well." She turned to see a tall handsome man, who she recognised as a Clerk of Works for Salford Council, by the name of Robert Johnson. Not expecting this response, she was unsure how to respond.

"Perhaps we could discuss this further in my office over a cup of tea, it's just at the other end of this building."

The secretary made an excuse and left the room. Mary was instantly attracted to him, so agreed. Once inside, it was obvious he had a senior position, the office was large, with all kinds of file drawings and paperwork in neat rows and stacks, she was impressed. She had attended a number of meetings before in his presence, but failed to really notice him, but on closer inspection she found him to be quite good looking. He told her he had been impressed that she had managed to get over her initial uncertainty, but was now more than holding her own in negotiations.

Mary hadn't realised that her lack of knowledge had been noticeable, but was now glad that her abilities were being acknowledged. They talked for about twenty minutes about non-work issues and she really liked that he seemed to be genuine and a warm personality, but she made sure she found out about his married status, she wasn't falling for that again. He gave credible responses, so she agreed to go to the cinema on Friday night.

The Appollo was closer to her house and he had to walk past it to meet her so she agreed for him to collect her from home. As they walked the couple of streets they talked about various topics, she mentioned how she found herself to be working in buildings and he told her about his middle-class upbringing in the relatively affluent part of Droylsden. He was 3 years younger than Mary, but that did not bother Mary. She didn't mention her age and he didn't ask.

The film was enjoyable and as they walked back, they discussed the various characters and how the plot evolved, in no time they found themselves outside her house, so she asked him if he would like to come in for a drink, which he accepted.

She poured them both a whiskey and they sat down to talk some more. He was a very dull person and the conversation went on for another couple of hours. She was however feeling sexually attracted to Robert, it had been a long time since she had been satisfied and so she decided to take the initiative. She put her hand on his knee, leaned forward and kissed him, long and slowly. He responded and they kissed for a few minutes before he stuttered that perhaps it was time he left.

"I don't usually take the lead, but with all that's happening in the world now, I just feel that we should act on impulse." She wanted him now, he wasn't going anywhere.

She guided his hand to her breast and kissed him again. "Erm, ok, it's just that I wasn't expecting it to go anywhere tonight," his face was flushed and as she reached down, she could feel him getting hard. His nervousness was turning her on.

"Come on, let's go upstairs," she led him to the stairs, where he hesitated.

"What's the matter, don't you want me?" She was getting agitated now, she wanted him badly.

"I have never done it before, I am not sure what I am supposed to do." His response was unexpected, but it just spurred Mary on.

"I promise I will take very good care of you, just leave everything to me," Mary was rampant now, she dragged him up the stairs and threw him on the bed. She was trying to undress both of them at the same time, such was her rush to get him inside her. After 5 minutes of wrestling with each other's clothes, they were naked and entwined on the bed. Mary started to stroke him but he was clearly nervous and failing to rise to the occasion.

"Just lie back and relax and everything will be fine," she murmured as she moved her head slowly down his body and wrapped her lips around his cock. She felt him start to grow and his breathing became heavier. She squeezed his balls and he was now a full length, she was just about to take him out of her mouth so she could sit stride him when he gasped, twitched and filled her mouth with his juices, she was not expecting this and nearly choked.

Mary was not impressed but didn't like to spoil his first time so just asked him if he was ok. She looked up and he was breathing heavily and staring at the ceiling, as if in shock.

"I am fine, I have never experienced anything like that in my life," he eventually replied.

Mary wasn't satisfied and wanted her pleasure now, but he was reluctant to go down on her and no matter how she tried, he just couldn't satisfy her. She wanted his cock and made her mind up he wasn't going anywhere until she had her fill. She told him he would fine in a short time and that they had all night together, so they drifted off to sleep for an hour.

Mary woke up to find Robert stroking her breast, so she pulled him to her nipple and told him to suck it. She then reached down and felt he was hard again, now it was her playtime. They played with each other for a short time before Mary climbed on top and started to grind slowly back and forth. She dug her nails in his chest and rode him hard, increasing the speed until she was ready to come. She grabbed his hands and told him to squeeze her nipples as hard as he could, her nails were digging deeper and he was saying she was hurting him. She rode him for another 5 minutes before she exploded, an orgasm that had been building up for months suddenly erupted and she gushed everywhere. When she had finished shuddering, she looked down and saw that she had drawn blood on Robert's chest and that he was looking at her with a look of bewilderment and horror, his hands still on her breast.

Mary then started to giggle as she realised she had just provided this poor man's first sexual experience, an experience he would never forget. They lay there for a while just talking, she asked why he had never had a woman before, even though he was 37 years old. He informed her he had considered becoming a vicar and had spent a long time studying religious matters, his family were very keen for him to join the clergy but he decided against it in his late teens. He then studied at Salford University and gained his professional qualifications, but as he was living at home his private life was controlled by his parents and the opportunities to meet ladies were limited. He had only left home in the last year and was now coming to terms with the opposite sex. He had been on a few dates but nothing had happened so far.

Mary felt sorry for him and decided to make amends and let him have a slower, more comfortable ride in the morning. They awoke at 6am and Mary took the lead once more and gradually got him aroused, she then lay on her back and guided him into her and let him fuck her at his own pace. He pushed and pulled, his lack of experience was shining through and eventually she turned over so he could mount her from the rear. She was bored by now and just wanted him to go. Eventually he came inside her, a sad little moan confirming the completion of the act.

He had a quick wash in the bathroom got dressed and left in quite a hurry, obviously embarrassed by his inexperience. No arrangement was made to meet again, Mary decided that Robert was a little too naïve and unworldly to keep her interested.

It took a few months for the Manchester area to recover from the December bombings, it was just getting back on its feet when another disaster struck. The air raid siren went off just after midnight on 1 June 1941 and Mary headed straight to the Anderson Shelter. Once inside she was just settling down when Billy came in with a child wrapped in blanket.

"This is my son, Patrick," he explained. Looking down she could see that the child was half awake with a bewildered expression on his face. He was a chubby child with big red cheeks, Mary noted he was not the most handsome child she had ever seen.

It was difficult to sleep when all you could hear was the sound of explosions everywhere around you and they were all glad when after a couple of hours, the all clear sounded.

"Looks like we will be busy again," said Mary as Billy gathered up their belongings. Billy nodded and left to back into his house, while Mary just sat in the dark, wondering when it would all end. It was at this point she also realised she had not had a period for two months and her body was also giving her all the tell-tale signs that her that she was going to have a baby!

She emerged from the shelter suddenly stunned by the reality of her situation, she didn't need a doctor to tell her, she already knew. As she turned the key to her house, Billy shouted to her and crossed the road with little Patrick wrapped in a blanket.

"I have to go to Pendlebury, it's important, can you watch the boy for me?" It was more of a statement than a request and he pushed Patrick towards her and then sprinted to his truck, "I will be back as soon as I can."

"Of course, why the rush?"

"I will explain when I get back," with that he set off, the truck going faster than Mary had ever seen before.

After making them both some breakfast Mary went into the office, sat Patrick down in the corner with a pencil and some paper, then began her daily routine.

Billy returned in the afternoon, his face ashen. Mary could immediately see there was a problem and asked if he was ok.

"She's dead, his mother, she is dead," Billy bent down and picked his son up, hugging him tightly. "Her house was bombed last night, direct hit, no survivors."

Mary wasn't sure what to do, there was nothing she could say, so she sat there quietly as the tears flowed down Billy's cheeks. After ten minutes he put Patrick down, wiped his face and stood up.

"I always hoped she would come back, I never loved anyone else, never will. Now it's just me and my boy, but we will survive."

Mary could feel herself welling up, the whole range of emotion, the bombings, the realisation she was pregnant and now Billy's situation had become an avalanche that she was struggling to contain. After asking Billy if he had eaten and been told no, she took herself off to her own house to get herself together and make him something to eat. When she returned, she was more in control and told Billy to eat then go rest, which he did taking Patrick with him.

Mary then began to think of her own predicament and knew she needed to act soon. She was now 41 years old and this was probably her last chance at motherhood, so she was grateful for the opportunity, even though her future was so uncertain. She didn't want Robert involved, he was a wet lettuce and she knew he would never make her happy, so being a single mother was the only option.

The first thing she needed was confirmation, which she got the following week. The date was confirmed for 25 November, so she was now 14 weeks into her pregnancy. She knew she needed to let Billy know, she still had some savings but wasn't sure how long it would last and she would have to stop working at some point, even if only for a short while.

Billy had taken his ex-wife's death badly, he was still working as hard as ever but there was no spring in his step, no banter, no smiles, nothing. Mary was concerned about him and the effect it would have on Patrick, who was beginning to ask where his mother was. She was beginning to show now so decided she needed to let him know about the baby and wasn't sure what the outcome would be.

Her worries turned out to be unfounded, Billy was happy for her and wished her luck and crucially informing her that her job was not under threat, that he valued her as an office manager as well as a friend. Comforted by this, Mary started to accept her pregnancy and relaxed into her role as a mother in waiting.

As Mary got bigger, she was reluctant to attend the meetings at the council for fear of meeting Robert again, there was no chance of him being involved in her life, so she avoided going into the offices whenever she could.

But some meetings were inevitable and she soon found herself sat across from him at a planning committee meeting to discuss some restoration work. She tried to make sure she was first there and sat down before any of the others entered the room and stayed until last before leaving, so as to try and hide the ever-expanding baby bump. Unfortunately, on this occasion she didn't make it on time and as she entered the room Robert was already sat down, he looked at her and smiled, then looked down and as his eyes saw her size, the smile turned to that of a startled animal. He then looked down at the paperwork on his desk, where his gaze stayed for most of the meeting.

Robert's contribution for the meeting was minimal, as was Mary's and they were both glad to see the meeting closed. Mary was in a rush to leave, but Robert headed her off and asked her to remain as he had a couple of matters to discuss. When they were alone, he asked her how she was in a very diplomatic manner, trying not to discuss her obvious situation. Mary decided the only thing to do was confront the situation head on.

"It's not yours, if that's what you're thinking," Mary was determined to sort this out once and for all.

"How many weeks are you?" It was obvious Robert was trying to pin down her dates to see what the possibilities were.

Mary decided to lie, "I had already missed one period when we were together, I know who the father is and it's not you."

"Oh, ok, I just wanted to be sure. If it was mine, I would certainly have made sure I would be involved in its life and taken care of its future."

Robert was almost imploring Mary to say the child was his, but Mary was having none of it, "Very kind of you but I know who the father is and he is already involved, thank you. I am very busy so I will say good day to you." She then set off down the corridor, glad that this awkward encounter had been faced and resolved.

The bombing from the previous weeks had destroyed the Royal Salford Hospital and Billy was working there for a few weeks. Mary casually asked what remained of the hospital, to which Billy replied, "There's nothing left, it will have to be rebuilt. It's a shame about the number of staff losing their lives, apparently it has sent the head nurse crazy, they say she has completely lost her mind."

This comment grabbed Mary's attention. "How so, why is she crazy?"

"She just sits on a bench opposite all day just staring, doesn't move and doesn't speak."

Mary was a little startled at first, then realised that the previous experience Claire had endured during the Great War had obviously impacted on her reaction to the recent bombings, she decided she needed to speak with her.

Later that morning, after sorting out the paperwork and paying some invoices Mary took a cab to the Royal Salford. She was amazed at the devastation. As she stood on Adelphi Street surveying the scene, she could not help but be moved to tears at the thought of the hundreds of deaths inflicted. At the end of the street facing what was the main entrance to the hospital was a bench, sat on that bench was the tall figure of a slim woman that Mary recognised immediately, it was Claire.

She sat down next to her and slipped her hand into Claire's without saying anything, Claire just looked up and Mary's eyes met hers, lifeless eyes, her face showed no expression, no hint of recognition.

"Hello Claire, how are you?"

There was not a flicker of response, nothing registered, she just maintained the dead face and she obviously did not recognise who Mary was.

A passer by commented that she sat there every day in the same position and sometimes never went home.

"This woman is ill, why has nobody bothered to take care of her," Mary was furious, Claire had obviously not eaten for a long time and was painfully gaunt.

She took Claire home and found the door unlocked, she lay her down on her sofa, then went into the kitchen to prepare some food. There was very little food in the larder, which was to be expected as food was rationed, but what was there was rotten and mouldy, Claire had obviously not eaten properly for a long time.

She managed to make a cup of tea with some dried milk and found some dry egg so scraped together an omelette.

Still Claire said nothing, just staring at the floor as Mary spooned the omelette into her, trying to create, but failing, to make a conversation.

Eventually Mary managed to get her to eat it all then took her upstairs and undressed her and lay her on the bed. Her body was always thin, but now it was gaunt, almost skeletal, she had obviously been in this state for a number of months. Mary was furious. She got her into the bathroom, run the bath then bathed her, her body smelled of odour and urine, what used to be an immaculately groomed woman who took great pride in her appearance had turned into a living corpse.

After putting Claire to bed, where she promptly fell asleep, Mary took Claire's ration book and keys and locked her in the house for her own safety. Then she sought out the hospital management to see why nobody had addressed Claire's issues. She managed to track down Richard Grice in his office and asked him if he knew about Claire's plight. Mary knew Grice was not a nice person, but the response she got really rattled her.

"Matron was asked to leave as the hospital has been destroyed and there is no longer a position for her here. We offered her a temporary position in Oldham but the management board there felt that she was not of a fit state of mind to fulfil that role, so she was released," Grice showed no concern, no empathy for Claire's plight, in short, he did not care at all about Claire.

Mary was furious. "This woman went through hell in the trenches of the Great War and has now seen her hospital and many of her nurses killed, she is obviously a sick woman, why has nobody seen fit to take care of her needs?"

Grice was unmoved, "A great many people have suffered, there is only so much that we as a hospital board can do, perhaps she needs to be referred to an asylum, as she is clearly beyond normal health recovery methods. I am sorry but there is nothing more to discuss, I need to be somewhere else now, goodbye." He then asked her to close the door on her way out.

Mary called in to buy Claire some provisions then returned to make sure she was ok, before making her some supper. She had slept most of the day, Mary decided to prop her up and tried yet again to indulge in small talk, but yet again there was no response.

She needed to get back to the office, it was now dark and Billy would be wondering what was going on, so she made sure Claire was ok then went home.

When she got back Billy was unloading the lorry and sorting a few things out in the yard, she started to help, then explained about Claire and how she came to know her through the uniform work, omitting the personal details of their previous relationship. Then she got around to mentioning Grice and the comments he had made about Claire, Billy suddenly stopped what he was doing and turned around slowly.

"Do not under any circumstance piss that man off. AT ALL, UNDER ANY CIRCUMSTANCES, IS THAT CLEAR?" Billy's face was purple she had never known him that angry.

"Ok, ok, why, what's so special about him?" Mary was curious, why would Billy know such a slimeball anyway and why would he defend him so much?

"I can't explain now, just trust me, you don't want to upset him."

The following morning, Mary went to get Claire dressed and breakfasted, there was a barely audible whisper of a thank you as she put some bread in her hand and placed a cup of tea at her side. Once Claire was comfortable, she went the nursing home in Eccles to see what they could do for Claire. They were completely unaware of Claire's condition, but promised to find her a room and take care of her. Mary gave the address and returned to the yard.

She had been looking for someone to help in the office, but with one thing or another had not got around to it. She was now getting quite big, so this became a priority that needed immediate attention. She only had 13 weeks to go and she could not possibly keep up with everything without assistance.

The previous experience with Mac had taught her that she needed to fully check out any prospective employee, she was never going to put herself in that position again. An ad was placed in the Manchester Evening News and there was a substantial number of applicants. She wanted Billy involved in the interview process, as whoever was successful would need to get on with him. When she approached him, he was very reluctant, this was not an area he felt comfortable with, but reluctantly allowed her to read the applications to him and he would give his opinion.

They agreed to discuss it at her house the following evening, so Mary agreed to make some dinner for them. They sat down at the dining table and Mary produced a sheaf of applications. When Billy saw it, his eyes rolled. Mary saw this and explained she had had a quick look and most were unsuitable, did he want her to show him everything or just the ones Mary thought would be a good fit. Billy opted for the latter and within ten minutes the list was down to eight.

Mary read each application out loud and Billy would ask a couple of questions, but it was apparent he didn't have a clue about some of the work experience.

"What's the difference between a bookkeeper and a librarian?" He asked at one point. Mary soon realised that she would have to be the one to make the decision, but she went through the motions and whittled it down to three potentially suitable candidates, whose backgrounds were easily referenced.

They then relaxed and had dinner, Mary was always comfortable in Billy's presence, he was a good, kind-hearted man and very funny when he was on form.

The following morning, Mary set about sorting interviews, they both agreed that Mary was probably best left alone to sort out the final stages and so Billy went off to work. As he was leaving, he said, "Thank you for last night, the food was very good, we should do it again sometime."

Mary smiled. "Yes, we must." Then she realised it was a genuine compliment, after all he could hardly be after her fat bloated seven-month pregnant body.

Mary interviewed the following week insisting that references were supplied, but more important was the fact they had to be checkable. The successful applicant was Mrs Pauline Winters who had worked as an Office Clerk at Boddingtons Brewery for the last 18 years.

Her boss had recently retired and she could not get along with her new boss who was a colleague that had been promoted from another department. Wendy had hoped for the job and as she was unsuccessful, she felt there was a need for a change. When Mary asked why she thought she didn't get the job, Wendy chuckled, "Look at me, Love, I am fat and over forty, the new boss is 28 and knows how to use her slim sexy body to get her own way." This honesty tickled Mary, she immediately took a liking to her and offered her the job, subject to references, which proved to be totally genuine.

Wendy started work 2 weeks later and Mary could now relax a little and was looking forward to the birth.

Chapter Thirteen

David Knox arrived in the world at 3pm on the 18 November 1942, a week early and to a room full of concerned medical staff at Pendlebury hospital. Mary's previous miscarriage had caused some internal trauma and the only option available was a last minute Caesarion Section. As Mary lay there with her newborn son in her arms, she promised him he was going to have the best life ever and that she would never leave him, then after handing the baby over to the nurse, she promptly fell asleep.

When she awoke, she was fully aware of the pain in her stomach and feeling sick. She was asked to sit up and breastfeed, which was an immediate success.

Mary was suddenly overwhelmed, all manner of emotion going through her mind. She thought about her parents, her sister, Toni and all the heartache she had endured in her life, all the while Robert was suckling away without a care in the world. Looking down, she felt an immense sense of maternalism, nobody would ever get the chance to hurt her boy, who she named Davey after her father. It was at this point she realised just how alone in the world they were, she had no friends, no relatives to share her joy with. But she now had a purpose... To make sure her boy had the best she could give, no matter what she had to do to achieve it.

They stayed in hospital for the next week and then were allowed to go home. Before they left, the doctor told Mary she would not be able to have any more children, such was the damage caused, in fact they were amazed she managed to carry the baby as long as she did.

Mary recovered quickly and was able to visit the office in the week before Xmas. Wendy had settled in well and seemed to be on top of most things, but she had a query about a monthly invoice that puzzled her. It was for one hundred and twenty pounds a month to a firm called Malcolm Glazing Ltd. She knew where this firm was and they didn't appear to have the turnover to warrant such an amount. It was just a one-man band that was more a picture framing outfit than a construction business. Mary remembered how she had queried this with Billy as well, the amount was the same every month and never varied. Billy had told her it was for a loan he had taken out when he first arrived from Ireland and needed money to set up his business. Mary just accepted what he had said and thought no more of it. She told Wendy not to worry about it.

The day before Xmas Eve, Mary asked Billy what he was doing about Christmas lunch, Billy predictably said he hadn't even thought about it and Mary's offer to cook was readily accepted. The day itself was quiet, just the four of them. After lunch Billy opened a bottle of Irish whiskey that had been brought over by one of his lads from Ireland. Mary didn't like it, but drank it anyway diluted with a little water. About 6pm after Mary finished feeding and changing Davey, Billy put Patrick on the sofa and they both sat drinking and gradually emptying the bottle. Mary felt fulfilled now, she was quite content to just sit in front of the fire and feeling its warmth and glow.

Mary was the first to speak and asked Billy about his background, he had never really spoken about his past or his family to anyone. The whiskey loosened his tongue and he told of his rough upbringing in Cork and the effects on the family of his father's drunkenness, of how he became the main victim of his violence and how he ran away at fifteen years old and had virtually brought himself up, working on Construction Sites and developing his skills. His mother died a few years later and he had not seen his brothers or sisters since. It was a tragic tale and made Mary realise that life was hard for a lot of people, not just her.

He also told her about how he came to be working in the northwest and his trip over from Ireland. Mary listened intently, she was genuinely interested in his life, she commented that he had done well for himself and was in a very handsome financial position. This reminded her of Wendy's query about the invoice for Malcom Glazing, so she told him what she had said about the company being so small. Billy sat there and chuckled to himself, the whiskey was in his system now and he was a lot more mellow and open to talk.

"That invoice generates a lot of work for me, and you, and Wendy." This cryptic comment had Mary baffled. Before she could ask why, Billy told her the company was a dummy, it belonged to the person who allocated all the work to the various contractors for the War Damage Commission via the local various councils.

"But I don't understand, I attend all the meetings where work is agreed and I submit all the invoices as well, so what is the purpose of this dummy invoice," Mary was perplexed, nothing made sense.

"It's quite simple my dear, all the work is pre-allocated, the meetings are just to finalise, rubber stamp the works and then orders are raised."

Mary was completely baffled by now. "Who decides what work goes where and what is the purpose of the invoice?"

"It's quite simple, we make a one-hundred-and-twenty-pound payment to the main man at the Commission and he ensures we get a set amount of work every month. We all do it, there are at least six other companies paying every month. We pay it into Malcolm Glazing, it is a genuine company and nobody queries any payments. You sit in these meetings but the contracts are already sorted."

"Who is this man that controls everything, why have we never seen him?"

"You have seen him on several occasions, but he never gets involved on a day-to-day basis, his name is Richard Grice."

Mary jumped at the sound of his name, she knew the horrible Mr Grice was influential, but hadn't realised just how powerful he was.

Billy realised he had said more than he should, so when Davey woke up for a feed, He told Mary he needed to take Patrick home and go to bed, he was working the following day. He kissed Mary on the forehead and told her she need not come as well, there would not be much for her to do. Mary was still reeling from the news and after feeding and changing Davey promptly poured herself another glass from the nearly empty bottle and sat thinking in front of the fire, she was learning more about how the business world works with every day that passed.

By February 1943, most of the clearance work had been completed and things were returning to normal, but Billy was still as busy as ever. Mary was now back in the office and on Valentines Day, just as she was stepping out of her front door with Davey in her arms, there was a delivery of a beautiful bouquet of flowers for her, which was a total surprise and had her baffled as to who might have sent it. There was a message with the flowers that simply read 'dinner tonight, I will call at 7pm.'

The writing seemed familiar but she could not place it, this was a complete mystery. It couldn't be Billy, he was not the romantic type, anyway he couldn't read or write, so she concluded it was from Robert Johnson. She hoped not, she was not happy to be bringing up her child alone, but certainly didn't want him involved in her or Davey's life.

This irritated her no end and she was unable to concentrate on any work in the office, which Wendy noticed.

"You ok Mary?" Mary admitted she was not ok, she was totally perplexed, this was not the type of thing that happened to her.

"I can't be in when they call, I can only think of one person it might be and there is not a chance in the world I would have dinner with him," Mary was really getting worked up about this situation and told Wendy about Robert.

"You never know, it might be a handsome admirer who wants to whisk you away from all this," said Wendy flourishing her arms about and spinning in her chair.

"Not funny, this is worrying."

"Its only dinner, what harm can there be?"

Mary spent the rest of the morning checking and authorising orders and invoices and was just about to leave to get some lunch when Wendy asked her to check an entry she had put in the ledger. As she looked at the entry, it was clear as day that this was the same handwriting as was on the message. Looking up she could see Wendy smiling from ear to ear.

"You?" Wendy was giggling away.

"I had to promise I wouldn't tell you who it was from… and I haven't."

"Promise who?" then it dawned on her, it was from Billy, he had got her to write it.

Mary was even more confused now, why would Billy want to take her to dinner and why would he send her flowers, he wasn't the romantic type.

That night promptly at 7pm Mary opened the door to find Billy there with a bottle of cognac, some meat wrapped in paper along with a basket of vegetables.

"Ah," said Billy when he saw her standing there in her finest. "I think my message didn't come across as I wanted it to, I thought we could eat in as we had the kids to consider, so I bought everything for you to cook at home."

The day was getting even more crazy, Mary ushered him into the lounge where Wendy was sitting, as she had offered to babysit.

Billy walked in with his basket of goodies and placed them on the table. "I got the finest steak, I had to pull a few strings at the abattoir, but there's two lovely pieces of fillet."

Wendy took one look at Mary's confused face and couldn't help but fall about laughing. "Best take your posh dress off and get your pinny on, girl, I will leave you to it." She was struggling to put her coat on she was laughing so hard, then she waved and let herself out.

"Where's Patrick?" She suddenly realised that he was missing.

Billy laughed, "It's ok, he is with Tony Maloney's wife for the night."

Mary, still nonplussed, went upstairs and changed into something less formal, while Billy poured a couple of drinks. When she came down, he stood there smiling and handed her a large glass of cognac.

"What is all this about?" a confused Mary asked as she picked up the basket and walked to the kitchen.

"Can we eat first? I am starving, then I will explain." He looked a little nervous, Mary was also hungry and the meal was cooked in silence, all the time Mary was wondering what the hell was going on. They sat down to eat, Billy still looking nervous, Mary still looking perplexed. Mary did not particularly like cognac but it was a big improvement on the Irish whiskey, so she managed to finish the large glass Billy had poured.

Billy went to refresh the glass but Mary covered it with her hand and looking up at him asked, "What is going on Billy, this is totally unexpected, why are we here?"

Billy cleared his throat and unable to look her in the eye, his eyes dropped to look at his meal, then with a trembling voice he started to explain, "I am not the most romantic man. I am not someone who finds the company of women easy. You are a fine woman, someone who is smart, someone that any man would be proud to have at their side. We work well together, we are both alone, we both have responsibilities and we both deserve to have a decent future. I would like to have that future with you." He then lifted his head and looked her in the eye. "I am not the smartest, but I think I am a good man, I also think I can make you happy… will you marry me?"

Mary sat there with mouth open, her expression was that of a startled rabbit, her mind not quite apprehending what was going on. After a short pause, she stuttered.

"Erm, ah, wow, erm, I wasn't expecting that, you have really surprised me, I don't know what to say."

Billy then went on, "I understand how you feel, I only came up with the idea the other week, just seems like a good plan for both of us."

Mary then started laughing. "A good plan, you think it's a good plan?" This was getting surreal, was she dreaming all this?

Billy then explained his logic, he explained how they both needed each other, they work closely together, they have a responsibility to their own children, Patrick needs a mother and Davey needs a father. They got on well, he realised she didn't love him but this was about practicalities. Finally, he said that if she agreed, she could have her own bedroom. He admitted he was not a sexual person and just wanted love and companionship, but he did have a great affection for her.

Mary listened intently, a lot of what he said was true and it would make sense, but she still couldn't digest it all, this was too much too soon.

"Thank you, Billy, you are a good man, there is no doubt about that. I was not expecting this, you have never given any indication of any feelings for me. I don't know what to say."

"Ok, I understand it's a lot to think about, don't hurry with your decision, just let me know when you are ready with your answer."

The next ten minutes were very tense, neither speaking, neither finishing their meal, finally Mary reached over and poured herself a large glass of cognac, topping Billy's up at the same time.

As she cleared the table, Billy stood up and said, "Right then, I'll be off, see you tomorrow," almost as if the monumental conversation had never taken place.

Mary put the plates down and walked towards him, "Thank you Billy, it's a fantastic offer from you, but this is not an answer I can give you tonight." She then hugged him closely and was surprised at how emotional she felt.

Almost on cue, Davey then woke up crying and Mary had to attend to him.

Billy then stroked Davey's face, "He is a fine strong lad; you will make him proud."

Mary cleaned and fed Davey then sat in front of the fire and contemplated what had occurred, still not sure what her decision was going to be.

The following morning Wendy was already in the office when Mary arrived and as she placed Davey in the crib next to her desk, she was desperate to find out what had happened.

"Well?"

"Well, what?"

"What happened last night, Billy was out of here like a Greyhound out of a trap this morning, there was smoke coming off his wheels," Wendy was smirking away, the suspense was killing her.

"Stop being a nosey old mare, I am sure you have got work to do," Mary snapped, she wasn't going to share her private moments with her staff.

Wendy looked surprised, then without speaking returned to the pile of paperwork on her desk and they both worked away quietly with not a word being spoked for the rest of the morning, Mary not being able to concentrate and Wendy upset at the abruptness of Mary towards her. Finally, Mary broke the silence.

"I am sorry, I have been made an offer I don't know how to react to and its playing on my mind," Wendy went to make a cup of tea and when she returned offered Mary some advice.

"Sometimes we need to need to talk and get an alternative perspective, sometimes we cannot see what is right or wrong. Whatever it is, I will always listen, I am not the brightest button in the box, but I might still be able to help."

Mary knew she was right, if she had family she would have talked it through with them, but she didn't, she needed to find a voice to listen to and Wendy was the closest thing to s friend she had.

"Ok, but not now, can you come to the house after work?" She didn't want this discussion to be in the office in case Billy came back, it could take some time to walk through this minefield of emotion.

Billy came back about 5:15 just as they were locking up and popped his head through the door. "How are we ladies, been a busy day?" Without waiting for an answer, he headed back out to the yard.

They locked up and crossed the yard to Mary's house. After putting the kettle on to boil, Mary explained everything about the previous night. When she had finished Wendy took a deep breath and exhaled. "Well, that was an eventful night, What's your answer?"

"That's the problem—I don't know what the answer is," Mary then went on to say she knew it made sense from a practical point of view to marry Billy that he was a good man, they both need a parent for their children and it was financially a good move. "Well, that's all the good points, now what's the bad points?"

Mary suddenly realised the good far outweighed the bad, "But I don't love him, I have never thought about him as lover or husband material."

"Listen Mary, I have been married for 24 years, when we first got together it was all love and roses, but bit by bit, year by year, the realities of life take over and love takes a back seat. Your future and your son's future can be secure, love may or may not follow, but I do not think love is the answer to everything. I love my husband but am not in love with him, if that makes sense."

Mary suddenly thought back to Sophia and her comment about 'All of your future is because of your past' and realised what she meant. Her past had been difficult and she owed a duty to her son to make sure that everything that had gone on previously was not forgotten, but that lessons were learnt for the future. She had never had the same opportunity her son now had, everything now had to be make sure his life was the best possible.

Wendy wasn't finished yet, "There's more good than bad can come out of marrying Billy, if you say no, what will the future hold?"

Wendy was right, it would be the right thing to do, she had now made her mind up, she was ready to become Mrs Reddy.

The wedding took place on Saturday, 17 April 1943 at Pendlebury Registry office, a small affair with just the bride and groom, 2 children and Wendy, her husband, Tony Maloney and wife as witnesses. This was followed by drinks in the local pub, then back to the house for a meal and a few more beers and some Irish whiskey. Rationing meant that a lavish spread was out of the question.

At the end of the night, they were finally alone with the children, Billy had taken in a few beers too many and was wobbling a little.

"Which room will I stay in? You don't have to sleep with me if you don't wish it?" Billy said.

"Don't be a fool, Billy, we are man and wife now, you will sleep in my bed." She then ushered him upstairs where he promptly fell asleep. But Mary was unable to settle, the grunting and snoring that Billy let out was so loud that sleep was impossible. What the hell have I done, she thought as the incessant noise emitting from the other side of the bed was overwhelming.

Davey woke up at 5:30, which was a blessing, so she got up and fed him, she then made a cup of tea and relaxed in the chair and dozed for an hour before being woken up by Billy.

"Good morning my dear, that was a fine night's sleep I got there," Billy was up bright and breezy.

Mary just shot him a dirty look, which he noticed. "Ah, I was snoring a bit, was I? don't worry, that only happens when I get drunk."

What a start to a marriage, thought Mary, things have got to improve if this is to succeed.

Over the next few months, things didn't improve as Billy drank most nights, so eventually he was banished to another room and the boys finished up sharing. Billy seemed quite happy with this arrangement, his feeble attempts at lovemaking had consummated the marriage, but he was no stallion in the bedroom. Mary too had lost her Libido; the effects of the birth had left her dry and she was uncomfortable with her body now she had a large scar across her stomach. They both settled into this arrangement and concentrated on putting their energies into the business. For Billy, it was because that's all he was good at, for Mary it was to ensure sure Davey's future.

Chapter Fourteen

Eventually the war ended and Britain concentrated on rebuilding the nation, especially in the area of housing.

Patrick was now in school and Davey was an inquisitive toddler that demanded a lot of attention.

Reddy Construction was thriving, they had been awarded a lot of contracts, refurbishing areas of Liverpool after the main Manchester work was over. Mary didn't ask how Billy had managed to acquire this work, but the payments to Malcolm Glazing Limited continued so she figured Mr Grice was still pulling the strings.

There was a great demand for new housing after the war, no new houses were built during the war period and there was now a hunger to demolish old Victorian streets and replace them with modern housing. The government allocated massive funds to local authorities and a massive rebuilding programme developed.

Throughout the northwest large areas of green fields were allocated for new housing projects and building whole communities, Billy was being given a lot of work but it was impossible to expand from where they were now and they needed more workers if they wanted to become bigger. Mary could see the possibility and they discussed it, but Mary was reluctant to get into debt to do it. She knew full well what could happen if they defaulted on a loan.

Billy was keen though and after yet another discussion in which Mary stated her reluctance, he grabbed her hand and said, "Come on, got something to show you." He took her down to the yard and opened the door that he had previously said contained specialist tools. He dragged a large box out and opened it. As Mary peered inside, she was amazed, it was crammed full of gold rings, watches, chains, all sorts of valuables.

"What the hell is this, where has this come from?" She was staggered.

"That's not all, come and see this." He opened the door fully and there were paintings, candelabras, statuettes, all kinds of artwork inside.

Mary stood there totally amazed. "Where's it come from?"

"This is the part you might not like, I call it the spoils of war, you might call it something different. When we were called in to prop buildings up or even demolish them, there was quite often a chest of drawers or a cupboard or table that wasn't damaged, but would have got buried after demolition, so I saved it, well the contents anyway."

Billy looked sheepish as he told of the source of this new found treasure.

"You mean you stole it," Mary was shocked, a little bit of deception was one thing, this was outright theft.

"It would have been lost anyway and the insurance would pay out on. Someone else would have claimed it, so I just look on it as good fortune."

"What's it worth?" asked Mary still in a state of shock.

"A lot of money, I don't know how much, shall we get it all out and see," Billy was completely calm about it all, Mary on the other hand knew that the penalty for looting was a prison punishment and she did not want to be involved at all.

"Just put it back, if anyone sees this, we are doomed."

They put everything back and Billy locked up, then went into the house. Mary was shaking, she was frightened, this was a serious situation.

Billy then explained, "I can't take it back as I don't know where it all came from. The people who it belonged to have probably written it off anyway as most of the houses were flattened. Especially the ones in Liverpool." Billy was still very calm about it all.

Mary had a sleepless night, she knew Billy was right about not being able to return it, he would be arrested and nobody would get their goods back anyway unless they had absolute proof of ownership. They did need the money and there was a lot of money in that room. The following morning over breakfast she asked how he would dispose of it all if he could sell it.

"Already thought of that, anything with a jewel would be separated, I have a friend in Birmingham who will buy scrap gold and another from the jewellery quarter in another part of town who would buy the diamonds, emeralds, etc. All we got to do is split them and drive down there."

Billy sounded quite confident and what he said made sense, it would be too risky to try and get rid of them locally. Her moral compass was telling her this was all wrong, but her financial mind was thinking about becoming a bigger company.

"How much could you get for it all?"

"Enough for a bigger yard, two new trucks and a crane. The future is in precast building and a crane would be a must buy."

"Ok, let's just see how much there is once we have split them, we can do it tonight after work," Mary's greed was winning, she convinced herself this was for Davey's future.

That night Billy dragged the box into the house and placed it on the floor next to the table, it was heavy and as most of it was gold it looked like a good haul. Most of the jewellery came from big houses of wealthy families in Liverpool, old wealth founded from the boom times of shipping between Britain and America.

He grabbed a handful and spread it out on the table, Mary could see some of it was very valuable, she was beginning to have second thoughts.

Billy started to prise diamonds from their clasps and separated them, putting the gold back into another box on the floor. At first Mary just sat there and was unable to handle anything, but eventually picked up a gold necklace with a large Sapphire, surrounded by Burmese rubies in the centre.

"This is sensational, it's a pity to sell it as scrap."

"We have to, it would be traceable otherwise." Then Billy nodded at her to make a start.

It took nearly two hours and at the end there was a big pile of scrap gold in the box and about 60 jewels of varying type size and quality on a plate. They then divided the gold into to piles 9 carat and 18 carats Mary didn't have a clue how much it was worth so asked Billy, "I reckon there's enough here to sort out a new yard, buy a crane and get a decent size lorry, but don't know much about jewels so not quite sure."

Mary was feeling less guilty by now, this could really make a difference to their life, so she was prepared to go along with it. They put everything back in the yard and locked up, but Mary still didn't sleep easy that night.

The following day, Billy rang his contact in Birmingham and arranged to go down at the weekend. He caught the train and was back later the same evening. It was a successful trip and resulting in over six hundred pounds for the gold and 1900 for the jewels, He also informed her of a sale of ex-military vehicles at Burtonwood airfield. But before they could buy new equipment, they needed a new yard as the present one was too small to hold any equipment for large scale projects. They eventually settled on a disused farm on the outskirts of Liverpool which was strategically well placed to cover both the Manchester and Liverpool areas. It was little more than a field with a farmhouse with a couple of outbuildings.

It was in a sorry state and a lot of refurbishment work was required. But it did have one advantage, there was 200 acres of land close to the road networks. Mary knew that you couldn't build on this land so queried why they bought it, but Billy assured her that a lot of changes of legislation was coming in that would allow houses to be built, not yet, but sometime in the next couple of years. Mary was aware there was talk of this but nothing had been confirmed.

The next few months were spent sorting out the roadway to the farm, widening it so trucks could enter freely. The workshop was created in the barn and the farmhouse split into offices at the rear and storage at the front. There was also a freestanding outbuilding that was converted into a house and the Reddy's moved into it in the summer of 1947. Billy's yard and the house were kept on as there was still work to be carried out and a local yard was needed, but the house was locked up and secured. All the artwork, statues, etc, were transferred to an upstairs bedroom, which Mary wasn't happy about, she would rather they were disposed of.

As Billy had forecast the work was coming through thick and fast, there were new developments everywhere, the move paid off as there was work in both Liverpool and Manchester. They hired extra labour locally and set up two teams both with their own foremen, Billy was running about like a madman and the amount of money flowing through the company was becoming substantial.

The building methods also changed, the emphasis was on building houses as quickly and cheaply as possible and the company began to hire Surveyors and take on teams that were familiar with what came to be known as 'system-built' properties. The system-built method was proving very lucrative, Houses were simpler to build, a lot were single storey with pre-built walls that were factory made, then bolted together on site.

This was all becoming too complicated for Mary so she left the meetings to the experts and took a position that was looking at an overview of the big picture, which she quite enjoyed. But at the back of her mind loomed the bad experience with Mac, so she was constantly asking questions and probing, trusting nobody.

Billy on the other hand was like a madman, he was very much hands-on and driving himself forward every single day.

There were now 8 people working in the offices, Wendy had stayed on and was now the office manager. She had separated from her husband and had decided she would move with the company, so took a small cottage a couple of miles up the road where she would cycle to work every day. Mary had her own office and all major decisions had to be run by her.

Davey was thriving, he had just started school and Mary dropped both boys off and collected them from the local primary school every day. Patrick was struggling however, he was now seven but could not write his own name or read, he was struggling just as Billy had done all his life. When Mary mentioned this to Billy, he just shrugged, "We are all like that in my family, it's in the blood, don't worry about it, we can always find something for him to do around here when he leaves school."

They now had a full time accountant who had his own office next to Mary, he advised that they were now too big and needed to be restructured, so after discussions between Mary and Billy the business was renamed as Reddox Construction Ltd with Billy keeping 51% and Mary getting the other 49%. Reddox being the first 4 letters of Billy's surname and the last 2 of Mary's. They also formed a board with Billy as honorary president, with no real office responsibilities, which suited him. Mary was appointed as Chief Executive Officer (CEO) and they also recruited a new finance director and operations director responsible for all construction elements.

Just before Easter 1948 Mary was sat in her office looking at a contract that needed to be signed off, when the accountant George Kay came into the office with an invoice in his hand. It was for Malcom Glazing and was in the sum of two thousand pounds. "Hello Mary, sorry to bother you but this company keeps appearing and I can't trace what work they do or what this is for. I checked previous payments and they were fairly steady regular payment s but this is quite large. I spoke to Wendy and she said to speak with you."

Mary looked at the paper and told George she would get back to him, so just leave it with her. After George had gone, she went out into the yard to look for Billy, but was told he had gone to Liverpool, he was spending a lot of time over there. When he returned later that day, she caught him in the workshop and showed him the invoice.

"Oh, yeah, I meant to talk to you about that," was Billy's response.

"Its 2000 pounds, why the hell are we doing giving him 2,000 pounds." Mary was not happy, Grice was still about and she hated him.

"Well, it's like this, you pay for what you get and we have just got not one, but 2 big rewards for this money," Billy seemed totally unconcerned.

He then showed her outside to the fencing next to the fields, He faced the fields and with arms outstretched said, "Remember when we bought this, I said one day we can build on this land, well the outline authorisation will get approved at the next planning meeting and then we can submit a planning application. Just imagine, on this land we will be able to build 1000 houses."

Putting his arm around her he whispered, "That's not all, there is a large expansion of housing development to be erected in the Wythenshawe area of Manchester, another 4000 houses, guess who will win the contract?"

This was really big news, it would mean another complete review of the whole company, Mary was worried they might be getting too big and not be able to handle it, but Billy had complete faith in both his own ability to get the work completed, but also Mary's ability to ensure the overall running of the company was smooth and efficient.

It was a difficult time as they could not divulge what they knew to the Surveying and Construction Teams, they could only go through the motions and wait until it was formally announced. Mary attended the more important meetings just to make sure that everything was to her satisfaction, she was quite pleased because the recruitment had gone well and these were serious professionals who knew their stuff, everything was looking good. Eventually contracts were signed for the Wythenshawe contract and work proceeded in the spring of 1950. A temporary office was set up on site and Billy spent a lot of time here.

The planning application for the farm land eventually went through and Mary had concerns that they would be living on a building site, so they agreed they would buy another house and move away. The accountants informed them they could buy a large house and class it as the office providing office facilities were present. When Mary asked how much they could spend she was told it didn't really matter as it was a tax-deductible expense for the company. Billy said he would leave it entirely to Mary to sort out as he was too busy. After much searching around She finally found a large Georgian detached house in its own grounds on the outskirts of Northwich. It was an impressive building, 6 bedrooms, a massive kitchen, 2 large reception rooms, with a large front and even bigger back garden. Mary pinched herself, could this be really true? Billy too was impressed, it was in a great location and office space could be discretely provided without impacting on the building as a home. There was a coach house and stables at the rear of the building, which were of a good size and easily converted. The move went ahead over the following weeks.

The dividends from the company were providing a very good income for Billy and Mary, so she registered both boys at a local private school, their education was a priority. While Davey was high flying and getting really good results, Patrick was still struggling. Eventually the school called Mary in and informed him that in their opinion he suffered from word blindness (today that is known as dyslexia) and he needed to be referred to a doctor for confirmation. This was duly done and confirmed, however, Billy still didn't seem bothered about it.

"Not telling me anything I didn't know," was all he could say.

The house was a lot larger than the farmhouse and Mary told Billy she was going to look for some new furniture, Billy just nodded, he wasn't very materialistic so didn't really care one way or another. Mary purchased some new sofas and beds; she was loving it. The boys now had a bedroom each so they were allowed to contribute as to what they wanted. She made sure that Davey had a desk and pens, pencils, paper etc and that she kept his mind occupied. Patrick on the other hand just wanted toys.

One Sunday morning, Mary was relaxing at home, Billy had gone to work and she was alone in one of the lounges reading a magazine. Suddenly she heard the sound of a motor coming up the drive, so she put the magazine down and opened the front door. A van appeared and out jumped Billy; he was alone. He usually worked 7 days a week and came home covered in mud, today however he was quite clean.

"Got some presents for you," he stated in a matter-of-fact manner.

"I like presents, what is it?" as she walked around to the back doors. As Billy opened the doors, her heart skipped a beat. Inside was all the stolen statues, artwork etc. that Billy had acquired and had been stored in the house.

"I have decided we need some office space at the yard, so will be using the house. You said you need to fill this place, so here we are… all for you," Billy was grinning, Mary was mortified. "You can't bring that here, its stolen goods, we will go to jail." With that, she slammed the doors shut. "Take it back, it's not coming in here."

"I can't, the lads are knocking walls through right now, I managed to load up before they got on site. There's nowhere to put them, they got to stay here."

Mary was starting to panic, so Billy tried to calm her down. "I will put them in the cellar and make sure they are securely locked up. I will get rid of them in the next couple of weeks."

He was still calm, Mary knew they didn't really have any option.

"I want them gone in the next two weeks," she stated, turning back towards the house. Billy never got around to selling the items and so Mary insisted he brick up the doorway so nobody would know they were there, but it was never done. Instead, a strong lock was put on the door and they never went near it again.

The Wythenshawe contract was completed on time and to budget, The Reddy's were now a wealthy couple, but an odd couple. They remained in separate bedrooms, Billy still a workaholic and Mary now settling into a nice routine as wife, mother and business partner. The first 2 elements were easy but she always had worries about the business side of things and kept her finger very firmly on the pulse, spending time in all departments looking for faults, flaws or more importantly deceptions. She hadn't found anything of concern, but she was never going to let up, this was her boy's future.

Halfway through the farm project, they made the decision to demolish the farm and build new properties on it they could get another 20 houses on the site. Initially they were refused permission but eventually, once a sum of money had been gifted to the planning officer, it all went through and another profitable venture was concluded.

It was now 1953 and councils were building houses everywhere, things had never been so good. Liverpool council in particular were very busy and new Estates were springing up everywhere, system-built properties were now the accepted norm. Redox were invited to attend meetings about some more work, by now they were a well-respected company with a good reputation. Mary tended to get involved at the initial stage of every project, just so that she understood what was involved and who were the main representatives of the various councils. After that she stood back and let the management team take over and run with the day-to-day stuff. There were regular office meetings and she always made sure she followed expenditure to ensure things were running smoothly.

Billy very rarely attended these meetings, he was kept up to date by Grice and already knew what work was coming their way, so wasn't really interested in the detail.

By the summer of 1955 the company was running at full speed and they were looking at setting up a permanent second office in Kirkby and leave the house as the flagship headquarters, which it was already as there wasn't any work being carried out from there. Mary and one of the Surveyors spent a few weeks travelling around the Merseyside area looking for a suitable site, when they found an ideal spot on a disused airfield. When Mary asked about buying some of the land, she discovered that the whole airfield was up for sale at a very reasonable price. She made a few phone calls to various contacts and discovered that planning permission would automatically be granted as it created employment in the area.

The new office would only take up about 10% of the area, so she asked about what they would be able to do with the rest of the land. Mary was thinking about it being land for houses, but when she was told that it may be allocated as housing, but they would likely get automatic permission if it was for business use. This made Mary think, there were hangars and very large buildings on site, these could be adapted very cheaply and there was plenty of space to build extra units. It was a no-brainer, so the land was purchased.

The prefabricated modules meant that once they had produced drawings they could also get an office designed using the same formula. After visiting the factory that produced the modules and agreeing a design the office was prefabricated and built in record time. The drawings were used as a template for the other units and another 20 offices were built to the same design. With the hangar and outbuilding refurbishments, it meant that 28 new offices in total went on the site. The position was strategically good as the Liverpool road network was expanding and it was a good catchment area for business. Rather than sell the units it was decided to rent them out. Thus, another arm to Reddox Construction was created.

This proved to be very profitable, business rents were always higher and a good long-term income was established. Previously they had only been concerned with domestic dwellings but from now on they made sure Reddox was allowed to tender for the ancillary works to an estate such as new shops, school, medical centres, etc. These were managed separately and Richard Grice was not involved so they won some and lost some, but they were still getting plenty of work.

This expansion was such that it was impossible for Billy to be totally hands-on, they had a team that was very good and he couldn't get his head around the fact that although they had never been busier, he was surplus to requirements. There were constant improvements in working methods, Billy's old time skills were only really in demand at a basic level, he was getting really frustrated. Mary said he should slow down, he wasn't getting any younger. She encouraged him to ease up but he wasn't having it and used to get very angry, so Mary let him be. He had a habit of just turning up on site and barking orders to the lads on site, which frustrated and irritated the Site Managers.

One of these meetings resulted in an argument with one of the groundworkers who was working and doing as he was told by his manager, but Billy turned up and told this lad to go somewhere else. This resulted in a very heated argument with the Site Manager who told Billy to fuck off home, he was just a nuisance. Not the best thing to say to the boss and Billy sacked him on the spot. There was then an even bigger argument in which Billy suddenly collapsed holding his chest and blacked out.

He woke up in hospital with Mary sat by the side of the bed holding his hand.

"What happened?" Billy had no recollection at all of what had happened.

"You have had a heart attack; the doctors were working on you all day yesterday. You died twice," Mary was close to tears as she recalled yesterday's events. Billy was still not fully conscious and could not fully comprehend the magnitude of what had happened.

"Give me a couple of days and I will be ok."

"We will talk about that when we get you home, for now you need rest. The doctors want to carry out more tests, so you will be here for a couple of weeks more," Mary knew the that Billy would hate the thought of not working.

Two weeks later, Billy was back home and making life hell about the house. He kept on muttering about the fact he was only 60 and had worked his whole life. This was beginning to irritate Mary. They had been married 13 years and although it was basically a marriage of convenience, they did love each other in more of a brother and sister relationship than man and wife.

Over the next 2 months, boredom got the better of Billy. Mary banned him from work and with all the extra time on his hands he began to drink more despite the health warnings from the doctor and Mary. He then had a second attack and was back in hospital for a month this time. The doctors told Mary his heart was in a very bad condition and that another attack would probably kill him.

Billy could hardly walk now, as well as the heart condition, his body breaking down, all the years on building sites had resulted in severe arthritis throughout his body, he was going downhill fast.

Life at Reddox was still busy, the board met every month and reported on what was live work and what was in the pipeline. The main revenue stream was the local council work and while they were currently busy it looked as though there would be a reduction of work over the next year or so. Mary queried this and was told that for some reason they had stopped being the preferred contractor and had lost a few tenders recently. They had checked the costs involved and they were still as competitive as ever, it didn't make sense.

As soon as the meeting was over, Mary sought out George Kay and asked if they were still paying Malcom Glazing. "Yes, it's a standard order, they invoice every month and it gets paid immediately."

Mary didn't want to bother Billy so she sought out Richard Grice and after a couple of days, managed to get to see him in his office.

"Mrs Reddy, how are you, you have come a long way over the last few years," Richard Grice sat back in his chair puffing away on a large cigar, he never asked about Billy, just stared at her through thick lensed glasses.

"I am here to query why there appears to be a drop in the amount of work we are being allocated for next year." Mary was in no mood for small talk with this vile person.

Grice stopped puffing and leaned forward, "My dear, why would I know the reason for that?"

"Because we pay you a 'Consultancy fee' to ensure we are given preferential treatment. My husband tells me everything. I have checked and Malcom Glazing are still receiving the same amount every month." As Mary spoke Grice winced, he was not happy that his private dealings were known.

"There are others that feel my contribution to the housing sector need to be better rewarded. But as your husband is not here, I cannot discuss it with him."

Grice was getting irritated now. Mary was also not happy.

"Well, I am here now, you can discuss it with me," Mary stared at him until Grice dropped his head.

"Sorry but I am happy with my new arrangements and most of the work has now been tendered. We did give you a couple of schemes to work, but I appreciate it is less than before and less than you were expecting, but that's business for you."

Grice smiled displaying his yellow tobacco-stained teeth.

"If that is all then please give my regards to your husband, I take it he is still alive."

Mary tried to keep calm; she knew Grice was deliberately trying to get her angry. "No, that is not all, I haven't finished yet. My husband is a very sick man and is unlikely to live more than a couple of years at best. I am now responsible for Reddox Construction and I want the previous arrangement you had with my husband to continue through me."

"Impossible, I am not dealing with you, my relationship was with him, we both understood each other." Grice was ruffled, he did not trust Mary and had other contractors already lined up.

Mary was not giving up. "I really think you need to consider. I will not put my husband in jeopardy, but when he dies then we have a scenario where if someone decides to inform the police and local authorities that bribery and corruption were responsible for who built all these houses and all the money that went to Malcom Glazing Ltd for consultancy fees, then prison sentences would surely follow. My husband would be dead so they can't prosecute him… but you on the other hand…"

"Don't you threaten me, you fucking jumped-up seamstress, I am a man of influence and could destroy you." Grice's face was screwed up spit coming out of his mouth.

"Yes, a man of influence, but what use is influence in a prison cell," Mary was in control now—her calmness had paid off, he was on the backfoot.

"That would ruin your company as well, you won't risk that," Grice was still raging.

Mary was determined to make Grice squeal, "My husband would be dead; he can't be prosecuted. Reddox will survive we have a lot of different spheres of work, yes it will hurt, but nobody will go to jail. I am but a bystander so they won't come for me. Even if it destroyed the company, I am a very wealthy woman now and have all I need, but if that happens then I will make sure every resource at my disposal will be used to lock you up."

Grice was trembling with rage but they both knew he was defeated, so Mary gave him an ultimatum, "We will raise the payments by 10%, but I expect that over the next few months that our workload will increase to previous levels. I know there is more work in the pipeline, you just decided not to make us aware of it. Reddox Construction look forward to resuming our mutually profitable relationship, good day to you."

Then, without waiting for a response she headed out of the door.

Sure, enough over the next 3 months, the contracts were restored to previous levels, leaving the Operations Director scratching his head at how there had been this lull in the first place.

Billy's health was deteriorating and Mary was now waiting for the inevitable, she was just as concerned for Patrick, who adored his father. He was always going to struggle through life and without a father figure life would be even harder. He was now 18 and they gave him a job working on sites. Office work was out of the question, but he was a big lad and using his hands on site was the only outcome, but as the boss's son he came in for a lot of ridicule, it was a difficult decision to make but realistically it was the only one.

As Billy got worse, they knew he needed to make a will as the inevitable was not too far away. Because of the structure of the company and there only being two shareholders involved it was agreed that Mary would be given Billy's share, except for 10% which was to be held in trust for Patrick until he was 25, with Mary becoming the executor of the trust. Billy made Mary swear she would always take care of Patrick and guide him through life, which Mary promised but she would have done anyway, Patrick was family. This meant that on Billy's death Mary would have 90% and Patrick the remainder. Mary decided to give 10% of her shares to Davey in trust as well to balance things up.

Billy lasted another 8 months and passed away in the summer of June '59. He didn't want a fuss, but they were now a prominent company and there were representatives from all areas of business mainly, there were very few there on a personal level, mainly colleagues he had worked with over the years from Ireland. Mary had tried to locate relatives but gave up when it was apparent Billy had long ago severed all ties with his home country.

Patrick was obviously upset and very quiet, just stared out of the window all the way to the crematorium. He didn't speak for most of the day, Mary decided to leave him alone and speak to him tomorrow. He didn't speak much at the best of times and Davey wasn't close to him. They had been together all of Davey's life, but they were never close as brothers. Davey liked spending time socialising at the local youth club, he also played cricket for the school and was very popular and starting to get interested in girls. Patrick was very much a loner, they were complete opposites. Davey did invite Patrick along on a couple of occasions, but when he did go, he just sat in a corner and never mixed. Eventually Davey told Mary he didn't want to go there with Patrick, apparently, he liked to put his hand up girls' skirts. This was later confirmed when Mary got a phone call from the youth club to say Patrick wasn't welcome anymore.

After the funeral and they were alone back at the house Davey asked about his real father, he knew he was not Billy's. Mary was a little surprised at this and was unprepared.

"Your father was a clever man, a handsome man, we had a brief relationship but we were not really compatible and we agreed that marriage wouldn't work between us," was the best she could come up with, Davey sensed this was not the time so didn't say anymore, but he was curious his mother had never mentioned him in all his 16 years.

Mary didn't enter Billy's room until a week later, except to strip the bed. When she did go in, she was surprised at how little possessions he actually had. There was just one wardrobe that was half full and a lot of the things in there he had owned for years. The chest of drawers was not exactly full either, just some underwear and a few socks. In one of the top drawers there was all sorts of bits and pieces, a watch, pair of cufflinks, a few keys and some cash. She closed this drawer and emptied the rest into a case and put it down in the cellar out of the way. It wasn't valuable and she wasn't sure what to do with it.

When she was in the cellar the locked door at the end reminded her of the Art work inside and she needed to get rid of these as well at some point, she didn't want them hanging about.

Life gradually got back in order and nothing was really changing in the world of Reddox Construction. Some of the Managers were a little relieved that Billy wasn't about to disrupt things but they dare not say anything. It was now the school holidays and Davey was made to work for the first time in his life. Mary had made her mind up that as this company would one day be his he needed to be able to understand how it worked and the sooner the better. He was due to study for his 'A' levels over the next two years, so Mary wanted him to get some work experience in first.

Patrick had by now passed his driving test so he was now just delivering materials and equipment to and from site every day, which suited him to the ground.

Davey was put in a site office in Maghull shadowing the manager and getting to learn the ropes from a hands-on point of view. He spent all the summer there and loved every minute of it. He even asked if he could give up his studying, but Mary was never going to allow that to happen. Davey was so keen that every school holiday was spent at work, he was popular and very adaptable.

Eventually he passed his 'A' levels with top marks, the reward for which was a brand new Mini and driving lessons to go with it. At first Davey wasn't too keen. He was now six foot tall and it was a bit cramped, but gradually the sense of freedom won him over. Mary didn't want him to get a bigger car until he was confident on the road, so the Mini was a sensible option.

Mary knew that Patrick would be jealous so dipped into his trust fund and bought him a Triumph Herald for 700 pounds, which delighted Patrick, but annoyed Davey. She had to explain that Patrick had a few years driving experience and that Davey could buy whatever he wanted in a couple of years, but for now the Mini was a good fit.

It was now 1961 and Davey was going to university. He had plenty of options, because of his excellent grades. Eventually he settled on Bristol University, Mary wanted him to select somewhere local, there were plenty of options in the northwest but Davey was ready to spread his wings and wanted to get away. Mary still wanted to see what the area was like and had said she would buy a small property for him to live in. This annoyed Davey he was looking for some fun and wanted to mix, he had heard great things about Bristol social life and wanted to party, so he put his foot down.

"No Mum, I want to live with other students, I don't want to be seen as an outsider." He was adamant, so Mary backed off and said nothing. He was growing up and she just had to accept it. It was a difficult day for Mary when Davey loaded up his little car and sped off down the A6 heading southwards to a new life. She felt a knot in her stomach, but knew he had to do it.

There was still Patrick to consider and she now began to think about his future. She had promised Billy she would look after him, but how far does that extend? She didn't want him under her feet for the rest of her life, but he severely lacked social skills and didn't show any intention of moving out in the short term. She needed to think about what was for the best.

He was ok for work, he was earning good money and he was also getting the dividend from the profits being paid into his trust. He was quite a wealthy young man, but Mary wasn't sure how he would handle it. He had another 2 years before it was all handed over to him, so Mary needed to think carefully. She eventually decided he needed a degree of independence but be close enough for her to keep an eye on him. She sat down and asked his thoughts for the future, but was met with a blank stare and a shrug… He was definitely Billy's son.

She asked if he would like his own house nearby, they could fit it out with his own design of furniture and Mary would call in now and again to keep an eye on him. This seemed to please Patrick so she arranged to see if there was anything suitable in the immediate area. He said he would like a small cottage with its own drive and garden. Mary worked out a reasonable budget and took the time out to visit a few potential properties, which she visited alone so she could have a good look around without Patrick distracting her.

She eventually found one she quite liked just outside Winsford. It was close enough but also far enough away so they both had some independence from each other. Mary found Patrick to be hard work at times and he was getting worse as he grew older. She could sense the jealousy towards Davey, who was smarter, better looking and had friends. Patrick didn't seem to have any friends, which was a worry. She also had concerns about his ability to cope in a house alone, he couldn't cook and was not the most hygienic person to have around.

Patrick liked the house, but didn't know that he owned it and had been paid for out of his trust fund. It was near the main road for work and there was some shops and a pub just up the road. Mary said she would call in twice a week to tidy up and sort his laundry out, Patrick was happy with this arrangement, so the house was bought and over the next few weeks was furnished and carpeted with new appliances and a bathroom upgrade. Patrick eventually moved in, Mary thought she could relax, but unfortunately that was not the case. Patrick had a habit of calling into the pub every night after work and getting drunk. He had fell out with a few locals in there and was on the verge of being banned.

News of this reached Mary and she went to see him to read the riot act and to try and get him to see sense. In the end she threatened to cut all ties with him and he would be left alone in the world to self-destruct. This had an effect, Patrick had nobody, Mary was his mother, she was all he had. He stopped drinking and behaved himself. He wished he could go back to living at her house, but at the same time Mary knew he had to grow up, he was 23, still a virgin, no friends and alone, not the best situation to find yourself. On the plus side he had money, no mortgage or rent, surely, he thought there must be somebody out there for me.

He knew there were women selling their bodies in Manchester, he had heard the lads at work talk about it, so he started to hang about the railway station at Deansgate. Sure enough, he found a fat older woman in her late forties to lose his virginity to, it was over in seconds and he felt a great sense of relief when it was over. This became a twice weekly event and he liked to try different women. All was well until he developed an excruciating pain when he went to pee and a visit to the local Venereal Disease Clinic was required.

After that he decided that now he was a man of the world, he needed to find a regular girlfriend, so he started to hang out around the local shops and market. He eventually plucked up the courage to speak to a very plain girl that worked on a market stall selling cheese and dairy products. He arranged to meet her after work and they went to the pub for a few drinks. Conversation was small, in fact hardly a word was said and after two difficult hours they parted company, with a promise they would meet again later that week. This went on for three more meetings, during which she managed to find out he had his own house, a regular job and was related to the Reddox outfit.

She in turn confided in him that her name was Fiona, she lived at home and shared a bedroom with two other sisters and a dad that had brought them up alone after their mother had run off with a local garage mechanic, she seemed perfect, thought Patrick, she would be happy to share my house and more importantly my bed. He asked her to be his girlfriend and she accepted, she didn't get many offers after all.

It was agreed that on Sunday, he would pick her up and drive to his house, where she would make him a nice dinner. Good idea in theory, but it didn't quite work out the same in practice.

After obtaining the ingredients for the meal they made their way to Patrick's house and placed the goods in the kitchen. Fiona took off her coat and as soon as she had put it on the hook behind the door. Patrick pounced on her. He went to kiss her, then put his hand up her dress. She begged him to stop.

"Please Patrick, can we eat, I am hungry." She pleaded. But Patrick had a different agenda.

"You're my girlfriend now and I want to take you to my bed."

"Patrick, I am a virgin, I have never been with a man before, please stop."

But Patrick was insistent. "We can eat later; I want you now."

He then bent her over the kitchen table, raised her dress and entered her from behind. Fiona squealed and begged him to stop, but Patrick was not in a listening mood. After half a dozen thrusts, he grunted then leaned into her and spurted inside her. He then buttoned his trousers up and casually asked her to make a nice meal.

Fiona was distraught, this wasn't how the first time was supposed to be. She knew she wasn't the prettiest but she never thought someone would not only violate her, but do it with such casual disdain. She somehow managed to compose herself and make the meal, after which Patrick casually asked her to go upstairs with him. It was now 10pm, too late for a bus and too far to walk. She asked him to take her home, she said she had to get up early to go to buy goods for the stall. To her relief, he agreed and dropped her outside her house.

"Can I see you on Tuesday?" He casually asked.

"Yes, ok," she just wanted to get into the safety of her house.

When she got in her sister was still up and she took her coat off, collapsed in her arms and told her what had happened. They went to the police the following morning and Patrick was arrested and taken to the station. He was questioned for about an hour, he said she agreed having sex, she said he raped her. In the end, nothing could be proved one way or another. He was released without charge and immediately went home. When he got there, he found Mary tidying up and washing last night's dishes.

"I see you had company last night, anyone I know?" Mary was intrigued, Patrick was not a popular person around town and she was curious.

Patrick looked shifty. He tried to be evasive and change the subject.

"Are you ok Patrick, what's wrong?" She sensed all was not well.

Keeping his eyes firmly looking down at the floor he recounted his version of events and how Fiona agreed to sex, then went to the police. He claimed he had done nothing wrong and that she was a crazy bitch who didn't know her own mind. After getting more information about Fiona, Mary decided she needed to talk to her. She was also reminded about Patrick being banned from the youth club all those years before.

"Ok Patrick, why don't you take your mind off it all and go back to work, maybe she is not the right girl for you." She then finished off tidying up and went in search of Fiona, but in the back of her mind she knew Patrick was in the wrong.

She found Fiona on the stall and asked her if she could have 5 minutes, so they went to a little café around the corner, Mary explained that she was Patrick's mother and just wanted to know what had happened. Fiona tearfully told Mary the full story, she believed every word she said. Mary knew Fiona had no reason to lie.

"My advice to you is to stay away from Patrick, he is a complicated person and not easily understood. I don't think he meant to harm you, but he looks at the world through different eyes than you and I."

Fiona nodded and told Mary she needed to get back to work, her father didn't know what had happened and she didn't want to arouse suspicion.

Mary now had a problem; it was obvious Patrick was not capable of self-survival but she didn't want him under her feet every day. She decided to ask him to come back to the house for a while until she could figure out what to do with him, but there was a bigger problem looming in the foreground.

Patrick was only a year away from receiving the money from the trust, God knows what he will be like when he gets all that money. Mary realised she had not looked at the value of the trust for a while. Patrick was living off his weekly wages and apart from buying the car and the house it was largely intact. All the dividends for the last few years added up to a substantial amount and the shares themselves were worth nearly a hundred thousand pounds.

That night she went back down to the cottage, they both arrived at the same time. Mary asked if he was hungry, which he was, so she told him to get cleaned up and she would get some fish and chips. She got back and was just unwrapping when he came downstairs.

"Why are you here, did you go to see Fiona?"

"Yes, I was concerned about you being arrested so I needed to speak with her to see what she had to say about what happened."

"I ALREADY TOLD YOU WHAT HAPPENED, DON'T YOU BELIEVE ME?" His voice was loud and threatening, she had known Patrick since he was a toddler and never felt threatened before, but he scared her now.

"Patrick darling, please calm down, I am concerned about you and need to make sure I do everything I can to be there for you," she appeared calm and that calmness seemed to bring him back down.

This was going to be very difficult, he needed to be handled carefully. They just chatted about work and various small talk as they ate and just as she thought he was more stable, she suggested that he moved back to the house.

"NO, NO I will not leave here, this is my home now and I am happy here." He was getting worked up again. He went on, "I am sick of being treated like a child, all my life I have not been able to do anything for myself, everyone always decides what is best for me. That's it. I have had enough, from now on I decide what's good for me and fuck everyone else."

Mary could see there was no reasoning with him so cleared the table and told him she had to go, but would he please think about it. She was only thinking about his welfare.

"Fuck off and leave me alone," was his response. She hesitated at the door, trying to think of something, but then thought better and went home.

Chapter Fifteen

Davey was having the best time ever, free away from the expectations at home he threw himself into student life at full throttle. He had a good living allowance to support his lifestyle, thanks to Mary's generosity. He shared a large terraced house near Clifton Park with 3 other students. He was studying building surveying, which was a sensible option when you consider that his life was already mapped out for him. He appreciated the hard work that had been done by his parents to get him to the privileged position he was in and wasn't not going to waste it. He was a hardworking student, but he also started to play hard.

The others in his house included a philosophy student from Leeds named Seb, a Londoner by the name of Tommy, who was studying electronic engineering and a small timid history student, who they nicknamed dormouse on account of the fact he never left his room and appeared to sleep all the time. It was 3 months before they found out his name was Norman.

Davey, Seb and Tommy automatically bonded, as they were all strangers in town and didn't know anybody else when they first arrived. Davey wasn't really a drinker, but Tommy and Seb certainly were and many a night Davey was unceremoniously dumped on his bed fully clothed after a boozy night.

By Xmas, Uni life was in full swing, the novelty of the pub life had quietened down, but certainly not stopped. One night they decided to have a night in and Davey was taught how to play poker, which he enjoyed. As they played Seb mentioned there was a young lady in his class who was always asking about Davey. When Davey realised who it was, he was definitely interested, he had seen around town and she was stunning. Seb agreed to make sure they were in the same bar over the weekend.

On Saturday night, they headed to one of the campus bars, where sure enough the lady in question was sat talking to some friends. She saw Davey, smiled and beckoned him to sit with her. Her name was Michelle, she was from Taunton and the same age as Davey. They talked long into the night, she was staying in the halls of residence and there was a curfew of midnight after which the doors were locked. The halls were near to his house so they walked to the halls, talking all the time. As they arrived at the entrance doors Davey was half hoping that the doors would be locked, but unfortunately, they had a habit of going beyond midnight before locking up, so she made it in time. They agreed to meet the following night, Michelle made it quite clear she wanted to go back to his house.

The following day, Davey told Seb and Tommy, he wanted them out of the way and gave them enough money for a few beers down the pub to ensure they did not disrupt his night. Although he had spent some time in female company back home, he had only enjoyed a fumble and a hand job. He was still a virgin at 20 and he was determined to change that status tonight. That Evening Michelle looked stunning, she had long auburn curly hair and an impressive curvy body. She made it clear that she wanted it as much as he did and they didn't bother with any small talk, but almost immediately jumped into bed. They clumsily felt each other, Davey could tell she was inexperienced as well. After a lot of writhing about he eventually found himself inside her and was struggling to hold back. Somehow, he lasted five minutes, then unable to hold back he came with a grunt, just about managing to pull out before ejaculating.

As they lay there quietly in the dark Michelle confessed, she was a virgin which did not come as a surprise, they were both novices and it showed. She stayed the night, and they had sex again in the morning before he drove her to the halls, after first stopping off to have breakfast in a local café.

The following day was the last before the Christmas break, he wasn't going to see her before then but promised they would get together when they got back.

The drive back to Northwich was long and slow, the roads were busy and snow was on the ground. He eventually got home after a gruelling 8 hours on the road.

Mary was up early that day, she was so looking forward to having Davey back, the house had been empty without him at home. He had never been away before and she was worried about everything, his health, could he cope living alone, was the workload stressful?

She needn't have worried, he walked into the entrance hall of the house like a returning king. He was confident, looked well and had filled out a little. He had been a little skinny but now had more meat on his bones. He had returned as a man, the boy was no more.

Davey asked where Patrick was and didn't look surprised when Mary recalled what had happened. "It's probably true, he always acted strange around girls, they all thought he was weird."

Davey's response didn't surprise Mary, she had also thought he assaulted poor Fiona, but had never said anything to anyone.

"He won't come back to the house and has got a little more distant, God knows what will happen when he gets his inheritance," Davey could tell Mary was very worried about Patrick, He knew she had an obligation to take care of him.

"I wouldn't worry about him, he will either sort himself out or get further into trouble, either way you can do nothing about it, it's all up to him," Mary was surprised at Davey's apparent lack of concern, but she knew that what he said was correct.

The recess lasted 3 weeks, Davey was getting a little bored, so after the new year, there was a week before he had to return to university. He decided to work in the offices with the surveyors to get a feel for what projects were ongoing. He could see they were busy and that things were going to get busier. The surveyors were talking about there being complete new towns being built in Skelmersdale and Warrington, thousands of houses. There was also going to be massive investment in roadworks with something called a motorway running the length of the northwest, all the way to Birmingham.

He spoke about it to Mary over dinner, she was aware of the new town developments but knew nothing of the motorway project.

"We have never been involved in roadworks, not where our skills lie so we shouldn't be interested."

Davey had been thinking about it and realised that the amount of equipment needed was massive, this was on a scale never known before in England.

"I wasn't thinking about getting involved, but just think of all the dump trucks, tractors, cranes, etc that would be needed. Not to mention all the tools, concrete, etc. There is a massive amount of money involved. If we can supply all this equipment, think how profitable it would be." Mary was staggered, she had never thought of that aspect of it. If they can buy out a lot of these suppliers before the work is tendered then they would strike gold.

"Davey, that's a brilliant idea, we need to get the team together to discuss."

The following day they went to see the finance director to see how feasible it was from a financial point of view.

"We have the financial clout to do it, but it is risky gambling on something that has not been confirmed yet. If you want to pursue this, I will put together some figures, but be warned this is a significant amount of money and I advise you to progress with due caution."

Davey listened intently, then added another dimension. "But surely, the worse thing that can happen is we have bought established companies anyway, if they are already successful then just how much would we actually lose."

Everyone around the table just sat there looking at each other, this youngster was showing great confidence and also a good head for business, this was a future leader for sure. Mary sat there, so proud of her son. She felt a lump in her throat, the business was going to be in good hands when she handed over the reins, but not yet. She was still in overall control and was determined to stay there until she felt the time was right.

It was agreed that another meeting would be convened in a month, once a feasibility study had been carried out.

Davey only saw Patrick once during the holidays, he went over to the cottage one Sunday morning and he was still in bed. They sat having a coffee, the talk was minimal, Patrick wasn't interested in Davey's time at Uni and Davey wasn't interested in Patrick's mediocre life.

"How's the driving, still enjoying it?"

"Fuckin' hate it, will be glad when I get my dad's cash, then I am going to see the world and enjoy myself."

Davey could see Patrick was serious, he knew Patrick would not be able to handle all that money. He could also see that Patrick didn't want him there, so he made an excuse and left.

He mentioned it to his mother, who just raised her eyes and said she wasn't surprised. "But what if he sells the shares to someone else, the money from the saved dividends is enough to live on for a couple of years but not in the long term and Patrick will blow the lot and have to sell the shares, we both know that," Mary did not want 10% of the company belonging to outsiders and she knew Patrick was not capable of being responsible, but she had not thought about him selling the shares.

"Leave that with me, we have another year to consider what to do."

She had a plan, but could do nothing yet.

Davey was back at university and having a great time, He saw Michelle for a while, but then decided she was a little clingy, she wanted to be with him all the time, so he finished it. This devastated her and for a while she was following him everywhere he went, which resulted in a number of arguments. Eventually she gave up, but they remained friends. He found the study interesting but moderately easy, he was a highflyer and very popular. Davey was also very rich, but all the money, like Patrick, was in trust until he was 25 and he relied on an allowance form his mother, which was generous and more than he needed, but also just the right amount to keep him grounded and on the same level as his peers at Bristol.

He never talked about Reddox Construction or the family wealth, so nobody treated him any different, he was just plain Davey Knox from up north. At the end of the first year Davey reflected, he had enjoyed himself, he loved the independence and his new friends. He had learnt quite a lot and was looking forward to a break, maybe a holiday. He was also looking forward to spending some time back at work.

The feasibility study was completed, it was a very expensive venture but they targeted a large tool and equipment supplier and also 6 independent outfits. Approaches were made, 4 of the independents were quickly snapped up and they decided not to bother with the other 2, they would concentrate on developing the 4 and expanding so they would be the preferred supplier, thus eliminating the opposition. The large tool hire company was a harder nut to crack, they had also heard of the development and were anticipating a lot of work coming their way and their branches were handily located. Reddox made two offers, both of which were rejected, so Mary decided on a different approach.

After making a few enquiries, she discovered that the owner, Mr Paul Thomas, had been talking about retiring for a while and wanted to sell, his only son and heir was irresponsible and would just run the firm into the ground so there was no sense in continuing as a family business. Once he found out about Reddox interest and the new infrastructure projects he suddenly decided to up the price by 30% which was a gross overvaluation of the firm's true value. She also discovered he had 2 weaknesses. One was gambling and he was also rumoured to have a couple of mistresses. Mary decided that she needed to exploit this and hatched a plan. She made arrangements to visit Mr Thomas, she wanted to see if there was any room for negotiation, but he remained steadfast in his asking price. If she was to make any headway then there needed to be some movement.

Mary made the first move. She booked a corporate entertainment box at Chester races for the May meeting. She then made a few phone calls to people in the entertainment business in Liverpool. When this was done, she invited Mr Thomas to the races, which he readily agreed to.

On the day she invited him to meet her at the Grosvenor Hotel for a pre-race lunch, where she informed him she had booked a room there.

After lunch they took the short walk down the hill to the racecourse, engaging in small talk. She informed him that they unfortunately would be alone as other guests had cancelled due to personal circumstances. When they got there, he was delighted to see there were two young ladies who had been recruited for the day as hostesses. One was tall and statuesque with a very large chest, the other was small, petite and very pretty. He quickly made himself comfortable, making good use of the free alcohol and as the afternoon went by, he placed several large bets and finished the day slightly losing, but he was in a good mood.

This was made better when the buxom lady, whose name was Rose, started to pay him a lot of attention. Mary made her excuses for an hour and said she had to see someone, she wanted to make sure that Mr Thomas and the girls got very friendly. She wandered around the course for an hour, stopping to take some photos and have a drink in one of the Bars, then returned. When she got back Rose was sat on Thomas's knee and he had his hand up her skirt. The alcohol had kicked in by now and he didn't seem bothered about the situation she had found him in, "I trust the young ladies have been looking after you alright, Mr Thomas." She smiled.

"Very nice, they certainly know how to please."

As she looked down, she could see Rose stroking his hard cock over his trousers. There were two races left, Thomas didn't seem interested and now had the other young lady sat on his knee.

Mary then made her move, "I am sorry but I have to attend to some personal business and need to go home. I have paid for the room at the Grosvenor, perhaps you would like to go and relax there after the last race, you can put any food and drink on my bill. My friends here are in no hurry and perhaps you would like them to dine with you?"

Thomas's eyes lit up. "Thank you, that's very generous of you," he could think of nothing better.

As she left, she summoned the little lady, who was called Eva, over to her and handed her a camera, "There are about 6 photos left on this film, make sure you get some of him in bed with at least one of you. No nudity, I need to be able to process the film, but I want you to make it quite clear what he has been up to. Tell Rose I want the full story on what happens. I will meet you tomorrow and pay you half now and the rest when the work is completed and I get the camera back."

Eva nodded, Mary handed the camera over and went home.

The following week she returned to see Mr Thomas and asked if he had enjoyed himself, to which he replied he had. She decided this was not the time for small talk, so she began to talk about whether he would reconsider his asking price as it was highly overvalued.

"Just because you treated me to a day at the races does not give you the right to expect me to reduce my price, I am not changing my mind."

"Are you sure about that, Mr Thomas?" queried Mary as she dropped 3 photos on his desk.

His face dropped and he blushed a deep red. The photos showed him entering the hotel with Rose, then another of them entering the elevator and finally him lying under the bedclothes with an obviously naked Rose next to him.

"There are others that are far more incriminating, but I will save you the embarrassment of showing those… for now." She lied.

Thomas put his head in his hands and groaned. "I should have known it was a set up, they were far too friendly and obliging."

Mary let him sit there and think about the situation for a few minutes.

He finally picked his head up, "Ok what do you want?"

Mary was not trying to ruin him, she did not want to attract unwanted attention. If she was unreasonable then questions could be asked.

"We stick to our valuation, which is a fair one. All the acquisitions we are making will form a separate company as part of the Reddox group, we will give you 5% in shares for that subsidiary". It was a fair offer and Redox as the parent company would decide what the dividends would be anyway. It was always anticipated that all profits would be reinvested for the first five years, so nothing extra would be paid out in the short term. She gave him 48 hours to decide then left him alone, with his head back in his hands and shaking his head.

The contract was duly signed and all the other acquisitions made, they were now in a position to discuss matters with the roads and bridges contractors to form a partnership, but it had proved to be an expensive venture and their working capital had been greatly reduced. Approaches were made to a number of the favourite tenderers and they received a helpful response to a becoming a preferred contractor, should they win the contract.

Eventually, all the legislation was passed and the motorway extended down from Preston in Lancashire and down into Cheshire. At the same time the road network was being developed to encompass the creation of Runcorn New Town.

Reddox were invited to attend the inaugural meeting, but this time however there was a new face sat as Chairman. He introduced himself as Mr Christopher Metcalfe and he was replacing Richard Grice who had now retired. This sent a mixed message to Mary, on the one hand she detested Grice, but on the other hand as long as he had been getting his cut, he had proved a very lucrative provider of work. By now, Reddox were one of the bigger players in the region and they received the good news they had won the contract, which would keep them busy for a few years. The work continued to pour in, there was new roads and roads and bridges being created, the purchase of the plant hire companies was proving very lucrative and they were still getting plenty of local authority work.

Mary now had to deal with the Patrick and his money, she was not particularly bothered what he did, he could blow the lot, but the shares needed to be kept in house. A month before his 25th birthday, Mary asked to see him, so he came up to the house to discuss his future. She tried to get him to invest his money, but it was clear he had decided he was going to go and enjoy himself and she was wasting her time.

"Ok, then let me buy your shares once they are in your hands. I cannot do anything at the moment as I am your trustee, but next month they will be yours, please let me buy them from you."

Patrick thought about it, he was not sure how much they were worth, he didn't have a clue about the value, but he did know it was a large figure and that it would be easier to take the money and run.

"Ok, how much?"

"I will pay the appropriate rate at the time of your birthday, I will get George Kay to work out the value and pay you accordingly."

Mary just wanted this meeting over, Patrick was now a liability and once he had gone, she considered her promise to Billy to have been honoured in full.

On Patrick's birthday she staged a dinner at the house, there was just the three of them and also George Kay, she needed to ensure all the legalities were tied up, Davey was back from the Easter Break and reluctantly agreed to attend.

After a quiet meal, Mary unceremoniously handed Patrick an envelope, inside there was a cheque for 98,765 pounds, the sum even surprised Davey who had a good idea of what the shares were worth. George then made him sign a number of documents, including the transfer of the shares.

Patrick looked at the cheque, signed the documents, throwing the pen on the table in the process. Then he smiled and stuck all the copies of the paperwork in his pocket, stood up and walked away from the table.

"Right, that's me sorted then, I have places to go and things to do."

Then he turned and informed them, "I won't be in work tomorrow, the day after, or any other fucking day, you won't be seeing me again."

The next couple of years rolled by, Patrick was now out of everyone's mind. They heard he had disappeared to Hamburg, having told everyone in the pub he was going to fuck himself to death in the Reeperbahn.

Davey passed his degree with Honours and he was now ready to join the company on a permanent basis. He knew that his degree was only a first step, he had a lot to learn so he decided he would spend a few months working in different departments. He was now 23 and bursting with ideas, but older heads within the organisation kept him grounded. There were more high-rise blocks being built, these were relatively easy to build as they all followed the same basic design, the local authorities loved them as less land was required. Reddox had tended to shy away from them as it was not an area of strength, but it was very popular, it was agreed that Davey needed to take a very close interest in this method of construction and so he worked mainly in the design office.

By the summer of 1967, he was well established and the trust that Mary had set up for him had now matured, she presented it to him with pride, he was now an articulate caring person, very popular and had a sharp mind. As they went through the detail of the trust payments, she also gave him some more good news.

"I have discussed it with the board and we all agreed, now is the time to make you a working director of the company, but we are not totally sure what the title and responsibility should be, any ideas?" Davey was obviously delighted, it was agreed his title would be development director, with a remit of ensuring growth and developing long-term strategies in a rapidly changing construction world. Mary was now nearly seventy and she was gradually easing back, but she wasn't ready to sit back and retire just yet.

Davey had noticed there was big increase in the demand for plant for road building and concrete products and met with a couple of the Civil Engineering

Contractors to see what their requirements were likely to be in the future. Yet more capital was invested, which very much annoyed Mr Thomas and no dividend was paid for a second year.

Mary was taking more of a backseat and had time on her hands, so she decided to reinstate the herb gardens in the house. They had been abandoned during the war in favour of supplying mainstays like potatoes, carrots, onions, etc. Originally the house would have had its own supply of herbs like rosemary, lavender, sage, thyme and the like. Mary now wanted to restore the garden to its former glory. She remembered there had been some glass frames in the cellar so went to seek them out.

She found what she was looking for, but then got curious about what Billy had brought back before he died. She went upstairs, got the key and apprehensively opened the door. There were about 30 objects, most were paintings but also some statuettes and art deco figures, which Mary was very fond of. The pile consisted of 4 sacks and a large trunk.

Opening the sacks first, she could see they were fine art, obviously family commissions. Mary assumed these had been taken from the large Georgian houses in Liverpool owned by the traders, who made their money transporting cotton and such things from the Americas. They were beautiful paintings, but Mary decided they were too traceable so put them in a pile to be burnt with the garden rubbish. This accounted for about 40% of the total. There were some exquisite statuettes, some signed but most not. She took a liking for a few of these and decided they were too nice to throw away, she would find room for them in the house.

She then moved on to the trunk, inside which there was a mixture of items including some more statues, some fine miniature paintings of country scenes and animals. Which she quite liked. Tucked away in the bottom she saw a small bag, she opened it up and gasped. Inside was the Burmese blood ruby necklace that Billy had said had to be broke up and sold. It was intact, Mary smiled, it was obvious Billy had intended to give it her at some stage.

After finally deciding what was staying and what was going, Mary made two piles and closed the door. She then took the necklace and hid it in her bedroom. She disposed of what could be burnt over the next few weeks, what was left she reluctantly threw in the canal at various places.

Over the summer of '67, Mary was still busy in the garden, she got a couple of landscape gardeners in and working from old photos she restored the gardens to their former glory. She was revelling in it all, but was very tired and ready for a holiday. She had never been in a plane before and had seen pictures of the Cote D'Azur and always wanted to go there, so booked a flight at the end of September. Davey was surprised as she had never been away from either him or the business in all his life. He was glad, he could see she was getting tired, things were running well and there was no need for her to be so attentive.

He wasn't keen on going so didn't offer to accompany her, but did ask if she would cope alright.

"I have seen many things in my life, I have been in many situations in my life, so what makes you think I can't manage a month in France," Mary was irked at Davey implying she was a doddery old fool, Davey knew that he needed to backtrack immediately as he knew when she was in an argumentative mood there was only one winner… and it wasn't going to be him.

Mary flew out to Nice on the 28 September, a cab was arranged to pick her up and take her to the Anantara Hotel situated on the seafront. She relished the autumn heat on her body which reminded her of her days in Italy. For the next month she relaxed more than she had in her whole lifetime, she was a wealthy woman, her son's future was secure and she found herself sometimes not getting up until 10am. She slept long and soundly. She met people from all over Europe and enjoyed watching the sun go down, washed down with some delightful wine. At the end of her perfect month, she was ready to return home totally refreshed and recharged.

Once home she was her usual self, charging about everywhere in the office, asking questions, querying decisions and Davey found himself having to justify everything that had gone on, he was getting agitated at the constant interference. Mary was happy with the answers she got, but also a little peeved. She was getting the impression she was surplus to requirements and this was annoying.

Davey listened to her account of her holiday, it sounded idyllic but he wasn't going to go with his mother. At 25, he was ready to look at where his future lay, he had previously had a number of girlfriends, but nobody special.

He had kept in contact with Seb and Tommy, so asked them if they fancied a trip to France, Tommy was unable as he was now married, but Seb leapt at the chance. Neither had been abroad before so in the spring of '68 they drove down to Calais and crossed on the ferry. Davey had by now upgraded his Mini to an MGB GT.

Davey wanted to drive and see the 24 hour Le Mans Grand Prix, a flight was quicker but not as much fun. Arriving in Le Man, they struggled to find a hotel but eventually managed to get one thanks to a generous donation to the receptionist at the Mercure Hotel who managed to find a cancellation.

The race was a thriller, eventually won by Jack Brabham, an Australian. After the race the whole town seemed to be celebrating, every bar and restaurant was full, everyone was enjoying themselves. They eventually decided they needed to eat and managed to squeeze into a corner in a small bistro and ordered. As they sat there Davey looked around and his eyes kept wandering over to a pretty blonde about twenty years old with the most amazing smile, sat two tables away. She was with her family and her natural elegance made him assume she was French. She noticed his gaze, smiled then turned away.

Seb noticed Davey keep wandering over and commented, "Yes, she is very nice, why don't you go and talk to her?"

"I know about five words of French I don't want to make a fool of myself."

"You won't she is English, I heard her talking before."

Davey was usually confident when speaking to anyone, but she was different.

Eventually, she got up to go to the toilet and Davey waited until she was just coming back and timed it so they met halfway back to her table.

"You here for the race?"

"Isn't everyone?" she smiled, Davey felt himself blush.

"How long are you here for?"

"We are going to Cannes tomorrow for two weeks, with my mum, dad and sister."

"That's a coincidence, so are we. I am with my friend," lied Davey, gesturing over to Seb, who could feel Davey's discomfort from where he was sat.

"Where are you staying, we are in the Carlton?" Davey did not have a clue, he had never been to Cannes.

"I can't remember, but it's one of the big ones on the front," Davey was floundering a bit now.

"Ok, see you there, my name's Helen," he replied, telling her his name. Then she flashed another smile and went back to her table.

Davey was smitten, he went back to his seat and told Seb that plans had changed, they were now going to Cannes, Seb just shrugged and ordered another wine.

The drive from Le Mans to Cannes was a 1000km so they stayed over in Lyon after driving for over 6 hours. Davey was quite happy to try and get there in one trip, but Seb insisted they stop off, he was still hungover from all the wine from last night.

Eventually after another 6 hours ride, they arrived in Cannes, neither had a clue about what to expect, but they were quite impressed with the drive along the seafront. They drove past the Carlton, Davey did not want to make it so obvious so they settled on a nearby hotel, the Martinez, a classy hotel 4 minutes away and both handily located on the Boulevard de le Croisette.

They booked into their respective rooms, Davey realised that this was a more expensive hotel than Seb could afford so he offered to pick up the bill. Davey sent all his dirty washing to the laundry, then realised he had nothing to wear that night, so went out shopping. Seb decided to take a walk down the beach.

Later as they sat outside a bar on a terrace near the Carlton, they relaxed and watched the world go by. Seb watched the world go by, Davey was on Helen watch. They wandered up and down the front, having a few drinks and stopping to eat at a small bistro. This went on for another four days with no sign of the elusive Helen and Seb was getting very fed up.

"I am going to take a look around tomorrow, all we have done so far is wander up and down this bloody road," Davey realised he was making himself ridiculous, so agreed and put thoughts of her out of his mind.

They had a few days on the beach, then had a run up the coast stopping off at some beautiful coves and swimming in the stunning waters of the Med. He started to relax and could appreciate why his mother loved it on the Cote D'Azur. The wine was good, the food stunning and even just sitting there soaking up the atmosphere was so peaceful.

On the nineth night, they were in a small bar in a side street, when Seb started to smile for no apparent reason.

"What's tickling you?" Davey asked.

"Nothing, I am fine," said a smirking Seb.

"Hello Dave, was wondering when I might bump into you."

Davey turned around and Helen was standing there in a white cotton dress, she looked stunning.

"Er. Um, its Davey actually, nobody calls me Dave."

He was sounding like a right idiot. Seb was loving his discomfort.

"Would you like a drink?" He gestured and offered her a chair, which she accepted.

"My parents are always late so I decided to take a walk and saw you, I have ten minutes or so, so thank you."

She sat down and after getting another glass, Davey filled it up from the bottle they already had. Seb made an excuse about needing something from his room and finally he was alone with her.

He discovered she was 22, a final year student at Nottingham University, on a business studies degree. She asked what he did and he decided to be upfront and honest with her. With most other girls he had met he played down what his job was and never talked about the company. He didn't tell her about the fact that the family owned one of the biggest construction companies in the north, merely telling her about his position within the business.

They finished up having another glass and chatted for about 40 minutes. When she finally said she had to go he asked if he could see her the following day. She said she was going to the beach with the family, but he was more than welcome to join them, to which he immediately agreed.

The following day he dragged Seb to the beach, Seb moaning all the way about being piggy in the middle. Helen's family were solid and hardworking, her father, Derek Tanner, was a town planner with Nottingham Council, so Davey found he had a lot in common with him. Her mother, Eva, was a doctor and he could see where Helen got her looks from.

The day went well and they agreed to meet for dinner that night, Davey found himself under scrutiny from Derek, who remarked he was young to be a director, he was giving the impression he thought that Davey was talking bullshit.

"Yes, well, I have to confess that maybe the fact that it's the family firm that helped me up the ladder a little," he replied modestly.

Derek said nothing and just sat thinking about this polite young man that had such a strong interest in his daughter.

As the evening went on, everyone relaxed and a good evening was had, Seb didn't have a lot to say, merely sipping his wine and chilling out.

Helen and Davey were getting on really well and talked way into the night, the rest of the family went back to the hotel, Seb disappeared and they found themselves alone. They went for a walk along the front, eventually stopping and sitting on one of the many benches. Eventually they kissed, at first just a small meeting of lips, then after a few seconds a long smouldering one that took them both by surprise.

Helen was usually a bit picky about the men her life, she had only had one sexual encounter before, which was with another student after a boozy night out. She had no intention of sleeping with Davey yet. But she was definitely attracted to him. She told him she wanted to go, so he walked her back to her hotel, they kissed again and he left her in the lobby.

There were now only 3 more nights before Helen was leaving and Davey wanted to make sure he spent as much time with her as possible. Davey and Seb went to the beach, but they weren't there, no sign of them at night either.

"Looks like you have blown it, mate, she doesn't want to see you." Seb's comments were not helping.

"I can't understand it, we got on really well," Davey was bewildered.

At the end of the two weeks, Davey had to accept the inevitable, she was deliberately ignoring him. So, with a heavy heart they spent two long days driving back to northwest England.

Chapter Sixteen

Davey concentrated his work for the next 2 years, he had invested a lot of time developing the high-rise element of construction and set up a team of experts and engineers, this was starting to pay off and work was gradually picking up. They won a contract to erect three 15 storey blocks of flats in Kirby, this was progressing well. They also won some large contracts to build shopping centres on 6000 housing development. They were now at full capacity and it was agreed they would consolidate for a few years, the order book was full for the next 3 years.

Mary took a few more holidays in France and was increasingly becoming less and less involved in the business. Eventually she told Davey she was going to step down altogether when he was 30. It was an irrelevant statement as she wasn't really involved anyway, but nobody dare come out and say it.

Davey was a wealthy man, he now wanted to settle down and get married, but there was only one woman he wanted and she had rejected him.

Reddox were gradually spreading their net wider, they had projects in Lancashire, Cheshire, Staffordshire and Yorkshire. They were among the top 5 companies working for local authorities in the country and offers to tender were coming in daily.

One morning at a regular operations meeting, it was mentioned the Nottingham Council had enquired if Reddox were interested in some new Deck Access flats, quite a big chunk. It was at this point that Davey's ears pricked up. He said nothing but went to speak with the Tenders Team after the meeting.

"I know one of the town planners there, let me go and see how the land lies."

Nobody objected, they knew Davey could be trusted to make the right decision. After a few phone calls he managed to get an appointment and after a week he found himself sat in reception at Nottingham City Hall. He was then shown into a room with a large oak table, sat around which were four officials, one of which was Helen's father.

Davey was well used to such meetings and his experience carried him through a very polished and informative demonstration of Reddox capabilities and experience, which took him 40 minutes. This was followed by another 20 of questions, answers and clarification. He could see they were impressed.

"We had already decided to invite Reddox to Tender, so why the presentation now?"

This was a question he had anticipated would come up; it was from Derek Tanner.

"Because we have experience of high-rise, general housing, shopping centres, business units and road building, we are being asked to supply a quote for housing work. The purpose of my visit is to let you see the diversity of our operations."

At the end they thanked him, clearly impressed they left one by one until only Derek remained, "You really are the real deal young man, when we met, I wasn't sure if you were genuine or not. I can see you clearly are." Then he extended his hand for Davey to shake.

Davey thanked him, then asked if he knew why Helen wouldn't see him again, as he thought they got on well. "It wasn't a case of wouldn't, more a case of couldn't. I received a telegram to say my father had died. She wanted to say goodbye, but I needed to get home as quickly as possible as my mother was heartbroken." He sounded genuine, Davey was in a way relieved, at least he hadn't done anything wrong.

"If you are not in a hurry then please feel free to call on her, she will be back from Uni by 4pm."

He then scribbled down the address and went off to his office. It was now 2pm, he decided to get something to eat, then tracked the address down. He got there at 4:20 and knocked on the door. There was no answer so he went back and sat in his car and waited. A short time later he saw her get off the bus at the end of the street and waited until she had turned into the path leading up to her door.

"You want to go to the races?" was all he could say just as she was putting the key in the door.

Helen stopped, then turned very slowly, was it really him? "Hello Dave, how did you find me?"

He walked quickly towards her and picked her up and swung her round, then he kissed her.

"It's Davey actually, you must be thinking of someone else."

They held on to each other for a good five minutes, before she invited him and made them a cup of tea. Davey could see she was glad to see him, he had been worried that she would reject him. She explained that they got the message about the death at 9am and by 10 they were on their way back to them UK, there was no time to contact him. The house started to fill up, first her sister, Maddy came back from school and then her father. She said her mother would probably get back about 7pm.

Her father invited him to stay to eat with them, but they both wanted to be alone so they went out to eat at a restaurant. They talked for hours, totally engrossed in each other. Eventually at ten o'clock Davey realised he needed to get home. She gave him her number and agreed to talk the following night. The drive home was 3 hours, but Davey didn't care, he was a happy man.

They spoke every night for two weeks, then she agreed to come and stay with him for the weekend. Davey had already spoken to Mary about her and Mary was intrigued, she had never seen him so infatuated before.

He picked Helen up from the station and they drove back to the house.

"Wow, nice house," was all she could say as they entered the driveway.

Mary was at the door waiting, she greeted them and they went inside to the lounge, after gesturing for Helen to leave her bag in the hallway. They talked a little, for about ten minutes, mainly Mary asking the questions about her family, the university, just general chat. Mary warmed to her and could see that she was smart, confident and also very pretty. It was obvious why Davey liked her so much.

Davey then asked Helen if she was ready to sort her bags out, she nodded and he picked the bags up and headed up the stairs.

"You have a choice of rooms, one facing the front or one facing the back garden," he explained.

"Which is yours?"

He showed her his bedroom which was a corner room with dual aspects. She took the bag and threw it on his bed.

"This will do nicely," and then closed the door and kissed him. "I am passed the stage of pretence, we are not children, so let's act like adults."

This threw Davey, he was wondering how he was going to approach the subject of sleeping together, but Helen had just sorted it for him.

"But not now," she said. "I want to see what life is like around here, starting with a tour of the house," They did the tour then he took out to see the area and finally they finished up at the offices in Haydock.

The building was large, around the back was various large items of machinery and vans, it was an impressive site.

"We have two other offices, both with yards, but this is the main place," Davey was proud of the company, this was his domain.

Helen was impressed but said very little, she could see how much he loved his work. After an afternoon of driving about, they got back to the house about 6pm, Mary was waiting.

"I take it Davey has given you a tour of his empire," she chuckled.

"You must be tired by now. I was thinking of booking a table at The George, you both ok with that. 7pm seems a good time?"

It wasn't so much a question, more of a statement. Mary wanted to know more about this young lady.

The evening went well, Helen was obviously, bright, confident and easy going. She didn't try and dominate the conversation and was prepared to listen to what everybody had to say. Mary was particularly pleased about the way Helen spoke to the hotel staff, thanking them and being polite at all times. For Mary this was a sign of character, she had obviously been brought up well.

Mary was also curious about her father, he was in a similar position to Richard Grice, she was curious to see if he had similar 'attributes'.

"How long has your father worked at Nottingham council?" Mary slipped the question in when the time was right.

"He has been there for thirty years, since he finished university. He likes it but says that once Maddy finishes at Uni he may think about retiring, but at the moment he needs to work. We are ok, because Mum is a doctor, but we certainly couldn't live off the one wage at the moment."

Helen was very open, Mary knew the money that Grice had scammed, obviously Derek Tanner was not operating in that league.

They got back to the house late that evening, Mary made her excuses and left them to sit in the lounge with a brandy. It wasn't long before they were wrapped around each other on the sofa, they both wanted the same thing, so without speaking went straight upstairs.

There was an instant spark between them, they both seemed to sense what the other wanted and they pleased each other all night. Neither had experienced this sense of intenseness before, Helen had only had one lover previously, but she was eager to please. Davey had a few experiences, but this was different, he couldn't get enough of her. They woke up late, the previous day had been long and the night even longer. They lay there spooning, Davey with his arms around her and she holding onto him.

"Thank you, I wasn't sure how the first time would be with you, but it has been perfect." She lay there, so comfortable and relaxed.

"You make it so easy for me, I have never felt such a sense of oneness as I am with you."

"Oneness, is that actually a word," she laughed, teasing him.

They drifted off again, when they awoke it was nearly noon.

"Bloody hell," said Davey looking at his watch. "Time to get up."

He jumped up and went to the bathroom to have a shower, she giggled, wondering what Mary would be thinking about her kidnapping her son and holding him hostage in the bedroom.

The rest of the weekend was perfect they went out for the day to Chester, shopping and seeing the sights of the old city. Sunday night came and he dropped her off at the station, with them both promising to see each other the following weekend. For the next few weeks, they had alternate weekends at each other's house, things were perfect. The weeks turned into months and before they knew it the summer holidays had arrived.

"Let's go to France, I would love to go back. We could fly down and be there in no time," Davey wanted to go to Nice.

"Ok, good idea, but I can't fly." Helen then went on to explain that when she was a child they had flown to Paris and the planes undercarriage failed to open and they made an emergency landing. The plane had bounced off the runway, lurching and rocking before finally landing. The experience had traumatised her and she refused to fly anymore.

Davey agreed to drive there, so their first holiday together was in a villa near the Prom Des Angles in Nice, it was set slightly up a hill with a sea view, a perfect place to relax.

It was there that Davey proposed, he had been thinking about it for a while, he was ready he was coming up for 30 years old, it was time. More importantly he was in love, for him it was the obvious thing to do.

They were in the habit of staying in alternate nights and eating simple meals like local bread, cheese, local charcutier dishes and wine. They would sit there watching the sun go down and sip wine and get pleasantly drunk. On the last night, they went to the market as usual and purchased their items.

Davey was sorting the Salad and getting the plates ready.

"Can you slice the bread, while I am sorting this out," he asked.

"Sure, no problem."

She grabbed the bread knife and started to cut. She felt a resistance as she inserted the knife. Not sure what it was she pulled the bread apart and inside was a very small piece of muslin.

"Looks like they messed up with this one."

She pulled it out and it felt hard inside, so she opened it up. As she unwrapped it, she gasped. "Wow, look at this, it's beautiful." She looked at Davey with mouth wide open and showed him a beautiful diamond ring sat in the middle of her palm.

Davey leaned forward, took the ring and placed it on her finger. "It fits, you may as well wear it if you want to." He was smiling.

Helen suddenly realised what was happening.

"Will you marry me?" Davey was now all serious, she could see the intensity in his face.

"Yes, yes, yes, OH MY GOD," she shrieked, then threw her arms around him.

They somehow managed to get the food on the plates then sat outside on the patio, eating, laughing and planning their future. Davey explained that he had made an incision in the bottom of the baguette and pushed the ring in, he also confessed he wasn't sure how she would react and he was scared she would reject him. He hoped he had chosen the right kind of ring, to which she replied it was perfect. The rest of the night was spent in bed talking about their life together, in-between sessions of lovemaking.

They arrived back home at the end of September and told their parents, which went down well with everyone. Mary now knew Davey was now ready to take over the family business. She was feeling a little bit sorry for herself, she thought Helen was perfect for Davey, but she felt she was losing her son. She also knew her days as chairman of the board were numbered, she was at a loose end and not sure where her place in life was anymore.

On 18 November 1972, Davey's 30th birthday arrived and as promised Mary had arranged for Davey to hand over the running of the company to her son. He already owned 10% and Mary signed over another 50%, he effectively owned 60% now and Mary the other 40%.

A meeting was convened to officially hand over, this was to be followed by a board meeting to validate Davey chairmanship. At the first meeting they signed the documentation and Mary made a short speech where she paid tribute to Davey and how proud she was of him, she also mentioned that she wasn't sure what to do with herself anymore.

Davey thanked her and said, "I am sure you will always find something to do, I think we have something that will keep you occupied as a grandmother… next June," With that he put his hand around Helen's shoulders.

"We are having a baby," Helen announced. The room fell silent for a few seconds, then squeals of delight followed and everyone rushed forward to congratulate the happy couple. At the official Board meeting it was unanimously voted to accept and welcome Davey and his new title of Chief Executive Officer or CEO for short.

Davey and Helen were insistent they wanted a quiet wedding, which was now being brought forward due to time constraints. Mary was pleased with this, there was no family to invite from their side and she did not want to appear a hypocrite by attending a church wedding. Helen's family would have preferred a lavish day, but it was accepted that this could not be organised in the short term and a heavily pregnant bride would not make for a good photoshoot.

The date set was Thursday, 21 December at Nottingham Registry office, with a reception at the Cockliff house restaurant. There were 20 guests, The Tanner family and immediate relatives and Davey and Helen. The were the usual speeches, but it was the quite event that the couple had asked for. After the meal, as they all sat around the lounge drinking and talking, Mary was taking it all in and observing everyone. She came to the conclusion that this was a good family and she was pleased that Davey had made a good choice. She caught Helen's eye, who came over to sit beside her.

"Thank you, for making my son a happy man," she said, taking Helen's hand in hers.

"I am a very lucky lady, I love him so much," Helen said with genuine tears in her eyes, which in turn made Mary well up.

"You will make a wonderful wife and mother, welcome to our small family."

Mary didn't want to make a scene by breaking out in tears, so she excused herself and went to find a toilet, but Helen sensed that the woman who appeared so resolute and strong had a soft underbelly, she could see there was a lot of heartache in the background.

The happy couple spent 5 days on honeymoon in the Lake District before returning home.

On 1 June 1973, the third generation of the Knox family entered the world, a bouncing baby boy, Richard Derek Knox.

Mary was the first to arrive and as she held him in her arms, she could only stare down and smile, not saying anything for a good five minutes. Eventually she looked up and smiled at Helen, "Looks like you have done a good job here, he is an absolute beauty."

Mary beamed as she handed him back to his mother.

"He looks like his father, I hope he grows up to be as clever and handsome," said Helen as she took Davey's hand.

They were released from hospital 4 days later and a new form of normality began. They did not holiday in France that year, but promised themselves they would spend a longer time there the following year.

Davey settled into his new role as the main man at Reddox, with Mary now spending all her time at home and getting bored. She was now struggling to fill her day, even though at 74 years old she deserved to sit back and enjoy life.

Helen too was not too keen on Mary being at home all day, she felt that she had no privacy and that Mary was spending too much of her time trying to mother the baby.

One night after dinner she decided to speak with Davey, but knew it was not going to be an easy conversation as she was the one that moved into his life and his mother had always been there for him.

"I need to bring up a subject and you might disagree with me, but I am going to say it anyway," Helen tried to pick her words carefully.

"I am at home every day with Richard, so is your mother. We are tripping over each other all the time, even though it's a big house."

Davey looked quizzical, so she tried to explain, "You know I think the world of her, but I see twice as much of her as I do of you. There is no sense of privacy, sometimes I just want to be alone with Richard. Please understand what I am saying."

She was getting a little tearful now and Davey could see she was unhappy.

"What do you want to do, or rather, what do you want me to do? Do you want me to speak with her?"

"This is her house, I am the trespasser into her space. We need to move out into somewhere else and make our own home."

Davey could see that what she was saying made sense, so promised to look at other properties in the area. What neither of them realised was that Mary had been passing, caught the beginning of the conversation and had heard every word that had been said.

Davey decided there was no point speaking with his mother about it until they had found somewhere else to live, to which Helen agreed. They spent the next 3 weeks looking at properties, money or a mortgage was not a problem so they could select literally anything that took their fancy. Eventually they found two properties that were perfect and Davey then told Mary he needed to talk to her. Helen insisted on being present, she wasn't going to hide behind Davey and she also wanted Mary to know that she adored her and this was nothing personal against her.

As they sat down in the lounge Mary was the first to speak, "I have been giving things a lot of thought lately and decided I need to change a few things now I am officially retired." This took Helen and Davey by they wondered what was coming next.

"As you are both aware, my circle of friends is rather limited and always has been, I am not what you call a social animal. This means that I have a lot of time on my hands and nobody to spend it with who is of a similar age. I love my holidays in France and always find I am engaging in various conversations and filling my time every day with older people in a similar situation."

Mary had them both mesmerised by now as she delivered her final comments, "In addition to that, the weather is kinder and my rheumatism doesn't bother me… so… I have decided to spend my final days on the Cotes Da Azure. I will be buying a villa there and moving before the cold weather sets in over here."

This took the wind right out of Davey's he didn't know what to say.

"You wanted to speak with me?" Mary asked with a wry smile, she knew what Davey had to say already.

"Never mind what I have to say, where has all this come from?" He was bewildered and confused at the same time. They then spent a while discussing the finer points of Mary's plan and agreed it was a good thing for her health and wellbeing. Helen sat there admiring this wonderful, incisive, thoughtful woman.

She had been aware of the circumstances all along and been brave enough to confront the issues and deal with them, she was in awe of Mary.

Plans were made and Mary went to spend the next couple of months in the South of France, relaxing and looking to see where to purchase a property. She had to return at some point to finalise her financial matters, so it was agreed she would return for Christmas.

Mary spent a productive couple of months in France, she had found a small villa, she had made a couple of friends and enjoyed herself immensely. She estimated it would take about a month to sort out her affairs in England and she booked a flight for 20 December. Davey, Helen and Young Richard met her at Manchester airport. Davey could see she looked well and commented on it.

"Yes, I have kept myself busy, made a few friends and am really enjoying life." The rest of the 30-minute journey was taken up by Mary describing the new villa she had purchased.

As they drove up the track to the house the car headlights picked up a figure hunched up in the doorway. "Who the hell is that?" asked Helen. Mary looked at Davey through the reflection of the rear-view mirror, they knew who it was likely to be. They pulled up outside, the hunched-up figure slowly got to his feet. As the figure reached its full height, he removed the hood of the parka to reveal a very gaunt, weary looking Patrick Reddy.

Helen sensed that this person was trouble, by the reaction of both Mary and Davey, she knew he was not a welcome visitor.

As Davey carried Mary's bags from the car Helen opened the front door and turned on the lights. Patrick had not spoken a word, instead he followed her in and sat down on a chair in the hallway. Mary followed carrying Richard and headed to the lounge, quickly followed by Helen, who did not want to be left alone with this strange man.

"Who is that?" she asked when they were in the lounge.

"That, is my stepson, Patrick, he left a couple of years ago, I was hoping I wouldn't have to see him again. But obviously he has got himself into some trouble and is seeking refuge. No doubt we will soon find out."

Mary did not want him there, but she couldn't turn him away.

Meanwhile Davey dropped the bags off in the hallway and confronted Patrick, "I am surprised to see you, why have you come back?" Davey wasn't going to waste time with small talk, he didn't want Patrick anywhere near his family.

Patrick finally lifted his head and in a very hushed tone muttered, "I have nowhere else to go, I need my family," At this point, Mary had returned from the lounge.

"You look terrible, when was the last time you ate. You smell, where the hell have you been?" She didn't mince her words either.

Patrick began to speak, but his mumbled words made no sense, so Mary took him upstairs and ran a bath, handing over a dressing gown. She ordered him to bathe and went down to the kitchen to sort out some food. Helen was in the kitchen now, giving Richard a little supper before putting him to bed.

Helen knew of Patrick, his name had come up in a few conversations, but nothing that was complimentary, so she knew his arrival was going to cause problems. "He scares me, I think he is a bit creepy."

Mary was a little surprised, Helen never really had a bad word to say about anyone.

"Don't worry he won't be here long, maybe a night or two at the most."

"Too bloody right, he won't be here long, he is going tomorrow," Davey had a face like thunder when he came in the room.

Mary finished plating up some supper and Helen left to put Richard to bed, as she did so she passed the large bulk of Patrick in the corridor, she turned side on to him and scuttled off.

"Who is that?" Patrick asked.

"THAT, is my wife," Davey was getting wound up now.

Mary tried to diffuse the she could see Davey was agitated. She pushed a plate of food in front of Patrick.

"Here, eat first, then we want to know what your situation is." She could see he was not well.

Patrick stuffed the food down his throat, he clearly had not eaten for a while. When he finished, they sat down on the opposite side of the table and began to question him. Helen did not feel comfortable in Patrick's presence and did not return to the kitchen, preferring to stay in the lounge. Patrick was rambling and not making a lot of sense, but it appeared that he had gone to Germany when he left England, spending all his time in hotels and brothels. He spent a lot of money in a short time and in a drunken session agreed to buy a hotel he was staying in. His logic told him it was a good idea, except the hotel he bought was not the one he was staying in, but a rundown wreck of a place with a similar name a few hundred yards away. Because of his word blindness he couldn't understand the paperwork and just signed the documents.

Once he realised his mistake, he then spent a lot of money on a legal case, which he lost. He then met a couple of dodgy builders who gave him a price for renovating it, they demanded a large deposit, supposedly for materials, but they then vanished. The authorities told him the property was in such a bad structural condition he had to either renovate it or demolish it. The refurbishment work was not practical so he had to demolish the hotel. It was then that he discovered that he did not own the land but had bought a thirty-year lease, by now his money was down to a few thousand.

He then met an Algerian woman who talked him into taking her to Marseilles where she robbed him and disappeared on a boat to Algiers. He has spent the last month making his way back to England. He looked a sorry state as he told his tale, Davey found it incredible that anyone could be so stupid.

They told him to sleep in his old room which was still empty, they then agreed to sleep on it and make any long-term decisions in the morning. Patrick was so tired he didn't argue and left his bag of clothes in the hallway and crawled off to bed. Patrick slept for a long time and didn't surface until well into the afternoon. By then Mary, Davey and Helen had the chance to discuss what they were going to do with him.

Mary was the first to speak, "I don't think he realises the cottage he lived in was bought by the trust and is in his name. I never mentioned it or gave him the deeds for the very reason we are discussing his situation now. He can go back there, but he mustn't know he owns it or it will get sold."

Davey smiled, his mother was a cunning old bird, she had thought of everything.

"Agreed, but what of his overall situation, he now has no money. I don't want him working for us again. Everything he touches turns into trouble."

Helen could see that Davey was adamant, but Mary held her palm up and told him to calm down, "I know how you feel, but I made a promise to his father that I would make sure he was ok, I just didn't think it was going to be a long-term commitment. But a promise is a promise, I gave my word and so have to abide by it." Mary obviously didn't want to be in this position, but was determined to make sure its impact on the family was minimal. "I have an idea, but we need to discuss it with Patrick first."

Davey left to go to work and Mary made a few phone calls about making appointments to see various people. Helen took Richard for a long walk and stayed out of the way as much as possible.

When Patrick woke up, he found that his few clothes had been cleaned and ironed and left outside his room. He came downstairs where Mary was cutting some vegetables up in the kitchen. As soon as he came into the room she was on the offensive.

"Right, Patrick, let's not beat about the bush. What have you come back for?" She wasn't going to hear sob stories she just wanted to deal in facts and sort this problem out.

Patrick was really down, the long sleep hadn't done much for his mood, he didn't really know what was going on. He told her he was back because he had nowhere else and nobody to turn to. He slumped into a chair and just sat there, silent and not making any eye contact. Mary realised she was dealing with a mentally destroyed man, he was incapable of any form of a logical thought process.

"While you were sleeping, I have had a few discussions with various people and think I have a plan that will help you out… but you must agree to everything I propose or you can leave right now."

Patrick raised his head, even in his confused state he realised that whatever the plan was it had to be better than the options he currently had, which was no plan at all. Mary told Patrick what was expected and that he would have to see a few people over the next few days. In the meantime, he would move back to the cottage. She still had no intention of telling him he owned it already and Patrick was extremely grateful he could return there. They went to the shops and bought some food, turned the electricity back on and settled him in. She made him some lunch and told him to stay out of the pub and to have a quite few days resting. He didn't really want to go anywhere anyway. Mary left him sat by the fire and returned home, now she had to explain to Davey and Helen what the plan was.

Davey arrived home at 6pm and promptly poured himself a drink, he knew the evening was going to throw up some interesting comments and he also knew Mary was committed to helping Patrick.

The evening meal was eaten in relative silence, as they finished Helen immediately got up to clear the dishes, but Mary stopped her.

"Let's clear everything up at once, I have a plan that we need to agree to." Helen sat back down and Mary explained what she was hoping for.

"Let's examine the facts. Firstly, none of us want him here. Secondly, I have made a commitment to make sure he is taken care of. Thirdly, he is a sick man, there is no doubt about that. He is incapable of thinking straight and making sensible decisions. So, let's look at our options."

Mary clearly knew where she was going with this, Davey and Helen just sat back and listened. Mary continued, "We need to help him with his mental health issues, I have agreed with Patrick he will see a psychologist and get treatment and continue that treatment for as long as it takes. He needs to be managed, he cannot function alone, but we don't want him here, so we need to make sure he has everything he needs at the cottage. He needs to work, so we must find him a job. Driving appears to be the only skill he has, so let's let him drive."

She looked at them both, from their expression she could see they were not happy with what she was saying.

Davey was the first to answer, "We know what he is like, he can't change, he will just be the same stupid moron that's annoyed everyone in the past, so why continue to put up with it?"

Mary was beginning to get angry now. "Because I promised his father, I would make sure he was looked after, that is non-negotiable, Davey. Remember your future is because of your past. If it wasn't for Billy, we would have none of this."

He could see she was getting irate so tried to calm the situation down, "Ok, when does he see the head shrink?"

"After the new year, I am employing a prestigious doctor from Manchester to check him out. We will have a better idea after that."

They agreed not to do anything else until Patrick had been seen, but Davey wasn't happy. Helen admired Mary's loyalty to her promise, but was very worried about sharing any part of her family's life with Patrick.

The visit to the psychiatrist comprised of eight sessions over a six-week period. Patrick agreed that Mary would be totally informed of what went on in these sessions, but she was not allowed to attend personally. After the last session, they all met in his office and he outlined what he thought the problem was and what treatment was required.

He concluded that Patrick was suffering from a psychotic borderline personality disorder (BPD) that was made worse and aggravated because he was on the Autism Spectrum. Patrick needed to not be put in situations where his dyslexia triggered his psychosis. This was not something that could be cured, but it could be moderated by medication.

He then handed over a prescription for a months' worth of tablets, telling her it would take about a week for the drugs to become fully effective.

Davey agreed to see what effect the tablets would have before making any further decision and for the next month Patrick spent all his time at the cottage relaxing.

Eventually the issue could be avoided no longer so Mary, Davey and Helen went to the cottage to see Patrick. The first thing Davey noticed was that he seemed very placid and relaxed, not the coiled spring he usually was. They talked about different things trying to assess his mood and he responded in a very agreeable manner. The tablets seemed to working very effectively. Mary was pleased with his progress but Davey had reservations. Helen still didn't trust him, but said nothing. She felt that this decision needed to be sorted out by the two of them.

It was eventually agreed that Patrick would work as a general errand boy/driver for a few weeks to see how he got on, based around the head office.

While all this was going on Mary knew she couldn't possibly go to live in France permanently, so was pondering what she should do. Davey would not be pleased if she left him alone to deal with Patrick, so she decided to go and have a holiday in her new villa for a few months and take Patrick with her as general dogsbody. Davey was furious and refused to allow her to go, but she insisted he was harmless now he was on medication. Eventually he relented, he knew he wouldn't win any argument with her.

At Easter in '74 Mary and Patrick flew down to Nice, she had 3 bedrooms so he had somewhere to stay with her. He was very compliant and obedient, Mary had described him as her new Labrador which made Helen smile. The medication also suppressed his sexual frustrations, which had been a major problem previously. In fact, he did actually become useful, she was ordering new furnishings and furniture and he came in handy for carrying and fetching.

Chapter Seventeen

Life continued and Reddox expanded once more. The work they picked up in the Nottingham area had a knock-on effect and they were starting to be invited for tenders all over the East Midlands area to the extent they opened another depot and acquired some more plant hire firms. This meant that the head office was also expanding, there was a need for new payroll staff and the accounts office was being stretched. It was at such a meeting to discuss this extra resource requirement that George Kay announced he was retiring, he had worked over retirement age but now it was getting too much for him.

Now was also the time for a complete restructure at the top, they were too large to continue as they were, they needed to introduce another tier of management and to start to delegate responsibility further down the line. Davey used to call Mary on a weekly basis to check on her and at one of these calls he mentioned about George leaving. The phone went quiet then she said, "He will be missed, he is a good man and hard to replace." Davey then explained that they were restructuring and outlined what the new management format would look like. The phone went silent for a few seconds, then Mary simply said, "I am coming home," and put the phone down.

The following day she walked into Davey's office at 2pm.

"That's quick, was expecting you in a couple of days' time. Why have you come back anyway?"

Mary was a worried woman. She was concerned because she had been very badly burnt at Castlefield and didn't want a repeat. Davey explained there would be a very intense recruitment procedure, overseen by specialist head-hunters who drilled down into every aspect of a candidate, that all departments would have budgets they couldn't exceed without authorisation from higher up the management structure and that everything was well organised. This still didn't satisfy her so he sat down and drew up a flow chart to explain how everything would work. This still didn't satisfy her, she was older now and new business management techniques confused her, but she knew she had to let Davey have his way, so eventually gave up. She stayed a few more days then flew back to Nice, she had left Patrick there with firm instructions on what was expected of him. When she arrived, she was pleased to see that there was no disruption apart from the general untidiness that she had expected.

Davey wanted to surprise Mary with a visit to see her at Christmas, but the break was only for a week and it wasn't practical for them to drive or get the train down as there would be no time left. He somehow managed to persuade Helen to fly down and they arrived at Ringway Airport in plenty of time for the 10am flight. Helen was having a really bad time, she couldn't breathe, she was sweating and panicking. Davey took Richard from her and booked themselves in. Helen could feel she was ready to collapse. She sat down and was hyperventilating. Davey could see she was in no fit state to fly, so they turned around and went home.

Xmas was then spent at Helen's parents where they explained that her previous flying experience had really brutally affected Helen, who he promised to try and get treatment as it was not practical to get the train down every time they wanted to go to France.

By the following summer there was cause for more celebration in the Knox family as they announced the pending arrival of their second child. Mary was spending more time in France, she was now settled there and had made friends and had a good social life. Patrick however struggled with the heat, his medication didn't help as it induced sweats, in addition to which he had bloated up and put a lot of weight on and Mary could see he was struggling.

She discussed with Patrick who admitted he would rather be in England, but by now he was reliant on Mary and he had finally realised he could not function alone. Davey agreed that he should come back to the cottage during the hot months between May and November and he would find him some work in the firm. He had softened towards Patrick who was now a lot milder man, that didn't appear to offer any sort of a threat, he was tolerable. Patrick was in a happier place now and as long as his medication held firm he could be managed. Helen however was still very wary of him, she had noticed him staring at her when he thought nobody was looking.

William Knox's arrival in April '75 really lit up Mary's life. She had watched Davey grow up without a sibling and he lacked a brother to bounce off, she didn't count Patrick because they were never close. She was so proud of her family, everything was perfect. Well nearly perfect, young Richard was not too happy about having to share his time with his mother and wasn't exactly welcoming to his new brother. Mary had come back for the birth but was now planning to go back to France. She loved being home, but knew if she stayed, she would want to get involved too much in the children's life. She knew she needed to stand back and let them develop as a family, she had done her bit, now it was up to Davey.

The pattern remained the same for the next couple of years, Mary spending a few months a year in England usually May to September, then back to France for the winter. Davey and the family tried to spend the whole of September in France.

Helen had failed in her effort to overcome her flight phobia, so they had to develop a different strategy to get there. Davey would fly down with the children and she would follow on the train, not ideal but to ask the children to behave for such a long time was not really practical, especially with all the luggage. All she had to do was carry hand luggage so it was an easy trip for her, Richard had all the hard work to do.

The September trip of '78 proved to be one they would never forget. All was well for the first two weeks, they relaxed on the beach during the day, walked the Promenade and had lunch. Mary had been to visit them for a few days then she went back to her home 30 kilometres away. They had now found their favourite restaurants and become very comfortable in their surroundings. On the Tuesday of the third week the sun was beating down and they decided to take some lunch and shelter in a little bistro near the sea front. Richard was complaining of a headache, he was also sweating.

"Looks like the sun has got to him, best keep him hydrated and out of it. We will take them home after eating." Helen was concerned, but Davey just put it down to a bit of sunstroke.

Over the course of the lunch, Richard started to get worse. He started to vomit and developed spots on his arms and legs. "He has got a rash, let's get him home," They asked for the bill and as they were paying the man on the next table informed them, he was a doctor.

"Can I take a look at him; this might be very serious?"

Davey nodded and the doctor had a close look at Richard. After a couple of minutes, he informed them they needed to take him to the nearest hospital, he suspected Richard had caught meningitis. He then told them he could drive one of them there with Richard and his wife would follow on in the Knox's car, to which it was decided that Davey would go first.

As they drove the doctor introduced himself as Paul Gilbert, who had worked at the hospital for over twenty years. Davey could only look down at Richard who was laid out on the back seat of the car and was not looking at all well. They were travelling at speed and reached the hospital in about twenty minutes, Paul Gilbert pulled up outside the main entrance and started to call out in French. A trolley and a porter arrived and immediately Richard was taken to the emergency department. Paul then summoned a doctor over, they had a brief discussion, which Davey did not understand and then they moved him into a side room, where a nurse came to attend to him.

"What's happening, what are they going to do to him?" Davey was very worried. Before Dr Gilbert had time to explain Helen had arrived and was in a tearful state, carrying William, so he explained to both of them.

"They are going to test for meningitis, this means they will give him a lumber puncture and remove fluid from the base of his spine and get it tested for sugar and also if there is an increase in white blood cells."

"What happens if he has it, what's the treatment?" Davey was asking all the questions, Helen couldn't think straight.

"It depends on whether its viral or bacterial meningitis. If its viral then all we can do is give him plenty of fluids and some injections to reduce the chance of swelling in the brain. If its bacterial, then we will prescribe antibiotics and also give him the same injections. Controlling the swelling to the brain is the most important thing. We should get the tests in about an hour, but we will try and reduce brain swelling anyway." Doctor Gilbert was obviously a very good doctor.

He showed them to a side room where they sat waiting very nervously until the results came back. Doctor Gilbert spoke to the doctors, then came over to speak with them.

"It is bacterial meningitis, so they have started him on intravenous antibiotics straight away. Because it's bacterial, it won't have spread to any of you. It has been caught early, so although he will be a very sick little boy for a couple of weeks, he should make a full recovery in due course."

Helen burst out crying, "Can I see him?" She was distraught at not being able to help her son. They were led into the room and Richard was on a monitor with a drip in his arm, he looked helpless.

By now, William was starting to play up, so Richard left her there and returned to the villa where he put William to sleep for an hour. He decided not to tell his mother until they knew exactly what the status of Richard was, she would only worry and be there getting under everyone's feet. His thoughts turned to the doctor and he realised that if it wasn't for his quick action his son could have died. Davey didn't know a lot about meningitis, but he did know swift action could save a life. He was extremely grateful and he hadn't thanked him for everything he had done.

With William rested and fed, they returned to the hospital, Davey took some spare clothes for Helen as just in case. When he got there the doctors were by Richard's bedside and talking in French. These were not the same doctors and Doctor Gilbert was not present. Helen was still sat there, her face ashen and looking extremely tense.

Neither of the doctors spoke English, but there was a nurse who could speak a little, so she interpreted what they were saying. She told them that they were pleased with Richard's progress but it was still early. The antibiotics would take a couple of days to work, they were going to transfer him to the ward and let him rest. There was nothing else they could do for now, so they may as well go home and rest. Helen was having none of it and insisted on staying, so she found a room to shower and change. They went out to a nearby restaurant to eat, then she returned to Richard's bedside and Davey went back to the villa with William.

The next few days were nervous, Richard slept most of the time and when he was awake was complaining of headaches. Doctor Gilbert called in a couple of times and assured them he was definitely getting better, but it would be a slow process.

Davey thanked him, "Your actions may well have saved our son's life. I cannot thank you enough."

"It's my job, so no thanks required," he replied modestly.

Richard got progressively better and after ten days was allowed to leave. He was told that he had to rest and take things easy, he didn't look as though he was in any rush to do otherwise.

After paying the medical bill, Davey asked if Doctor Gilbert was around, nobody was sure but they gave him directions to where his office was. As luck would have it, he was in sorting a few papers out. His door was open so Davey walked straight in.

"He is being discharged today and we are taking him home. If it wasn't for your quick action, we might have been taking him out in a coffin."

Davey was getting a little emotional, but carried on, "Please accept this as a token of our gratitude." He then handed over a bottle of wine.

Doctor Gilbert thanked him and looked at the label, it was a very expensive vintage from Chateau Margaux.

"We would also like to invite you and your wife to have dinner with us before we go back, would Saturday be ok with you?"

Doctor Gilbert said he would confirm with his wife and let him know, which he did.

Davey rang his mother to tell her what had happened over the previous week, as expected she was on the next train. She was livid that Davey hadn't told her about Richard and she made sure he knew it.

Helen by now was back to her serene pragmatic best, she wasn't going to get involved, she didn't want to feel any heat from Mary.

Davey explained about the doctor and the swift action he had taken and said he wanted to treat him to a nice meal. Mary agreed to stay with the kids, so on Saturday night they arranged to meet at La Negresco Hotel, which had a famous reputation for its food.

Davey and Helen arrived first and made their way to the lounge bar, where they settled down with glass of wine. Paul Gilbert and his wife arrived shortly after and they sat down and Paul reintroduced his wife, as the last time was a very rushed occasion. Helen noticed how elegant she was, even the way she drank wine was sophisticated, but like her husband she spoke perfect English. When Helen commented on it, she explained that her father was a diplomat and she had been educated in International Schools. Paul had travelled as a student and spent a lot of time in England, he was fascinated by the relationship between the English and the French in the Middle Ages. The evening was a great success and the beginning of a friendship that was to last for decades. They promised to stay in touch and Davey said they would be back next year, but if they wished to come over to England for a break then they were most welcome.

The stay in France was extended by a couple of weeks due to Richard's illness and it was late October when they finally managed to return home. Richard had been due to start school for the first time, but it was to be after Xmas before he had fully recovered.

The new year in '79 was a very busy one for Reddox. The recruitment process had begun, there were several director posts to be filled as well as a number of senior Managers. Once these had been appointed then they would in turn recruit the lower Managers, it was a very long procedure and it occupied a lot of Davey's time. He was well aware of his mother's concerns and was desperate to ensure it was going to be a painless restructure. He was glad they had used a Headhunting Agency, who were very thorough and saved a lot of Davey's time and energy. They were now a renowned company with a good reputation and the quality of candidate was exceptional. Over the next few months, the posts were gradually filled and the new executive team settled in well.

The next stage was the middle management, the restructure forcing the redundancy of some positions and the creating of new ones. This meant that a number of the existing team having to apply for their own jobs. Davey insisted that wherever possible the outgoing applicant should be given the new alternative posts by default, unless they were clearly unsuitable. This caused a few discussions at board level, Davey's gut feeling was that the new Executive had their own preferences in the form of employees from their previous roles that they would prefer to work with. The existing teams had served Reddox well and he wasn't going to desert them. They had plenty of work going on and it made sense to consolidate, rather than ploughing on chasing work, so the rest of the year was spent easing into transition.

Mary was starting to feel her age and at 78 she was definitely slowing down. She had been getting chest pains, so went to see the doctor who confirmed she had high blood pressure and coronary artery disease and was prescribed tablets for both. Her mind was beginning to slow down as well, she was forgetting things and kept referring to Patrick as Billy. She always made sure Patrick took his medication, but he had run out a couple of times and it was only when his mood started to change that she remembered to get a new prescription. Davey too was aware that Mary's mind was sometimes slipping, a few of the phone conversations had been difficult. His mother had always been very sharp and didn't miss a trick, but lately she was repeating herself and when Davey was trying to explain about the restructure it was obvious she didn't understand what he was saying. He was considering asking her whether she would come back to England as he wasn't sure if she was safe to be over there alone anymore. He also noticed Patrick was becoming a little more erratic and Davey was determined that he see a doctor the next time he was home to see if his medication needed revising.

There was however an incident that accelerated that position.

Mary had a housemaid called Lisa, who was spending more time at the villa to assist Mary to get about, she and Patrick had a few arguments about various things, including going shopping. Mary had taken to letting Lisa do the general shopping and Patrick didn't like it, he enjoyed going around the markets, it got him out of the house. Lisa preferred to go alone it wasn't far and she liked the walk instead of Patrick driving her. She was also wary of Patrick and didn't like his company. One day Lisa spoke with Mary about what she wanted then left the house without speaking to Patrick, when he found out he was livid. Who was she to say when he could and could not drive her, she was only a maid, not his boss. When she returned, she was putting the food away in the kitchen and Patrick walked in and started an argument which quickly escalated into a full-scale row, with Patrick lashing out at Lisa and splitting her lip with a slap to the face. Mary heard the commotion and entered the kitchen to find Lisa on the floor with blood coming from her mouth.

"Patrick, what have you done? Lisa, are you alright?" Mary was shocked and ordered Patrick out of the room.

As she helped Lisa get up off the floor, Mary could see how shocked and scared she was. She sat her on a chair and Lisa in very broken English explained what had happened, that she was scared of Patrick and she didn't think she could carry on working for Mary. She Liked Mary she liked her job, but she felt threatened by Patrick.

At this point Mary knew that Patrick needed to go back and see someone, she noticed that he had changed, she realised that if he get treatment then more serious situations might arise. She promised Lisa that it wouldn't happen again and that Patrick would go back to England for treatment and that she wanted her to stay. She also knew that Lisa was more helpful to her than Patrick, so it made sense to get him out of the way.

After a couple of phone calls to Davey, a flight was arranged and Patrick was sent back and returned to the cottage. It was now the week leading up to Xmas and an appointment was made with a specialist, but nothing could be done until the end of January.

Davey and the family now always went to Helen's mother's for Christmas, it was a bit cramped, but they usually had a good time. Mary now insisted on spending nearly all her time alone, she was becoming a bit of a recluse, Davey worried about her but also knew that if that's what she wanted then nothing would change the situation. Lisa was now living in permanently, so he knew there was always someone with her.

Davey had suggested they stay at home this year as Patrick was alone, this was very quickly dismissed by Helen who wasn't going to disrupt her family celebrations for that obnoxious man.

On Christmas eve as usual, they all piled into the car and arrived at the Tanners house. By the time they got there it was early evening, so after the usual greetings and the Tanners playing with the grandchildren, it was time for the children to eat. While Helen sorted the children out Davey and her father went for a drink down the local pub and generally chatted, mainly about work. Derek announced he was about to retire now that Maddie had finished university. They said they would be also be moving to a smaller property but hadn't made their mind up where yet. Helen's mother was also retiring after 35 years as a GP. They were hoping to finish in the next year. Davey wished them well but knew if they were too far away then it would upset Helen.

They returned home to find Helen and Eva in the kitchen. Christmas eve was traditionally a casual buffet, so the table was full of all sorts of goodies. They sat around eating and drinking and gradually got pleasantly drunk, and had a nice time. Eva then announced about her impending retirement and possible move, Davey looked across at Hellen and could see she was genuinely shocked, she had not been expecting it.

Helen smiled and wished them well, but Davey could see she was troubled. Later that night in bed she confided that she thought her parents too would go and live in France, her trouble with flying meant she would see very little of them.

Christmas Day was always hectic in the Tanner household, Maddy arrived with her new boyfriend, Eva's sister called in and at 11am the Tanners went to morning service at the local church. Helen also went with the children. Davey stayed at home, religion was a very strange creature to him, his mother had instilled a sense of contempt into him and he preferred not to go. He had already decided he would leave all matters such as that to Helen, she wasn't at all religious, but it was a family tradition to go, so she went along with it. None of the children were baptised, it was agreed that if they wanted to seek spiritual guidance then they could do it of their own accord when they were of an age to think independently.

He decided to telephone his mother and after a short while it was answered by a very tearful Lisa who said she had been trying to contact him at home.

"Your mother is very sick, she is in hospital. I found her on the floor yesterday. I have been trying to call you but there is no answer," Lisa was very tearful.

Davey managed to calm her down and tried to piece together the story. She had collapsed yesterday afternoon and Lisa found her an hour later. She then called an ambulance and she was rushed into hospital, where she remained in an unconscious state. Davey immediately rang Paul Gilbert who told him that he also had been trying to reach him, He described Mary's condition as very serious, she had suffered a heart attack and was very ill.

After finishing the conversation, he tried to arrange a flight, then realised it was Christmas Day and everywhere was closed. He started to pack a bag, he needed to be there, he was just finishing when they all returned from the church. Once he explained what had happened, they agreed that he should go home and pack some clothes and book a flight. Helen also wanted to go, so the Tanners offered to keep the children with them and she could catch a train down. The ride home was a sombre one, Mary had always been there for Davey, she was strong. This was new territory and he was clearly upset.

The following morning, Davey tried to book a flight, but again it was a bank holiday so nobody answered the phone. He then had the idea of going directly to Ringway Airport to see if he could fly directly with the airline. He was in luck there was a 12:15pm flight going that day, which he booked immediately. Helen was going to catch the train to Dover, then the ferry, then the train in France, but due to weather conditions there wasn't a ferry available for another 2 days, she would have to wait.

Davey arrived at the hospital in the afternoon to see his mother in a very bad way. She was looking very frail. She wasn't eating and was drifting in and out of consciousness all the time.

He called Paul who met him at her bedside. He informed Davey that she would not last longer than a week and to prepare for the worse. He stayed another couple of hours, then realised he hadn't eaten all day and was very tired. He went back to Mary's villa and decided he needed to speak with Helen about it. Helen listened, choking back the tears, she had grown to adore Mary, she loved her strength, her resilience and her no-nonsense attitude. They talked for about an hour, then Helen said she was going to fly down, time was running out and she wanted to be there. This surprised Davey, he knew a flight was terrifying for her, but was also glad that she would be with him, he needed her there.

After putting the phone down, Helen then began to realise the magnitude of her decision and poured herself a very large Gin and Tonic, then she went to have a bath. She came back down in her dressing gown and made something light to eat. Then she had another Gin and Tonic, then another, then another. She knew there was a flight at 12:15 the following day and it was not likely to be full so she knew she had to wait until the morning to book as the Booking Agents would now be closed. She could feel herself getting agitated so took a Valium to calm her nerves, then had another Gin and Tonic. By now, Helen was totally drunk and forgot she had taken a tablet, so took another one. She laid out on the large chesterfield and fell into a heavy sleep totally oblivious to the world.

Patrick's day had been a bad one, he had been alone for Christmas Day and was not in the best of moods. Not having any friends meant that he had been totally alone and he wasn't pleased with Davey, who he thought he should have invited him to stay at the house. Boxing Day was spent in the pub, but when that closed at 3pm, he made his way home.

He made himself a sandwich and a cup of tea, then settled down to watch the TV, planning to go out again later. At 6pm he had a shower, got changed then went back down to the pub, where he settled down in a corner and had a few drinks. At 8:30 the pub was plunged into darkness, there had been a power cut. After waiting for an hour there still was not any electricity so the landlord decided to close for the night and everyone was sent home. The cottage was on the same power grid as the pub, so when he got home, he was faced with the same situation. After 30 minutes of sitting in the dark, he decided to see if there was any electricity on at the house, it was a couple of miles up the road so there was every chance he would be alright. He jumped in his car and by the time he got halfway there he could see that everywhere was lit up. He entered the driveway and as he approached the house, he could see there were lights on and Davey's car was parked outside. He hadn't been told about Mary's condition so didn't know that they had returned early. He was a little puzzled, so knocked on the door, there was no answer so he let himself in. He still had a set of keys to the house. He shouted out but there was no answer so entered the main sitting room to see Helen fast asleep with her feet up, lying down on the sofa.

"Hi Helen, I thought you were staying with your parents for Christmas?"

No answer, so he repeated the question. Still no answer so he wandered into the kitchen looking for Davey, he wasn't there, so Patrick went upstairs. After a couple of minutes wandering around he realised the Helen was alone, so he went back into the living room and asked Helen where he was. It was at this point he could see the empty glass tumbler and the bottle of Valium capsules.

He shook Helen, but she was completely out of it, there was no response at all. As he nudged her the top of her gown opened a little and he could see she had not bothered getting dressed. Once he was convinced, she was completely unconscious, he ventured further. He opened the gown and her breast were exposed. He couldn't help himself and slipped a hand over them, rubbing her nipples and eventually stooping down and putting one in his mouth. He had always liked Helen. He didn't feel guilty because Davey had left him alone all Christmas and had never made him feel part of the family.

He opened the gown robe and fully exposed her body, which showed she was wearing only a skimpy pair of panties. He was getting excited now and stroked his cock over his trousers as he played with her perky nipples. He unzipped his trousers and got his cock fully out, then asked Helen if she was ok. Still no response, so Patrick moved his hand down to her panties and slipped a finger inside her. Helen hadn't moved, so now he spread her legs open on the sofa and began to play with her pussy, at the same time he was rubbing himself.

By now Patrick was too excited to stop and undid his trousers, he then pulled them down past his knee. He moved Helen around so she had her legs apart and her feet were on the ground. He pulled her panties to one side and rubbed his stiff cock up and down her pussy. He could not hold back now and put it inside her, this was a dream come true. After a couple of thrusts, he realised he was going to come, he didn't want to chance her realising someone had come inside her when she woke up, so started to pull out. He only just made it, as soon as he was outside her he spurted all over her thigh. He then went into the kitchen and got a dishcloth to clean her up with, he couldn't chance there being any semen odour.

Luckily for him, Helen was still completely unconscious and he managed to clean her up without her realising what had just taken place. He readjusted her gown and slowly lifted her legs so she was in the same position as when he first entered the room. He thought it better if he went back home, Helen would not then know that he had been there.

At 6am the following morning Davey was back at Mary's bedside, she was a little more lucid today and realised for the first time exactly where she was.

"How did I get here, what happened?" Her voice was very weak and she had a very grey, pale look about her. She had never been big, but Davey noted how thin and frail she was now.

"Just rest, we can talk about it later," Davey could see she was not going to last long, he gave her a sip of water and repositioned her pillows.

"I am not stupid Davey, I know I am near the end. I can accept it; You and your family are the future now."

Mary's voice suddenly got a little stronger. "But you must promise me one thing, please can you make sure Patrick is cared for. I know you have your differences, but I still have an obligation to make sure he is alright."

Davey had been dreading this, he had already thought she would ask him, but he didn't want to carry on with his mother's pledge to Billy.

"Let's not talk about this now, you need to get your strength back, then we can get you home," Davey was trying to dodge the subject, but Mary persisted.

"I think we both know I won't be going home, this is my deathbed." She gripped Davey's hand.

"Please, promise me you will take care of him, he cannot cope alone, we both know that… Promise me, Davey."

After everything his mother had sacrificed in her life, he could not refuse her last request. He nodded his head, "I promise I will make sure he is safe and secure for the rest of his life."

Mary's hand relaxed in his and she laid back and fell asleep with a serene smile on her face. Davey then went out for a coffee.

As he sat drinking his coffee, he thought about his promise, he knew Helen would not be pleased and he knew there would be even more disruption to come over the coming years, but a promise is a promise and he had to honour it.

He returned to Mary's bedside and sat with her for another hour, at 9am am she woke up and was offered breakfast, which she refused despite Davey's plea for her to eat something.

"I know I am dying and I am at peace with that. My main purpose has been to ensure you grew up happy and successful, which you are. You have a good wife and 2 lovely children and your future is assured. Now that I know you will also care for Patrick, I can die a happy woman."

She then closed her eyes and with a contented look on her face, the life of Mary Reddy nee Knox, was over.

Davey watched her go and although he knew it was coming, the pain was not diminished. He sat there for a while and eventually the doctor came along and declared the death. They then said there would be an autopsy the following day and took her body to the morgue. Davey sat and had another coffee, still a little dazed. Then he realised that Helen would be leaving for the airport soon, he needed to tell her that she need not rush now, there was no point, she could get the train.

Helen woke up about 8am, with a fuzzy head that ached. She looked at the bottle of half empty gin and the tablets, then realised why she felt so bad. After a couple of cups of coffee, she made a slice of toast which she took into the lounge. She was about to call the agent to book a flight to Nice when the phone went, it was Davey.

"She's gone, went about an hour ago, so no need to rush here, just get the train as normal."

Davey's voice was soft, almost whispering, Helen could feel the pain in his voice. "No, I want to be with you I will book it anyway." She so wanted to be with him, but Davey intervened.

"The next week is going to be very stressful anyway, there is no point you stressing out even more. Just pack my black suit, I have a lot to arrange, so can get most of that done while you are travelling." Helen was in two minds, she wanted to be there but she knew Davey was right about the flight stressing her out. They talked a little more about what plans needed to be made before Davey realised that Patrick didn't even know about Mary being in hospital.

"Can you tell Patrick what's happened, he will need to get a flight down here sometime this week."

Helen agreed and Davey promised to call her back before she set off for the train and ferry. The forecast was to clear up a little in two days' time.

Patrick had gone home the previous night and found the electricity was back on. He had poured himself a few large whiskeys and then took himself off to bed. He awoke about 10am and had just got up, when there was a knock at the door. He very rarely got visitors, so curiously went and opened the front door. As he opened it, his face was ashen when he saw Helen stood in front of him.

"What, what. What do you want?" he stuttered.

Helen was equally taken aback, Patrick looked totally flustered. She looked at him suspiciously.

"Can I come in; I need to talk to you?" Patrick was breaking into a sweat, if she realised what had happened, he would lose his job, house and probably go to prison for a long time.

"But what do you want?" His voice was now desperate.

"Mary has died this morning in hospital, Davey said to call you and for you to book a flight down there as soon as possible."

"Oh, is that all, oh ok then."

What do you mean is that all? "Your mother has died and all you can say is that all." Helen could not believe the insensitivity Patrick was showing.

Patrick was relieved, he was safe, so he regained his composure. "No, I mean I am sorry, you just confused me for a second. You know I am not good with words."

Helen couldn't be bothered talking to this idiot, so she said she would book him a flight for the following day and he could collect the tickets from the travel agents, to which he agreed. As she was walking away, Patrick smiled to himself, he had got away with it.

Davey got the death certificate and made the arrangements for Mary's funeral, she was to be cremated and her ashes placed in the garden of her villa. Helen finally arrived and they stayed at a local hotel and arranged for Patrick to do the same. Helen said she didn't feel comfortable being in the villa until all Mary's personal items had been removed. Lisa the maid did however stay there.

The funeral was a quiet affair with only the family, Lisa and the Gilberts in attendance. Patrick hardly said a word the whole week and Davey was concerned this would tip him mentally, but in actual fact, all Patrick was thinking about was how much money he might get.

After the service, they then returned to the house, Helen was missing the children and wanted to go home. There were still a number of outstanding matters to deal with and Davey was going to stay another week to clear things up.

One matter that needed to be addressed was Lisa, there was now no longer a need for her, but both Helen and Davey liked her. They discussed the house and depending on what was in the will they would decide whether to keep the villa, in which case they would ask Lisa to stay on. He could afford to continue to pay her and if and when they decided to keep the villa, or buy a bigger one for their own personal use, then they would be looking for someone, so for now it was agreed she would stay on.

Patrick was asking about Mary's will, but Davey could not answer him, he did not know what was in it. She had it drawn up a couple of years previously with the firm's accountant and it would be read when they returned to the UK. Patrick then flew home, still not saying much and Helen caught the train back.

Once they had gone Davey had a quiet reflective time looking back on his life, he realised he had been privileged and it was all because of his mother's sacrifices. He was wealthy and had a good lifestyle, the business was doing well and the restructure meant he didn't have to work as long as he previously had. He was in his 40th year, too young to retire and anyway, he didn't want to stop working altogether. Looking around the villa, he could see there was massive potential, although it was small, there was a large garden and drive at the front and an even bigger garden at the rear.

As he was sorting Mary's possessions out, it was apparent that she really liked living in this quaint little village, everything personal to her was here, there was very little back in England, only clothes and some bits of jewellery, it was all here.

He decided he would not sell the villa, he would expand it and make it into a home big enough for his family, his mother would have liked that.

He wasn't sure what to do with everything once it was packed up. There were 2 piles, one he was keeping as family mementos, the other was to be disposed of. He asked Lisa if she wanted anything, she took a couple of things, but Mary was a lot smaller than her so she asked if she could take it and give it to the church, which Davey readily agreed to.

He then asked Lisa if she would stay on at the villa, to keep an eye on the place. Lisa was confused and pointed out there would be nobody here, so what would she do? Davey informed her he had big plans to renovate and he would need someone here full time, she gladly accepted his offer.

Chapter Eighteen

When he got back home it was time to sort out Mary's finances, she had died a wealthy woman. She was not a big spender and with the dividends from Reddox and her savings she left a substantial amount of money. George Kay had retired but was still the executor and Mary's will was read out in the Boardroom at Reddox.

In it, she left all of the shares to Davey, but also left instructions for a trust fund to be set up for Patrick, this was a substantial amount but with many restrictions on how it was to be managed and how much could be withdrawn at a time.

The house as expected was to go to the family, with a proviso that Lisa be retained, if possible, which made Helen and Davey chuckle. She was still one step ahead of them in death. Lisa also received a cash settlement as a thank you.

Patrick was listening to all this but was struggling to take it all in. He knew he was getting something and that it was a lot of money, but didn't understand the complexities that surrounded it. He asked George how much his trust fund was worth and was pleased when he was told it was several hundred thousand pounds. But as George explained he could only have so much a year and was not allowed to cash it all in, his face dropped.

"But if it's my money I can do what I want with it," he exclaimed.

George went on to explain about how a trust operated, that did not go down well with Patrick who then sat sulking for the rest of the meeting once he realised the cash was long term and not easily accessible. He was even more annoyed when he realised that the trustee was Davey who had to approve every transaction.

Eventually, he could contain himself no longer and stood up shouting and pointing a finger at Davey, "This was my dad's firm, he made it, but you get all the money, your nothing but a thief." Helen was scared, Patrick was a big man and very unpredictable.

Davey just sat there and let him rant. When Patrick had finished, he responded, "Your dad had a little builder's yard until my mum joined his firm. She was the one that sorted him out, she was the one that organised the paperwork and paid the invoices. She was the one that attended the meetings and won the work, your father was only good for glorified labouring, we would all have nothing if it wasn't for her. So, I suggest you shut up and be grateful that you are still here and not rotting in some dingy cellar somewhere."

Davey was getting angry now, he wasn't going to let this moron besmirch his family name, "I had to promise my mother on her deathbed that I would ensure you were cared for, I didn't want to, but I respect her wishes. Even as she was dying, she was looking after you, you ungrateful bastard."

Helen was shocked, Davey had not mentioned this to her and she wasn't pleased that Patrick was still going to be around for a long time.

"If you're the trustee then you can sign the money over then I can fuck off away from here," Patrick was still ranting.

George explained it was not that easy, Mary had put stipulations in that prevented that from happening. Once Patrick realised he was not getting anywhere, he stormed off, leaving the Knox's and George Kay to finalise matters.

Later that night after the kids had been fed and put to bed, they opened a bottle of wine and settled down in the living room, "Why didn't you tell me about what your mother asked you to do with Patrick." Helen couldn't let the matter rest. Davey sighed.

"I wasn't sure myself what I was going to do and I knew you wouldn't like it, but I promised and we are stuck with him, for now anyway. He will be kept out of the way as much as possible, I am going to get him reassessed and let him continue to work as a driver until I can work something out."

He then went on to explain what his plans were for the villa in France and how he was going to make it a lot bigger. Add a swimming pool and make it a family home. Helen was happy about that; she liked the villa and the area it was in. They threw a few sketches about and drank some more wine, then went to bed totally relaxed and had the best sex they had for a long time.

The following day, Davey went in to work as usual and informed various board members he was going to take a sabbatical for a few months. The business was beginning to take care of itself so he wanted to spend time at home and working on the villa in France. He would still be available for important decisions and would come back for the monthly board meetings.

A week later they were all on the Cote de'Azure and Davey was in discussion with an Architect and various Building Contractors. St Paul De Vance was a small village and he quickly discovered that if you wanted to get anything done in the area then sharing a few bottles of wine and a lunch with the mayor was the easiest way to achieve it. They quickly settled into the area, everybody was friendly and life was perfect. Helen loved France it was just the travelling she hated, so to spend an extended period there was most welcome.

The year passed quickly and was the happiest they had ever been, the villa was finally finished, they had spent quality time together and all of it was capped off by the arrival of a long-wanted daughter, who they named Marie in respect of Davey's mother and also a nod to her love of France.

Richard took an even bigger dislike to his sister than he had to his brother, who he had grown to begrudgingly accept. He was now ten and like his father was academically very bright. William had now started school and was proving to be a handful. He was a clever child as well but more inclined play the clown than concentrate on all matters educational.

After Davey's sabbatical it was back to business as usual and they agreed that they needed to stay in England for the children's education, but when the long holidays came at Easter and the summer it would be in France.

Patrick had come to realise that without Davey, he would struggle financially and that the terms of the trust meant that he was tied into whatever Davey decided was good for him. He did briefly consider taking the matter to court to get more independence but then accepted that he may well lose and that actually he needed someone to guide him through life. He was now in his forties and very vulnerable, he would never amount to much and it was easy to let someone tell him what to do, rather than make decisions himself. He returned to work at Reddox, but was now Davey's run around man, not doing much except driving.

The Knox's had become more involved in charity work and joined the Rotary Club, attending various functions and generally being benevolent in the community.

One night they attended a charity dinner in Runcorn and Helen noticed an elderly lady kept staring at her, which was making her nervous. She mentioned it to Davey who had also spotted her looking over.

"That woman won't take her eyes off me, who is she?" Helen said nervously.

Davey shrugged. "I don't know, I will try and find out."

The woman eventually wandered over to her table. "What an amazing necklace, where on earth did you pick up such a beautiful object?"

Helen explained that it had belonged to Davey's mother, but didn't go into any detail.

They had discovered it when they had been clearing out Mary's possessions from her room and found the beautiful blood red ruby surrounded by sapphires with a gold chain.

Davey didn't have a clue where it came from, but assumed Billy had bought it for his mother. Helen really liked it and wore it on several occasions at various functions.

The woman reached down and peered intently at the ruby. "That's a very unique ruby, there are not many of those about, based on the size and deepness of colour it will be very valuable."

Helen didn't like the way this woman was scrutinising her and put her hand around the ruby. "Thank you, yes, it is very pretty. My name is Helen Knox, and you are?"

The woman looked down her nose at them and snorted, "I am Mrs Esme Starkey, my family are part of the shipping folklore of Liverpool. My family were once one of the biggest transporters to the United States." She looked annoyed they had not recognised who she was, Davey was struggling to contain a smile.

Helen found it equally funny, "Well we know now, don't we?"

The woman could sense she was being mocked, so returned to her table, but kept looking over. Helen adjusted her chair so that she was not in her line of sight and they carried on with the rest of the evening.

Aweek later, Davey was sat at his desk when he received a call from a tearful Helen, who asked him to come home. She wouldn't explain over the phone but said she needed him there. Fearful that something had happened to the kids, he sped home arriving about 30 minutes later.

"What's all this about, are the children ok?" Davey was worried, Helen never rang him at work. Helen opened her hand and inside was the ruby necklace.

"The police have been around, they say there has been an accusation that this has been stolen from a family in Liverpool. It must be that horrible woman we spoke to. I told them it was in your mother's wardrobe and that it was a likely a present from Billy. They took a statement from me and took some photographs. They want to speak to you as well." She handed him a card with a number on it.

The card was actually from an insurance company and they had been contacted by Mrs Starkey, who informed them that she believed it was her mother's chain that they believed to have been destroyed during the WW2 bombings in Liverpool. The family had been paid out, but Mrs Starkey was prepared to give the money back in return for the chain. She remembered it vividly and swore it belonged to her.

A meeting was arranged in the insurance company's offices in Manchester, it was a fairly informal atmosphere with two employees from the insurance company setting their case out. In it, they insisted the description fully matched the necklace claimed by the family. It was so unique it couldn't possibly be otherwise. They had checked the gold assay mark on the chain and it matched where the chain was originally bought in Mayfair London. The fact that Davey could not establish where the chain came from added to the belief that it was stolen goods. It was a good case and Davey said nothing at first. When they finished, he merely said, "As far as I am aware this chain was bought for my mother by my stepfather during their marriage. There is no photographic evidence to demonstrate it is the same chain. Furthermore, there is no evidence to say it was stolen. So, I refuse to accept that Mrs Starkey has any claim, as far as I am concerned the matter is closed and we are the rightful owners."

The room was silent for a short while, then one of them finally spoke. "The necklace is very valuable and we cannot just write this off. If you are not prepared to return the necklace then firstly, we will go to the police and believe you are handling stolen goods, then secondly, we will take you to court and take out a civil challenge that will ultimately end up with expensive court costs and ultimately, I feel sure we will win." He sounded very confident, but Davey was standing his ground.

"Ok, we will see you in court and await the police's arrival."

At that point, the meeting was closed. On the drive home, Helen asked why he didn't just give the necklace back, she liked it but didn't want all the trouble.

Davey angrily responded, "That necklace was a present to my mother, why would Billy steal it? To admit that would undermine his and my mother's integrity. I refuse to allow her name to be disrespected. Also just think of the adverse publicity this would generate for the firm if the CEO was accused of theft."

Helen didn't say anymore, she knew when Davey had a principle to defend nothing would get in the way.

The following week the police arrived and they made a statement. Davey pointed out that it had not been proved the goods were stolen, the police said as far as they were concerned it was a civil matter, there was nobody to bring charges against, the insurance claim was over 40 years ago.

Nothing more happened for over six months, then out of the blue the insurance company sent a letter to say that after due consideration of the facts, it was decided that there was a case for the return of the chain and that they had 28 days to respond and agree to return the jewellery or legal action would commence to recover the stated goods. Davey's response was to get his legal team to respond to say they refuted the allegation that this was stolen goods and that if his reputation was brought into question then he would counter sue and seek punitive damages.

Davey knew that Billy had been working in the area that the jewellery was listed as lost, but wasn't prepared to let his family name be dragged through the mud because of an unsubstantiated accusation.

He found out the original jewellery makers were still active, so made an appointment to meet them and went down to Birmingham to see what he could find out. The firm was in the middle of the jewellery quarter, they had an old frontage and were obviously a long-established company.

He sat down with one of the directors, Mr John Ibbotson and explained the reason for his visit. He opened his case and placed the chain on the desk in front of them. Ibbotson picked it up and examined it very closely with his magnifying glass and smiled as he put it on the table. He looked up at Davey and nodded his head. "Yes, it was made here, I can tell you exactly who made it as well. Every Jeweller adds his own personality to a piece, almost like a fingerprint. This piece was made by a Mister Andrew Ibbotson, he was my grandfather and I also remember my father telling me about it when I was a child."

Davey wasn't sure if this was good news or not and as he was thinking this over in his head Ibbotson got up and went to cabinet where he drew out a number of files and placed them on the desk beside the gold chain. After 5 minutes of working his way through each file, he came to a number of drawings and sketches in a separate file and upon opening it Davey could clearly see the necklace was there in a sketch, along with another necklace that contained 3 rubies surrounded by diamonds and sapphires.

"I knew it was here somewhere, this is your chain, is it not?" and laid out the sketch for comparison. Davey could clearly see it was identical in every way, this was not looking good.

"A customer came in and asked for this necklace to be split up and 3 more necklaces to be made from the original. He then presented the sketch of the necklace with three rubies in it."

"He said he had 3 daughters and wanted each of them to be given a necklace as a Christmas present," There is only a drawing of the original and the one that identifies as your necklace, so it's highly possible that there are 3 identical ones, yours is not an original, "I am afraid."

Davey asked whether all three were made at the same time and who ordered them to be made.

Ibbotson proceeded to start going through the files and not finding anything, he went back to the main files and eventually emerged with a ledger. Running his finger down the pages he eventually stopped on a line midway down.

"The customer was a Russian Diplomat called Nedved who paid in cash on 26 August 1928 and took all three necklaces with him for the grand sum 5000 pounds, but he had supplied the jewels. The value of your necklace today would be in the region of 80000 pounds."

"What happened to Mr Nedved?" Davey was intrigued.

"Who knows, but it's safe to say that the origin of the necklace and whose ownership it is, is certainly open to question. My guess is that as a diplomat, Nedved would be close to the hierarchy in Russia, these jewels could well have fallen into his hands. If so then he probably thought a piece as grand as this would attract too much attention and so wanted it to be broken up. Probably proceeds from the Russian Revolution."

Davey was buoyant now, there was no proof that the necklace was the actual one, there were two others in contention, certainly not enough to support the claim being made against them. Mr Ibbotson was prepared to make a statement and also to testify if required so Davey thanked him and went back home to celebrate.

Helen was relieved and when Davey told her the value of the piece, she was astonished.

The following morning Davey spoke to his solicitors and asked them to contact Ibbotson for the report and to contact the insurance company. A week later they agreed to drop the case, the cost of legal fees far outweighed the risk of not winning. Davey was in two minds, he was tempted to sue them for bringing his family name into disrepute or he could let it slowly die and be soon forgotten. He opted for the latter, there had been too much publicity already.

In September of 1993, Richard, at twenty years old, was ready for university. He was obviously going to enter the family business, but in what capacity? Davey had specialised in the construction elements of the business, but Richard was more focused on financial and strategic matters. In the end he decided on becoming an accountant and enrolled at the University of Salford, which meant he would be able to stay at home, which suited him. He was not a very sociable person and had few friends. He was however very focused on all matters mathematical and had glowing reports and exam results. Helen tried to get him to go out more but he wasn't interested, Davey used to shake his head and wonder how his son was so different.

Never a person to engage in idle gossip, Richard surprised them all at the dinner table one night by commenting on one of his lecturers.

"One of my lecturers looks just like Dad, they are so similar its uncanny," he proclaimed.

"Handsome fella then, is he?" Davey asked. It wasn't often that Richard commented about anything so he had to keep this conversation going.

"Mr Johnson, he lectures in Economics, he is about the same age as you, maybe a bit younger."

The subject then turned to other matters, William was taking driving lessons and gave them all up to date information on his progress and Marie was moaning about settling into her new high school.

Life was very good in the Knox household, they were wealthy, healthy and enjoying all the benefits that they had accumulated over the years.

Patrick too seemed to have finally sorted himself out. He had been referred back to the hospital and they had recommended further changes to his medication. The new prescription made him more alert and certainly not as angry as previously. He had calmed down to such an extent he was now working as Davey's driver for most of the time. Davey had found he was getting headaches and being tired when driving long distances, so it worked out a convenient move for all concerned.

William was now taking exams and although he knew the answers, he didn't apply enough application to get himself top marks, he just did enough to get him through. He was happy with that, he knew his future was secure anyway so why push yourself when you don't need to. This drove Davey mad, not because he had bad results, but because he knew that William was complacent and didn't try. They had a few arguments about it, but William always talked his way out of it and had Davey smiling by the time he was finished. Davey tried to point out that the family business was an institution, that it had grown through the hard work of the family and that it should be treated with respect, not taken for granted. …But it fell on deaf ears.

Helen knew how much it meant to Davey and also tried to get William to understand, but to no avail.

She was also fed up with the amount of phone calls there was to the house from William's various girlfriends, who he let down on many an occasion. He was the hardest of their children to manage, but also the one who made them smile the most.

He lived and loved life to the full and managed to upset Helen by taking girls into his room to study, then they would still be there in the morning at breakfast. They were both glad he was still at home, though, he did brighten the place up. They had also both seen this type of teenager before from their own days at university and knew the more you pushed the less response you were going to get back, so they both hoped he would calm down eventually.

Richard was still working for the company during his holidays and even cut short his annual holiday to France to work in the office. They could see how driven he was and the Managers in the office commented how much knowledge he had picked up over the course of his degree. Richard progressed well, the time passed quickly and the four-year accountancy degree was passed with a 1:1 with Honours.

When Richard was in his third year, William had now progressed to being eligible to start university as well. He had struggled through his A levels and only just got enough marks to be accepted for a University Course. After much deliberation, he opted for business studies. He decided he was going to work to his strengths which were his social skills, he was very much a people person, bean counting or working with bricks and sticks was not really for him.

This pleased Helen as it was the same as she had studied. She hoped he would let her provide him with advice and was also curious to see how the course had developed since the decades before, when she was at university. But William had his own ideas, he wanted a gap year before he did anything.

Davey wasn't bothered too much, but Helen was opposed to it. She wanted him to graduate first then they would reward him with a nice year of travelling to get used to the 'real world' as she put it. It would also give him time to mature as a man before he plundered the planet.

This caused a few arguments but William stood his ground and refused to go to university, he was adamant he was travelling around Europe first. He had his own money from his grandmother and he got a generous allowance from Davey and Helen, so they couldn't really stop him, at 21 he was an adult now. A couple of his friends were also going that Davey and Helen knew, they were from decent families and at least there was somebody to try and keep him out of trouble.

At the beginning of July 1996, they all met up at Manchester airport, the first place they were going to was Amsterdam. They had a vague route of where they were going but nothing was set in stone.

Marie too was growing up, but unlike William she had already decided she didn't want to be involved in the company business, she had her heart set on fashion and design. She didn't like studying and found her concentration levels were low, she preferred it where she could work at her own pace. Helen was pleased with this; she could see there would be problems between her and Richard if they were both working in the same office. She was dreading the day that William would walk through the doors at Reddox Construction Ltd.

Graduation day arrived for Richard and they all presented themselves at Salford University where Richard went off to rent a gown and Davey and Helena wandered around the various buildings, stopping for a coffee in the refectory and chatted about their own experiences and how much it had made them grow up. Davey needed to go to the toilet and wanted take a further look around the place. Helen decided she would go looking for Richard, they both agreed to meet up in half an hour back in the refectory.

Davey wandered around and eventually found himself by the Accountancy and Law block, where there were some interesting photos on the walls of previous graduates going back to the 1930s. Davey was fascinated by how serious everyone looked, not a smile amongst any of them. One particular photo suddenly grabbed his attention, the year of 1934 showed a group of about 15 people, all male and wearing a very stern look on their face. Right in the middle was a young man who on the photo looked to be about the same age as Richard was now. As he peered closely, the likeness became even more uncanny, apart from the fact that the man in the photo was wearing a moustache, it could quite easily be Richard. He read along the names on the bottom of the photo, this particular person was called Robert Johnson.

He didn't think any more of it, then realising he had been gone a while went to look for Helen and Richard.

After graduation, they all went for a nice meal at a very fashionable Italian restaurant in the middle of Manchester where they congratulated Richard on his achievement and how much they were looking forward to him joining the firm on a permanent basis. They had taken the train to go to the graduation ceremony, they didn't want to drive as they knew it would be all day and they would be drinking. But when they were ready to leave Davey called Patrick and arranged for him to pick them up. Richard had arranged to meet some of the other graduates for a celebratory drink and arranged to get a later train back which surprised Helen, so they went home alone. As they drove back, Davey told her about the photo on the wall. Davey chuckled as he told the tale.

"You would swear it was Richard, same build, same features, it was unreal. Somebody called Johnson."

Helen then remarked, "Wonder if he was as serious as Richard is now."

When they got home, they had a couple of more glasses of wine and eventually rolled into bed about 10:30pm.

The following morning was a Saturday and unusually for a weekend Davey had an early meeting and was in the office first thing. It was a tricky meeting as the board were to discuss what Richard's role was to be within the organisation. A number of options had already been explored, some were still under discussion, some already discarded. It was tricky because it meant a reshuffle of the finance department and it was impossible to create a post for the sake of it, so someone would have to make way for the newcomer.

Ultimately it was Davey's company and he could do what he wanted, but he realised there was no pointing upsetting the whole office because of Richard. He remembered how there was some hurt feelings when he was introduced to the company, he knew there was some resentment and he needed to minimise the disruption. He also realised that although Richard was a very capable person, he did not have the experience yet to operate at the very top end of the management structure and would have to learn the requisite skills before being given that opportunity. After two hours of weighing up the options a decision was made about the role and the salary and they left it with Davey to finalise with Richard.

Helen woke up as Davey was leaving and went downstairs to make a coffee, the coffee had just finished percolating when Richard came downstairs. She made them both a drink, then asked how his night had been.

"Had to do it I suppose, but didn't really enjoy it, too noisy for my liking," he muttered, then he asked where his father was.

"He had a meeting with the board, should be back later this morning."

She knew why Davey had gone to work but said nothing to Richard as she knew Davey would tell him later what the plan was.

"Dad went for a wander around the accounting block yesterday and said he saw a photo from years ago and there was someone that looked just like you."

"Bet it's not as weird as Johnson, my Economics lecturer who is the double of Dad."

Helen then asked what he wanted for breakfast, then made them both a bacon sandwich.

Although they were wealthy, they had never found the need to have staff around the house, apart from the gardeners who came in weekly during the summer and fortnightly in the winter. Helen liked to look after her family, it made them closer. As she was stood over the cooker frying the bacon, she realised there was something niggling away in her head that she couldn't shake off, but she couldn't quite get her head around and it troubled her.

When Davey arrived back, he sat down with Richard to discuss his future, the result was not what Richard was expecting.

"As you know, Reddox has 3 arms to its structure, Reddox, the main construction company, Reddox Plant and Tools Supplies Ltd and RMS, Reddox Materials Supplies company. Each is an independent company in its own right with a separate management setup."

Richard nodded, he wasn't sure why this was being explained to him.

Davey went on. "The finance director of RMS will be stepping down and retiring in 18 months' time, so what's proposed is that you work under him until he retires, then you will become the finance director at RMS."

Davey was quite pleased with this outcome as it ticked every box, Richard thought otherwise.

"I don't want to be stuck out in Runcorn, counting bags of cement. I want to be in the heart of it at head office, with you," Richard was seething, he hadn't expected to be offered such a minor position.

Davey explained that he needed to gain experience and the only way to do that was by learning on the job. They had looked at all options but the post had to be within the finance department, as that is where his skills lie and that having a degree was only the beginning of his career, he still had a lot to learn. He then handed him a sweetener. "It has also been agreed that you will become a non-executive board member, you will be involved in the major decision process, but without a vote… For now. Eventually you will become integrated inro the board proper, but not yet. You are the future of Reddox, but learn to walk before you run."

Davey looked across at Helen who could see Richard's disappointment, but she knew Davey had made the right decision. Richard was impatient, but he had to learn that hard work pays off, not being fed with a silver spoon.

Finally, she spoke, "When you look at the others that graduated, what level of responsibility do you think they will be allowed in any jobs they get? I suspect most if not all of them will be working as basic bookkeepers for the first few years. You are to be assistant director in a company that trades tens of millions of pounds a year, that is some first job to have, young man."

Davey smiled, as per usual Helen had nailed it! They talked a little more about the role then Richard said he accepted what they were saying and took himself out. He had recently been told that golf was good for business contacts, so had started taking lessons.

When he had gone Helen casually asked what the name of the man on the picture was that he had seen yesterday.

"R Johnstone or Jonson, something like that." Helen tried to look nonchalant but inside her head was spinning, it was the same surname as Richard's lecturer. This was bızarre.

The rest of the year faded away, William had promised to come home for Xmas, but they all knew deep down he wouldn't. What was concerning was that there was no contact whatsoever, no phone calls or postcards, nothing. Helen was worried and Davey tried to calm her down by saying if there had been a problem his friends would have been in contact. She called his friends families and apparently, they were all ok and William was last heard of heading towards India.

Richard had eventually reluctantly come to accept that there was more to running the financial aspect of a company than a degree allowed for, he was on a steep learning path. Luckily, his new boss was very experienced and competent and taught him well. Once Richard had accepted what the position was, he became a sponge, soaking up every piece of information he could, he was a quick learner.

Marie left school at 16, she wasn't interested in A Levels. Like William she said there was more to life than studying. She had already made her mind up about university, she wanted to do something creative, but wasn't sure what it would be.

Helen had met a Mrs Sweeney at the Rotary Club who had a couple of clothes shops and Marie was working there until she could figure out what her future was. She would take her out to the various warehouses to look at what fashions were available. Davey commented that his mother would have approved, she had told him about her fashion businesses she had before he was born.

William had been due back in June of '97 but didn't arrive, all his friends had got back and one of them rang Helen to say he was ok, but he wanted to go and see the Philippines and would be back in February the following year. Helen was furious, Davey knew this was always likely to happen but had said nothing.

"This means he won't be able to start Uni… and another Xmas away." Helen moaned.

"That's why he did it, I don't think he ever intended to go this year."

Davey gave a wry smile; it was typical William.

The rest of the year was fairly eventful, Helen's father passed away unexpectedly, having had a stroke while working in the garden. Helen was distraught, but accepted that at 88 years old time would eventually catch up with him. She was now more concerned about her mother who was a year younger and also in poor health. Helen was spending long weekends with her, sharing the load with her sister. Eventually the travel got too much and they arranged for her to be placed in a residential home where she could receive more attentive care.

In November, Davey received a call from the Managing Director from one of the biggest construction companies in Europe which proved interesting. They wanted to buy out Reddox and made an offer of 150Mpounds, which was a lot less than it was valued at, it was obviously an opening enquiry to gauge an opinion. Davey was very blunt in his reply.

"Sorry, not for sale now, or at any time. We are a private family business and intend it to remain so."

The offer was improved, "What if it was 200m?"

"You're wasting your time and mine, thank you for your offer but it's not going to happen, goodbye." He then ended the call.

He told Helen, but said nothing to anyone else.

"That's an awful lot of money," she responded.

"I don't care how much they offer, I will never under any circumstances sell out all the hard work Mother and Billy put into it… that's the end of it."

Helen could see he was adamant, so never mentioned it again.

The following month was the last meeting of the year and traditionally Davey hired a local hotel with conference facilities, where a lavish lunch was laid on after the meeting was finished. Before the meeting, Davey received another call that said the final offer was for 235m pounds, which again was rejected.

The meeting went through the same formal motions and at the end under 'any other business' Davey mentioned the buyout offer from Pollock Enterprises. A few eyebrows were raised including Richard who was now allowed to attend meetings but without a vote.

"That's probably near to the true valuation," said Davey. "But it's irrelevant anyway. I don't want anyone to worry, your jobs are safe, we can withstand any offer because I hold all the shares and can state categorically, there will be no sale."

This went down well with everyone in the room except Richard. He had been promoted to finance director at RMS, but it wasn't enough for him. He found the work tedious, it was all too straightforward and routine for him, he wanted more. He had been dabbling in the stock market using his own money and been quite successful. He hadn't said anything to anyone, but now had built up a decent portfolio and wanted to expand. He wasn't interested in the cost of roof tiles or bricks, he wanted the cut and thrust of the stock exchange, his aim was to become a billionaire. To do that he needed capital and if the company was sold, he would no doubt be given a substantial amount of money to play with, he wasn't happy at all.

Helen always tried to cook a proper family meal at least twice a week and the following Saturday the four of them sat down to enjoy a roast dinner. As Davey poured the wine and Helen sliced the meat, Richard who had been stewing all week about the buyout offer, could contain himself no longer.

"It was a very good offer for the company, Dad."

Davey just gave him an intense stare. "I never said it wasn't." Helen could sense Davey did not want to discuss the matter so tried to change the subject, but Richard persisted.

"Then why will you not consider it?"

"I have considered it and rejected it, now can we please let the matter drop," Davey looked at Richard.

Helen knew the signs, she glared at Richard. "This is not the place to talk business, Richard, please do as your father says and shut up." She was now also getting wound up.

"But just think of what we could do with all that money, we could start new ventures, create new empires, we could make even more money," Richard was not listening. Davey said nothing for the next minute or so, but Helen could see he was building up to say something, he was just getting it clear in his head what he was going to say. Then Davey began.

"Just how much money do we need? We have everything we need in life, any more money will not make us happier. In 100 years, we will all be gone, we will be short term memories. But this business will still be here and all our future Knox's will always remember how it started, they will always remember who we were. If I sell then nobody will remember anything about us… AND THAT IS WHY I WILL NEVER SELL. NOW SHUT THE FUCK UP AND DON'T MENTION ANYTHING ABOUT A SALE AGAIN OR YOU WILL BE OUT OF THIS FAMILY, ARE YOU FUCKING LISTENING TO ME."

Davey was now raging, but his message certainly got across to Richard, who visibly winced. Marie who had said nothing, could only sit there open mouthed, she had never heard her father swear in front of her. Helen too was shocked, Davey very rarely lost his temper and she had never seen him as angry as this in all the time they had been together.

"Ok, I am sorry, I won't mention it again," said Richard holding his hands up.

The rest of the meal was eaten in total silence, Helen couldn't wait to clear the table and Marie scuttled off to her bedroom at the first opportunity. The matter was never raised again and Richard went back to the job he resented and kept his head down for a while.

Meanwhile William was having a great time, he spent Christmas with his new Filipino girlfriend and family and life was a beach. He knew he would have to go back and face the music in February, money was not a problem but he knew he needed to spend some time with his family and start to live normally. He had been on a good run for his money, but 18 months is a long time and it was time to face reality. On 28 February he booked a flight and 20 hours later was back in Manchester.

He didn't call anyone, he just got a taxi from the airport and turned up with his rucksack full of smelly clothes. There was no-one there to meet him so he filled the washing machine, but didn't know how it worked so left it and went up to his room exhausted after a long overnight flight, where he fell into a deep sleep.

Marie was the first one back, she went into the kitchen to make a drink and noticed the smell of sweat, and soiled clothes, pulled a face and took her drink into the lounge. Helen was next home and she went straight into the lounge and sat down opposite Marie.

"There's a funny smell in the kitchen, like someone has died," said Marie screwing her face up.

"Probably a blocked drain, I will sort it out." Helen got up to take a look and was in the kitchen for about 30 seconds, then let out an almighty scream and rushed up the stairs. She threw open the door to Wiliams room and found him fast asleep, then rushed over and grabbed him in her arms.

William, who was completely out of it, was jolted back into reality and didn't know where he was.

"What the fuck!" He momentarily lashed out, then realised where he was. Helen was hugging him like a new born baby, William was in a daze.

Eventually she let go and sat beside him on the bed. "You have lost weight, but you look well," she observed.

"And you smell, go and get a shower and I will make you a drink and something to eat," then left the room.

The rest of the day was question after question from Helen, William was beginning to wish he hadn't bothered coming home. Marie was also glad to see him, she had missed him. When Davey arrived, he didn't bother asking too much he knew Helen would fill him in later, he just hugged him and asked about his welfare.

"You have lost weight, son."

Willim nodded and whispered when he though Helen couldn't hear, "Yeah it's all that shagging and eating coconuts, great diet."

But Helen had heard and she had a little chuckle to herself as he left the room.

Nothing was said about William's plans for about a week, but he knew they would want to discuss it with him. He still didn't have a clue what he wanted to do, but did at least accept that he needed a career. Applications for university would not be open yet so he had time to confirm his options. A few months later, he applied for and was accepted for a position at John Moores University in Liverpool, which of course meant he would be living away from home.

Marie was enjoying herself working in the clothes shops, she had now progressed to actually ordering the new stock. She loved the sense of freedom she had been allowed and appreciated the trust placed in her. There were 5 shops and she had a floating brief to supply them with whatever she thought was fashionably suitable. An opportunity then came up in a conversation with Mrs Sweeney that was to create a fantastic opportunity.

Marie mentioned that she wanted one day to own her own shops and was surprised to learn that the owner was considering retiring and she could have the first chance to buy. Marie was only 19 and although she enjoyed her work, she was worried the overall responsibility of managing the whole process was too much for her at such a tender age. She asked how much it would cost and they were asking for 250k for all five shops. They explained that the buildings were all leased and what she was buying was the stock, fixtures and fittings. This seemed like a good deal, so she decided to look into it.

She mentioned it to Davey, who wasn't very keen, it seemed like too good an offer. He was prepared to go along with it for now and said that before anything was done, they needed to get the accounts for the last 3 years and run them by Richard, but Marie didn't want him involved so it was agreed another accountant within the company would take a look.

The books appeared to be ok, with nothing that would cause concern. There was an issue about the leasehold being renegotiated in the event of the company changing hands, but Mrs Sweeney said that was a minor matter that could soon be resolved. Davey still wasn't convinced though and insisted the leasehold matter be discussed and agreed before any contracts were signed. Marie had wanted Davey to support the deal financially but he refused and said he would only partially fund the project if all the right terms were in place.

Marie thought she knew better and agreed terms with Mrs Sweeney and renegotiated the lease thinking her dad would support her anyway. She tried to get a loan from the bank but they said she didn't have enough experience and was therefore a bad risk and refused. She was very frustrated now and went back to her father and pleaded for help. Davey had mixed feelings, on the one hand he wanted her to succeed, but on the other he needed her to be realistic. In the end he relented, Marie never really asked for anything and if it was a foothold on to better things then he had to help her with the finances.

The deal was done and Marie was now the proud owner of 5 shops, which were renamed 'Marie Marie' which came with the strapline 'so good they named it twice'

Apart from the new advertising and shop signage, nothing else changed. She had a tour of the shops and informed everyone there would be no difference, all their terms and conditions remained and it was business as normal at the front of house. She did however need to get new accountants, set up credit accounts and change banks, there was a lot more work than she anticipated and she was working long hours to get herself into a position where there was a full transition from the old company to the new.

Because of all this back office work, she was neglecting to go and buy new stock and the shelves were running down. She also realised that her investment was a lot more expensive to run on a daily basis and her cashflow was limited. The suppliers refused to extend to her the same payment terms as Mrs Sweeney because she was a new venture, which affected her turnover. After 3 months she was forced to ask her father for a further loan of 25k to keep things running. Davey warned her this was the last time she could expect him to bail her out and deposited the money in her bank account. Gradually things settled down and she was ticking over, not making a massive profit, but enough to gain a little stability.

Richard was not happy that Marie was getting what he considered to be favouritism, He was the one putting in the real work while she played at being a shopkeeper. He had kept his head down since the dispute about selling the company, but he was still angry. Davey had made the effort to make sure that Richard was aware that he had a big future at Reddox, he was going to be the financial director of the whole group in a couple of years, with great responsibility. He was told he was a valuable asset that was to be nurtured, but Davey also knew how ambitious Richard was.

Richard was still buying stocks and shares and his investments were rewarding him with a steady return. He had thought about asking Davey for some extra money to invest, after all he had subsidised Marie, but then thought better of it.

In September 1999 William enrolled at John Moore University and quickly settled into his new routine at Liverpool, as usual, he was the life and soul of the party.

He surprised himself when he realised he actually liked studying there, it was a good mix of education and a nice lifestyle.

William started off in the halls of residence, but quickly moved out. The room next to him was taken by a Chinese student who complained about the noises from his room in the early hours after the bars closed. William's response was to knock on his door and invite him in for a drink at 3am. The student declined but was dragged into his room anyway where there were 2 girls waiting in a preplanned arrangement to embarrass the poor man.

William then locked him in his room with the girls and went and waited in the Chinese student's room. Within five minutes the said Chinese student was heard screaming to be let out as the girls made themselves available. They let him out and he bolted into his own room and locked the door. William thought this would stop him complaining, but it actually made things worse. He was reported and it was the talk of the university. Chinese students were a great source of revenue and this was not appreciated by the hierarchy. He was on the verge of being expelled but as usual talked his way out of it and agreed to live off campus.

He settled down and eventually reached his goal and achieved a 2:1 in Business Studies in 2001

Chapter Nineteen

The new millennium arrived without any major dilemmas, all was steady in the Knox household and even Patrick was not causing problems anymore.

Helen's mother unfortunately had now died at 90 years old, which caused Helen to contemplate her own and Davey's future. They were coming up to 60, a time when a lot of people were considering retirement. They did not need to think about finances and Helen wanted to spend more time at the villa in France. She was beginning to suffer from rheumatism and the warmer climate would be of benefit. They discussed it and Davey agreed they should spend more time in France, they still went for a month in August and they still both enjoyed it there.

"Your right, we do need to wind down, but the timing has to be right."

Davey wanted to sit back a little, but didn't think Richard was up to it yet, but he didn't mention this thought to anyone else.

Helen, however, knew exactly what he was thinking, Davey was scared of letting go.

"You should give Richard more responsibility, you know he lives for work, he would relish it." Helen was testing the water.

"Why don't you take a year off and make Richard temporary CEO and see how he copes." Helen looked intently at Davey. "If after a year, he has done well, then you can relax and get ready to handover."

"And what if he doesn't manage, what then?" Davey replied, but he could see there was mileage in the idea.

"Then you look at the areas he is failing and point him in the right direction, to prepare him for the future."

Davey smiled to himself she had done it again, Helen was so much like his mother when it came to thinking things through.

"That actually might work, I will see what can be worked out," Davey was quite pleased with this outcome, it would give him the chance to assess Richard's capabilities and frailties.

Over the next few weeks, Davey worked out a strategy for the next 12 months, then when he was satisfied, he spoke to Richard and let him in on his plans.

He asked him to a meeting in his office, where he outlined the proposal which was that Davey was going to take a full year off and hand over to Richard. He would have the same control as Davey and he would chair the meetings and generally run things without interference. Richard was delighted, this is what he had been waiting for, even though it was only for a year it would give him the opportunity to demonstrate he had what it takes to manage a large organisation. The agreed date for the handover was the beginning of the following tax year in April.

What Richard didn't know was that Davey had spoken to a couple of the other directors and told them to keep him informed of the important decisions that Richard wanted to make.

Richard casually asked about what would happen if and when Davey died, which he thought was a bit morbid and told him so.

Richard nonchalantly said, "We must face facts, that day will eventually arrive, so we need to know what your long-term plans for the company are."

Davey reply was instant. "This is a family firm and will remain that way. The shares will be distributed equally amongst you all." This appeared to satisfy Richard's curiosity.

Helen was delighted, now they could sit back and relax and enjoy life on the Cote D'Azur. But she also knew Davey would be worried about what was happening back home and would never totally switch off.

It was now April 2002 and the train was booked, ready for a new phase of their life. Because there was no hurry, Davey took the train with Helen, he had all year to do what he wanted so a leisurely first-class ticket on the TGV was just the start he needed. He was surprised at all the improvements made since his last train journey all those years ago, it now only took six hours from Paris to Nice and the ride was exceptionally comfortable. Previously he had to insist he flew as time was important, but now time was irrelevant.

They arrived in Nice at 4pm and got a taxi to the villa, where they unloaded their bags. They always travelled light as they had a permanent wardrobe of clothes that they retained at the villa, so they were in holiday mode within half an hour.

Davey had bought a Mercedes a few years ago and was checking that out as Helen unpacked. They arranged to meet Paul and Claudette for a meal that evening where Davey outlined their plans for the future. The Gilberts had watched the children grow up over the years and Davey was hoping to get their opinion on the what he had proposed.

"There's no doubt Richard is a capable young man, who is very intently focused when he decides he wants something," were Paul's first comment.

"Yes, but is that good or bad? He has tunnel vision when it comes to getting what he wants, he can never see alternatives… that is not good leadership!" Davey clearly still had reservations.

Helen then mentioned that this year could be the making of him.

"We have a good team of executives who could lead him into making the right decisions, he can learn a lot about being part of a team and showing he has what it takes, it's a great opportunity for all of us."

Helen was optimistic, but Davey held up his hand and stated, "Only if he is prepared to listen. If he messes up it will be a long time before I will trust him again." Helen then changed the subject and they enjoyed the rest of the night.

As Davey was settling into life in Nice, Richard was beginning to feel more confident. He could finally see the day when he would have control of the company, was only a matter of a couple of years away. He decided to ease his way in before exerting any real control, after all the company was well run and the key players in the executive team were loyal and trustworthy.

The board all knew it was a matter of time before Davey retired and his heir was installed and accepted Richard's installation as CEO without question. There weren't really any big egos to massage, they all knew their job and accepted the changes that were coming.

The next few months came and went William was now on board as a manager in the Human Resources, dept responsible for day-to-day recruitment and general matters relating to personnel. He had no financial or operational responsibility, he just dealt with people. This suited both of the brothers, Richard didn't want his younger sibling sitting by his side. In Richards eyes William was totally irresponsible, whereas William took the view that Richard was a total prick.

Marie, by now was struggling with the clothing shops life was harder than she imagined, with so many matters that needed to be dealt with at any one time, she was overwhelmed with paperwork and cashflow problems. She was drowning and needed help, this was making her ill.

She had a meeting with her accountant, who warned her she was getting into serious problems and recommended she dispose of at least two of the shops that were losing the most money. In his opinion, the turnover they generated were never going to realise a profit and if they were disposed of then the others could possibly be salvaged.

Marie reluctantly agreed and informed the leaseholder of her plans to terminate the rental agreement, at which point she was informed she still had 8 years left on the lease which would have to be paid regardless of whether she operated or not. Marie was trapped, the rents were a substantial part of the problem. Her father had warned her, but she hadn't listened.

She got her solicitor to take a look at the overall situation with the shops including what was required in terms of redundancy details for the 5 members of staff. She was waiting for a response but suddenly got a call from the previous owner Mrs Sweeney who wanted to meet up with her at the Widnes shop.

As Marie sat in the back room of the shop, she looked around and it was obvious she had paid more for everything than it was actually worth. She had paid retail prices for the stock, when it should have been the trade value. Her rent had nearly doubled since she had taken over.

'What a bloody fool I have been it was a stupid decision and now I am stuck with it,' she thought as she pondered her stupidity Mrs Sweeney came into the shop and made a cup of tea for both of them. She then sat down and explained the purpose of her visit.

"I expect your wondering what I am doing here, well I won't mess about, I will come straight to the point."

She then took a sip of tea, before resuming. "You are looking to relinquish your lease, which means you are probably going to close the shops, am I correct." She did indeed get straight to the point.

"Yes, the rent is too high and turnover has dropped by 60%, I have tried to see why it has dropped, but there doesn't appear to be any main factors that have caused it. But I cannot continue like this, something has to give." Marie was close to tears as she explained.

"You still have 8 years on your lease as well so even if you close then you are still obliged to pay that," Mrs Sweeney had done her homework.

Marie was puzzled as to how she knew all this.

"I am prepared to offer you a way out, which will save you any further losses. If you agree you walk away from the shops and won't owe any money," Marie was listening, she needed some form of escape.

"If you handover the shops to me for nothing I will take on the leases and keep the staff employed."

Marie thought about it, the leases were the main cause of her problems and paying them for another 8 years was not something she was looking forward to.

"Ok, let me discuss it with my accountant and I will get back to you."

This could be a way out for her, Marie was definitely considering it.

Mrs Sweeney then dropped the bombshell, "Just so you understand, that is all five shops, not just these two."

Marie was shocked, she hadn't anticipated this result. "But I was only discussing the two, I don't really want to sell them all."

"Its 5 or nothing, take it or leave it. Please discuss with your accountant and let me know within the week," Mrs Sweeney was certainly ruthless.

As Marie sat there stunned, Mrs Sweeney had a parting shot, "Your debts are only going to increase, my dear, get out now before you owe a lot of money."

She met her solicitor and sat down and explained the offer that had been proposed. When she had finished, he looked up and gave her the bad news, he informed her she was in serious financial trouble.

"The five shop assistants have all been there for a number of years and are entitled to a redundancy package running into several thousands of pounds. The leases were watertight and will still have to be paid." This was not encouraging news.

"But I have only been there for less than two years, they were not working for me all those years ago."

"Doesn't matter, you assume full responsibility for their rights when you bought the company," he explained.

"I think you need to speak with your accountant, financial matters are not my responsibility, I only provide legal advice."

Marie took that to mean he was hinting that she was in a bad situation and needed to find the path of least financial pain as soon as possible.

The meeting with the accountant was even worse, he informed her that having delved further into her situation, it was unlikely she would ever make a profit from all the shops and getting rid of the two was not going to solve the problem. Turnover had dropped significantly in all areas, he suggested that because of her inexperience and the fact she was trying to manage every aspect of the business, then standards had dropped.

Marie had to accept that whereas she had previously been able to predict what was fashionable and trendy, recently she had not been ahead of the game. This had resulted in buying stock that was not up to date, therefore sales were down.

He listened to the offer Marie had received and then offered his opinion.

"If you ignore her offer and close the shops down, you will still be liable for the rent and also redundancy pay, which at the moment you cannot afford to pay. You are at the limit of your overdraft, your debts will mount month on month and I cannot see where you can retrieve the situation. I cannot tell you what to do, but I can forecast what your financial position will be if you don't accept her offer… and it will be a lot more expensive than rejecting her offer."

Marie knew she was beaten and had no choice, she had to accept or face further losses. The telephone call was made and the documents drawn up. A month later and 'Marie Marie' was no more and had reverted back to Mrs Sweeney, complete with all the stock. Marie was still faced with a mountain of debt.

Marie couldn't understand how Mrs Sweeney could make a profit and would want the shops back but she got the answer a couple of months later.

Mrs Sweeney's husband had a number of commercial properties and was in court, he was accused of drug dealing and laundering money through his subsidiary companies one of which owned the lease of the shops. It appeared that he set a rent for Mrs Sweeney's shops, but she never paid because he laundered the cost of the rents through these dummy companies and also laundered dirty money into her shops as purchased stock and sales. The shops had never made any profit and were just fronts. Mrs Sweeney had wanted out of it and sold the business, but they needed somewhere to get rid of the money so he made her get it back.

Marie had never been in a position where she would make a profit. In all the time she was working there, she never once suspected what was going on.

She was now ruined, the bank was on her back, her accounts were a mess and she owed thousands. She knew she could ask her father but she didn't want to trouble him, he had warned her and she chose to ignore him. He had already spent a lot of money, she dares not ask for anymore.

By September, Richard was getting restless, even though all was well at Reddox. He still wanted to make his mark, so he set up a plan to expand and impress his father. He was still investing on the stock market and had acquired some shares in a company called Aztec Electronics who manufactured motherboards for various companies including well known household appliance manufacturers. They had expanded quite quickly over the last couple of years and he had kept a close eye on their results. He did some private investigation and discovered they could be bought out for 20 million pounds, which he thought was reasonable.

After an initial contact he was invited down to the factory for a tour and a meeting with the directors. He went alone at this stage, he wanted to tie everything up before he presented it to the board.

He did not understand a lot of the technical jargon and although impressive it was too much for him to take in at this stage. He asked if he would be able to see the accounts, this was approved on the Proviso that an official Memorandum of Understanding from Reddox was received. He went back and prepared a comprehensive report outlining the need for Reddox to diversify and expand into other areas. He also produced graphs to show the improvement in turnover and profit from Aztec over the last 5 years of expansion. Finally, when he was ready, he had it added to the agenda and presented it to the board at November's monthly meeting.

There were plenty of puzzled faces as he made his pitch, nobody had been consulted, nobody had a clue about electronics and everybody wondered what the hell was going on.

Richard was on his feet for about 20 minutes giving his PowerPoint presentation and when he finished, he asked if there were any questions. At first there was a stunned silence until eventually the first question was asked by the Operations Manager, quickly followed by a flurry of others.

"Why are we getting involved with electronics, this is a completely alien area?"

"They would appear to be totally reliant on being a company subcontracted to others, they have no direct outlet themselves."

"Why have they suddenly been profitable when for years they seemed to have mediocre results?"

"If all this success is down to the current owner, what happens if he leaves?"

The questions kept on coming Richard was barely able to keep up. In the end, he requested that a special meeting be set up to discuss the offer, but he made it quite clear to them all he wanted this acquisition to go through. The special meeting was quickly called a couple of days later and after thinking it all through it was obvious that the board in general opposed it. Richard could sense this and decided he needed to make a stand.

"Of course, I understand your concern, but we need to diversify and spread our wings into other areas. This will not be the first move into a new direction, nor the last and if there is anyone here who does not share that ambition, then maybe they should consider their future."

Looking them all in the eye as he said it, this was a clear warning not to stand in his way. They took a vote and most of them were of the opinion that it wasn't a good move, there were too many areas of concern and the proposal was rejected. Richard was furious and as they all vacated the room, he was left alone with the vice chairman of the board Martin Livesey.

"You are making a mistake, Richard, we operate within parameters we understand. You are talking about a fledgling company that's not fully established, there is so much that can go wrong." He tried to reason with him, but Richard was past discussing anything, this was going to happen one way or another.

"It's the future of this company whether you like it or not. We WILL buy this company." He pointed at Martin, who sat there very calm and refused to get into an argument.

"Does your father know about this move, I can't see him agreeing to it?" Martin calmly asked.

That was the last straw for Richard.

"I, me, Richard Knox am in charge and I have decided we will buy it, my father has nothing to do with it." He raged.

"But you don't own it, your father does and you would need his permission first," Martin was still calm which seemed to make Richard angrier.

"No, but I do decide who works for me and as of now that's not you, your fired."

"Ok, but I think you will find your making a big mistake," and very calmly Martin left the room.

As promised various members of the board had kept in discreet contact with Davey and when they first told him about the proposed offer for Aztec, he asked them to contact him after the special board meeting. He was confident it would be rejected he knew his executive team well and they would never go along with it.

One of them was Martin Livesey, who called him straight after his dismissal.

"Not sure if I can talk to you, Davey, seeing I am now an ex-employee."

"What the hell you talking about, what went on today," Davey could sense this had not gone well.

Martin went on to explain the full extent of the meeting, the insistence of Richard and his implied threat to anyone who crossed him. Then finally he outlined the conversation he had alone with him. Davey was stunned, how could Richard have been so stupid.

"First of all, you're not sacked. I will travel back tomorrow and we can discuss further then. I am going to call Richard now and make sure he is well aware that nothing will happen in terms of this debacle he has created," Davey hung up and booked his flight for the following day.

When he told Helen what had happened, she asked the question to which Davey had no immediate answer.

"What happens now then? You will go back and slap him down; he will feel humiliated and he will lose face with the rest of the executive team. So, what will he do then?"

Davey could not answer that yet, he needed to speak to everyone concerned before he could make a decision. He called Richard but he wouldn't take his call. Richard knew he was in trouble, but as far as he was concerned, he was doing the best thing for Reddox and would not be backing down.

All the way on the flight back he was turning it over in his mind, this was a very bad situation. Richard had let him down badly. The board will have lost all trust in Richard and they would be questioning what the future held for them if Davey was not there.

Patrick met him at the airport and drove him home, it was 4pm and he decided to wait for Richard to come home and speak to him before doing anything else.

Richard arrived home at 7pm and was confronted by his father as soon as he entered the house.

"I thought you might turn up, no doubt your spies have informed you I have been a naughty boy," he said sarcastically. "Before you have a go at me, I know I am right."

It was not the right thing to say to Davey who was simmering already.

"I am trying very hard to stay calm right now, but you acting like a petulant brat is not going to do you any favours," Davey needed to keep his cool and think this through it was a very delicate situation.

"What made you think that such a magnificently stupid idea would be accepted by either the board or myself?"

Richard tried to justify himself, "I have been following them for 3 years, there stock has gone up significantly year on year, it's a no-brainer."

He then explained about his investments and how he tracked them, but still Davey was unconvinced and quickly dismantled Richard's reasoning.

"In order to control these types of companies you need to know how they operate, who is pulling the strings, there is more to it than three years of good profits. You need to know about their research and development strategies, what the supply chain is like, none of which we understand. We are construction, that is our expertise, our knowledge and our strength."

Davey was trying not to get angry. Finally, he delivered the knockout punch, "I found out about your proposal within an hour of your presentation and started asking some questions about the current owners. What do you know about them?" Richard confessed very little, so Davey carried on.

"The current owner took over four years ago, he was previously research engineer at De Wilder a major electronics manufacturer in the Netherlands. He is alleged to have stolen some significant new technology and bought out a little company over here. He has used all that technology to supply major household appliance manufacturers in the UK and central Europe. However, he does not have anything new in the pipeline and as with all electronic devices the motherboards he supplies are rapidly becoming superseded."

Richard was crushed, he knew nothing of this. Before he could say anymore, there was one last kick in the teeth.

"On top of all that, he is being sued for intellectual copyright theft in the Netherlands," Davey was now finished.

Richard was totally demoralised, but had one last question, "How could you possibly know all that?"

Davey had been in contact with his old university friend Tommy, they had kept in touch over the years. Tommy was now himself a lecturer and as such kept an eye an all things current in the electronics world. As soon as Davey mentioned Aztec, Tommy tried to warn him off. Richard made an excuse and left the house and jumped into his car, Davey decided to let him lick his wounds for a few days before tackling the repercussions. He decided he didn't want to make any food so headed down the pub for a nice steak and a couple of pints.

He got back about 11 and Marie was up watching television. He poured himself a glass of wine and offered some to her but she declined. Davey could see she had lost a lot of weight, her face was thin and she had almost a haunted look.

"Are you ok, you don't look well." He tried to talk to her but she wasn't in the mood and decided to take herself upstairs.

The following morning at breakfast he told Richard to go off for a few days, he would cover for him. They discussed what was in his diary for the next week, there wasn't anything terribly urgent, so it was an easy switch. Richard wasn't happy about it but knew better than to try and reason, he just accepted the decision and made an appointment for a golf lesson.

When Davey arrived in work, the first thing he did was to get his PA to arrange a board room meeting for later that day. He said he wanted all the executive team to attend, but if they already had important meetings then don't cancel and he will get around to meet them individually. All but one accepted, the Operations Manager had a handover meeting on site and couldn't attend.

At 2pm they all assembled in the Boardroom, Davey knew this was an awkward moment and he had to be careful with his words.

"Thank you for coming at such short notice, I know you are all very busy. We all know why I have called this meeting and there is only one item to discuss."

As Davey looked around, he could see there were some very anxious faces, nobody was sure which way this was going to go.

"First of all, I want to thank you all for the action you took, you showed loyalty to the company and worked in its best interest to ensure this buyout didn't happen. You also did it for the right reasons, you could have easily just gone along with Richard's decision, but your head told you it was a bad move and collectively you opposed it. I am proud of you all, once again I thank you," There were some relieved faces in the room.

"I have spoken with Richard and we agreed that he was due some time off, he has been working long hours and he never takes a holiday. I have asked him not to come in for a week or two, so now you are stuck with me for a while."

Davey had won them over. He went on to say that there were no plans at the moment for any acquisitions in the foreseeable future and that it was business as normal. He didn't expand on Richard's position because he wasn't sure what he was going to do. It was obvious that he was not ready to step up yet and possibly would never be capable enough to run the company. The meeting was ended and as they were all leaving, Davey asked Martin Livesey to stay behind.

"I think you have managed to retrieve the situation, for now. But what are the plans for the future?" Martin was a steady pair of hands and never flustered, but he knew there were some big decisions to be made.

"I am back for the next few months. Let the dust settle on this crap and then I will see where we go. I would welcome any thoughts you have on the matter though."

Martin sat there pondering and eventually spoke, "You still need Richard, he is the finance director… and a very good one. There is no doubting his talents in that area. But as for CEO, I think his actions have proved he still has a lot of maturing to do yet, even though he is now 34. What he needs is a wife and kids to bring him back to earth."

Davey chuckled, "He has never had a girlfriend, never mind a wife." He had often wondered about Richard's sexuality, or rather non-sexuality, he did not appear to be interested in any relationships, or indeed friendships for that matter. He was a definite loner.

Davey thanked Martin again and as he went back to his office he thought about Martin as a possible CEO. He would prefer it to be family, but if there were any doubts, then Martin would be a very good fit.

Davey realised he hadn't seen William since he got back, so went off to HR to seek him out. He found him in his office and he was on the phone as he entered. He finished the call and coolly asked, "Am I to prepare an exit interview for my brother," with a big grin on his face, it was obvious everyone knew what had happened.

"Not a funny matter, I am here to see how you are, I never see you nowadays," Davey could never understand how everything was a joke to William, he never took anything serious.

William let him know he had got himself an apartment in Salford Quays, which was why he was never at home now.

"You could have let us know, your mother would be worried about you."

"That's why I never mentioned it, she would be camped on my doorstep every morning," Which Davey knew was probably accurate.

When Davey got back home, he arrived to see Marie still in her pyjamas.

"You ok, are you sick?" Davey was concerned, she looked terrible.

Marie couldn't hold back, she threw herself into his arms and held him tight, then she started to cry. This went on for a good five minutes. Davey said nothing but knew this was serious, Marie was a strong character and something bad has happened. She eventually pulled away.

"Let me go make us a coffee, I need to talk to you." She went off and Davey was standing there totally bemused. She came back, handed him a cup, then sat down on the sofa.

Davey took a chair opposite her and she told her tale of how her business collapsed. As she told it, he looked at her and could see that this had mentally crippled her. He didn't care about the money, it was small change to him nowadays, his concern was that his little girl was hurting and she looked really ill.

When she finished, he assured her the money didn't matter, the main concern was she needed to look after herself.

After establishing how much she owed on her overdraft and various legal costs, she agreed to go and stay with her mother at the villa and Davey promised that he would clear her debts. He then booked a flight for her and rang Helen to bring her up to date.

Marie started packing and was massively relived at the outcome. She knew she had let her family down, but at least she was now debt free and able to resume a normal life. She also thought about how lucky she was to have such a caring dad. He had warned her against it, but when it went wrong, he didn't criticise, he just sorted her mess out.

As Davey explained everything Helen listened intently, there was so much going on, but it looked like Davey had sorted it all out. When he told her about Marie's business collapse, she wasn't surprised, but was concerned about her welfare.

"I have booked her flight, she will be with you tomorrow, she is ok now but needs fattening up, she obviously hasn't been eating properly."

Davey then told her he would have to stay on for a while until he had a plan, which he confessed he didn't have at the moment. He would come back down to

France in a week or so for a few days, but would need to spend more time back in England for the next few months.

He put the phone down and started to try and make sense of what he should do about Richard. His fixation with his career and making money was overload, he needed to step back and create a life outside of work, but how? He had never shown any interest in anything, he only played golf because it was a form of networking for him. But he didn't use it for that and preferred to go and play a round alone when the opportunity arose. He knew Martin was right about him being a good finance director and he was considering letting him go back after a week. The longer he was gone the more awkward it would be for everyone.

At that point, Richard's car pulled up and Marie came downstairs at the same time, so Davey decided he would treat them to a nice Italian meal at the restaurant down the road. This didn't really go down well with Richard or Marie, they didn't want to be in each other's company, but neither felt able to refuse, so a very quiet meal was had by all. Davey commented about William's carefree attitude.

"I haven't really spoke to him at all for the last few months, I think he might have moved out. He has rented a flat in Salford Quays," as Davey told of William's present position.

Marie's response was a shrug of the shoulders. Richard said nothing, after all William's life was totally alien to him. He wasn't particularly bothered if he saw him or not.

Davey could only wonder at how all three of his children were disinterested in each other.

The following morning when Davey got up, Richard was on his laptop looking at his stocks and shares. Davey peered over his shoulder.

"Anything interesting, any future acquisitions?" He mocked, then realised Richard didn't have a sense of humour.

Richard closed the lid and sat back. Then with a really serious face he asked Davey when he could go back to work.

"Next week should be ok, let the dust settle a bit first," Davey then informed him he was coming back as CEO and Richard was to return to being finance director, which Richard was expecting anyway. He also said he wanted Richard to attend some management training courses on developing leadership skills. Richard did not like this at all.

"How long are you back for?" He was quizzical to see what the future was.

"For as long as it takes, could be months, could be years," Davey was deliberately being evasive, mainly because he wasn't sure himself.

Marie then came down asked to be taken to the airport, her flight was at noon. Davey threw her the keys and told her to put her bags in the boot and he would be out in a minute.

"Shame about Marie's business going belly up," he said to Richard as she was putting her cases in the car.

"Didn't know it had, but not surprised, she hasn't got a clue about business," was his curt response. Davey shook his head, Richard did not have a clue about the world outside his head, he hadn't even noticed how obvious it was that Marie was having problems.

"I suppose you know everything then?" Davey replied sarcastically.

After driving Marie to the airport, he went into the office, and read a few documents. He was finding that his vision was getting really blurred just lately, which probably accounted for the headaches he was now constantly getting, so he made a mental note to go and see a doctor. He decided to go back to France at the weekend, he didn't want Helen to feel lonely and he also knew she would be fretting as soon as she saw Marie.

He was also trying to work out how he could manage his role as CEO as well as living in France and came to the conclusion it wasn't possible, he would need to come back to the UK until he could get a replacement, but that was a difficult position to fill, so it wasn't likely to be in the foreseeable future. After checking with Martin that there was no pressing business, Davey informed him that he was going back to France for the rest of the week, but would be back on Tuesday.

After booking his flight he found he was still tired, so went home and fell asleep in a chair for a couple of hours, only waking up when Richard came back in.

He got up from the chair and immediately felt dizzy, then his nose started to bleed so he went and got some tissue paper. He was cleaning up the blood when Richard came back in and immediately asked him to sit down and talk.

He ignored the blood-stained tissues and asked Davey if he could come back to work straight away, he was bored and it served no purpose to be at home doing nothing. Davey reluctantly agreed, he couldn't be bothered arguing about it and Richard did have a point. He did however have one stipulation.

"Ok, I agree. But only after you have apologised to Martin Livesey, what you did to him was appalling."

Richard agreed to see him the following morning. Davey then rang Patrick and asked him to be at the house for 9am to take him to the airport.

Helen met him at the airport the following day along with Marie, who seemed a little brighter. They stopped off for lunch at a little bistro they liked and Davey brought Helen up to date on the developments at work.

"We are going to have to go back, for now at least," Davey explained.

"I know, I have already started packing," was Helen's response, which raised a smile from Davey.

"Marie is going to stay on a while and rest, she will be back for Christmas though," Davey looked at Marie. "How are you feeling now, you look better?"

"I am sorry I let you down. I should have listened to you. I will make it up to you," Marie knew the money was irrelevant, it was her not listening to him that would have hurt him the most and she genuinely was sorry.

Thy took their time and had a leisurely lunch, returning to the villa about 4pm, by which time Davey was tired again and went to the bedroom.

Helen looked at him asleep on the bed and felt sorry for him, the last week had been exhausting, no wonder he was tired. Davey woke up with another headache and feeling sick, he should not have drunk that extra glass of wine at lunchtime.

They spent the last few days in France just relaxing and enjoying the last of the warm autumn sunshine before catching the train home. Davey slept on and off, all the way back. Helen had noticed and she decided he needed to sort out the future of the business then sit back and retire as soon as possible. He was getting too old for this now and at 62 she was concerned for him.

Davey settled back into work and Richard duly reluctantly apologised to Martin Livesey and all the problems eased off for the next couple of months. Marie arrived back mid-December and even William managed to put in an appearance for Christmas Day.

Reddox was closed for a week every Christmas holiday break and 2005 was no exception. Davey decided the year needed to be seen off in fine style after all the heartache of the year, so booked a hospitality suite at Aintree Racecourse for the Boxing Day meeting and invited the board and spouses. He laid on a coach that picked them up from Reddox and an envelope with 200 pounds in for free bets, which went down well.

Davey knew there was still some repair work to be done after Richard's behaviour and he was determined to draw a line under it by the end of the year.

He spoke to Richard before they departed and told him he had to mingle, make small talk and generally make a good impression. Of course, Richard, being Richard, had worked out a spreadsheet and from the racing post did calculations for every race about form, jockeys, everything. It was a very successful formula and after 3 races he was 400 pounds up. As a consequence, he then became very popular with the others and was asked for tips for the next 5 races, of which 3 were winners and 1 placed. The day was a great success only marred when Davey lost his balance and tripped up the steps while getting on the bus, bruising his knee. The bruising was slow to heal and lasted until the middle of January. Davey also noticed that his breathing was more erratic and the dizzy spells were continuing.

Helen decided to go shopping in the January sales and asked Marie to go with he. Money was no object, but she just liked the thrill of the chase, hunting down Bargains. She was never comfortable around Patrick so they decided to catch the train. As they approached Salford Crescent Station, they noticed all the students returning to the university after the Xmas break and then saw a man walk past where they were sitting. Marie also saw him.

"My God, I thought that was Dad for a second, same hair, same build, even walks just like him."

Helen was spooked, it was a slightly heavier version of Davey, "Its uncanny," she remarked.

While Helen was shopping Davey called Paul Gilbert for some advice and told him about the headaches, blurred vision, nosebleeds, being very tired and nauseous. Paul listened intently then asked him a few questions one of which was did he bruise easily.

"As a matter of fact, I do, had a bruise on my knee for nearly three weeks now, bloody thing still not healed up."

Paul asked a few more things and then told Davey he should see a doctor straight away. Davey said he didn't want to alarm anybody at home and he preferred it if Paul would take a look the next time they were in France.

"No, this might be serious, you need to see someone as soon as possible." He sounded very serious.

Davey said he would find an excuse to come down in the next week or so and let Paul carry out some tests. When they got home later that night loaded down with bags full of clothes, Helen poured herself a large glass of wine and slumped down in the chair. Davey was already in and had nodded off, but woke up when he heard her come in.

Davey didn't mention the phone conversation with Paul, he didn't want her worrying, it might be something and nothing.

At breakfast the following morning, he told her he was going to an international seminar in Paris, something to do with new legislation from the European Union that affected companies with more than 350 employees and that he would be back in a couple of days. These things came along every now and then, so Helen wasn't really paying attention or particularly interested.

The following week he was in Paul Gilbert's office and after an initial medical check they sat down and discussed what the possibilities were.

"You will need a few tests, but I am certain it's a blood related issue," was Paul's assessment, "I would like you to take a blood test and also a bone marrow biopsy."

"Bone marrow? That sounds serious," Davey was now concerned.

Paul explained that all the symptoms were that his body's red cells may be deficient and the best way to check was a complete blood count or CBC.

Davey agreed to the test and it was arranged the same afternoon. He was then informed it would take a couple of days for the result, so Davey decided to go back to the UK and await the outcome.

Chapter Twenty

The sound of the 6am alarm was irrelevant as Helen lay in bed contemplating the dilemma she now faced. She had been awake for most of the night analysing the recent behaviour of her husband and there was only one conclusion she could arrive at; she was thinking the unthinkable. The man she had been married to for the last 35 years was having an affair. All the symptoms were there, the furtive phone calls, the uncharacteristic behaviour, the changes in temperament, it all added up.

Unsure of what to do, she thought her best plan for now was to try and keep life as normal as possible. She got up, combed her hair and opened the curtains, to reveal a grey overcast morning that did nothing to lift her spirits. She then went downstairs and made the morning breakfast, as she did every time Davey had a business trip abroad.

Davey heard Helen get up and as he adjusted his eyes to the light, he too began to wonder where his future lay, he knew that today would be the most influential day of his life and that no matter what the outcome, his life and that of his whole family would never be the same again. He sat up in bed and reached for the phone on the bedside table and dialled a foreign number that was answered by Claudette Gilbert. He made a request for her to purchase some items, then headed for the bathroom. On the way there he passed the mirror and looking into it he sighed as he realised the face looking back at him was that of a man past his prime and at that moment accepted his life needed to change.

As she made the morning Coffee Helen could hear her husband in a telephone conversation but could not make out its content. She suspected it was not a business call.

Her mind however was elsewhere and she went over the events of the last 24 hours in her head to try and make some sense of it all. Davey had told her that he was going to France on business, not to Paris where he usually conducted business, but to Nice. There was also the unresolved matter of the return air ticket to Nice she found in his pocket that was taken last week, when he had supposedly been in the Algarve.

Davey usually spent the evening before a trip in his study looking at papers and ensuring all loose ends were tied up. Last night however, he sat in darkness listening to his favourite classical music, managing to drink a full bottle of wine. Davey was a creature of habit and this was certainly not typical.

As he showered Davey thought about his relationship with his wife and the strength of his love for her and their three children. He knew that Helen suspected something and that the deception was hurting her, but it was better that she did not know the full details until he himself knew what the future held.

Breakfast usually consisted of a little cereal, toast and fruit juice, with conversation at a minimum as Davey was not at his best first thing in the morning, but this morning there was an especially subdued atmosphere with neither of them in the mood for eating.

"What time will you be back tomorrow?" asked Helen as she sat half-heartedly trying to force down a slice of toast.

"I'm booked on the four o'clock flight so I'll be back for dinner, why not see if we can get a table at Sidney's for about eight," replied Davey.

Forcing back the tears, she thought about her husband possibly sleeping with another woman and the deceit and humiliation being inflicted upon her, she turned to clear the table.

"Let's just see how you feel when you get back, its midweek, there shouldn't be any need to reserve a table."

Just then the silence was broken by the sound of the phone ringing, Helen answered, "Its Patrick, he will pick you up in 10 minutes," she said as she replaced the phone on the wall.

She briefly wondered if Patrick knew what was going on, then discarded the thought.

"Got to get dressed, ring me tonight," she whispered, kissed him on the forehead and then left for the bedroom.

As soon as Davey had left the house Helen pressed redial on the phone to check who Davey had called and recoiled when she heard the voice at the other end of the line, "Hello?"

She only had to hear the voice once to know who it was, Claudette, one of her closest friends and someone whom she had shared some of her happiest moments with. Helen was shocked, how could her husband and her friend do this to her?

She then switched off the phone and sat in silence stunned at what she had just heard. After 5 minutes, she picked up the phone and called the airline to see if there was a seat on a flight to Nice later that day.

"Yes, we have a seat would you like to book now?" said the officious female voice on the other end of the line.

"Yes please... er... no... I'll call you back!"

She was barely able to replace the receiver with her quivering hand. Her heart was beating faster and faster, her breath becoming uncontrollable as she started to hyperventilate. She could feel herself start to go dizzy and she knew she had to calm down. Slowly she regained control of her body and she began to try and reason with herself. Flying was an everyday occurrence that involved millions of people all over the world every day, travelling from A to B without incident, she told herself. Why should anything happen to me?

She knew that she had to try and save her marriage and the only way she could think of doing it was to confront the treacherous bitch that threatened 30 years of rock-solid happiness.

After an hour of self-analysis, with the backup of tranquilisers and a couple of Gin and Tonics, she finally found the strength to redial the airport and make the booking, she was due out at 4pm.

The flight for Davey was uneventful, although he had to wait for half an hour at the terminal entrance for his transport to arrive.

Sitting in a coffee bar, he suddenly felt very tired and was beginning to doze off when a silver Lexus pulled up and Claudette arrived to collect him.

"Sorry for the delay, my husband forgot to let me know that he had bought a new car and needed to pick it up from the salesroom," she said in a soft apologetic tone. "Besides, I had to take a trip to the market to pick up your food order, are you sure you want to cook tonight?"

Davey looked her in the eye, "Claudette, I don't know what today holds but good news or bad I need something to occupy my mind, besides you know I enjoy cooking, I find it very therapeutic!"

Claudette knew this was true, Davey had over the years produced some delightful dishes and she and her husband had many happy memories of nights sitting around the dinner table at each other's houses.

The short drive from the airport was punctuated with small talk, they had known each other for over 30 years and Claudette was usually sparkling company and their personalities gelled, but they both knew this was a difficult time.

They stopped at the villa to place the food and wine in the refrigerator and then carried on their journey eventually arriving outside the Pasteur Hospital where Claudette pulled up in the carpark.

"I will catch a taxi, take my car and will see you later," she said tossing him the keys, before crossing the road to hail a cab.

Once inside, he worked his way along the corridors until he found himself outside an office in the haematology department. Walking through the door into a room of soft warm colours that contrasted sharply with the cold clinical décor of the rest of the hospital.

Davey observed Paul coming towards him, then stood up and gave him a warm handshake, "Nice to see you again, Paul, it seems a long time ago that I was last here for the tests, I hope you have good news for me."

"I see you have not lost your touch when it comes to straight talking," said Paul. "So, I will get to the point, please take a seat," gesturing Davey towards a seat in front of his desk.

Reaching into his filing cabinet he withdrew a file, 2 glasses and small bottle of cognac, nodding for Davey to acknowledge the bottle which he did, then sat down in his large leather chair that seemed to wrap itself around his slender frame.

Paul then recalled the previous week's events. "The symptoms you were showing indicated there was a blood disorder and as a precaution Dr Vallete ordered a bone marrow biopsy and a blood count. The test results show that you have a very low cell count and that your bone marrow does not contain normal blood forming tissue."

Paul looked across at Davey to see his reaction, which was studious, trying to take in the information but at the same time remaining calm. This was the reaction Paul expected, Davey was a very pragmatic man who would absorb the details and then assess the impact it would have on him.

"Does this mean I have Leukaemia?" Davey eventually asked.

"No, the condition you have is called aplastic anaemia and carries three classifications, non-severe, severe and very severe. Yours is very severe, which means that your bone marrow is what we call hypoplastic with a low platelet count," Paul then went on to explain that the condition can be treated by restoring the function of the bone marrow through blood and stem cell transfusions and that great strides had been made in this field and that there was a good chance of a full recovery, but this could not be guaranteed.

"When do I start the treatment and how long does it last?"

"I will book you in here with Dr Valette straight away if you wish, the sooner we start the treatment the less chance there is of you picking up an infection that could affect the immune system," replied Paul, looking Robert in the eye, he added, "You have a very serious condition and although you are fit for your age, you are going to take a long time to recover from this."

Davey sat stunned as the reality sank in. Now that he knew the severity of the situation he needed to plan for the future, the first thing he needed to do was speak to Helen, but it was not something he could do over the phone. He knew he had to stay in Nice to sort out his treatment plan and that he would be here for a couple of weeks, so he decided to ring anyway but only to ask her to come and join him, he would explain everything when she was here. Picking up the phone, he dialled his home number and when there was no answer, he tried her mobile, but there was no response there either.

Paul could see that Davey was shaken, but knew that his old friend would not be seeking sympathy, so he asked about Helen and how much she knew.

"The last few weeks have been horrendous, I didn't want her to know anything in case there was nothing to worry about, you know what she's like."

Paul did indeed know what she was like and how much she would have worried, he also wondered how she would take the news now.

"I need a drink, in fact a few drinks and whether I'm allowed them or not I'm bloody well having them!" said Davey snapping out of his state of shock.

Paul wasn't going to argue with him, "Are we still on for tonight or do you want to cancel, we understand if you would rather be alone."

"No. No, please, by then there will probably be a few questions I need answers to. Tonight is not the night to be alone."

Taking the short journey home to the villa, Davey was beginning to feel a little weary and on arrival he threw his bag in the bedroom, snatched a beer from the fridge and flopped onto one of the massive Chesterfields in the lounge. As he sat facing the doors that opened up onto the balcony he smiled in appreciation of the fantastic views of the Riviera below, the sight of which he never failed to wonder at. They had spent many nights relaxing as the sun went down and the golden glow ebbed away, to be replaced by the evening calm and the sounds of crickets as the evening emerged.

Looking at his watch he realised he still hadn't managed to trace Helen, so picking up his phone he tried again. There was still no answer, it was only five thirty, she always had her phone with her and was always available to take a call. As he sat relaxing, he could feel his eyes closing and gradually, unable to keep his eyes open, he started to drift off into a gentle doze…

Suddenly Davey awoke with a start and looking at his watch he realised he had been asleep for an hour and a half and that his plans for the evening meal were in tatters. He jumped up and headed for the kitchen to try and reclaim the situation. He had originally intended to cook leg of lamb slowly braised in a red wine jus but there was no time for that now, he would have to settle for a plain roast.

Preheating the oven and preparing the meat, he cursed the affliction he was now suffering and realised that he had no choice but to be ready for a different kind of lifestyle. Throwing the meat in the oven, he prepared the vegetables, then grabbing another beer he showered and changed, ready for his guest's arrival.

Paul and Claudette were, as always, punctual and arrived at exactly 8 o'clock.

"Sorry, but slight change of plans," apologised Davey.

"Tonight's menu is a much simpler affair than originally intended," as he explained that he had fallen asleep.

"Don't worry, but don't expect a tip," replied Paul before handing a vintage bottle of Barolo over and then walking over to the cloakroom to hang their coats up.

As the flight from Manchester landed at Nice airport and ground to a halt outside the gate, Helen's trembling hand undid the buckle on the seatbelt and gathered her small overnight bag from the overhead locker.

"Are you all right, Madam?" enquired the Stewardess as she saw the state that Helen was in. "would you like some assistance?"

"No thanks," she replied with a shaky, tremulous voice and gathering herself together she stumbled off the plane and through into the arrivals area. The flight was an ordeal, made worse by the fact that it was an hour late.

Once she was through immigration, she sat down in one of the bars and ordered a large Gin and Tonic to try and compose herself before finding a taxi to take her the half hour drive to the villa. Pulling up outside the front gate, she stopped the taxi and paid the driver. As she slowly walked the 60 yards up the drive, her feet crunching the gravel beneath, she saw that Claudette's car was parked there along with another that she did not recognise. Probably Davey's hired car, she thought, as she approached the front door.

"Drink?" asked Davey as he began to open the Barolo, then offering a glass to Claudette, he filled it to the brim before reaching for another glass.

As he did so he heard the sound of the front door opening and the sound of footsteps on the marble tiling in the hallway. Turning to face the doorway, he was amazed to see a distraught Helen standing in the entrance.

The sight of Davey and Claudette standing together sharing a glass a wine was a sight that she had expected to find but when she caught sight of Paul walking into the room out of the corner of her eye, the whole day's events suddenly caught up with her.

"Will someone please tell me," she softly muttered. "WHAT THE FUCK IS GOING ON." She suddenly screamed before throwing herself at Davey with both fists flying.

Davey didn't know what had surprised him most, the fact she was there, the state she was in, her swearing, or the sudden onslaught, all of which were definitely not the normal actions of his wife. Holding her tightly to contain her rage he whispered in her ear to try and calm her down and eventually her fury subsided to be replaced by incessant sobbing.

"Please, please tell me what's going on, why are you acting like this, what are you doing here and why are they here," she said, sitting down on the chesterfield and placing her head in her hands, her hair obscuring her tearstained face from view.

Davey then slowly began to explain exactly what had happened over the last few months, the way he had been feeling and describing the symptoms and that he had avoided discussing it with her, as he did not want to upset her unduly. He admitted that this had been the wrong decision and he was very upset at the effect all this had been on Helen.

After a couple of minutes, Davey asked Paul to explain about the condition and what the next steps were going to be. Paul then described what the effects of aplastic anaemia were and the treatment that Davey was to undertake and finally Helen was able to piece everything together and make sense of it all.

Sensing that the couple needed to be alone, Paul and Claudette made their excuses and left after an hour, Davey poured them both a large glass of wine and they sat down to discuss what the options were for the future. He informed her of his decision to stand down from the business and to definitely spend more time with Helen and of his intention to create a legacy to stand the test of time. She listened intently and knew that this was so important to him and to withdraw from the business was an incredible decision to take and that she would support him no matter what. Her feelings had by now turned to guilt as she felt ashamed that she could have doubted him.

The smell of the lamb began to drift in from the kitchen and they both realised that neither had eaten all day and so transferred themselves to the kitchen.

"You hungry?" Davey asked as he carved the meat into thick slices.

"Yes, but not for anything fancy," she replied.

Davey split a large baton lengthways, filled the bread with the meat and cut it into manageable lengths. After pouring more wine into the glasses they settled down around the table and discussed how this legacy was to be created. Finally, at 3am and a second bottle of wine later, they both stumbled into bed and collapsed unconscious, comfortable in the knowledge they both knew where the future lay.

Chapter Twenty-One

The following morning, Davey and Helen woke up with a sore head; they had drunk far too much the night before. But at least now they both knew that Davey had to look to retire; this was a very serious illness they were dealing with and his immunity was low.

They went to see Dr Vallette and he went over the treatment which would mean a stem cell replacement treatment from a suitable donor, then various drugs to be given over a long time to stimulate red cell production. He explained that it would be a long slow process and he would be severely weakened by the whole experience.

When he finished, Davey said they needed time to digest the information and they would get back to him in the next couple of days which he understood.

They returned to the villa where they weighed up all the possible alternatives, but kept coming back to the same conclusion. They had to be in the UK for treatment, the timescale and the effect on family was too much. Christies Hospital was a world-famous cancer treatment hospital just a few miles from their home, where he would get the best possible treatment.

They invited the Gilberts for dinner, but Davey decided a restaurant would be the best choice, so they met later that night and discussed Dr Vallette's findings and also informed them they would be going home.

"I perfectly understand, the most likely match for a stem cell transfusion would be from the family and the follow-on treatment is a long process," Paul was, as always, pragmatic.

Davey then insisted they change the subject and the talk wandered onto other more trivial matters and the rest of the evening was the usual enjoyable time. They said their goodbyes at the end of the night and promised they would be back as soon as Davey's health allowed.

The train back to the UK was uneventful and Davey arranged for Patrick to pick them up from the Euro Star Train at Paddington.

"Must have been an important visit for Helen to catch a flight to Nice."

Patrick was fishing but neither of them wanted to take him on. "You will find out all about it in due course, Patrick," was all Davey could muster.

The following day he went into work and called an emergency meeting, where he explained that he needed some medical treatment and would not be available for a couple of months and that Martin Livesey would be the stand in CEO during his absence. He had previously sat down with Martin and explained everything to him and offered him the role, which he gladly accepted.

"Just don't sack the finance director, will you?" Martin was glad Davey still had a sense of humour.

The following day and Davey contacted the family doctor and made an appointment. The meeting was fairly short, the doctor read the files over a couple of minutes, then informed them he would refer this straight to the main blood specialist at Christies.

One week later, they were in the offices of Mr Joseph Bentley, one of the major experts in the field of haematology. He too looked at the file and said he wanted to carry out some more tests and Davey would need to stay in hospital for a few days. They had predicted this and had brought a bag with pyjamas and toiletries with them already.

They were led off into a side ward reserved for private paying patients. It was a very pleasant room with cable television, coffee facilities and a fridge.

Helen stayed a while, then eventually left and Davey was left alone to sit and ponder. He realised now he was in a very serious predicament and was naturally worried.

The rest of the afternoon was spent having various tests including giving more blood and lumbar puncture to confirm the results from France. The following day the consultant appeared with his team to give an update and confirmed the original diagnosis.

In the couple of weeks since his original tests, the cell count had reduced further and Davey was now in need of a bone marrow transfusion. They were checking the National Bone Marrow Donor Register to see if there was a direct match but nothing had come up. They now were looking at blood relatives to try and find a suitable match. Richard was first to give a sample, followed by William. Marie arrived later that day to give hers.

Helen also donated, more in hope than expectation. In the meantime, Davey was receiving tablets which made him extremely drowsy as well as blood transfusions on an almost constant basis. Helen was really concerned and she mentioned to the consultant that Davey seemed to have deteriorated since he came into hospital. The consultant explained that this was normal as his body was now having to deal with the effects from the medicines and treatments, but they had no choice because Davey's body was now not able to support the amount of red blood cells he needed and his immune system was under extreme pressure.

The following day, the results came back and as expected there was a low percentage of the possibility of the children being a suitable donor. Richard and William were assessed to be a 29% match, Helen and Marie both a mere 5% match.

When he read them out by the bedside Davey was not really conscious and was unaware of the results. Helen asked why Marie was so much lower than the other two and was surprised when he asked if Marie had been adopted.

Looking very quizzical, she replied she was not, then she asked him why he would say such a thing.

"Looking at the makeup of the blood and its molecular breakdown, it is extremely unlikely, in fact some might say impossible, for your husband and Marie to be blood relatives."

Helen was stunned. "No, this is impossible, there must be a mistake. I know this is my husband's daughter."

The consultant then went on to mention about further treatment for Davey, but Helen wasn't listening, she was still trying to absorb what she had just been told. She looked down at Davey who was oblivious to everything around him and just held his hand. She sat there silently for a while and eventually Davey came round a little. She informed him there was still not a suitable donor but they were looking and not to give up hope.

Evening came and Helen went home to an empty house, so she had a quick shower then made herself a little pasta and sat down in the kitchen with a glass of wine, still trying to come to terms with what she had been told. She was convinced there was a simple mistake, she knew she had never been unfaithful. She tried to track down the dates she might have conceived, but it was all so long ago. She remembered it was about the time that Davey's mother was ill and he had to rush off to France and she had booked a flight for the following day, but didn't have to take it. She also remembered getting really drunk that night and passing out on the sofa… then she remembered going to Patrick's house the following day to tell him about Mary passing away… and the sheer look of panic when she knocked on his door.

Surely not, she thought as she recalled the events in her head, this was not possible, then realising that she was extremely drunk the night before, she was now thinking the impossible and that Patrick Reddy fathered her child. She felt sick and leaned over the kitchen sink and retched, that animal had been inside her, the person in the world she most detested could be Marie's biological father. She poured herself another glass of wine and just sat there, her head spinning trying to absorb this sordid possibility.

She could not sleep at all that night and vowed to try and find out one way or the other. She had to find out, this was eating away at her and so the following morning looked on-line and found what she was looking for, then had some breakfast and drove over to the hospital. When she got there Davey was sat up in bed and looked a little better, he had just had breakfast and was awake and smiled as she entered the room. She wondered if he recalled the conversation with the consultant the day before, but there was no sign he had any idea what they had spoken about.

They talked about blood relative matches, but Helen didn't mention about the percentages, only that none of them was a close enough match. She wasn't going to disturb Davey when he was so sick, she needed to sort this situation out first before she said anything to him.

Richard came in later that morning and immediately started to talk about work, but Helen shot him down.

"Do not come here burdening your father with problems, let him rest and recover." She was furious with him, her mood was not the best at the moment and she did not welcome this intrusion.

Ten minutes later Patrick entered, he didn't particularly want to be there but he knew it was expected, so appeared for about 15 minutes then left. As he sat by the bedside Helen could feel herself getting angry, but then realised she needed to keep calm, so went for a walk and got herself a coffee. She returned as he was leaving.

"What's your plans for today, Patrick?" She nonchalantly asked.

"Got to deliver some documents in Leeds, that will take up all my afternoon."

This response was just what Helen needed.

Davey was constantly being monitored and by mid-afternoon was having yet more tests, so Helen decided to go home for a while.

Once at home, she went to the cabinet where all the keys were kept and took out the spare pair for Patrick's house, they had always had a set from the days when Mary used to make sure he was ok.

She drove down and let herself in, she was looking for something that would be able to provide a DNA and immediately found it.

Patrick's coat was hung up on the back door, on the collar was a short length of grey hair that was obviously Patrick's. She picked it off and placed it in a small plastic wallet, then locked up and went home. Back home, she went into Marie's room and found a hair in her hairbrush and placed it in the same bag.

She then rang a laboratory that specialised in DNA matches, luckily there was one in Manchester. They told her if she dropped the samples off the following day, she could have the results in about 3 days.

Once she had dropped off the samples, she went back to the hospital where Davey had improved a lot. The consultant was very pleased with the results so far, Davey's cell count had greatly improved and he was able to walk around the room.

"How long will I be here?" He asked, hoping he could be out in a few days.

"Not for at least a couple of weeks, your improving, but there is still a long way to go," the consultant then explained that the medicine he was now taking was helping with the development of new cells and building up his immunity, but he was starting from a low base so it would naturally take longer. He then went on to say that he wanted Davey to undergo chemotherapy to kill the white cells that were attacking the bone marrow, which should speed up the healing process.

Davey reluctantly accepted the fact he was going nowhere, so asked Helen to get Martin Livesey to come and see him, but Helen refused.

"You only have one job at the minute and that is to sit back and get better. If there was anything going wrong, I would have heard about it by now from Richard."

Helen hated hanging around hospitals and so was glad when Davey needed some more treatment and she could leave the ward. She was not achieving anything just hanging around and Davey would quite often just fall asleep, so there was no point hanging around.

The laboratory where the DNA test was to be done was not far away, so she dropped it off and asked if they could email her the results as well as post them, which they agreed to do. This was preying on her mind as much as Davey's condition and she was desperately hoping it was all a mistake.

The results from the DNA test came back, but Helen didn't open the letter, she didn't want to face any further turmoil, she had enough going on in her life at the moment. She hardly ever read her emails so that wasn't a problem, best let sleeping dogs lie at present was her mindset.

The next few weeks followed a familiar pattern of going to the hospital, staying a couple of hours, Davey nodding off every now and again and various treatments being administered. Helen could see Davey was improving and as he got stronger, she sensed the day he could go home was getting closer.

Davey had now been in hospital for a month and he was bored, when he was really sick, he didn't really take any interest in anything and just went along with whatever was suggested. But now he felt more alive, he needed to be up and about. He was furious when he realised the Helen had taken his phone to stop him calling work and tried to call Martin Livesey on a payphone, but Martin wouldn't take his calls, Helen had begged him not to speak with him and Martin agreed. Davey needed rest.

Helen always went to the hospital about 10am and stayed for a couple of hours, then returned later in the day about 6:30pm. It had become a bit of a routine, but that routine was about to be broken.

She arrived at the bedside as usual, only to find Davey was running a high temperature and his breathing was fast and shallow. He had also developed a red rash on his skin. The doctors and nurses were looking very concerned as they hurried about his bedside.

"What's wrong, where has this rash come from?" Helen could see this was a very serious situation.

"We have taken a blood sample and we will know in the next hour or so, but we are taking the precaution of administering some antibiotics to fight a possible infection," was the only response she got.

Helen sat in the corner of the room out of the way, but she saw the anxiety in their faces as the worked on Davey. The results came back quickly and Davey was diagnosed as having sepsis. The doctors explained that this was because his immune system was low, the sepsis was attacking his auto immune antibodies. In other words, his body was attacking itself.

Helen could only look on as Davey appeared to be deteriorating rapidly. His heart rate was increasing by the minute and his body temperature was high. By now he was oblivious to anything going on around him. This went on for the next 5 hours, then his body began to react to the antibiotics and everything started to calm down to a manageable level. Eventually he levelled out and the nursing staff felt a bit easier.

"He has stabilised for now, but we will need to keep a constant eye on him over the next few days," one of the doctors told Helen. "There is nothing more you can do, I suggest you go home and we will call you if there is any change."

Helen could see she was just getting in the way, so decided to go and let the rest of the family know what had just happened.

She asked them all to come home for a meal that night, after what she had been through, she wanted her family to be around her.

That night she explained what had gone on and that Davey was a very sick man.

"Will he die?" was Richard's first question.

"Let's just say, he is in a critical condition, the next few days will be crucial." Helen knew there was no point trying to avoid the position they were in, they were not kids anymore.

Even William wasn't cracking any funny lines, he looked very concerned and Marie was silent the whole time.

After the meal, William went back to his apartment and Marie helped Helen clear up and load the dishwasher. As she was helping Helen kept looking at her, she was looking for some sort of feature that would identify who Marie's father was.

Marie noticed this, "Are you ok, why are you looking at me in a weird way."

Helen apologised and just said she was a bit distracted tonight. When they finished Helen took the laboratory letter from the rack and went up to her bedroom, but still couldn't open it, she could not face any consequences at the moment. She put it in the drawer and went downstairs to try and watch some television, but she could not concentrate and took herself off to bed at 10pm.

At 2am her mobile phone went off, it was the hospital, she needed to get there as soon as possible. She woke Marie and Richard and rushed to the hospital. She tried to ring William but there was no answer.

When they arrived, the doctors were gathered round bed administering defibrillation, Davey's heart had stopped. They managed to get it going again, but there were anxious looks everywhere. One of the doctors saw Helen and came over to her.

"I am afraid your husband has deteriorated and now has septic shock," as he was speaking Davey's heart started again.

Helen was stunned into silence, she knew septic shock can kill, especially in someone with a weak immune system. She didn't know what to say, but just kept looking over at Davey's unconscious body. Eventually she pulled herself together enough to ask some questions.

The doctor went on to explain that septic shock attacked the organs in the body and that this had caused the heart attack, but the kidneys, lungs and liver were also under threat. It was impossible to say at this stage if he would recover, but it was unlikely that Davey would need to survive the next 48 hours if he was to have any chance.

Over the next few hours Davey had another heart attack and even when they restarted it, Helen could see from the monitors that he was only just staying alive. She could do nothing but sit there and hold his hand.

At 9am it was all over and Davey slipped away without gaining consciousness, Helen watched as they undid the monitors and removed the transfusion equipment, too numb to comment, she just sat there completely unaware of anything happening in the room. She could only think that her beloved Davey was no more. Marie hugged her and tried to offer words of comfort, but she didn't hear her. She only reacted when she heard William's voice as he entered the room.

"Sorry I am late, I only just got the message."

Helen raised her head and looked at him, "You knew how sick he was, you knew we could expect a call at any time. But yet, as usual, you could only think of yourself. You should be ashamed of yourself."

Then she stood up and walked down the corridor, with Marie following in her footsteps.

Richard then told William what had happened over the last few hours and William was devastated.

Davey was cremated on 14 April, it was a quiet affair. Although Davey was a popular figure, he didn't really have many friends, certainly no close ones. The Gilberts attended, as did the members of the board. Helen's sister was there as well and Helen said she needed to talk to her after the funeral.

Back at the house, they had hired caterers to provide some lunch and a few drinks, but everyone had gone home by 2pm. Helen ushered Maddie upstairs to her bedroom where she retrieved the letter from the lab and then told her what had happened about the blood tests carried out for compatibility for donating bone marrow.

"They said it was practically impossible for Davey and Marie to be blood related," Maddie was struggling to understand what Helen was talking about and she had to explain it a couple of times before she could fully comprehend the situation.

"They said the compatibility ratio for Marie was less than 5% compared to the boys who were in the late 20s."

Maddie was still confused, but Helen carried on, "So, then I had to track back on the dates and the only date I was unsure about was the day before I was going to take a flight."

"Did you have sex with someone else?"

Helen went on to explain how drunk and tranquilised she was that night and that she didn't have a clue about what had happened. Helen then told her about how she had to go to see Patrick at his house the following day and the terrified look on his face when he opened the door to her.

Maddie couldn't believe what she was hearing, she knew Patrick was a slimeball, but surely even he wouldn't stoop so low as to rape a sleeping woman.

Helen then explained how she submitted a sample of hair from Patrick and Marie for DNA analysis, then she waved the envelope in the air, "Here are the results, but I have not been able to face looking at them with everything that has gone on. But I need to know and cannot hide any longer."

She opened the letter with a trembling hand and pulled out the results. She just sat there with it still folded, but couldn't bring herself to read it.

"Let me do it," Maddie took it off her and opened it out and just stared at the results in front of her. Helen looked up and could see by Maddie's reaction it was not good news as she read it out to her.

"The result from the two samples submitted for DNA testing have demonstrated that the compatibility is a 96% match," Maddie put the letter down. "Oh my God, Patrick is Marie's father."

She then rushed over to Helen and held her. The past few weeks had been hard for Helen and she was spent in terms of tears, there were none left. What was left now was bitter hatred, she hated the fact that her husband had been taken away from her, she hated the fact that she was now alone, but most of all she hated Patrick Reddy, a hatred that had brewed up over many years and had now developed into a need for revenge, a savage revenge that would destroy him once and for all.

"It's ok I can deal with it," she was amazingly calm under the circumstances. "At least Davey didn't have to go to his grave with this knowledge, He loved Marie and that's all that matters."

Maddie looked at Helen, she had a disturbed appearance, "Will you tell Marie about it?"

"Are you serious? Why would I do that? She doesn't like Patrick and adored her father, why put her through that agony. Nobody will ever know and you must swear you won't tell anyone either." Helen was deadly serious, this was a secret to take to the grave.

Maddie agreed and they sat there on the bed, not saying anything for at least half an hour. Then she said she had to go, she left Helen alone with her thoughts and headed back to Nottingham.

Richard had anticipated that Davey's Will would allocate the company shares between Helen and the three children, with perhaps Helen getting a small majority of them. So, in expectation of this, he was canvassing William and Marie to see what they would do with them once they got them.

Marie told him to fuck off, she wasn't going to do anything with them, the dividends were enough for a good life, that was enough for her.

William said he might consider selling at some point in the future, but out of respect for Dads wishes he wouldn't do it for a while. This deflated Richard who was hoping to be able to get an overall majority and control the company with a view to selling at some stage.

The end of the week saw the reading of the will and they all gathered around as the family solicitor read out the detail.

As expected, the villa in France was transferred to Helen.

There was a gift of 20000 pounds to Paul and Collette Gilbert as gratitude for their friendship over the years.

The children were each to receive 250,000 pounds each and the balance of his private monies to be transferred to Helen, this was a couple of million pounds.

There were a couple of other minor donations until finally there was only two issues to address.

The first was Patrick's trust that Davey had complete control over, there was a statement that the solicitor read out loud.

"I am aware that the terms of the trust state that I, Davey Knox, am the sole executor of Patrick Reddy's trust and as such I can decide who administers it in the event of my death." The solicitor looked up before carrying on, "This has been a burden to endure as a result of a promise I made to my mother when she died. This burden should end now, both my mother and I have spent a lifetime ensuring Patrick's welfare and I don't think it would be fair to expect anyone else to inherit that burden. Therefore, all the proceeds of the trust will be handed over to Patrick Reddy and he can self-administer as he sees fit."

Patrick smiled, even he knew that meant he was getting a substantial amount of money.

The last part of the will related to Davey's shares. He changed his will after Richard's performance and Marie's business collapse, neither of them was fit to be given any amount of control within the company. In it he left all the shares to Helen, which surprised her as she was always under the impression that on his death, Davey would redistribute his wealth through the children.

Richard was fuming, but sat there saying nothing, William and Marie just shrugged, they were happy enough with the payout they got. There were a few forms to sign to complete the formalities, then everything was complete Davey Knox's fortune was no more.

Patrick had to stay and sign the handover documents for the trust, he didn't know what he was signing but knew it was for money so didn't care. As soon as he had signed and stood upright, Helen whispered in his ear.

"As of this moment your sacked. I don't want to see you anywhere near my family or Reddox again," she hissed.

Patrick wasn't bothered and just nodded, "Ok, no problem."

Richard was straight over to Helen when everything was completed, "Who will be the new CEO now Dad's gone?" He was still pushing his own agenda.

"I discussed this with your father just after your performance, when you had temporary control. We both agreed that you were not ready yet. We also were of the opinion to see if Martin Livesey would stay on, I have spoken with him and he has agreed. He expects to retire in about 4or 5 years' time. By then you might be mature enough to take over."

Richard stormed off, this was not his expected outcome, he felt betrayed by his mother and his father.

Helen sent an email to all the executive team to tell them it was business as usual and that she was not planning to change the existing status quo. The was a great source of relief for a number of members as they had been dreading Richard taking over. Richard had one last throw of the dice and threatened to leave and use his inheritance on other business ventures. Helen called his bluff and said that Reddox was a family firm and if he walked away, he would never be allowed back or inherit any shares. He never mentioned it again.

The whole paternity incident with Patrick was still eating away at Helen, the loathing was always there, it consumed her thoughts on an hourly basis. Finally, she could take it no longer and decided to have it out with him. She went around to the house and knocked on the door. Patrick answered it dressed in boxer shorts and a tee shirt.

"What do you want?" He sneered. He had obviously been drinking heavily and his breath reeked of whiskey. She wasn't sure whether she wanted to go in or not, but decided she didn't want any chance of the conversation being overheard so pushed her way into the lounge.

"I am here because a memory of something that happened a long time ago has been brought to the surface of my mind." She looked at Patrick who didn't blink, it was that long ago he wouldn't be able to remember anyway.

"A night where I was alone, asleep and drunk at home and you came into my house and raped me. Do you remember that?"

Patrick did now remember but still wasn't fazed. "No, sorry, don't know anything about it." He guessed she would be unable to prove anything after all this time.

Helen was really getting angry now, she was never going to tell him about Marie, but she wanted him to know she knew what he had done to her.

"Think you have been dreaming, I don't suppose you have any proof, do you?" He was smirking at her, which made her feel even more angry.

She wasn't sure what to do, she came here to expose him, but it was all unravelling for her instead.

"You're feeling frustrated because your husband's dead, how about I ease the pain for you?" He lurched towards her and she side stepped him. But now he had his back to the door and she was trapped.

"Come on, Helen, you know you want to," he lunged again, but this time he fell to the floor and banged his head. He lay there slightly concussed, Helen's only thought was that she wanted to hurt him, she ran into the kitchen where there was a large wooden cutting block. She picked it up and ran back into the lounge where he was just picking himself up off the floor. She raised it as high as she could then slammed it down onto the back of his head. Patrick instantly collapsed; she thought about hitting him again but realised he was unconscious. She stood there over him for a couple of minutes, but he hadn't moved. She checked his pulse and he was still alive, she wasn't sure what to do now. If he recovered and the police were involved then the whole sordid history might become public knowledge, she could not allow that to happen. She realised she must end it once and for all now.

There was a half a bottle of whiskey on the table, she undid the stopper and tried to pour the contents down Patrick's throat, but he couldn't swallow because he was not awake. She knew Patrick smoked cigars so she lit one then placed it so it looked as though it had fell from the ashtray onto a cushion and next to the curtains. She fanned the ember of the cigar until it was smouldering Helen reasoned that the cushion would set fire, then spread to the curtains. It would then look as though Patrick had fallen in a drunken stupor and set fire to the house himself.

She then sat outside in her car waiting to see the result. Sure enough, after about ten minutes she could see flickers of flame, eventually creeping up to the curtains. As soon as she was sure it had taken hold, she drove off. She began to feel guilty about her actions, not because of what she had done, but because of her lack of remorse. She was glad he was dead and she hoped it was a long, slow, lingering death.

She smiled to herself as she drove home, her family was safe; now, all she had to do was ensure that the Knox legacy lived on.

The End